USA TODAY BESTSELLING AUTHOR

DALE MAYER

A Psychic Visions Novel

GARDEN OF SORROW

GARDEN OF SORROW
Beverly Dale Mayer
Valley Publishing Ltd.

ISBN-13: 978-1-988315-66-9
Print Edition

Books in This Series:

Tuesday's Child
Hide 'n Go Seek
Maddy's Floor
Garden of Sorrow
Knock Knock…
Rare Find
Eyes to the Soul
Now You See Her
Shattered
Into the Abyss
Seeds of Malice
Eye of the Falcon
Itsy-Bitsy Spider
Unmasked
Deep Beneath
From the Ashes
Stroke of Death
Ice Maiden
Snap, Crackle…
What If…
Talking Bones
String of Tears
Inked Forever
Psychic Visions Books 1–3
Psychic Visions Books 4–6
Psychic Visions Books 7–9

About This Book

After a brutal year, trying to cope after the loss of her sister, Alexis Gordon knows she needs to get on with her life. Only, instead of the normal workday she'd anticipated as the means to begin her journey back to the land of the living, reality as she knows it disappears …

Kevin Sutherland is a detective and a psychic. Recognizing Alexis's gift and aware she has no idea what's happening to her, he calls his friend and frequent case consultant, Stefan Kronos, an artist with psychic gifts. Stefan leads a community of psychics, able to help Alexis understand and develop her unique skills.

Alexis has unwittingly become involved in a case unlike anything Kevin has ever seen before. The killer seems to have a personal vendetta against Alexis herself. He intends to eliminate her, before she uses her psychic gift to discover not only his identity but the location of his garden of sorrow, where he's buried his long-dead victims.

Only Alexis can stop this madman, who fully intends to survive, … even after death.

Dedication

This book is dedicated to my four children, who always believed in me and my storytelling abilities.

Thank you!

Acknowledgments

Garden of Sorrow wouldn't have been possible without the support of my friends and family. Many hands helped with proofreading, editing, and beta reading to make this book come together. Special thanks to my editor Pat Thomas.

I thank you all.

PROLOGUE

IF ONLY HE could turn back time, … be there when he'd been needed.

The night was bright and clear. The moon full, happy. The opposite of what he wanted, what he felt. There should be thunder and lightning destroying the world, … just as his world had just been destroyed.

He sat in the borrowed truck and studied the funeral home. Inside the stone building lay that beautiful little one, cold and alone. He couldn't stand it—that she was dead, that he'd never hold her again, never play with her or bring her gifts or watch the sunshine break free with her smile. It broke his heart … and damn-near crippled his soul. To think of her inside that box, … alone for all eternity, … was too much to bear. For all its fancy brass and plush interior that coffin would seal her up and would keep them apart forever.

He couldn't lose her. He loved her too much. That said everything … and nothing. The term *love* was overused, misunderstood, and didn't begin to explain this ache so strong it had turned the pit of his stomach to a cavern of emptiness. How could one adequately describe the light of your life? The reason you got up each day? She'd been his savior in this dark existence. His reason for being.

She couldn't go into that grave. So dark. So far away. So alone.

It couldn't happen.

He wouldn't let it.

Irrational blind rage boiled inside him. She was a child, but she'd been the only light in his world. That she'd died *not* in an accident was just another wrong he couldn't prevent. It happened when he hadn't been there to look after her. He'd been away. He hadn't wanted to go. But he'd had no choice.

He couldn't fight everyone all the time. He and she had both had a shitty life, her and him. At least *her* suffering was over.

Now his was just beginning. He had to go on. With his new purpose—to make them pay.

But he couldn't do it alone. He had to have her at his side.

Somehow. Somewhere. Someone would help him make that happen.

CHAPTER 1

Many Years Later

SHE SHOULD HAVE stayed in bed.

"Un-freaking-believable." Alexis Gordon stood, hands on her hips, at the edge of chaos. Cops, kids, dignitaries, and everything in-between wandered through the green spaces of the park. She sniffed the aroma of hot buttered popcorn and hot dogs permeating the air.

Smaller communities, like theirs, got fanatical about local events—like today's groundbreaking ceremony for the new gardens. A ceremony to celebrate the completion of the gardens made sense to her. Too bad the politicians in the small community of Bradford, Oregon, used events like this to garner votes. Not just at the beginning of the ceremony but at the end too. Bradford was smaller than Portland but independent, like neighboring Gresham. And Bradford politics were a complicated issue.

Alexis blew out a gust of breath and ran her fingers through her long superfine hair. Why hadn't she stayed home? She was a gardener, not a politician, and it was Sunday, after all. At least she didn't have to wear her work boots today. But her presence, apparently, was mandatory, since she was employed by the city.

Tucking her yellow cotton shirt into her faded jeans, she headed away from the crowd and behind the cordoned-off construction area. Her crew had set up a makeshift bridge to cross the huge culvert, where the city was installing new sewer pipes. That ditch clearly resembled a wading pool after last night's rain. Scott McIver, her immediate boss and best friend and father figure and big brother, approached from the other side.

"Hey, Alexis, be careful! Without work boots, that thing's a bitch."

Alexis nodded at Scott's warning, refusing to let her lightweight sneakers keep her from crossing the bridge. She kept her eyes firmly glued to the slick surface in front of her. Once at the other end, she grinned in triumph, reached for his outstretched hand, and jumped the last foot. "See? No probl—"

The soft dirt edge fell away from under her foot, as she landed on the left one, and her fingers slipped from his grasp. "Shit!"

"Jesus, Alex!" Scott made a grab for her … and missed.

His voice rolled over her, as she tumbled in a mad downward scramble, clawing against the dirt wall for something solid to grab, but still in a slow muddy slide. A fresh puddle of muck waited for her at the bottom.

"Oh, hell!" The oath slipped out, as she pulled herself up on her hands and knees, grimacing, as slime oozed between her fingers. "I don't need this today." The smell of wet earth and minerals assailed her senses. It might be a new ditch, but it already smelled like a sewer.

Everything ached, but nothing appeared damaged. She was more pissed at herself than anything. Alexis glanced up to see Scott staring down at her, a worried frown deepening his heavily wrinkled face. "I'm okay. Just give me a minute."

Feeling more or less normal—if disgusting were normal—she attempted to stand. As she pushed against the ground to get up, something sharp dug into the palm of her hand. Her fingers automatically closed over it, only it squished out the top of her fist and back into the mud.

"Ouch." A thin stream of red oozed from her mud-covered fingers. Whatever that thing was, it had scratched her palm. She stared at the surrounding puddle. Where had it gone? There, beside her right foot. Alexis leaned over for a closer look.

It couldn't be.

Several voices called down to her. She ignored them and tugged the muddy piece free. Blowing away several strands of hair blocking her view, she swished the item around in the rainwater and cleaned off most of the dirt.

Small, white, and with a distinctive shape, it resembled a bone. More like several tiny bones barely connected by stiff mud. And, oh God. … It looked like … *a finger*!

Ice settled into her spine. She held a finger.

A tiny finger.

A child's finger, still wearing a toy ring.

Her fingers tightened around the fragile piece. Her insides warred to keep the precious item safe, while another part of her wanted to throw it far away from her.

Then something changed.

Dizziness and nausea fought for supremacy, as her vision blurred. Disoriented, she wavered, as the ditch before her suddenly lengthened and narrowed, morphing into an interior hallway.

Alexis froze, her horrified gaze locked on the changing scene.

Dear God, what was going on? Her mind raced to sort out the change. How had the dirt bank turned to gray paint?

And the sewer smell now smothered by heavy cooking odors? Fried chicken?

Where was she?

Alexis stared down the hallway. A young child, caught inside this peculiar scenario, stumbled toward her, with both hands clasped over her ears. Tears streamed down her young face, and her T-shirt was inches above the dirty shorts. Bruises decorated her lower legs, and, well, … dirt covered the rest of her. As if she'd recently been playing in a dirt pile. Alexis tried to run to her, to hug her tight, to protect her, … only to find she couldn't move. Her feet were paralyzed in place. Terror filled her heart.

She opened her mouth to scream. No sound came out.

Run. The scream seared through her mind.

Dimly in the background, loud crashes and yelling could be heard, as if someone gave chase. Fear of retribution accented every step the distraught child took. The sound and tone distorted.

Alexis shuddered. Tears clogged her throat, and pain choked her heart.

"Alexis. Alex? Alex!"

Scott's alarmed voice pulled at her from outside the vision that held her transfixed. Caught between two realities, Alexis jerked toward Scott, the object dropping from her fingers.

Instantly the hallway disappeared, as if a vacuum had sucked the dirt walls back into place, with a rush so powerful it forced Alexis to lean forward. Then, as if caught in a giant rubber band, the force suddenly released, throwing her into reverse. She flew backward and landed, once again, on her butt in the middle of the large puddle.

Her gut screamed, and bile tried to escape her throat.

She shuddered. What the hell had just happened? She swallowed convulsively, willing her breakfast to stay down. Tremors started at her toes and rattled up her spine.

"Alexis, damn it. Answer me!" Scott demanded.

"I—I'm fine." Was that croaking *her* voice? The finger. ... Where was it? More than a little daunted by the prospect of touching it again, she remained seated and eyed the surrounding mud.

There.

It rested on the muddy surface, ... waiting for her.

Eerie. She hated to touch it again, the last experience too horrific to repeat. She reached for it, but her fingers shook so badly that she stopped. Yet she couldn't force herself to leave it behind. Compromising, she pulled a tissue from her shirt pocket and gingerly picked up the finger.

The size bothered her. The vague image of the running child from a few moments ago slammed back. Ruthlessly she pushed the vision from her mind. She couldn't even begin to analyze what had happened. It had been way too weird. Alexis focused on what was important right this moment. *Where there is one finger ...*

She studied the high expanse of dirt wall. She dimly remembered digging her fingers into the bank on her downward tumble. But how high up had she been? The ditch stood eight to ten feet deep.

"Here's the ladder, Alexis," Scott said, as Mike, another coworker, arrived with the ladder. Scott held the long metal structure several feet off to the side.

"No!" she motioned. "Please, bring it over here. Where I fell in."

Scott shrugged, and the two moved the ladder to the right spot.

Alexis struggled to position it the best she could, near her original flight path. Once the ladder was secured, she moved upward, one rung at a time. At each new level, she stopped and searched. The bone must have come from somewhere.

"Oh, for the love of God. Alexis, what are you doing?" Scott peered over the ladder at her.

Alexis didn't answer. What could she say? Three, maybe four feet from the top, a speck of white caught her eye. Reaching between the ladder rungs, she gently brushed some of the dirt away. Another bone, possibly another finger. Vomit lined her throat. She rested her forehead against the steel frame of the ladder for a long moment. "Scott?" Her hands squeezed the ladder tight. She kept her voice low.

"Yes, beautiful. What's going on?" He crouched down for a better look, but he was at the wrong angle.

"Are any police close by?" She cleared her throat, tears suddenly clogging her throat. Willing him to not ask her any questions. "If not, go get one—*now.*"

Startled, Scott stared at her for a brief moment, before disappearing from sight, his heavy footsteps fading rapidly. Mike held the ladder steady. Alexis let her head remain on the rung and waited, her arm wrapped around one side of the ladder. The steel dug into her forehead, as she realized something important.

This wasn't just a ditch. This was a grave.

DETECTIVE KEVIN SUTHERLAND chose a spot off to one side, where he could watch the proceedings. He tugged at his collar and unbuttoned his one good suit jacket. If it weren't for his boss, he wouldn't be here.

This was so not his scene. The warm sun already sent sweat down the small of his back, and he had more hours to go. Irritation pulled at him. He had no time or patience for this. Up half the night on a domestic violence call, he should be catching a few hours of much-needed rest. Instead he'd been badgered into coming here to support his elected officials and to ensure everything went smoothly.

He snorted. Support, his ass. When would they support his request for extra manpower to keep the community safe?

"Kevin, it's good to see you." Mayor John Prescott approached, his hand out to shake. With a wary glance around, John asked in a low voice, "Everything okay?"

Kevin narrowed his gaze on the mingling crowd. "Everything appears fine." He paused. Except for one thing. The hairs on the back of his neck stood on end, a sure sign that something was wrong somewhere.

The mayor nodded. "Great. Let's keep it that way." He sharpened his gaze, locking it on Kevin's face. "Keep that other issue in mind today too."

With a curt nod, Kevin said, "I'm on it."

The mayor returned to the crowd, his politician smile firmly in place.

Kevin slipped farther back from the noise to the large stand of evergreens. He had his own special way of finding out where the trouble came from. Alone, he opened his mind, allowing his senses free rein. From this new perspective, he opened a special portal and reached out mentally, like a trouble-seeking probe, searching.

The music blaring over the loudspeaker mixed with the shrieks of children on the playground. Normal. Widening his perimeter, he checked the parking lot and side streets. That area seemed fine too. Turning slightly, he half-closed his eyes, sending energy behind him.

There.

Cold tendrils of fear crept toward him from the back of the construction area. He did another quick mental check. The energy was calm but insistent. Not static and flaming, which meant the problem wasn't violent or an emergency. But someone needed help.

After a quick survey of the crowd, he took off to answer the silent call.

ALEXIS SHIFTED HER sore butt, as she stood on the ladder. Fatigue like she'd rarely experienced had slid inside her bones. As much as she wanted to distance herself from what she'd found, she felt oddly protective of it too. She could have easily stood guard from above but couldn't leave that little bit of skeleton alone and exposed. It had been part of a person once. To be so lost all this time made Alexis's heart ache.

Rotating her tense shoulders, she waited. Her muddy jeans clung to her calves, and her shoes were a write-off. She shivered in the sunlight. Grief pulled at her for this lost child … and for her own sister. Memories slammed into her. Alexis slammed them back out. This wasn't the time or the place. Still, the trigger refused to be ignored. After all, she'd just found a child's grave, one year to the day when she'd placed her kid sister in one.

"What's the problem here?"

Startled, Alexis tilted her head and squinted up through the morning sun's rays to find a man at odds with his voice. The suit fit the tall muscled frame a little too well for her peace of mind. The angular face and tone of voice said business all the way. She couldn't take her eyes off him. He had to be media.

Better to get rid of him fast. "The media booth is on the other side," she replied, eyeing his suit, the perfect contrast to her fashion statement in mud.

"I'm a cop." He rested his hands on his hips, gazing down at her.

A cop? She reassessed him. Deep-set gray eyes. High cheekbones supported by a square jaw. This man had little patience for fools, regardless of what he wore. Damn, was that a silk shirt? Alexis shook her head. No way he was a cop. "Look. I'm not an idiot. My morning wasn't going well before I got here. Now it's pissed itself right down the drain."

"How appropriate, considering where you're sitting." He reached into his inside jacket pocket and pulled out his badge. "I repeat. What's the problem?" Exasperation sharpened his voice.

Alexis clambered up the last two rungs of the ladder. Seconds later, she stood before him, covered in drying slime. "Let me see that, please."

He held his badge before her face.

"Detective Kevin Sutherland." Okay, maybe he was telling the truth. She held out her hand. With her free hand, she gently unfolded the tissue.

His back stiffened, and his angular face sharpened as he studied the bone. "Where did you get this?"

"When I fell in, I must have dislodged it from the wall. I think more is down there." Alexis pointed in the general direction of the ditch.

"Show me." He was all business now. He stripped off his jacket and tie, discarding both on a spot of clean grass.

Alexis stared, as he started down the ladder. You had to appreciate a man who had his priorities right. She moved to the side of the ladder and pointed. "Search through the third and fourth rungs, off to the left."

A moment later, his heartfelt whisper floated up to her. "Shit."

CHAPTER 2

HOURS LATER, YELLOW police tape cordoned off the entire park area. Uniforms worked alongside the coroner. A forensic anthropologist had just arrived from Portland, and investigators were collecting trace evidence. In general, it seemed too many authorities were here, but everyone was doing something. The gathered crowd showed no signs of dispersing, the police guarding the area a draw instead of a deterrent. She had to love the curious mind-set of today's society.

Alexis grabbed her work coat from her red Toyota truck, but shivers still racked her body. A hot shower would be perfect right about now, but she couldn't leave.

Somber silence greeted the appearance of the tiny outline in an oversize body bag.

"It isn't right. It just isn't." Scott's Irish accent thickened with sadness.

Alexis tucked her arm through his, appreciating his support and happy to give some in return. She'd become a loner over the years, first from necessity, as the disease had slowly decimated her sister, then out of preference in the aftermath. But this barrel-chested Irishman hadn't let her hide in her darkness. He'd pushed, prodded, and propelled her back to life. She'd hated him for it then. Now he epitomized the father figure she'd never had, the older brother she'd always wanted, and the best friend she'd ever known. "Life isn't fair. Better to learn that now and save yourself some heartache," she murmured.

His disgusted snort washed over her. "You don't believe that drivel. Better to feel and to know you're alive than to walk through life as if you've never lived." His muscled arm wrapped around her shoulders in a clumsy, but caring, hug. "I know you're thinking of your sister. Be hard not to, with all this going on." He swept his other arm wide to encompass the hub of police activity. "Don't hold all that pain inside. Lissa is gone. Time to rejoice in her living. Don't focus so much on her passing." He squeezed gently before letting Alexis go.

Caught on an inward spiral of pain, Alexis barely noticed his intense gaze. Horrified understanding overtook her confusion. Was he right? Had she focused so much on her sister's death that she'd forgotten to honor her life?

Please, let it not be true.

One tear formed at the corner of her eye, hung for a brief moment, then slid down her face.

"Miss, … uh, sorry. I need to get some information from you."

A fresh-faced policeman interrupted Alexis's painful musings. She made no attempt to wipe the tear from her cheek.

"I need to take your statement," he said. "If we could start with your name and address, please."

Scott gently prodded her. "Alexis."

A sidelong glance at Scott's concerned face prompted her to speak. "Alex, … Alexis Gordon."

"What's your full address and phone number?"

Startled, she stared at the cop. He looked like he should

be selling raffle tickets for a Boy Scout trip. "Why?"

"You found the body. We need your statement."

Shaken, she quickly supplied the required information, as Scott stood silent at her side. Just as they finished, her irritating district supervisor strode toward them.

"Do you do things like this on purpose? Show up late, sneak in through the back, and wreak havoc on everyone's plans?" *Rick the Dick*, as the rest of them not-so-affectionately called him, glared at the mess of the opening-day ceremony. He too sported a full three-piece suit, although his was more designer than business.

Alexis scowled at the stinging unfairness of Rick's words.

"What a disaster!" her boss snapped.

"That's one way of putting it, Rick." The detective, now with his jacket back on and looking very much the worse for wear, joined their little group. "Hey, Scott. Haven't seen you for a while. Sad day for a reunion." He glanced down at his mud-encrusted clothes, flicking off small clumps still clinging to the material. "These pants are history."

She turned her back on Rick to speak to Scott, trying to ignore the unsettling knowledge that everyone knew each other but her. "Nothing for me to do here, so I'll go home and get cleaned up." She ignored Rick and had done so since he'd refused her time off for her sister's palliative care. She'd gotten it eventually, … after going through the higher-ups. At a price—her relationship with her boss. That Lissa had lasted much longer than the doctors had expected hadn't helped Rick's attitude toward the situation. For Alexis, every additional day had been a gift.

Alexis watched as Scott snuck a sideways glance at their fuming boss. "I'll walk her to her car. Back in a minute."

Scott ushered her toward the parking lot for their first

chance to speak privately. He waited until they'd reached the relative quiet of the area before the words exploded from him. "Now that we're alone, what the hell happened to you?"

Alexis stilled, almost convinced that the incident after her fall had gone unnoticed. "I don't know," she admitted. "Maybe I was just a little shaky from the fall."

"Well, you scared the bejeezus out of me." He clasped her face in his big mitts and studied the look in her eyes. "You've been in a fog all morning. If you hadn't let the paramedics check you out, you wouldn't be going home now either." His hands dropped away.

"I'm fine," she retorted. Taking a deep breath, she tried to make light of his concern. "At least *I'm* normally awake." She grinned at the heavily wrinkled man, who loved to nap at every opportunity.

His smile flashed and disappeared just as quickly. "You could've been badly hurt, falling like that." He glanced behind her and frowned.

Alexis pivoted. The coroner's vehicle had made its way through the parking lot to the exit, where it stopped before heading out onto the road. She shivered, tugging her work coat tighter around her.

Should she mention the vision? No. If she couldn't explain it to herself, how could she explain it to him? "Go home and rest." Scott nudged her toward her truck. "I'll go back and sort things out with Rick."

Alexis had an uncanny ability to piss off Rick within seconds of them being together. Scott had warned her several times to button her lip, and, for the most part, she had managed pretty well. This morning's lapse only proved how badly she'd been affected by what she'd found in the culvert.

Scott glanced behind him, probably to make sure she was really leaving. Something odd *had* happened down in the ditch, something besides finding a body, which was enough to rattle anyone. He'd have to wait until she recovered before quizzing her more closely.

But he would.

KEVIN AND RICK stood outside the perimeter of the crime scene tape, when Scott joined them. Rick glared at him, the words, obviously barely held in check, finally burst free. "Damn it, Scott. What the hell is her problem?"

Scott narrowed his eyes. Slurs against his friends were never allowed. Damaged and hurting, gentle Alexis needed his support. Her life had been hell for a long time. She deserved a champion. It didn't matter if she hid her hurt so well that others were fooled by her apparently caustic comments. Behind all that, Alexis had heart. Besides, she never turned on anyone who didn't deserve it.

He held up his hand, forestalling Rick's next outburst. "Her problem is that she just found the grave of a dead child. Come on, Rick. You know about her kid sister. Is it too hard to see that today might trigger some tough stuff for her? Hell, I won't sleep well tonight after this, and I didn't lose anyone."

"What happened to her sister?" Kevin stood off to one side, his gaze going from one to the other.

"She died of cancer a year ago." Scott stopped and frowned. He glanced down at his watch. "Shit. She was buried one year ago today." He glanced up at Kevin. "Such a shame. Just seventeen years old."

Kevin nodded. "Today will trigger all sorts of issues for

her. You might consider seeing that she gets some help."

"No room in the budget for stupidity." Rick stared ahead, a muscle in his jaw twitching.

Both men stared at him in surprise.

He glared at them both. "What? She didn't have to walk on that damn bridge. She knows the safety rules as well as anyone." Rick shoved his hands in his pockets. "Shit, I don't need this now. I'm heading home. See you both later."

Scott watched Rick storm off.

"Is he really that cold to her plight? Or is she really a loose screw?" Kevin asked Scott.

How to answer that? Scott didn't know. Was Kevin asking as a cop or as a buddy he'd shared a couple beers with every month? Was there a difference?

"Alexis and Rick have a feud going on. For myself, I side with Alexis, but Rick's my boss, and I don't want to lose my job. I'm not sure Alexis cares about that aspect anymore." He shrugged and glanced at Kevin. "I can tell you this. Their issue has nothing to do with the body part Alexis found."

Scott waited, as Kevin studied his face before he nodded once. "Good enough. If she's earned your loyalty, she must have something going for her."

Someone called Kevin's name.

"Excuse me, Scott. I have to go."

"No problem. Let me know what you find out."

Nothing was good about finding the remains of a child. But to find the child's family? … Now that would help.

ALEXIS MADE HER way to her vehicle. "Rest, he says. After this morning? He's got to be joking."

The crowd was breaking up and filtering through the

parking lot, making it difficult to drive. Alexis watched a young mother hug her child tightly to her chest. A grim heavyset man passed them. She sensed these people had experienced a paradigm shift today, one that could set in motion a complete reevaluation of their lives. Alexis didn't need that shift. Her world had been jolted years ago, when cancer had moved into her home.

Before Lissa's death, Alexis had lived for every moment. She'd savored every remaining hour she'd had with her sister, and still, the precious time had slipped away too fast. At seventeen, cancer had been a painful wasting away of someone so bright, so vibrant, and so full of life. It wasn't fair.

Lissa would laugh, saying, "That's why it's okay for me to leave. I find joy in every second and beauty in all things. Life goes on for both of us. You'll see. I'll find a way to come back and see you." Alexis had always hoped that Lissa had been right, and Alexis had to admit that she'd been looking for a sign from her sister ever since.

Alexis shook off the heavy memory, determined not to focus on any more death, as she rattled her red Toyota truck onto the main road. She just wanted to go home.

Long moments later, she pulled into her parking spot at her apartment building. Serenity Haven. What a joke. The cement building looked more like a juvenile correction center. She hated living here, but she'd sold the family home after Lissa's funeral, unable to deal with the memories. That aside, this place had no soul.

Maybe she'd rented it for just that reason, as a punishment. In what way, she didn't know or understand. Yet it felt like a punishment to drive home to this cold concrete box every day. Maybe it was time to leave.

The idea had merit. Maybe she could find another little house, one with a huge garden, where she could start her hanging-basket business again. She'd built it up, with Lissa's help, as an add-on to her full-time job. The long-term plan was to expand and to eventually make it full-time work. When her sister had gotten sick, Alexis had given it up.

With fresh eyes, Alexis examined her surroundings. The walls leading to the entrance were chipped, peeling, the elevator decorated with graffiti. Even the gray hall leading to her dismal apartment was dingy and showed a lack of care. It was essentially clean, but a sense of desolation permeated the place.

Alexis stopped as she reached her apartment door, casually glancing back down the way she'd come.

And froze.

Horrified recognition washed over her. Terror gripped her throat, before escaping in a gasp of shock. Uncontrollable trembling racked her lean frame. Her fingers lost their grip, and her keys tumbled to the threadbare carpet below.

The hallway. Dear God, it looked to be the same as the one she'd experienced in the ditch.

CHAPTER 3

IT COULDN'T BE!

Alexis bent slowly to retrieve her keys, keeping a wary eye on the hallway. She desperately wanted inside the safety of her apartment but didn't dare turn her back on the creepy space.

Her fingers trembled so much that she couldn't get the damn key to work. Finally the lock clicked. She flung open the door and raced inside, slammed and locked the door behind her. Alexis leaned against the door, shaking and sobbing. Her heart hammered in her chest. What the hell was happening to her? She rubbed away her tears. Her life had been normal up until today—sad in many ways but normal.

It took several long minutes before her legs could function. It took several more before her breathing calmed. Still shaky but no longer panicked, Alexis slowly moved to the bathroom.

"God, I'm cold," she muttered, turning on the water for a hot shower. And so tired. Steam filled the room, as she stripped off her clothes. Alexis scrambled under the hot water, where she tipped her head back and let the full force of the water pour down. The steam soothed her senses, the heat easing her aching muscles. Only when the water ran cold did she turn off the taps. Her legs trembled slightly, as the rough towel whisked off the moisture.

The images wouldn't leave her alone.

That poor child, lost and forgotten in the garden, discarded, … like garbage. Alexis dressed quickly, pulling on a heavy sweater and tugging her wet hair free of the wool. Shivers rattled her teeth. "Why can't I get warm?" Grabbing a spare towel, she twisted her hair inside it and headed for the kitchen.

She put the kettle on for a hot cup of tea.

While waiting for the water to boil, she gazed out at a world that appeared so calm and normal on the surface. Was she the only one who'd dipped beneath the facade? Had the years of enforced calm—holding it together at all costs, in a world so beyond her control—damaged her psyche?

Alexis.

The fragile voice broke into her musings. So clear, so sharp, yet so … whispery. Prickles rose on the back of her neck, goose bumps across her skin. *It couldn't be!*

Afraid to look—but more terrified not to—Alexis twisted with agonizing slowness.

Lissa!

A beloved and so familiar wispy vision of her sister sat at the table, as if waiting—like she had for so many years—for her cup of tea.

"Lissa," Alexis whispered, her voice aching with tenderness …

Alexis was petrified that the sound of her own voice would break the spell, … and the miracle of her sister's presence would disappear. She'd hoped for, prayed for, such a visit. Her heart swelled with joy … and awe … and fear. "Lissa, is that you?"

The apparition flickered, then slowly began to fade.

"No, don't go, Lissa!" Alexis cried out. "Please," she begged. "Please don't go!" Her voice faded, as the vision dissipated into the air.

It was too much.

Alexis crumpled at the table, her head in her arms, and sobbed out the last year of grief and loss. Pain, held in too long, burst free. Her shoulders shook uncontrollably, as her body weathered the storm.

Eventually the tempest expended itself, leaving a heavier exhaustion and an emotional devastation behind. Alexis laid her cheek against the cheap Formica tabletop, staring at the spot where she'd thought she'd seen her sister. The occasional hot tear still welled up to slide down her cheeks.

What was happening to her? Was she having a breakdown? That would make sense. She'd endured a horrific amount of stress and loss in her world. … But why now? On the anniversary date? The time to break down would have been the day she'd buried her sister. But for it to happen a year later? … That didn't make sense.

The teakettle whistled on cue. That was normal. After all, she'd put that teakettle on. She could accept that—unlike the rest of her day. Feeling as if she'd aged fifty years, she poured water over the teabag and watched the tea stain the liquid. Wafting her hand over the top, the steam warmed her fingers—as it should. This was the normal, the usual, and the right.

She'd survived Lissa's death because she'd depended on that normalcy. She expected it. She counted on it.

And today her whole world had been blown apart by—dare she say it—a vision, a body, and … a ghost.

THE WIND BLEW hard outside the double glass doors. Branches swiped the edge of the railing, making a faint scratching sound, … like a ghost asking to come into the private nursing home room.

The older man chuckled. No such thing as a ghost. If there were, he'd have been haunted years ago. Still, the concept had given him pause over the years, … for a moment or two.

He shifted closer to the prone man on the bed. He studied the man's slack features, as he twirled his balloon glass slowly. The rich aroma of his Glenfiddich whisky swirled in an ever-rising circle, bursting forth to assail his senses. His brother's favorite. He closed his eyes and breathed deep. He kept a bottle here in the room for evenings like these. He sank his thin frame deeper into his armchair, facing the glass doors to the gardens beyond. Heavy rain bounced off the patio, flattening the delicate rose petals.

Odd how that rain could be a blessing for grass, yet signal the end of the blooms on a rose. Such delicate plants. It was the same for people. What was a disaster to one was a gift to another. Some people were hardy and could withstand the harsh elements of life, and then the others, the delicate ones, needed protecting. He was good at that—the protecting part. Of course people didn't always understand or appreciate his protective method or didn't know what was good for them.

Stretching out his arm, he grabbed the remote and turned on the television. Maybe his brother would like the distraction. Had to be something to break up the monotony of lying there day after day. Personally this was his favorite time of day. A little peace and quiet, a little time alone, where he didn't have to pretend to be something he wasn't—

with his brother.

The evening news came on, the announcer bubbling about some large contribution to a local charity. A moment later, he brought up today's headlines.

The man straightened in shock. *What the hell?*

THE NEXT MORNING started clear and warm, with one insistent message rattling around inside Alexis's head—she needed help and soon. She didn't know who to ask or even what kind of help she needed. Still, just admitting she had the problem could be thought of as a big step forward.

Regardless, at the moment she needed to get to work. Her soul needed the comfort of the gardens. Only nothing was likely to be peaceful about them today. The damage from the excavation yesterday could be extensive.

Arriving at work twenty minutes later, Alexis cast a wide glance across the park. From the looks of them, the gardens needed her too.

They'd been trashed. She wanted to howl at the damage. Damn.

One officer stood off to the side. She nodded at him but stayed away. Some of the police tape had been removed, though most still sagged in place. Several long strands of it cordoned off the grave and the surrounding area. A few forlorn pieces blew aimlessly across the park. Heavy vehicles had left muddy ruts in the grass. Litter decorated muddy footprints. The carelessly discarded disposable cups and cigarette butts really burned her.

The park definitely had a morning-after appearance.

She exhaled hard, rolled up her sleeves, and tucked her shirt into her jeans. She pulled several garbage bags from her truck. After putting on her work boots, she stomped her feet a couple of times to settle in, then locked her truck and stormed around the site on her clean-up mission. Every area of the park came under her scrutiny, as she searched for offending human trash—every area but one.

When she finally realized what she'd been unconsciously avoiding, Alexis forced herself to walk toward the tiny open grave. The police officer stood to one side, his narrowed eyes watching her.

The grave remained achingly difficult to gaze upon.

Alexis couldn't stand the lonely uncared-for look of it. She had to do something.

She couldn't enter the area, but she stacked several rocks just inside the cordoned-off perimeter, where the ground held deep ruts from the vehicles. Maybe this location for her construction would reduce vandalism. Stepping back, she studied her handiwork.

As a memorial, it left much to be desired.

Plants. It needed the healing energy of plants. Chewing the inside of her lip, she surveyed her gardens. Her understanding of Mother Nature had been well-honed over the years. Her coworkers called her spooky because of the way the plants responded to her. According to them, she could bring any dead plant back to life almost immediately and could even make flowers appear out of season. That wasn't true of course. Not totally.

She couldn't save them all.

As for the plants flowering off-season, who said plants could only flower at specific times? Alexis couldn't explain why her methods worked. She only knew they did.

Alexis gave them the same loving attention she gave to animals and kids. Walking through the flowers, she called out softly to them. "How are you guys doing today? Yesterday was tough on all of us, wasn't it?" She stopped here and there, once to smooth a bent leaf, another time to stroke a particularly bright petal. "It's okay. It's all over. Everything is back to normal now."

She continued to speak to her babies, murmuring soft words of comfort, as she checked out each one. Her senses picked up on the energy levels of the plants around her. One small daisy plant with multiple white petals had a dark dull color to it. Alexis walked closer.

The leaves drooped miserably. It cried out for help. She couldn't resist. Gently her hands hovered over it. Years ago, she'd read several books on tricks to improve plant health, and she had to admit, with practice, it seemed to work better all the time. The more caring and attention she devoted to her plants, the better they did. Nothing magical about that. Common sense really. One of the books also mentioned something about playing music and using soft lights. She grinned. Like her boss would let her do that.

Within a few intense seconds, the plant brightened ever-so-slightly, almost appearing happy to have the company. Alexis laughed at that whimsical thought. She did have a good imagination.

That thought wiped the smile off her face. Had Lissa's ghost been a figment of her imagination? God, she hoped not.

Using another technique from the book, she focused a loving green—for health and healing—light around a different listless daisy plant.

"What else can I do for you, little one?" She chuckled at her words, for, in truth, it was a decent size. She glanced over at the grave and, without giving herself a chance to reconsider, she dug up the plant, making sure she kept a large root ball attached.

"Yep, they'll really think I'm nuts for this one." Alexis checked the surrounding area. Outside of the silent ever-watchful police presence, she was still alone. "I can always move you again, if you're not happy there," she murmured.

It would be the public that showed its displeasure. A lone flowering plant wouldn't be considered an artistic improvement. Yet, as a memorial, it was a start.

Using her hands, she carefully loaded up as much of the rich black dirt around the ball as she could then carried it over to the rock pile. After planting it deep, she rearranged the rocks in an artistic pattern, creating a backdrop for the daisy.

Scott found her almost an hour later.

"Alex?"

Bent over her tools, Alexis raked the footprints from the flower beds. She straightened and smiled up at him. "Hi, Scott. About time you showed up."

"Don't you be worrying about me. The real question is, how are you?" He studied her face.

Alexis grimaced and looked off in the distance to avoid his piercing blue eyes. He had a way of seeing things a little too clearly. "I'm better. It helps being in the gardens." She motioned to the mess around them. "We have a lot of work ahead of us."

"There's time. I don't know if the police are done yet." He studied the daisy flower memorial. "Did you do that?"

"What? Oh, yeah, I did." She searched his expression. "I had to do something," she added warily, hoping for, but not quite expecting, understanding. She needn't have worried. Scott was already nodding his acceptance.

"You're different this morning. What's the matter?" he asked.

Startled, she hid her expression behind the fall of her hair.

"Come on. What's going on?" Concern thickened his tone, making him harder to understand.

She didn't know how to answer him, so she said nothing, just looked quietly into his eyes. What could she say that he'd believe—that wouldn't make her sound on the edge of a breakdown? Accepting the visions seemed too far-fetched, even for her.

The intensity of his gaze changed. "Oh, wow," he muttered softly. "You've always had a touch of the Sight, but something's changed." He studied her face. "But what?"

She missed the last part, too startled by his first comment. "I don't have the Sight, whatever that is."

"Like hell you don't. Don't be trying to hide it. You've always had magical speakings with them little plants of yours." He did a sweep with his arm to encompass the whole of the gardens. "That's how you make this so glowing. Only someone with the Sight could accomplish all this."

Alexis flushed with warmth, followed immediately by an icy fear that he might know more than she'd intended him to know. "No, you don't understand. I just practice some exercises I read in a couple books. Anyone can do it."

"No way. I can't." He grinned. "But my gram sure could. That … and more. You probably see all their colors too, don't you? My gram could tell all kinds of things about her plants just by the colors she saw."

He was so matter-of-fact she could only stare at him in shock. She shook her head violently. "That's nuts!" She plunked down on the ground, her hand on her forehead. His words had shaken her very foundation.

A loud snort answered her. "That's your modern thinking interfering. Me? … I have a healthy respect for the Sight."

That she had the Sight, or whatever he referred to, so didn't make sense. She was a gifted gardener. *That* she saw and accepted. More than that? *Uh-uh.* Over the years, she'd had some indications that her abilities were out of the ordinary, but she really hadn't given it much thought. Her *skills* were a natural part of her world, so why question them? Besides, the Sight meant psychic stuff, premonitions, visions. Ghosts? Her world slowed. *The child in the ditch. Lissa.*

Oh, dear God.

She stared at the sky above, her mind blank, her heart pounding—but not in shock—more like after a revelation.

"What would make these skills suddenly change?" she asked, not really sure she wanted to hear the answer.

His clear gaze seared through her.

She shuddered at the sense of exposure. As if he saw what she could not.

"That's what yesterday was all about, wasn't it?" he asked.

Slightly afraid, she nodded—a tiny, barely perceptible movement—then said, in a small voice, "Maybe."

"Ah, lassie. … Scared yourself right and proper, didn't you?"

His words startled a crooked smile from her. "I don't understand any of this. Life was pretty normal, until I fell into the ditch. But now? … The things I'm seeing? … That's scary." She was confused and more than a little relieved to talk about it with someone.

"What did you see?" Curious, Scott sat down on the

grass beside her, close enough to be supportive and far enough away not to crowd her.

"I saw a little girl in a hallway. I think. I mean, I saw a little girl. Or I thought I saw a girl, … but she wasn't real. … It's like she was mist or something and in a hallway. … in the ditch." She stopped, confused.

Scott nodded. Keeping his voice low and calm, he said, "Start at the beginning and tell me what happened. Step by step."

Alexis checked around to make sure they were still alone. The sun was almost directly overhead. A few people walked around or sat on benches, but she and Scott were at the other end of the park.

She took a deep breath and began to explain. She left nothing out. Her voice wobbled, as she finished by telling him about her sister's visit. "I thought I was having a breakdown, Scott. My God, Lissa was so clear. She was right there in front of me. She said my name." Shock and disbelief colored her voice.

"Ah, lassie." Scott pulled her into his comforting embrace, squeezing her tight, before releasing her. "You should be joyous, not afeared."

What could she say to that? She studied his compassionate gaze. "Really? It's that simple to you?"

"Is *what* that simple?" A strong voice reached across the flowers to them.

Alexis pivoted. *Detective Sutherland.*

What was it about this man that made her back straighten and her knees weaken at the same time?

"Hi, Scott. Alexis. I need to speak with the two of you. But first, who put that memorial together? It's within the crime scene." The detective's stern face towered above her.

"Oh." Alexis snapped to her feet, brushing the dirt of her pants. "I did. I'm sorry. I'd hoped it would be far enough out of the way for you but deter vandalism because it was inside the tape."

His chiseled features eased. "The tape is there for a reason. We aren't done with the scene yet."

Alexis twisted around to look at the memorial in the distance. "I can move it outside, if you need me to."

Casting a quick glance at Scott, who now stood beside Alexis, the detective continued in a calmer voice. "Should you even be at work today? Most people would understand the need to take off a day or two after yesterday."

Alexis shook her head. "I'm fine. I'm better off doing something constructive." She hesitated. "Have you identified her yet? I can't imagine what her family has gone through all these years." Alexis stuffed her hands into her pants pockets, as she waited. Her insides trembled. She didn't know why his answer mattered so much, but it did.

Suspicion shone in his eyes, as he stared her, his jaw firmly locked in place.

His instant shift from casual stance to hardened investigator had Alexis asking, "What?"

"You called the skeleton a 'she.' What makes you so sure it is a little girl?"

Confusion clouded her mind. Good question. How had she known it was a little girl? Because she'd assumed it was the same child that she'd seen running in the ditch.

The men waited for her answer.

"I guessed," she answered lamely, not ready to share her bizarre vision with this man.

Skepticism washed over the detective's face, but thankfully he left it at that, at least for the moment.

Scott was a different story. He quirked his eyebrow at her, but she shook her head.

Detective Sutherland watched the silent exchange. Alexis could almost feel his mind cataloging her and Scott. Figuring who they were, what was their relationship, and if they were hiding anything. It was obvious this man missed little.

His body stance relaxed, in total opposition to the sharpness of his attention, and damned if her contrary hormones didn't find that attractive. What the hell was with that?

"Do I need to move the memorial? I just felt that the grave needed to be respected and marked." Her fists clenched deep inside her denim pockets. She wanted to wipe them dry on her jeans but didn't want to arouse his suspicions any more than they already were.

"I'll see. A crew will be here later today to map out the gardens to compare to aerial photographs." He glanced at Scott and gestured to the spot above the ditch. "Scott, you've been here a while. … How long has this garden bed been here? Do you know?"

"Since forever, it seems. I can't give you an exact year, but I've been working on it for over twenty years."

The detective nodded. "Right. And, in that time, has any major work been done? Work that would have brought the skeleton to light, if one had been here then?"

Both Alexis and Scott turned to study the bed. A beautiful blue spruce stood close to twelve feet tall in the center, with weeping maples and begonias filling in the bulk of the area beneath. Bulbs flowered and went with the seasons, and annuals were planted each spring for bright cheerful color.

"Even if we dug it over, like we do in the fall, we wouldn't go that deep," Alexis said.

"Aye, that's true enough, but this city park was upgraded with this spruce and new perennials around twelve to fifteen years ago. I'll have to check the records." He paused, a frown twisting his face. "But that spot where the body was found was part of this big bed here." He motioned to the spruce bed. "We moved all the smaller plants at this end of the bed last year, when we were notified about this job with the pipes. There weren't many big plants, so we didn't go very deep. It wasn't a big area and was fairly easy to shorten up to make way for the construction." He walked around the garden bed, studying the plants flourishing in the rich mulch. He pointed to the end where the grave sat. "And that spot had originally been put in about a decade ago, … maybe even fifteen years or so."

"Pictures and plans are on file," Alexis offered.

Detective Sutherland smiled. "Pictures and plans would help a lot. Help establish a time line. Scott, send over anything you have, and I'll add it to the file." He glanced at the large silver watch on his wrist. "I'm short on time. Make sure nothing else is disturbed in the crime scene. Don't be surprised if you come in one day to find your memorial has been moved. We need full access to the entire surface." He nodded to both of them and headed back over to the grave.

Alexis watched as he stood in front of the memorial for a long moment. *Don't touch the plant*, she pleaded in her heart. Instead, he pulled on thin rubber gloves and moved over to the open grave, where he sifted through the lightly packed dirt close to the surface. He filled several small vials and then repeated the process from lower, inside the ditch. Back on top again, he pulled out a notepad and started writing.

"Now what the hell is he doing?" she muttered. It shouldn't matter, but everything to do with this case affected her. She needed him to do his job and to find out who this little girl was. It was important. Alexis just didn't know why she felt it so strongly.

Finally he must have finished because he tucked his notebook back into his pocket.

With each sign that he'd soon be leaving, Alexis felt her tension drain away. It had been years since any male had rattled her cage, like this one did.

The detective walked toward the parking lot, but, instead of going to his car, he strode down a path that looped through the trees.

She relaxed. In the distance dark clouds gathered. Rain threatened.

"What's going on now?" Scott asked.

"I hardly know how to explain it." How could she? "It's like the little girl is real. Trying to say something to me, … through me. Only I don't know what she wants me to say." She cast a glance his way. "Scott, what if I'm losing my mind?"

"Why? Because the dead are speaking to you? They only do that when they have something important to say. They won't leave you alone, until you give them a voice." He shrugged, helpless to offer more comfort. "Maybe you should go study up on it?"

Alexis nodded. "I can do that easily enough. The internet is full of information." She silently wondered if she should do more, … like book an appointment with her doctor.

"Internet, now that's bad stuff. How can all that information float around in the air?" The huge man looked around uncertainly, as if words and pictures from the internet would jump out of thin air and attack him. "That can't be good for you."

Alexis snorted. "Listen to you. It's okay for dead people to be speaking inside my head, but it's not okay to send data through cables or fiber optics. Yeah, that makes sense."

"Don't you go being disrespectful of the Sight. It'll get you, if you do," he warned.

"Get me how?" This new worry stopped her cold. She rubbed her arms, brushing the first summer raindrops off her bare skin. She always carried rain gear in her truck but didn't bother to go after it. The horizon shone bright blue. This could just be a short squall.

"No way to know. Mostly it's demanding that you listen—or else." Scott studied her face.

"Like I need more to worry about." She changed the subject. "What do you think about the detective?"

He looked sideways at her. "In what way?"

At his teasing tone, her face warmed. "Do you think he's a good cop? You obviously know him. So what's he like?" she asked, exasperated.

"Oh, is that what you mean?" he drawled. He nodded, as if he believed her, but his cheeky grin said otherwise. She rolled her eyes at him. He shook his head. "He's a good man. Driven. Stands for the victims and their families and bulldogs through to see they get justice. Doesn't think much of politics, politicians, or any superior for that matter. Made himself a few enemies because of that. A loner too, just like you. He doesn't talk much about his past." Scott thought about it for a moment. "Come to think of it, rumors have it that he's a bit odd himself."

"Odd how?"

"He gets things done. No one questions him too much because they like the results."

That could mean anything. Not that it mattered to her. She didn't want to know the detective's methods—or his secrets for that matter. He meant nothing to her, and that was how she wanted to keep it.

"The energy around you two fair crackles. Be a shame to waste it fighting."

"What?" She rounded on Scott, caught his grin, and smacked him on his shoulder. She held her hand up to stave off any more comments. "Don't even go there. I've got enough problems to deal with, thank you."

"Can't ignore it though. Almost made me want to offer me van for a couple hours."

He couldn't go unpunished for that one. She raised her hand and smacked him lightly on his shoulder again.

A great shout of laughter was her reward.

"You damn well better be joking," she muttered.

"About the van? Maybe. About the crackling of energy going on around you two? No way."

Alexis shot him a dirty look. "He pisses me off."

"That's passion too."

"Not the kind that matters." She definitely needed to change this subject. Once Scott got going on her nonexistent love life, there'd be no stopping him.

"There's only one kind. How you use it is what matters."

Alexis turned and strode back to the gardens, her face warming in irritation. "Don't hold your breath. It won't happen."

"Never say never, Alexis." Scott's voice floated behind her.

"Like hell," she muttered to herself. "Not in a million years."

"NOT IN A million years, huh?" Kevin didn't know if he was amused or miffed at her offhand rejection. He'd taken a circular path and had ended up close enough to hear their conversation. Standing under a huge spruce tree, he'd stopped to watch Scott and Alexis. They were an odd pair. Yet an obviously strong bond held the two together. *Interesting.* Bonds like that usually developed over a seriously long time—or through shared hardship. According to his records, Alexis had worked for the city for just under five years. Scott, on the other hand, had been here for close to twenty.

Alexis intrigued him. Strong cheekbones, pert nose, slim to the point of being thin, with an abrasive personality that would turn off most men. And that hair. ... Long, flyaway, and blond. Yet according to a couple people he'd spoken to, she was a softie inside.

Now her boss, ... he had a different tale to tell. Rick didn't appear to be a fan in any way. Some hidden story there.

Suddenly Kevin's mind filled with erotic images of Alexis. Heat, pounding hearts, skin slicked with sweat, and ... satisfaction. He couldn't breathe, his heart blasting away against his ribs.

Just as quickly the movie trailer was gone. Leaving him stunned and more than a little aroused. Visions were a rare occurrence for him, but he knew better than to dismiss them. They'd never been wrong before. He grinned and headed to his car. Who knew the twists and turns life could take?

CHAPTER 4

WORK DOMINATED THE next day for Alexis, even though rain continued to pour. The wet weather had eased some, but, just when the sun started to poke through, the skies opened up and soaked everything all over again. The soggy weather didn't stop the work on the sewer line, although it commenced farther away from the grave.

By quitting time, Alexis's energy had crashed. She'd worked hard these last few days, finding it easier to exhaust herself with weeding and plant care, rather than leave any energy available for worrying. Her muscles screamed as she loaded the last of the shovels into the back of Scott's truck. She stripped off her raincoat and carried it over her arm. She hated wearing the damn thing. All coats—raincoats, evening coats, it didn't matter—suffocated her.

Alexis rubbed her sore back and yawned. She walked toward her truck. A vehicle drove in and parked beside hers. Detective Sutherland, in an unmarked police car. She stopped and frowned. What was he doing here?

"Where are you off to?" Detective Sutherland slammed his car door closed, before striding around her truck.

"Home." Tired, she turned her back on him and unlocked her truck. She didn't want to care what he did. Not wanting to care didn't stop the curiosity though. Resolutely she tossed her raincoat into the back seat and tried to ignore him.

Scott came up behind the two of them, carrying several large shovels. "Hey, Kevin. How's it going? Back to the scene of the crime, eh?"

The two men greeted each other with such a friendly rapport that Alexis turned to watch. She shook her head. She'd forgotten to ask Scott how he knew Kevin.

"Just walking around some." Kevin motioned to the gardens. "Get the lay of the land, as it were."

"Have fun. Right. I'm off. Alexis, I'll see you in the morning." Scott turned his bright blue eyes on her. "You're okay, right?"

Alexis smiled. "I'm fine. Looking forward to a hot shower, food, and a good night's rest."

Her friend nodded. "Sounds like a plan." His truck door creaked open. He hopped in, backed out, and took off, gravel spitting out behind him.

Alexis turned to get into her truck, but Detective Sutherland stood at the front of the grill, motioning for her to join him. She frowned at him.

He pointed to the right side of her truck. "You have a flat tire."

"What?" She slammed her door shut and walked around the front end. "Shit." He was right. She didn't need this right now. A few large drops hit her head. Alexis looked up at the sky, ready to explode again. "Lousy timing."

"Do you have a spare?" He squatted down to take a look. "It's not totally flat yet, but it's too low to drive on."

"Yes, but I have a can of inflating stuff, which should get me to the closest garage." She checked her toolbox in the pickup bed. She'd bought the stuff just a couple months ago. "Aha, here it is." She pulled it out, a big grin on her face.

The detective bent down and unscrewed the cap on the tire valve. “Here. Pass it to me.”

Within minutes, the tire started to reinflate.

Alexis laughed. “Just like magic. I love that stuff.”

“I’ve never used it before. Good idea for emergencies.” They stood watching the tire return to normal. Once it was fully inflated, he popped off the can and replaced the valve.

“I’ll head to the garage now, while the tire’s still holding air.” Alexis accepted the empty can, hopped into the driver’s seat, and shut the door. “Thanks, Detective.”

“Kevin.”

“Pardon?”

He walked to the driver’s side. “Call me Kevin.”

Alexis nodded, tongue-tied. What the hell was she supposed to say now?

“You’re Alexis, aren’t you?”

Alexis flushed. Stupid. She couldn’t even engage in a normal conversation with him. “Yes.”

“So, Alexis, what are you hiding about those bones?”

Her eyes widened. Alarm whipped through her. “What? Nothing.” This couldn’t be good. She turned slightly away, so she didn’t have to look him in the eye.

He lowered his head to the open window. His gaze pierced her to the core. Slowly he said, “I notice things. Sense things.” He narrowed his eyes. “And one of those things is that you’re not telling me everything.”

Heat washed across her neck and face.

Kevin’s gaze deepened, as if searching her thoughts. “Unfortunately I don’t know what you could be holding back.”

Thank God for small miracles. Alexis planted her hands on the steering wheel, tossing back her long ponytail. With a confidence she didn't feel, she snapped, "How nice for you. Make a lot of friends that way, do you?" She looked through the windows at the deserted park. How did she get out of this conversation?

Then it happened.

Something brushed the back of her neck. A gentle caress, a stroke of smooth fingers. Alexis twisted her head. "What … was that?" she asked. Her hand crept up to cover her nape.

She hadn't imagined it. She couldn't have. The sensation still burned. Could a touch of her hair feel that way? She shook her ponytail experimentally. No. Not even close.

Twisting, she confirmed that the back of her truck was empty; so was the front of the cab. She searched through the windshield. Everything appeared normal. She glanced carefully at Kevin. If the sensation hadn't been so creepy, it might have felt soothing.

"What's wrong?" Kevin asked. He straightened, shooting her a curious look. "What happened?"

"Something touched me. I swear it. Did you see anything?" She looked over at Kevin, more than a little unnerved. He stared at her—an odd look on his face.

Unconsciously she rubbed the back of her neck. The weird feeling was gone, leaving uncertainty and more than a little fear behind.

"*What?* I'm not crazy. I really did feel something." The defensive tone rang loudly in her own ears.

"You're just tired. I'm sure it's nothing."

Goose bumps rose on her arms in the warm evening air. Alexis rubbed the chill from her arms. "I need to get to the garage and get my tire fixed." *And get the hell away from him.* But she kept that thought to herself. "Thank you for your help. It's late, and I've got to run," she babbled, feeling like a fool. She started the engine, then gently reversed out of the spot.

Kevin called out, "You can run, but you can't hide."

He looked so eerily sure of himself, her nerves couldn't take any more. She slammed her gearshift into Drive and raced off.

LONG SHADOWS FELL on the empty parking lot, as Alexis escaped.

"Well, well, well," he whispered to the empty parking lot. That was a first. Occasionally a probe made someone feel odd, uncertain even, but that was after he'd had a good chance to check out their energy. Alexis was unique. He'd barely opened his senses, barely sent out a smidge of his consciousness before she'd noticed the shift in energy. *As a physical touch.*

Then she'd panicked.

Kevin considered some of the things he'd heard about her. Scott had said she was well-liked but a loner with a spitfire temper. That she wasn't afraid to call a spade a spade, a great friend to have on your side …

Whereas her boss said the exact opposite. Rick's comments had been caustic, and he basically said, "Alexis is walking trouble, with an attitude."

Mostly she was an enigma. One he had no intention of walking away from and for more than one reason. Psychic intuition had supplied the knowledge of an upcoming relationship—an intuition that had yet to fail him—and his imagination had filled in the rest. Images so vivid, they'd driven him half-mad last night. Which, considering she wasn't even close to enjoying a night in his bed, had frustrated him beyond sleep.

Thank God, she couldn't hide her response to him. He'd take some solace in that.

He grinned. He could expect one hell of a fight getting her into his bed.

That was all right. It would make the victory all the sweeter.

For both of them.

ALEXIS SHUDDERED IN relief, when she finally turned off the truck's engine at her apartment. Not the most pleasant trip to the garage and then home. She couldn't explain the continued sense of unease. It lived under her skin these days. She ran to the front entrance.

"Hey, Alexis."

She raced past her neighbor with a fast wave and headed for the stairs, knowing she still had to navigate the hallway. Afraid her nerves would overtake her if she slowed down, she ran up the three flights to her floor. The door to her hallway stood on her right, but her fear of a repeat of yesterday's hallway vision made her hand hesitate, hover over the handle …

Irritated by her lack of control, she forced herself to pull open the stairway door.

So far, so good. The hall looked normal. With a confidence she didn't feel, she strode down the length to her apartment. Just as she unlocked the door, a faint voice reached out to her.

Hello.

Alexis pivoted in surprise. "Who's there?"

A small rippling mirage wavered in front of her. Transparent and wispy, the outline of a child slowly appeared. Alexis reared back. It was the child from the ditch.

Help me, the voice intoned. *Please. ... Help free me ...*

Trembling and weak, Alexis shook her head in denial. Her mind screamed, even as she reached for a semblance of control.

"Who are you?" she whispered to the miniature apparition, so clear and yet so transparent. "What do you want?" She wiped her hands on her jeans.

Huge expressive eyes beckoned to Alex, drawing her closer. She noticed the odd brownish tint first, only to realize it was a dingy carpet showing through. The child's eyes were empty windows to an old soul.

"Dai ... sy. Help me ..." The voice trailed off as the image rippled, then faded into nothingness in front of her.

"Oh God, oh God, oh God." Alexis couldn't stop her frantic litany of a prayer any more than she could control the mad trembling that prevented her fingers from opening her door ...

Finally she made it inside. Alexis leaned against the locked and chained door, taking in deep gulps of air.

Talk about déjà vu. Adapting to ghosts was so not on her agenda. And helping them? ... She shuddered at the thought.

When she finally peeled herself off the door, she couldn't stop pacing. Nervous energy sent her storming around the tiny apartment. Her nerves couldn't take much more. Chills iced their way down her spine, sending her in search of a heavy sweater. She pulled it tightly around her. A cup of tea would be wonderful right now, but she was too scared to go into the kitchen, in case Lissa was there. Alexis didn't think she could stand to see her sister's ghost too. She'd loved her sister dearly, but seeing Lissa in ghostly form hadn't exactly been the warm bonding experience she'd so foolishly dreamed it would be.

But it could be.

"Who said that?" Alexis spun around, as panic coursed through her. She was alone—wasn't she? "Help. Please, someone help me," Alexis called out. Tears coursed down her cheeks. She brushed them away.

She had to talk to a doctor, before she lost it altogether.

The phone rang, startling her with its piercing demand. Alexis crossed the room to stare down at it warily. She picked it up. "Hello?"

"What's wrong?"

"Huh?" Heavy traffic noises filled her ear.

"Damn it, answer me, Alexis! What's wrong?"

"Kevin?" God, she was so rattled she'd actually called him by his first name.

"Who the hell were you expecting?" he snapped. "You've been calling for help out on the ethers for the last ten minutes."

She was? On the ethers? Oh God. Alexis closed her eyes in disbelief. What was he talking about?

"I'm less than two minutes away. Stay calm, and I'll be right there."

The phone went dead.

How did he know where she lived? *Duh.* She'd given her statement to the police after the garden incident. Of course they had it on file now.

His heavy pounding broke through her musings.

She unlocked the door but never had a chance to open it.

Kevin barged in. "Why the hell did you unbolt the door

when you didn't know who was on the other side?" he roared, storming past her.

The raging maniac in her living room was a little hard to understand, but his meaning was clear. Her back bristled. "And to think I actually let you in," she snapped at him, only to back up at his hard look.

"You couldn't have kept me out. Now what the hell is going on?"

Cold and deadly, this was a new cop persona she hadn't met. She'd only seen him a few times, and, each time, he'd seemed different. His changeability had stopped her from finding a level of comfort with him. "What makes you think something is going on?" She moved around the living room, straightening up magazines that didn't need it. She wrapped her arms tight about her chest.

"No more games."

Startled, she turned to face him. "I'm not playing games."

"Like hell you're not. I'd almost made it home when you started crying out in my head." He glared at her.

She blinked. This conversation was beyond bizarre. "Let me get this straight. You came here because you thought I *might* be in trouble," she said slowly, watching him. He straightened as if preparing for something. And it had damn well better be to provide an explanation. She had no clue what was going on. And she needed to understand.

"Sometimes I hear things." He shrugged. "I've learned to listen." He studied her carefully. "That means something *was* going on." He looked around at the tiny apartment. "Although what, I can't imagine." His gaze swept her from head to toe and back up again.

"You appear to be fine physically and no one …" He

swept his arm around the tiny space. “No one appears to be attacking you, so …” Again his irritated voice trailed off. He ran his fingers through his hair instead. “I can’t explain how I know, but you were afraid. I felt it.”

That he understood she’d been afraid was comforting in a way. It disturbed her to think that he could pick up her thoughts—and from miles away. The silence stretched between them, as she considered his admission. “I was upset.”

He sighed in disgust.

She shrugged. Okay, so he already knew *that.* She chewed on her bottom lip, as she considered what to tell him. Given what he’d just said, maybe he would understand. It was either that or book in with the doctor. And maybe both. “I don’t know what’s happening to me.”

“Explain.” His voice was curt, clipped, and all cop.

Alexis paced the small dingy room. She couldn’t bear to see the look of disapproval on his face, nor could she get out the words. Alexis changed direction and marched into the kitchen, not caring if he followed or not. She bustled around, making a pot of coffee. She needed a clear head for what was coming.

When she surreptitiously checked on him, she found him sitting at the old kitchen table, looking around at his surroundings with interest.

“Have you lived here long?”

“Just under a year. Although I’ve been thinking about moving lately. Why do you ask?” she asked.

He nodded noncommittally, still looking around. “Where did you live before here?”

What was he noticing, and what was going on in his mind? She looked at her grimy walls. The walls were bare;

she hadn't gotten around to putting up any personal mementos. The same dingy color covered the walls as when she'd moved in, which was probably the same color as the decade of tenants kept it before. Dull, boring, bland, … and, in truth, downright ugly.

"I lived in a little house with a big heated greenhouse in the backyard." Her face softened.

"With your sister?" he probed, searching her face and eyes for the truth. At her wide-eyed look, he added, "Scott told me."

She put two cups on the table and said, her voice now tinged with sadness, "Yes, with Lissa. She was a fighter. Lived much longer than anyone expected her too, but …"

"I don't mean to intrude …" He paused, a wry look on his face. "And I realize it must seem like I'm doing just that." After a moment, he added, "Try understanding my position. You're the strongest transmitter I've ever connected with. If I could understand the source of the pain you feel, then I might differentiate it from a different transmission. It would also help me if you'd apply a level of control."

Alexis kept her gaze on her cup of coffee, wishing it had something stronger in it. She could use the boost right about now. This whole conversation was too crazy. She studied Kevin over the rim of her mug. He seemed serious. Almost too afraid to ask, but needing to know, she asked, "Transmitter?"

His stunned gaze pinned her in place. Disbelief oozed from his voice, as he asked, "You didn't know?"

Alexis got up and walked over to the sink, where she turned around and leaned against the counter to face him. Putting distance between them didn't help. Confused and a little apprehensive, she had to ask, "Didn't know what?"

Bemused, Kevin could only gape at her. "You're one of the strongest psychics I've ever come across. And the only one, to date, who had no idea they were." At her look of total incomprehension, he added, "Look. I don't know *why* this is happening, but the *what* of it I *can* explain. When you feel strongly negative about something, you're actually sending out a distress signal to any receivers—psychics who can receive your signal—who are in range. That's why I called you a transmitter. You're transmitting or broadcasting emotions."

CHAPTER 5

TIME STOPPED.

A transmitter? Is that what she was?

She rolled the idea around in her head, trying it on. Did it fit? Maybe, ... in some ways. But there was so much more to it than just that. Like seeing the vision of the little girl, seeing the hallway shift, and even hearing the voices.

And, if she were transmitting, like Kevin said, how come no one else heard her but him?

Another thought struck—what about her plants? She'd thought she just talked to them. Was she transmitting when she talked to them? Yes, that made more sense. But what about her understanding of their needs, their colors, and even their sounds. Didn't that make her a receiver too?

Was there such a thing?

"Does everyone have this ability?" she asked cautiously. "Lying latent until something brings it to their awareness?"

"Researchers say we do, but only a small fraction of the population uses it or even knows those abilities are there to be used. It can also get more confusing because all receivers are transmitters but not all transmitters are receivers." He leaned forward, locking his hands together in front of him. "This whole idea *is* new for you, right?"

"Absolutely." And with the word came a question. Should she tell him everything or wait?

He cocked an eyebrow in surprise at her answer, but he continued. "Chances are something triggered this. Something like finding the body, maybe?"

"The finger," she added softly, needing to tell someone. Maybe he would understand. "Something happened when I picked up the bones and realized they belonged to a child's finger." The horrific memory made her wince. God, she didn't want to revisit this.

"Tell me," he urged. "Exactly *what* started with the finger?" He rose, neared her.

Slowly, haltingly, she related the weird series of events from the ditch. He let her get it all out, and somehow, in the process, her hand ended up cradled in his.

Mesmerized, she watched his strong, sinewy thumb stroke and slide over her palm, warming and comforting on a level she hadn't felt in many years. It moved over the rounded pad, sliding down the valley between her fingers, sensuous, sexy, and definitely seductive.

She ordered her hand to withdraw. But her long fingers had a mind of their own and refused to obey. They chose instead to nestle against his much larger and stronger ones. As if they belonged there …

Enough. Alexis broke the trance and snatched her hand free, tucking it into her pants pocket.

"What else?"

She glanced at him.

"Is there anything else?" His question prodded gently for more.

Alexis wavered, but no point in keeping the rest from him. As clearly and as succinctly as she could, she described her visions of the hallway, of little Daisy—and of Lissa.

"When you heard the little girl calling you, did it come

from outside your head or inside?"

She smiled without humor. "Believe it or not, I'd wondered that myself. I don't have a definitive answer."

Kevin seemed to consider her words. "Is that everything?" he asked.

She flushed.

"It would help if I knew it all," he suggested quietly, his gaze never leaving hers.

She wanted to believe in the understanding, the compassion, and the acceptance he offered. Taking a chance, she shared the last bit about her gardens and the need to transplant the suffering plant to the child's grave.

"You planted a daisy on her grave, and you're saying the ghost child said the same word was her name? That's odd and too much of a coincidence to ignore."

"I know. I'm presuming it's her body we found."

"Anything's possible." He pulled his sleeve back to check the time. "I need to leave. Let me know if anything else like this happens." He paused, gave her a wry look, and added, "Or else I'll find out the same way I did last time."

Alexis almost laughed, but, now that he spoke of leaving, Alexis found the thought of being alone disconcerting. How stupid. She hadn't wanted him here in the first place. Still, he'd gone a long way toward helping her tonight.

"Will you be okay here?"

"Of course. This is home." Even though she hadn't put much effort into making it hers. She cast an unhappy glance around the cold place.

"We need to talk some more about your abilities and how you can learn to control them. I have a friend, Stefan, who might help. I'll talk to him." He walked to the doorway, jacket in hand. She'd trailed behind him, helpless to abate the sense of loss already threatening.

Slowly she closed the door behind him and turned to look around the empty room. An odd thought struck. Outside of Scott, Kevin was her first real visitor in a year.

How pathetic.

When her sister's cancer had first been diagnosed, priorities had to be set. Everything had been about Lissa. Afterward, Alexis had remained secluded, inside a wall of pain that refused to ease.

When had that changed? When had the pain reduced her to the point that she'd just been hiding?

KEVIN WALKED OUT to his car. Given Alexis's skills and lack of control, he had one more thing to do tonight. He headed to Stefan's house.

Stefan lived in a huge cedar post-and-beam home on a couple acres just out of town. Evergreens lined the long driveway and ringed the property. But that was nothing to the damn plants surrounding the house that looked like they lived on steroids.

His psychic skills, many of them still developing and expanding, were extraordinary. Stefan had worked alongside most major police departments throughout the country. He had often quipped that he'd been forced to learn more and faster just to stay one step ahead of the criminals.

The door opened to a yawning Stefan, rubbing his fingers through his rumpled hair. He snorted at the sight of Kevin. "Did anyone ever tell you that your timing stinks?"

"Were you sleeping already? Sorry, but sleep is reserved for those not on guard duty, Stefan. You know that. You can go back to bed in a minute. I'm not coming in." He gave his friend another minute to wake up further.

Stefan was an artist who used his creativity to release the images and visions that haunted him. His art gave a deep insight into the extreme sides of his personality. His work hung in private collections all over the world. He painted when he required release from his emotional hell. Rare were the privileged few welcomed into his inner sanctum. Intensely private and eerily accurate, Stefan walked a path forged with his own boundaries.

"So what's going on?" murmured Stefan. "Oh …" An intuitive pause was followed with "You have girl trouble. How very funny." He really looked amused as he propped himself against the doorway. "So there *are* ladies in your world." After a heavy pause, his face leaned out, deepening with pain. "One of them is dead, the little one."

Kevin waited for his longtime friend to sort through the onslaught of impressions. That's what happened when you had an extreme psychic as part of your circle of friends. Nothing was private.

Stefan rubbed his eyes. "What do you need from me?"

Kevin knew Stefan had seen too much of this world and the next to be surprised by anything much these days. "If you have anything that can help on the child's case, I'd appreciate it. But it's the other female I really need help with."

Stefan grinned. "Is that so?" he drawled. "I never thought I'd see the day."

"I'm not sure you're seeing clearly now," Kevin said wryly, crossing his arms over his chest. "Take another look."

Silence stretched between them.

"Right." Stefan was all business now. "What's her phone number, and have you told her about me?"

"Yes." Kevin pulled out a piece of paper with Alexis's number on it. Like many psychics, Stefan had no luck remembering numbers. Occasionally he could come up with dates, but, more often, he couldn't recall numerals of any kind. He said it had frustrated him to no end at the beginning. Now he acknowledged that as a weakness.

"I'll call her in the morning."

Kevin grimaced. "Or you could call her tonight."

Stefan frowned, his eyes focusing inward. "Not everyone keeps your hours."

"Except I just left her, and she wasn't in any shape to sleep."

Stefan's long-suffering sigh brought a grin to Kevin's face. "Thanks, Stefan. Let me know what happens." He headed toward his car. "Also, if you learn anything about the little one …"

Stefan waved him off. "As always. I'll let you know if I pick up anything."

Kevin honked once and drove away.

LATER THAT SAME evening, exhaustion caught Alexis by surprise and startled a yawn from deep down. She closed her book, placed it on the paisley bedspread covering her and snuggled deeper into her bedding.

Hi.

Alexis bolted upright. She searched the empty room. What the hell was that?

My name is Stefan Kronos. I'm a friend of Kevin's.

Damn it. Alexis bolted from the bed and ran to the living room.

Alexis stared at the room, absolutely freaked. She spun

around in a circle. How did you run or hide from voices in your head? Shivers slipped down her body, and she wrapped her arms tightly around her chest. Her pounding heart had no place to escape and continued to knock against her ribs.

The voice in her head sighed. *Fine, we'll do it your way.*

The phone rang, scaring the bejeezus out of her again. She stared at her cell, like it was a bomb about to go off.

Cautiously she picked up the phone. "Hello?"

"I'm Stefan," said the voice on the other end.

Shit. Her knees knocked so badly she might collapse. Unintentionally she blurted out the first words in her mind. "Was that you?"

"Me?"

"In my head a minute ago?" Oh God, she shouldn't have said that. Alexis ran her shaky fingers over her face. She sounded like a lunatic.

"Yes."

"Yes," she shrieked. "Yes, you were inside my head? Why? How?" Alexis sat down on her couch with a *thump*.

"Kevin asked me to call."

"Kevin? You know him?" Alexis latched on to the one sane thing he'd said.

"Yes. We need to meet. Tomorrow would be good. Cardinal Park around six-thirty p.m. We'll talk then." He hung up.

Alexis gaped at the phone still cradled in her hand. "My God."

How had her life gotten so crazy?

Still troubled, Alexis knew any sleep would be a long time coming.

THE NEXT MORNING, Alexis pulled into the lot at the garden, tires squealing and ten minutes late. Striding over to Scott, she handed him one of the two coffees she'd picked up on the way in, hoping it would work as an excuse in case her boss, Rick, beat her to work.

Scott accepted the cup and flashed her a grin, before he quickly sobered, nodding toward something behind her. "Good morning, Rick. How're you doing?"

Rick? Alexis stiffened at Scott's address but then forced herself to relax. Rick was irritating but harmless.

"The mayor is very unhappy over the regrettable end to the ceremonies." Rick's voice washed over Alexis like lighter fluid.

Ever-so-slowly she swiveled to face him. "What did you say?" she demanded.

Rick took a defensive step back.

"Did you just say the *mayor* was upset at all this unpleasantness?" she questioned caustically. "How about the parents who, even now, are looking for their missing child? A child was murdered. Don't you people understand that?"

Alexis was warming up to rip into her boss again, when Scott placed a heavy hand on her shoulder—a gentle but indomitable warning. "Take it easy, Alexis."

Scott's intervention barely allowed her to regain an appropriate level of restraint, only it wasn't enough to still her piercing anger or the grief she felt welling up inside. She spun away from the men and walked off a short distance to be alone. She looked toward the makeshift memorial and gasped in surprise.

The grave was heaped with flowers, candles, and balloons. Teddy bears smiled out at the world, among the glorious blooms and ribbons festively adorning the jumble.

She couldn't resist walking over to stand in awe at the testimony to a much warmer humanity than she'd seen in a while. Tears formed in the corners of her eyes. Toys, cards, and notes spoke of a community mourning the sad resting place for the lost little girl.

In a small way, Alexis was proud of her contribution to the beautiful gardens. If the child had been tossed away so casually, at least she'd had one of the prettiest resting places while she endured the long wait for discovery.

Alexis could only hope it wouldn't be an equally long wait to find the girl's killer.

"Alexis, if you want to work on the south bed today, we'll go over some of the other work to be done later. I've got to go downtown with Rick for a meeting." Scott had walked up behind her. "Will you be okay?"

She knew what he was asking. "I'll be fine. Go on. Just make sure you take him with you."

"Go a little easy on him. He's the mayor's confidant. What affects the mayor affects him." Scott shrugged.

"I know. I know. But he's an arrogant, cold, brown-nosing asshole." Now she felt better.

Scott patted her back, before joining Rick and driving away.

When the dust settled, Alexis put her cup down and spread her arms wide. Time alone. Finally.

Her spirits lifted, as she did something she'd always done naturally, but only now understood for the intricate communication process it truly was. She sent out a wide belt of joyous green energy to her plants. Their glorious energy bounced back. Her heart embraced the bright colors and cheerful sounds exploding in her mind.

So that's what being a transmitter meant. She just hadn't known what it was called.

CHAPTER 6

AT THE END of her workday Alexis had stopped for a quick meal and then hummed contentedly as she drove to Cardinal Park. She was early for her meeting with Stefan, and, not knowing what else to do, Alexis wandered around the garden, admiring the plants. Their colors were slightly different than those she normally worked with, but they had a serenity she hadn't seen before.

While enjoying one particular arrangement, the flower petals brightened, almost as if a light had come on from within. How curious. Alexis compared them to the petals on other flowers. Now they all appeared to be lit up. What the hell?

That's the result of both our energies combined.

Alexis froze. That voice spoke inside her head. Again.

It's me. Turn around.

Ever-so-slowly, Alexis turned to look behind her.

That's right. I'm the one talking to you.

Alexis's mouth dropped open.

That brought a knowing smile to the man in front of her. Did she say a man? What an understatement. *Man* implied ordinary. ... This guy could pass for a GQ model. He was stunning!

Thanks for the compliment.

Alexis flushed. Not only was she hearing him in her

mind, but he was also reading hers! Oh, God. She closed her eyes in mortification. How embarrassing.

Proving her assumption, he spoke telepathically once again. *Don't be embarrassed, please. I wouldn't normally do this, but it seems like you are the type to need proof. I'll get out now.*

Instantly her mind felt empty—bereft even. She was mystified. How could she miss what she'd only just noticed?

He smiled at her. "It's the loss of a connection that you hadn't experienced until now, one that you'd always longed for, because, on some level, part of you knew you were incomplete."

Her gaze widened at the hypnotic-sounding voice. As he obviously could read her every thought, it would be best to be totally honest. ... But wow! "It's not fair. You're too gorgeous for *any* woman to ignore," she complained, startling a surprised laugh from him. "Could we start again?" she asked drily. Quickly recovering her composure, she held out a hand. "Hi, I'm Alexis."

When his chuckles calmed down, he shook her hand. "I'm Stefan. Kevin told me a little about you, but he didn't say that you would be a breath of fresh air to my jaded soul."

"If you can read my mind, I might as well speak it. I don't think I can communicate telepathically like you do."

"Wrong. If you can understand me as easily as you do, you are certainly capable of speaking your thoughts in the same way. And I heard yours. Remember? You just have to learn how to focus them, then send them." He tucked her arm into the crook of his elbow. "Let's walk."

They meandered through the twisting pathways. There was so much color that it distracted Alexis from her purpose.

"You love the plant world, don't you?"

She nodded at his question.

"Why?" he asked.

"I have no easy answer." She took a minute to gather her thoughts. "I feel better when I work with plants. They've helped me to heal, to grieve for my sister."

She stopped to smile down at a particularly valiant pansy, trying to bloom between the flagstones. "I admire the wild ones, like this little guy. In the face of all odds, he makes a tremendous effort to live his life the best that he can."

"Isn't that what you're doing?"

Startled, she stared at him. He was very intuitive, regardless of any psychic abilities. "My struggle hasn't been all that difficult."

He allowed that one to pass, for the moment. "Where do you see yourself going from here?"

She snorted. "It's all I can do to get through each day right now." Her fear and frustration bubbled over. She *had* to tell him. "All of a sudden, ghosts, voices, even weird visions have taken over my life without warning." She searched his face closely. She didn't know what she'd do if he laughed at her.

Stefan only nodded.

A weight in her chest eased. "I've talked to plants for years, but I hadn't seen that as odd. Many people have a green thumb. But, after finding those bones, well, I don't know if a green thumb explains it anymore."

Stefan motioned her in the direction of a large stone bench. "Now, start where you found those bones." He remained silent, as her words poured out ...

"Then you called me," she finished lamely, feeling a bit foolish at the end of her emotional spiel.

Stefan looked at her with admiration. "Kevin is an old friend, from a difficult time in my life when I didn't want friends. In truth, I didn't want anything—especially life."

Alexis turned to face him at his surprising confession. "*You* were suicidal?"

Her shocked disbelief brought a wry smile to his face. "Yes, I was. The reason, however, is all you've just said … and so much more. I saw dead people all the time. I answered questions in people's heads, under the assumption that they'd spoken to me. I knew things would happen before they did. The worst part was …" He paused for a moment. "Nothing I did stopped events from happening. I couldn't *do* anything to keep the bad things from coming to pass. I was helpless. That made me a victim myself." He fell silent.

Alexis watched his face darken, with the shadows of memories. He'd turned inward, as if staring off into a horrendous past.

"How did you get through it? My God, I've only been dealing with this for such a short time, and I didn't think I'd make it through *that.*" Alexis cringed at what he must have endured. His childhood must have been one long, lonely nightmare.

"I met someone, a parapsychologist, who recognized the mess I was in. After that, I studied, practiced, and learned to mentally control my abilities. At least to a certain extent. That helped me regain perspective." He smiled. "I was no longer a victim, and that made all the difference."

"What makes these abilities start up? No prior warning, just, all of a sudden, ghosts walk toward me? I don't get it." And she didn't. It was just too odd to think that, one day, she'd fallen into a ditch and had woken up like this.

Stefan patted her hand. "There are still so few answers. Your abilities with the plant world left a door open, which triggered the next stage of development. There seems to be no limit to how far these abilities can progress." He stood and pulled his jacket closer together in the front, before burying his fists deep into his pockets. "In my case, they are in constant flux. I never quite know what's next."

"So *just get used to it*, is that it?" The thought of the intrusion left a bitter taste in her mouth.

"You can learn to accept your gifts and eventually develop them, or you can fight them and slowly go crazy." He smiled a little grimly down at her. "The choice is yours." He started to walk away, leaving her sitting there alone.

"Wait."

He stopped but didn't turn around.

"I'm scared. This is pretty freaky stuff." She chased after him to stand next to him. "How do I learn to control all this? Please understand. I didn't ask for this." That brought a disgusted look to his face, rushing her back into speech. "I can't live with my life always being out of control. I need to know how to direct it."

"It won't happen overnight. But you can do some things to minimize the impact and to speed up your recovery afterward." He hesitated, his expression undecided.

"Please," she pleaded. "I need your help."

Finally a single decisive nod came. "We'll try to meet twice a week. But you have to work with it every day between. If you can't make that commitment, then neither will I."

"Agreed."

He considered her for a moment, then spoke slowly, "As time appears to be an issue, we'll start tonight." He pulled out his card and handed it to her. "Meet me at my place at seven-thirty. We'll cover some basics this evening."

Startled, Alexis took the card that read Stefan Kronos. Consultant. Psychic Investigator. When she lifted her head to ask him what kind of investigation could one do in that field, she found he'd walked off, leaving her to stare after him.

KEVIN SAT DOWN at his desk, determined to find some proof to support Alexis's vision. An eight- or nine-year-old girl and the name Daisy was all he had to go on. He logged on to his computer and set up a search.

Within minutes, he'd traveled deep inside the national data banks. He started locally, then branched out county by county, researching missing person files.

A grim realization settled quickly on his shoulders. He found so many cases of missing children, so many destroyed families who existed in an endless state of waiting and hoping.

By the time he'd run through all the searches he could, the name Daisy still had no hits. Kevin slumped in his chair. Fatigue screamed through his muscles as he stretched his arms overhead.

"Damn." He hadn't expected to solve this mystery in the first five minutes, but it would've been nice to score a little information. From his desk, he saw the black shadows cast by the old clock tower above the square. He found no comfort in the familiarity of the scene tonight, not when a different kind of darkness gathered in the deep silence.

His intuition screamed that this heinous crime related to a child buried in the park was just the tip of an iceberg. He had no idea what lurked beneath the surface. He'd find out though. This was what he was born to do. It defined who he was.

A hunter.

Every instinct flashed on red alert now.

Why that location? What drew a killer to that spot? A garden? Had it been the softest spot to dig up at the time? Or perhaps the prettiest spot to lay the child to rest? Did the place seem like a memorial to the perp? Surely burying a body, no matter how small, would have been noticed by the gardeners who worked there at the time. Or dogs in the ensuing years. Then again, if the gardeners used heavy chemical weed sprays or fertilizers, that could have kept the dogs unaware.

Wouldn't Alexis, with her abilities, have sensed something was wrong there, when she gardened close by? Although it's possible she might not have known or understood, on an energy level, what she'd received. She was a beginner in energy work.

Kevin was well past frustration. He'd walked straight into disgust. What had made him consider, for even one minute, that Daisy was the name of the child they'd found? It sounded more like a nickname than a proper name.

He shoved back his chair, stretching out his arms to rotate his shoulders. He needed a break. Glancing at his watch, he swore, stood, and raced from his office. He would be late for his meeting with the mayor—a very perturbed mayor, who'd just received another threat this morning, according to the early phone call.

The mayor's favorite café around the corner had become a steady lunchtime gathering place. Two blocks away, it catered to a varied clientele. The food was good and always came hot. Kevin didn't care about much else. This was their third such meeting at the same place. So far, the mayor had proven to be a creature of habit.

John Prescott stood, talking on his cell phone, outside the restaurant. Seeing Kevin, he finished his call and smiled at him. "Good to see you. Life is busy these days, isn't it?"

They walked in and were immediately seated in one of the far corners. At the exact same table as last time. "It's too damn busy. Our town is growing, and it's hard to stay ahead."

Kevin couldn't resist passing on a reminder that the town needed more law enforcement officers to keep everyone safe. "Could use more staff."

"Noted." John moved into the corner and took the far side of the table, his back to the wall, where he could watch the rest of the restaurant. He didn't look at the menu, choosing instead to order his regular hot sandwich and salad from the waitress.

Kevin waited his turn, then ordered the special, a hot roast beef sandwich and mashed potatoes. One good meal today would hold him for a long time. Who knew when he'd get home tonight? Besides, if their lunch meeting followed their regular pattern, they'd eat quickly and then go walk in the park, while they discussed personal stuff.

Sure enough, today was no different.

Once outside, John led the way into the large park in front of Bradford's Central Hall. Once away from the crowds, he wasted no time. "Any news?"

"Nothing, John. Absolutely nothing."

This whole blackmail mess felt wrong. There had to be more to it. Kevin felt it. To this point, the mayor had received threats but no demands, except to say that the mayor had better step up and tell the truth—*or else*. It was the last part that bothered Kevin. He hadn't spent all these years on the force without gaining a deeper, darker understanding of humanity. In this case, blackmailers usually had something to use as a bargaining chip. Only the mayor denied such a thing existed.

The mayor lowered his voice, his body almost vibrating with tension. "Kevin, this is unacceptable. I need answers. Hell. I need more than that. I need solutions, damn it." He clenched his fists, glaring at the bright sunny gardens surrounding them. "This asshole will ruin my life," he spluttered to a stop, then started up again. "I can't sleep for worrying. What the hell is going on here?"

John, as a politician, had faced criticism and verbal abuse before, but he told Kevin it was never like this. For the last ten years, he'd served the citizens of Bradford well. The public record showed he'd been a businessman in Redding, California, before that. The timing had been perfect for his move here, as the locals were more than ready to get rid of their corrupt politician. Through the years, John remained a popular figure, easily being reelected.

"I'm looking, but I haven't found the answers yet," Kevin stated.

"Then you'd damn well better find them fast," the mayor grumbled. "Before this asshole makes good his threat."

Kevin got the message. But he couldn't help wondering what the mayor might be hiding. He'd once probed gently to see if he could find out but had hit a wall immediately. It happened that way sometimes.

As he walked back to the office, Kevin's mind once again turned to Alexis. Had Stefan called her? Instincts said he had.

A twinge of unease settled in his stomach. Stefan's looks often stopped women in their tracks. It wasn't Stefan's doing and in no way did it affect their friendship, but Kevin found himself hoping that Alexis wouldn't react like all the rest.

Stefan kept his love interests private, but generally the relationships were short and intense. Stefan had said once that his potential partner wouldn't show up for another few years, and that would happen only if she found him. When Kevin had asked for an explanation, the answer had been even more confusing.

"Energy, like colors or musical notes, have to combine to make the right kind of music, or I don't go there, no matter how willing or how gorgeous the woman is. Especially for a long-term relationship."

Colors? What did that have to do with anything? It boggled Kevin's mind.

As did the thought that he wanted Alexis for himself.

He couldn't help but wonder if Alexis blended with his colors, creating the potential to make the right kind of music.

And, if they did, how long before they could start to sing their colorful song together?

~

ALEXIS DROVE CAREFULLY to the address Stefan had given her on his business card. The driveway, lined by tall trees, appeared well-kept and normal. She wasn't sure what she expected, but considering what this man could apparently do, it wouldn't be an ordinary home. She followed the curve of the road and hit the brakes.

What the hell?

The gardener in her was stunned. Both the transmitter

and the receiver in her were overwhelmed … with joy. Gently she parked her truck to the side and got out. She took several steps forward, tears in her eyes.

It was apparent in this setting that she was but a newbie student to a master when it came to gardening or plant health. All the bushes, flowers, even the trees looked like they were on steroids. The house itself twinkled through the greenery that both hid and guarded it from prying eyes. One side of Stefan's house was all glass that reflected the setting sun. The rest was crafted from logs. Some of them so huge she'd wished she'd seen the trees before they'd been felled. Evergreens bordered the property, and they glowed with some otherworldly shimmer.

Everything was alive in a way she had never seen before. Birds twittered and sang in the garden as she stood in awe.

"Were you planning to come in or to just stand there?"

Stefan. She didn't bother to glance at him. Her gaze was desperately trying to delve deeper into the miracle in front of her.

"Earth to Alexis."

"I'm here. I'm just … overwhelmed." She'd never seen roses with blooms so big. And the colors. Everything practically radiated joy. Wood carvings peeked out from parts of the garden, catching and holding her attention. Such craftsmanship.

"Don't be. You're very talented with plants as well."

That caught her attention. "No," she said. "I'm skilled." She waved her arms around her and added, "This … is talent. I don't even recognize some of these plants."

"I'm a bit of a collector. Have plants from all over the world." He grinned.

She stared for a moment, then grinned back. "And you

are too damn good-looking as well."

This time he chuckled. "But only temporarily. Once you get to know me, I won't look that way at all."

She frowned and walked closer. "Why? Does the troll in you shine brighter the better I get to know you?"

He stepped inside and motioned her to enter, but she couldn't. She stalled at the open front door. Made of wood, it was as if she saw Tolkien's tree Ents coming to life. Faces had been carved, making unique use of the wood grains. She shook her head and walked in. "You didn't answer my question."

She followed him through the house, loving the unique space, the bright lights, … and, oh my God, the stained-glass windows. She spun around, trying to take everything in, and realized she couldn't. The walls were covered with paintings that drew her in and wouldn't let go.

"I don't need to."

Had she insulted him? She hoped not. Damn her unruly tongue. She studied Stefan's features carefully. He didn't appear to be upset.

He motioned her to a chair. "We'll start right now. And we'll keep it short. I want to show you how to protect your space and how to run the energy you need for your system. I'll show you several techniques to help you meditate. From there, all kinds of skills can be worked on."

"Like?" Alexis sat where he pointed.

"Talking safely with ghosts, for starters."

She flushed. Dare she ask about the *safely* part? But he was already giving her instructions to sit comfortably and to take several deep breaths. She tried to let the questions go and followed along.

And hoped she could trust where he led.

Forty minutes later, she was still hoping.

"Okay, we'll try to put all this into practice right now, then call it a night. Close your eyes. Focus on deep breathing. One breath in. … Let it out slowly. And again. As each thought flits into your mind, acknowledge the thought exists, then let it slide away. Let it go. Let them all go. Let the thoughts drift in and then drift out. Just like your breath. Deeper breaths, longer exhales. Feel the tension drain away.

"Now think of a favorite place where you'd like to be. A waterfall, a beautiful meadow. One of your favorite gardens perhaps. See yourself there. Be there. Smell the fresh air. … Feel a breeze on your skin."

Alexis walked forward toward a waterfall she'd loved as a child. She was on the path through an open meadow. The grass was high, the sun hot. The sound of the water beckoned. She felt so alive. Strong. Vibrant. She tilted her face to the sun and smiled.

Feels good, doesn't it?

She turned to answer Stefan, somehow not surprised to see him in her meditation. *Yes, it does.*

Good. Now let's work on your energy pathways.

She followed his instructions and saw the energy in her body glow, as he pointed out how to move it up the meridians that crisscrossed her body. He showed her how the little hiccups in the meridians could be smoothed out and how to increase the energy as the two of them moved about.

She lost track of time in this alternate world, as if just the two of them were in a whole new world.

Actually it is a new world. It's a different facet of the old world—but in a whole new way. For you. For me and many others, this is a place we come to often.

She could believe it.

Someone else is here as well. Someone hoping to say hi.

She turned to look at him. Lord, he looked different. Surreal, glowing even. At the beginning of this exercise, he'd looked like he had when she'd arrived at his house. Now he looked, ... well, ... ghostly.

He laughed. *That's because we crossed into a new dimension. We're on the dead side of life, so to speak. The other side. An alternate plane of existence. And, because we are here, at least this much inside the energy field, someone wants to see you. Someone who has stuck around instead of traveling into the light. Someone who has waited a full year for this moment.*

A glowing purple-gold light stepped out from behind him.

Alexis stared. The form became more distinct. Clearer. More easily identified.

Her heart stopped. Then raced forward. Her feet unknowingly did the same. She ran into the wide-open arms ready to receive her.

Lissa!

CHAPTER 7

ALEXIS'S WEEK DISAPPEARED under a heavy load of work and practice sessions. She went to work each day, impatient to end her workday in time for her sessions with Stefan or to work on her lessons at home. And to have more visits with her sister.

Focusing on her day job, she raked, weeded, and hoed her way down the rows and the beds. The plants were reaping the benefits of her developing skills. The colors of her flower beds no longer erratically jumped and zinged around. As she practiced being calm, loving, and centered, the plants followed in kind. The colors of some were less exuberant perhaps, but all were healthier looking.

Who'd believe that stilling her mind and opening her chakras, a concept Stefan had shared with her, could happen in the first place? Or that, when the chakras were open, the energy moved through the body in a healing way that automatically spread outward to others?

If only she could learn to calm her thoughts. After just two sessions with Stefan, she'd already learned so much, but mastery of that knowledge was a long way off.

"Hey, Alex!"

Alexis turned to see Scott striding toward her.

"What's going on, Alex? Lately you're taking off like you've got a hot lover stashed somewhere. It's not like you."

Scott's long shaggy hair flipped in the wind, with his shaking head. He stopped to take a closer look at her. "You don't, do you? You'd tell your good buddy, Scott, wouldn't you?" he teased.

"Are you nuts? You'd post it in the newspapers, if I told you. I'm not quite that naive." Her heart warmed at the sight of him. "No, I've found someone to help me with the Sight."

His laughter stilled as he grew serious. "That's good, that is. Just don't be believing everyone out there. Plenty of charlatans in this world."

"This one isn't." She was dead certain of that. Stefan had such incredible abilities, and she knew he hadn't even found his own limits yet. Currently her practical psychic work centered on controlling her energy, so she could respond to Stefan's telepathy in the same way—with mixed success. She still didn't know if her telepathy would work with anyone else, although she suspected she might communicate that way with Kevin eventually. According to Stefan, Kevin had far more than just basic psychic abilities. Stefan had refused to elaborate, insisting instead that she ask Kevin herself.

Unfortunately she hadn't seen the irritatingly sexy detective in days.

LATER THAT DAY she arrived at Stefan's for their prearranged training session. She pulled up beside a truck and parked, a little nervous but excited to see him. She knocked on the front door and took a step inside, calling out, "Stefan?"

"We're in the solarium." His voice came from deep in the house.

Figured. Stefan appeared to live in that room. She headed to the room where she'd gone for most of their practice sessions. "Hi."

Stefan sat in his big corner chair and beamed at her. She glanced around for Kevin but found no sign of him. She raised an eyebrow. "Is that Kevin's truck out front?"

Stefan nodded toward the large deck beyond the open doors.

Her gaze searched, slipped past, then locked on the silent man, leaning over the railing. She didn't need to be psychic to know that something was wrong in Kevin's world. Quietly she asked, "Do you want me leave? We can do this another night."

"No, you might be good for him tonight."

Startled, she stared at him. "I doubt that."

A secretive smile played around the corner of his lips. She eyed him suspiciously. "Go say hi to him," he urged. "Or better yet, sit here and try to read him telepathically. Figure out what is bothering him."

Soberly she took up her meditative position. She distanced herself from the outside world and let her mind open, like she'd been taught. Thinking of a beautiful waterfall, she imagined herself floating gently in the warm pool of water beneath, and she relaxed. She let her mind empty of all thoughts, accepted when something popped in, then gently released it again. Hesitantly her consciousness stretched outward, past the walls and beyond. She floated lightly in Kevin's direction.

Keeping her concentration focused on Kevin, she said, *Hi, Kevin.*

As if she'd opened a door, strong colors surged into her mind, stretching her ability to see them, as the maelstrom filled her. The same reds, blacks, and whites swirled around

Kevin in an angry vortex. The force of the colors stunned her. She didn't need to open her emotional center to understand his feelings. They swamped her.

Fear! Pain. Anger. Frustration. Something was wrong, and he didn't know what. *Police, children, death, torture,* the words poured through Alexis's mind in an endless, horrific stream of ghastly movie clips that she couldn't turn off. She slammed that door shut immediately. The withdrawal jolted her painfully back to Stefan's living room.

Her hands trembled, as she shifted her position. She tucked them under her thighs to calm down the tremors, and her heart raced, even as she gasped for breath. Elated yet shaky, she evaluated her success. She'd done it, but what had it gotten her? A glimpse into Kevin's nightmares? That she didn't need. She had enough of her own to deal with.

"Satisfied?"

Startled, she looked over to see a disgruntled Kevin, leaning against the doorjamb, staring at her.

Worried, she asked in a small voice, "Did I overstep some unspoken boundary?"

The darkness on his features lightened. He shook his head. "No, I would have bumped you out if you had. What did you find out?"

Slowly she concentrated on formulating an answer. "That you don't know what's wrong yourself. You feel like something bad will happen, only you don't know what. Even if you did know, you couldn't change it, and *that's* what you really hate."

Cool gray eyes surveyed her. "Not bad, not bad at all."

She shrugged dismissively. "Those were the feelings that I could read. The words were much harder."

"What words?" he demanded sharply.

"*Death, children, pain, torment, blackness, torture* ..." She recited the litany blindly, ignoring the look of utter astonishment on his face. She tried to stay detached, but the utter bleakness of the memory and of the words themselves got to her. She fell silent, as her throat clogged with emotions.

She closed her eyes and shuddered, wanting to ease his nightmare but not knowing how. It took several minutes to regain her balance. When the heavy emotions finally receded, she opened her tear-rinsed eyes to find Kevin crouching before her.

Not able to help herself, she reached for his hand and held it up against her chest. She wished she could take his soul inside her own and chase away his darkness. She stroked his fingers, his arm. Wanting, wishing she could help him ... ease his pain, alleviate his sorrow ...

"You have to grow a tough shell in this business, or it will destroy you." He spoke simply but with conviction. "So much pain and suffering is in the world, you must find a way to detach, or the knowledge of it *will* kill you."

"Have you? Found a way, I mean?" she asked shakily, staring into eyes that were windows to a world she'd never known existed. And now that she knew what his job put him through, part of her wished she could return to ignorance.

"Sometimes. And sometimes man's brutality is just too much for any of us to handle."

"How can you bear it?" she cried out. "What outlet is there for all this poison?" Her heart ached with his pain. "How can you do this job? Live through these conditions?" Alexis closed her eyes, as emotions poured through her. Her fingers clenched, then soothed his fingers with soft strokes.

"Don't do that. You're not strong enough." Kevin's sharp voice cut through her.

She tilted her head and frowned at him. She wasn't *doing* anything. "Do what?"

"You were absorbing his pain," Stefan said from the doorway.

Shock coursed through her. She turned to face Stefan, now standing behind her. "I'm what?" *Was that possible?*

Both men's voices slammed into her mind. *Yes!*

Startled, she looked from one to the other. Had they both spoken in her mind?

They both nodded.

This so didn't make sense.

Stefan, his gaze on hers, crossed the room to squat in front of her. "You mentioned to Kevin how the doctors were surprised your sister held death at bay for so long. The seriousness of her condition would have put anyone else into their grave much, much sooner." Stefan sat down on the floor beside her, laying a gentle hand on her knee.

Alexis could only stare at him in distress. She lowered her trembling fingers to her lap, clenching them together. "She was always strong, even as a little girl," she whispered.

Kevin placed a soothing hand on her shoulder, as Stefan continued, "She did so well, … and you didn't," he said, then added pointedly, "because you took her pain away. She held off death for those extra months because of *your* abilities. You activated the receiver in you. You received her pain, took it from her." He waited a moment for her to absorb his words. "But you suffered every day. You didn't know how to dump her pain from your aura or how to protect yourself."

"No, that's not possible!" Shock hit her. She shook her head violently. "No way." Except, along with the wonderment and the disbelief was a faint touch of understanding coloring her voice. He had to be wrong.

Still, a flame of hope that she might have helped her sister brightened inside. Lissa had suffered terribly. If Alexis had helped ease that for her—even a tiny bit—she was grateful.

"Not only possible but, in this case, definitely. You've probably been developing your abilities for years, first with the plants, then with your sister." Kevin dropped his hand and stepped back. "Only now are you aware that this is something not everyone can do to the extent you can."

"This is too much." The overwhelming concept besieged her. Memories, thoughts, and confusion crowded in, saturating her already overloaded emotions. She wrapped her arms around her chest, rocking in place.

"No, it's not. It's just new. You can do this." Stefan smiled down at her. "You *are* doing this."

"Come on, you need a break. Let's forget your session with Stefan tonight and get you some fresh air." Kevin pulled her to her feet, half tugging and half pushing her toward Stefan's front door.

Stefan watched with a paternal benevolence on his face. "He's right. That's enough for now. Go home and rest. Give it a few days before we move on to other techniques." He stepped forward, as if to return to his solarium, but stopped and turned back. "Because your senses are open, you must protect yourself at the times when you can't consciously deal with them. Before bed every night, you need to meditate and to follow this ritual. It will allow you to sleep undisturbed."

She gave him a tired nod. "I'll remember."

"The only reason it hasn't happened yet is because no one has tried," he warned. "Some of these people are desperate for help, and some are just plain evil. A door has been opened. From now on, you must take care."

Kevin tugged her outside. "Come on." Nudging her in the direction of his truck, he said, "I know a nice little café down the road a mile or so. I'll drive you back here later to pick up your truck."

Alexis nodded, too numb to talk. Her bones ached like never before. Fatigue lived inside her. Information overload had set in. She sat, silent, as he maneuvered his truck down Stefan's long driveway, then onto the main road. A few moments later, after the countryside had blurred into a collage of images and colors, he pulled up in front of a small building with several large patios.

"Come on. You'll feel better in a little while." He guided her into a small cozy restaurant and on through to an open-air patio, where he tucked her in behind a table located by a cheery outdoor fire. Even though summer air blasted around her, she welcomed the comfort of the flames.

Two frothy coffee concoctions arrived quickly. She hugged the mug, while warmth slowly returned to her cheeks. Eventually a deep sigh escaped, bringing with it a lessening of her tension.

"Don't think about it."

She didn't bother replying. How many people had to deal with this psychic stuff?

Lots.

"So you can speak in my mind too?" At his nod, she added peevishly, "When do I get to speak in your mind? It's not fair that you get to do all the fun stuff." She winced. She sounded like a two-year-old.

He obviously agreed, if his deadly grin was anything to go by. God, she was tired.

"Did you eat?"

His question caught her unaware. She had to stop and think. "No, I don't think I did."

He shot her a disgusted look, before getting up to grab a menu from the front counter. He tossed it down in front of her. "Pick out something."

"I'm not really hungry."

"It doesn't matter. You need food. Choose something."

It was easier to order than argue. Afterward, she sat mesmerized by the fire, as he returned to the counter to place their order. There was an ironic element to this mess. As a child, she'd always wanted to be a witch with magical powers. As an adult, she knew better. Fairy tales were kids' dreams. Now she'd learned that the old adage was right—be careful what you wish for; you just might get it!

Anybody else would be excited to learn about these talents, wouldn't they? What was wrong with her? She should be happy that she'd helped her sister. Instead, this bothered her. *Why?*

"What are you thinking?" Kevin studied her face. "And, no, I won't read your mind without your permission."

She couldn't help but snort. "These abilities terrify me." She slumped back, as horrible fears filled her heart. "What if I screwed up?"

"You loved your sister very much. You were driven by your need to help, to ease her pain. Motive is everything here. If you came from a position of love, then love is what you transmitted and received." He studied her features. "And you loved her, didn't you?"

"Absolutely." The answer burst free. She smiled, as relief blossomed inside. "Thank you. There is so much to consider. To deal with. It's overpowering."

He grinned. A carefree motion that let her know his earlier unrest had eased. That he could live with all the stuff, said a lot about his temperament.

"That's understandable. All your beliefs have been challenged. This isn't a comfortable sit-back-and-enjoy-yourself type of ride. This is an intense, painful, and downright unnerving process."

"Were you scared? You know? When you first found out?"

A twinkle shone from his gaze. "Terrified."

His honesty disarmed her. "Really?" She searched his features intently for any attempt on his part just to make her feel better. He radiated only sincerity.

"Any normal person would be alarmed if ghosts suddenly showed up in their world. In my case, the ghosts were all connected to my work."

She hesitated to ask, then couldn't help herself. "You didn't have these talents as a child?"

"No, like you, I came into them after a major shock. In my case, I was shot. I died on the operating table. Luckily I didn't stay that way." His face pinched.

She grimaced. "Yeah, I can see how that might do it." She needed to know more. "Tell me."

His finger traced the scalloped pattern on the iron table, as he sighed and lifted his gaze to hers. "It was years ago. I was at the scene of a bank robbery. There'd been a standoff, before the two perps gave up. On their way out of the bank to surrender to the police, one of them pulled out a hidden gun and fired off several rounds before being shot dead. Two of his bullets found targets—in me."

Silence fell over them. Alexis stared down at the table. Without knowing it, she'd cradled his hands within both of hers. Subconsciously she'd reached out to remove his pain.

Her hands froze.

Stefan and Kevin had been right.

She didn't know exactly what she was, a transmitter or a receiver—or both, as apparently they went together for some people—or whether she was something else again. But she did know she'd mentally been siphoning off his troubled energy. Easing his aura. His soul.

She sat back, disturbed by a reality she could no longer ignore. This was no quirky gift that she could play around with for fun. It was a part of her identity that she hadn't known, hadn't understood even existed. A part of who she was.

During the lengthening somber silence, the waitress arrived with their food.

Alexis stared at her meal. She needed her strength, her health. With that new understanding, she ate ravenously. He sat back and watched. She barely looked up.

"Change of heart?"

"Maybe."

He watched as she polished off her sandwich and salad. When she eyed his remaining food, he quickly finished it.

"Just joking." She grinned hugely. That grin widened cheekily, as she watched his lips quirk with an answering grin.

God, he was sexy. After years of celibacy, the awakening of her hormones was excruciatingly intense. Like everything else happening in her world right now. It was like nothing fit anymore. Or after a long winter, summer clothes felt odd, leaving her more exposed than she was used to. She suspected Stefan would explain that the awakening of her other senses had awakened these ones too.

She turned to look around the room, afraid he'd read her

thoughts. Stefan had tried to show her how to put up a wall to block her thoughts from being read, but she'd not yet succeeded.

And Kevin wasn't relationship material, not with a job like his. She'd loved and lost too many times to ever contemplate going there again. At least that had been her position up to now.

Besides, could she trust her emotions right when they were in chaos? With her desire escalating every time she was around Kevin, did she have a choice?

"Alexis?" Kevin called out, his voice darkly sensual.

Slowly she turned and gazed at him. His eyes, like charcoal magnets, pulled her deep into their depths. She was drowning in sexual awareness and didn't even care in that moment.

They might have been the only two people on the patio for all the notice they took of their surroundings. Pure streaming energy flowed between them.

"Alexis?" he repeated, his voice velvety smooth and full of secrets. Secrets he invited her to share.

Oh boy. Alexis closed her eyes briefly and drew herself back, shudders sliding over her skin in withdrawal from his unspoken promise.

"Damn," his voice cracked in agonizing acceptance. His shoulders sagged. He turned to look out into the darkness. He swallowed convulsively, looking everywhere but at her.

She whispered into the agonizing silence, "I'm not ready."

He dropped his gaze, a pained grin showing. "I know, but I'd hoped."

Her lips curled knowingly, spiking the energy once more. "Thanks. And … I'm sorry."

The evening ended soon afterward. She was careful not to physically touch him, in case she risked starting something she wasn't ready for. The trip back to Stefan's was fast and silent.

After a quick goodbye, Alexis got in her truck and headed home, comfortable in her skin for the first time in days. If there would be ghosts in her life, then she wanted a say in when and where they appeared to her.

Lissa. Her name floated painlessly on the air—for the first time in over a year. Feeling lighter, sweeter, and so full of love, Alexis swore she heard Lissa's laughter tinkling around her. It had to be her imagination, but the memory of it brought tears to Alexis's eyes. She knew in her heart that Lissa was okay.

Alexis could finally move on.

"SO WHAT DO we know at this point? Caucasian female?" Captain Mark Gosling dropped the report on his desk, continuing to read aloud. "According to the initial report, the probable cause of death is a broken neck. Age …" He flicked a couple pages. "Approximately eight to ten years old, based on mixed dentition. Buried in a yellow dress and an *M* … is embroidered on the collar." The captain frowned. "Maybe the start of her name?"

Kevin stood quietly, his copy of the coroner's initial report in hand, waiting for his friend and boss to go over the more salient points. He shrugged. "Maybe. Anything helps at this point."

"I don't like the next bit though." Blustery, loud, yet infinitely capable, the captain had no problem showing his displeasure. "X-rays show the kid had multiple fractures …

on left arm, right wrist, and badly broken left tibia. Not to mention broken and badly healed index finger on the left hand and two cracked ribs."

Damn. Kevin knew the chances of those manifold injuries being accidental were slim. "All those had healed. So the assumption is that the child was possibly abused over a long time period. *Damn.*"

Kevin sat down in the armchair opposite the desk. "We're waiting on the lab results, possibly collecting DNA from the teeth. We also determined that the grave was not the primary crime scene."

"Which isn't unusual. But no proof that this is a murder case."

"No," Kevin spoke slowly, organizing his thoughts. "We're still waiting for more test results to come back to understand how long the skeleton was there." Kevin pulled out his notebook to check his notes. "According to Scott, those particular gardens have been there, basically undisturbed at that level, for fourteen years. Around that time, backhoes were brought in, and major work done."

"Therefore," the captain said, "the body has been there less than fourteen years, presuming the work went as deep as the bones we found. Identification is top priority. Do what you need to do. Keep me posted. A child's skeleton in our city gardens. What next?" The captain turned back to the tall stack of files, sitting on the corner of his desk.

What next, indeed?

CHAPTER 8

THE VOICE STARTLED her.

Alexis had spent a few happy days with no strange phenomena; she had almost convinced herself that the anomaly was over.

So focused was she on transplanting fresh color into the huge beds, she never paid any attention to the multitude of noises around her. The colors of the young plants were not as vivid as they should have been. They badly needed nutrients. Alexis mentally calculated the amount of nitrogen they'd need.

Help. Help me, please.

Alexis spun around, still on her knees. No one was there. Far off on the other side she saw another colleague working hard. But the voice had been too soft, sad even, to be him—and way too close to Alexis.

Something—or someone—was here. Another spirit? She took a deep breath and made a quick decision. Rather than just let things happen, she'd try to control how it happened.

Hiding in the shadow of a large bush, she sat down and closed her eyes, as Stefan had taught her to do. Slowly she took several deep breaths, letting the stiffness slide from her spine and drain into the ground beneath her. Feeling the stress and the nervousness ease, she visualized walking through a beautiful meadow, every step freeing her from the physical reality of her existence. She reached a waterfall, and a beautiful glistening pool waited for her there. She couldn't resist; she sat on one of the rocks surrounding the water. She dipped her toes in and felt more relaxed than she had in a long time. From this position of peacefulness she widened her consciousness ever-so-slightly.

Instantly sensations forced their way in—fear, pain, loss, grief, and sadness. Alexis slammed the door shut, gulping for air. It was one thing to practice, but quite another when reality kicked you in the stomach. Briefly opening her eyes, she was relieved to find herself still alone. Inhaling deeply, she closed her eyes and tried again. This time she opened the door just a smidgen.

The rush of emotions was still there but not quite so demanding.

Alexis opened her eyes and gasped. The world had a completely different look to it—surreal colors, with less definition but with a brighter, eerily translucent color blending.

A young girl stood in front of her—the same little girl Alexis had seen in the ditch. Alexis sighed softly. The cherub was tiny, blond, and beautiful. She appeared to be dressed in a yellow party dress, matching ribbons in her hair, except the grass from the park lawn showed through her dress, giving it an oddly alive look.

"Hello," Alexis whispered softly.

The angel smiled, creating a golden light that warmed Alexis's heart.

Hello, Alexis.

Alexis studied the waif intently. She was spectacular. No way Alexis wouldn't have remembered her if they had ever met. "You know my name?"

You're the garden lady who makes the plants laugh.

Alexis leaned back in astonishment. "Do I?" She loved the sound of that. "Do you hear them?"

I listen sometimes and watch, the child said.

A wistful longing crept from her voice, breaking Alexis's heart. "Do you have a place to go? You know, like a home?"

No, the little girl whispered in Alexis's mind forlornly. *I can't go home. Ever.*

Alexis struggled with that last single word. *Ever.*

Then the child spoke again telepathically. *I have to stay here, so he won't do it again.*

"Do what?"

He says, if I stay with him, he won't have to hurt any more little kids.

"Who? Who is hurting kids?" Alexis tried to keep her voice calm, peaceful. But damn it was hard. She hated to think someone was hurting children. And what would this little girl have to do with stopping him?

The translucent angel stared back, solemn but silent.

Alexis tried again. "Doesn't he like little girls?"

Oh, yes. He loves little girls … and boys.

That didn't make sense. Alexis didn't want to scare her off but needed clarification. Slowly she asked, "Then why does he hurt them?" The sunlight slid into something else, stormy, cloudy, and a little eerie. Shadows rippled in the background.

The little girl's form hitched and wavered, before rippling away in a fast fade-out.

"No, wait. Don't go."

The shadows shifted. Other little pale faces formed before dissipating in the fog.

I'll come back, … if I can get away, echoed the ghostly

whisper in Alexis's mind.

She was gone.

The blackness was absolute.

Alexis closed her eyes, trying to shift realities, and slowly returned to her surroundings. Icy chills filled her. Stefan had warned her that she might never feel warm again, as long as ghosts were among her closest confidants. Each person experienced a different reaction. Hers seemed to be freezing and tiredness.

Shivers raced down her spine. As much as she didn't want to, she also felt obligated to tell Kevin about her experience. Surely every bit of information counted. Not that she had much to offer. Still, the station was only one block away.

From a coffee shop situated beside the police station, she stopped to pick up two of the largest coffees they had. Walking inside the police station, sipping her coffee, she moaned softly as the warm cream-laced brew slid all the way down, curling her chilled insides with delight.

"May I help you?"

She took one more sip, before answering the police officer at the front desk. "Yes. Is Detective Sutherland in, please?"

"Just a moment. Who's inquiring, please?"

Alexis gave the female officer her name and sat down to wait. Maybe he'd be too busy to talk to her.

"Alexis, nice to see you." Kevin stood smiling in front of her. "Are one of those for me?"

She handed him the second cup. "I hope you like it black." She took a sip of hers, collecting her thoughts. "May I talk to you for a moment?"

He instantly became businesslike. "Sure. Do you want to

come into my office or take a walk over to the park?"

She perked up. "The park's a great idea."

Kevin held the door open for her.

They walked companionably for a few moments. When they reached the park, almost at the same spot where she'd seen the little girl, Alexis's words blurted out, "I saw her again."

"Who?"

"The little girl, Daisy."

He searched her face, as if to read what she *hadn't* said. "What happened?"

A sigh gusted out heavily. "I followed Stefan's instructions on opening the door consciously but just a little bit at a time. That made it easier." She rubbed her arms. "Except, after this time, the cold's much worse. I'm not as tired maybe, but definitely colder."

"Hence the hot coffee?"

She nodded at his astuteness. "Daisy said she couldn't leave. She couldn't leave until he stopped hurting little girls." Alexis paused, thinking. "No, that isn't quite right." She concentrated on the little girl's words. "She said, she has to stay, so he won't hurt any more little kids." She finished in a rush, relieved to have remembered.

She paused a moment, staring morosely at the beaded drops on the surface of her take-out lid before continuing, "She also said that he doesn't hate little girls and boys. He loves them." Alexis sipped at her drink, as despair wafted through her already muddled emotions. She'd never get warm at this rate. The child's odd words had sent another chill directly to her very soul. Maybe it wasn't the vision giving her the chills but more likely the concept of a child abuser. Like how wrong was that?

"Could be a serial killer, or could be something else altogether. Not sure if that fits what little we know—if that's her body we found."

"What did you find out?" Alexis gazed at him warily.

"The child had been embalmed. As far as we can figure, she was stolen from her grave right after burial—or from the funeral home before her burial—and then was buried here."

"What? Why?" Alexis froze in shock. Why would anyone do such a horrible thing? She sat down on the closest bench. This new information rocked her to the core. She shook her head in disbelief.

He shrugged. "I don't know why."

"So she might not have been murdered either, right?" The rest of the conversation came back in a rush. "She said, I'm the lady who makes the plants laugh. What are the chances that the gardens—and me, the gardener—are a connection between the children?"

Heaviness settled in the blossom-laden air.

"It seems a stretch, but it could be. Then again, it's probably too early to make a connection." He shrugged. "We've run a DNA sample through the database, in case her death was a criminal case. I'll check to see if any missing bodies are mentioned in the case files or if this has happened somewhere else. Another possibility is facial reconstruction. If we can get a picture of her face, created from her skull, then we can send that to the media, hopefully to identify her that way. But that is expensive."

Alexis hated to think the child had been there all these years, and yet no one knew. From what she'd seen in her visions, the child hadn't had a great life, and to think she might have been buried, dug up, and then reburied was just too much. This child had been through enough.

They had to help free her.

IT WAS LATE when Alexis headed to bed that night. She dropped into dream sleep immediately.

In her dream state, she walked through a beautiful wildflower meadow, with sunshine and yellow finches. Lissa walked beside her. It felt wonderful. The two of them were full of bubbling girl talk. Alexis couldn't tell her dream from her memories. They seemed the same.

She loved it.

Alexis ignored the subtle changes going on around her. The joy at spending time with her sister overrode any other worries. Then Lissa froze, staring into the growing blackness moving over them.

Where had that dark wall come from? The sun had been shining only seconds ago. *Lissa? What's wrong?*

Alexis spun around, looking for answers. She found nothing. Literally nothing. Only a smoky black fog surrounding the two of them. Lissa never answered. Alexis swiveled, searching Lissa's starkly pale face. Alexis placed her hands on her sister's shoulders and shook gently. *Talk to me. What's going on.*

Go! Get back. Lissa pushed away Alexis's hands and tried to turn Alexis around, shoving her forward. *You have to go back.'*

Go back where? What are you talking about?

The sun went out, as if on a switch, leaving the two of them in total darkness. A terrible sense of foreboding washed through Alexis. *Lissa, what's going on?*

He's here. Alexis, wake up. You're not safe. Wake up. Wake up!

Alexis woke up.

Her heart raced, trying to escape her rib cage. Her lungs gasped for air, while her mind pleaded to know what had just happened.

Only her nightmare wasn't over.

Someone was in her room.

Fear and sweat poured off her skin. Huddled under her covers, she shivered. Excruciatingly quiet, terrified of moving and attracting attention, Alexis desperately tried to calm her ragged breathing.

He hadn't moved. *Why? What was he doing? Who was he?* Fear shut down her ability to think.

Macabre laughter filled the tiny room—or was that in her mind?

You can't fool me. I know you're awake. I can smell your fear. That's very smart of you. Be afraid. But you're not so wise to talk with my Daisy. She's mine and don't you dare forget it.

The disembodied voice faded, taking with it the horrific sense of an intimate brush with evil.

Alexis waited several long minutes. When she was sure he wasn't coming back, she tried to sit up and turn on her light.

Only to find out she couldn't.

She wrestled uselessly inside her body, trying to force it to shift. Alarms sounded, until she relaxed back, gasping at the nasty twist. She could breathe and blink, but she couldn't move her arms or legs. Panic ripped through her.

Dear God. She was paralyzed.

She screamed—soundlessly.

Into the chaos of her mind came a voice.

Alexis. Try to stay calm. Stefan's voice brought an instantly comforting realization. She wasn't alone. Stefan had come to help her—at least telepathically.

That's better. Focus. Now. What's the matter?

I'm paralyzed.

In another part of her mind, she heard and felt the overwhelming emotions screaming to whoever heard. But it was disconnected from her, as if it were someone else. How odd. Then someone found her volume switch and turned it down. Whoever it was, adjusted it downward yet again.

Explain.

Calmer, with her mental functions allowing her to think, she tried to answer Stefan's question. Talking to Stefan with her baby telepathy skills demanded all her focus. Shakily at first, then with building strength, she gave him the details. She was forced to relive the horrible memories that were now permanently etched in her mind. And to feel them again.

You're not physically paralyzed. You're paralyzed by your fear.

"Feels the same," she muttered aloud. It took a minute for it to register. She'd spoken out loud.

See? The fear is easing. That's why you could speak that time. Continue to work on relaxing your mind and to know that you are safe. I'm here in your mind with you. Your muscles will slowly unwind, as you calm down.

It took another ten long, painful minutes before she could move her hands.

Good. It's improving.

She continued to calm her mind, relaxing her muscles. With the worst of her fright under control, she took one deep, ragged breath and released it slowly—only to freeze again at the powerful banging on her front door.

"Alex! Alexis, open this door. Damn it, open up."

Kevin.

"I can't," she whispered, knowing her voice couldn't reach the front door. She hadn't recovered to that extent. *Stefan?*

I'll tell him.

Emptiness filled her mind as Stefan withdrew. Terror resurged to the surface as she realized she was alone again. Shudders raced down her body. She grappled with the horrible sense of aloneness.

No, she could do this. She had to be strong—to control this. She was almost there.

The pounding on her door ceased.

"Alexis, I'm coming in."

Kevin could do what he wanted. She couldn't stop him. Within seconds, she heard the sounds of her door opening and Kevin rushing toward her. She lie here, waiting for his reaction.

What she received both stunned and touched her and brought hot tears to her eyes.

Kevin dropped to the floor at her bedside. In an incredibly tender movement, he lowered his head until his warm cheek rested on her cool one. "It's okay. You're not alone anymore," he whispered against her ear.

He shifted to sit beside her, before wiping the tears from her eyes. Pulling back slightly, he picked up her hand and stroked her arm in a calm, soothing motion. "You'll be fine. I'm here now. Everything will be all right. Just relax."

His comforting presence helped ease her rigidity. Her paralysis faded, leaving behind a coldness and a bone-weary exhaustion.

She'd never felt heaviness like this before, like her bones were made of concrete. She seemed to be part of the bed, sinking through the mattress to become one with the floor—

a rather disconcerting sensation.

"I think I'm okay." She shivered.

She attempted to sit up, but Kevin placed his hands on her shoulders to keep her down.

"Don't move yet. Even though it feels better, you'll experience a numbness, a time lag between your mind and muscles for a while."

The conviction in his voice explained his understanding. He'd been through this himself.

"This is no fun," she said peevishly. As she began to feel more like herself, irritation quickly replaced the trailing splinters of fear.

He grinned down at her. "No, it isn't, is it? With any luck, now that you've been through it once, that won't happen again."

Alexis couldn't quite understand how or what had happened in the first place. Thankfully he seemed to understand her confusion. He picked up her hand, holding it gently in his. His thumb stroked across the back of her hand in a slow, comforting movement.

"There are possible variations on how to explain what happened. The first is that you left your body, and you jumped back in too fast. The shock of that can paralyze you. The other is that fear snapped your consciousness awake too fast and created a state of temporary paralysis."

At his explanation, Alexis's attention shifted away from the odd feeling of having her hand cradled in his. "Out of body, … returning to the body. I don't think I like the sound of either of those."

"For many scientists, it's an accepted theory that you leave the body every night to astral travel."

A hard quiver rocked her body. Now she really didn't

like what he was saying.

"Stefan just hadn't gotten that far along in your education." Kevin shrugged. "Easy to understand. After all, no one expected your psychic development to move along so quickly." He patted her hand and stood. "You can try to sit up now. Expect your muscles to feel like rubber. I'll make you a cup of sweet tea. Back in a minute."

She watched him walk out of her room. Damn, he looked good. Casually in charge, he wore power like other men wore suits. A rush of sexual energy flowed through her, slowly reawakening her body. *Holy crap.* The sensations caught her unaware, leaving her open and unguarded, as erotic images whispered through her mind. Her body shifted restlessly on its own. Silk sheets smoothing over her bare skin. Sensitizing the nerve endings.

Dear God, if Kevin jumped in her mind now …

Breathe. Control. Detach. This was *so* unfair.

She sat up on the side of the bed again and consciously emptied her mind, which was easier to say than do. Focus. … *Shit!* She groaned at the constant stream of sensual images firing through her mind.

"Is something wrong?" Kevin's concerned voice carried from the other room.

"No," she yelped. She had to get up.

Moving as fast as her rubbery muscles would allow, she tugged an old terry cloth robe over her silk cami set, before wobbling from the bedroom. The living room clock read two in the morning. So much for getting some sleep tonight.

"The tea's almost ready. Are you moving around okay?"

She grimaced. "Did you feel like you'd been hit by a cement truck when it happened to you?" She walked slowly into the living room.

"A whole convoy of them." He nodded in sympathy but that grin of his? … Lethal. "It takes a while to get your balance back. You'll feel even worse tomorrow."

This time, his grin was pure mischief. She didn't know if she should believe him or not. The way she felt now, it couldn't get much worse. The exhausted feeling was a direct contradiction to the liquid lust, and both were battling for supremacy. She didn't dare look at him, afraid he'd read everything she was trying so hard to keep hidden. There had to be something to distract her unruly hormones.

"What were you dreaming about?"

That did it.

Her horrific nightmare surged back to the forefront. Ice raced down her spine, as she remembered Lissa's terror and her conviction that danger closed in. Even now, Lissa's screams for Alexis to wake up before it was too late echoed in her mind.

Yet waking up to that scary apparition in her room had been even worse.

The phone rang.

Its harsh sound startled Alexis, while grounding her back to this physical reality. Unconsciously she looked at Kevin.

He nodded. "It's Stefan."

She needed a pipeline like these two had. They were irritating.

She picked up the receiver. "Hello, Stefan."

"How do you feel now?" Concern tinged his voice, and she shuddered quietly in embarrassment. What if he'd been in her mind again, had seen the vivid sexual images playing through? She didn't think she could discuss those right now either. She looked again at Kevin, hoping he wasn't picking up on the vibes.

Stefan's velvet voice whispered in her ear. "Later. We'll discuss it later."

She closed her eyes. He *had* seen them. *Damn.* Regardless of the awkwardness, she knew she needed his help. Even more now. "Fine. Some weird crap's going on here." She took a deep breath. "Someone was in my room tonight."

"I know. He won't return tonight. I promise. We'll discuss that tomorrow too. You need to get some rest."

She snorted in disgust, the sound spinning Kevin around to face her. "And just how do you suggest I do that? I was asleep when it happened. Remember? I may never sleep again," she said bitterly. "I've never seen evil before."

"It's taken me a long time to understand the people out there. Some of them are twisted. Very twisted. I no longer see evil as an ungodly spirit but more as a person who does ungodly things."

"So these people are just the opposite of us?"

"Exactly." As always, Stefan knew what she needed. His soothing tones melted over her.

"It will be all right. You have to remember to follow the steps that I showed you before going to sleep now. Instead of it merely being important, after tonight, it's mandatory. It will prevent you from being tracked and located. Someone has picked up your signature." The soothing tones disappeared, and his voice returned to normal, then hardened. "I won't explain it all now, but you no longer have that option—not if you want to stay safe."

She replied in a very small voice, "I will."

"Good, now let me speak to Kevin."

Silently she handed Kevin the phone.

He searched her face as he answered. "Hello, Stefan."

Alexis tuned out the conversation, as she drank her

warm tea. She could still hear Kevin's voice. Oddly enough she could also hear a faint echo of Stefan's voice still in her head. This psychic communication stuff would take some getting used to.

God, she was so tired. She slumped down at one end of the couch, fatigue sinking her deeper into the cushions. Filling her mouth with warm tea, she leaned her head back and let her eyelids droop. Mentally she followed Stefan's instructions.

Minutes later, in a feat she'd never have thought possible, she was asleep.

STILL IN THE kitchen, Kevin continued to talk with Stefan, while keeping an eye on Alexis's movements. "I think she's out."

"Good. I did some energy work, easing her chakras. Glad it helped." Stefan paused for a weighty moment. "Will you stay the night?"

"Yes." Kevin volunteered nothing else. He didn't need to; Stefan already knew.

"Without taking advantage, right?"

Kevin let him wait, pissed he'd even been asked.

"Right?" Stefan's voice was no longer amiable.

It wasn't prudent to push Stefan's buttons too far. "You know I wouldn't do anything when she's this vulnerable. But ..." This time Kevin was the one pausing. "I give no promises for what happens tomorrow."

"Tomorrow she's a big girl again. She can make her own choices."

Kevin chuckled. "As long as she makes it through the

night, I'll be happy."

"You're also in danger of losing your heart."

"Like hell," Kevin answered amiably, as he walked into the living room to check on her.

"I know what I see and feel. I'll mention it to you again in a month, and we'll reevaluate. Have a peaceful night." With that, Stefan hung up.

Kevin wanted to move Alexis to her bed but satisfied himself with gently rearranging her into a more comfortable position on the couch. The apartment was cooling off. He walked quietly into her bedroom for a blanket.

Her real personality showed here. The sheets were emerald silk, the duvet sporting a matching embossed pattern. At least a dozen pillows were probably initially on her bed, before her nightmares had tossed them wildly to the floor. Her closet was open, showing myriad colorful fabrics he'd never seen her wear. Wistfully he wondered what it would be like to see her all dressed up for a night on the town. He nudged the closet door wider with his feet. His heart leaped with joy at the sight of bright red spike-heeled shoes.

At heart, she was still *that* girl. Life had boxed her into the caregiver persona, quickly followed by the loner and the lonely existence. … He could help her find this part of herself again. What he wouldn't do to see her in those shoes.

With another quick glance around, he took in the dresser, an old-fashioned mirror covering the back, and tiny perfume bottles laid out like soldiers, untouched. Yet ready. They spoke volumes about who Alexis had been and who she could be again. She just needed a gentle nudge, … a reason to live again.

Feeling a little like an intruder, he snagged the duvet and

returned to Alexis and covered her. She hadn't moved. In the huge armchair across from the couch, he made himself as comfortable as possible and waited for her to wake up.

CHAPTER 9

ALEXIS STRUGGLED INTO awareness. "Ouch," she murmured, shifting painfully on the couch. Rubbing the sleep from her eyes, she started and then bolted upright. Kevin sprawled out of her oversize chair, head tilted to the side, fast asleep. She winced at his position. His poor spine should be screaming right now.

What a gentle giant. He was a sweetheart to have stayed and watched over her.

Moving quietly, she slid off the couch and bundled up her duvet, returning it to her bed. Yawning again, she stepped into a hot shower. The heavy spray pounding over her tired body was painfully refreshing. Ten minutes later, she almost felt prepared to face the day.

Coffee would help. She tiptoed back through the living room and into the kitchen. Kevin still hadn't moved. While the coffee dripped, she rummaged through her cupboards. Between one thing and another, she hadn't taken time to shop. Now she regretted it. She had a sleeping guardian angel in the living room, who was liable to wake with a ravaging appetite.

Alexis grinned. Shivers rode up and down her spine, as another appetite stirred to life. While a weekend fling would be amazing, she didn't think she'd dip her big toe in, test the waters, and then walk away. Their weird psychic connection had the huge potential for delight … or disaster.

The latter might not be enough to stop her though.

Denial wasn't something she was good at.

As a child, she'd had a bubbly enthusiasm and a glowing optimism that matched Lissa's. The death of their parents had wiped it all away for the then-eighteen-year-old Alexis. She'd worked hard to build a warm protective cocoon to keep the two of them safe. That had worked fine until Lissa's diagnosis.

Alexis stared out the window, when a deep, growly voice disturbed her reverie. Alexis turned to face him.

"Good morning." Kevin stood hesitantly in the kitchen doorway.

Bare-chested, top button of his jeans undone, and the material clinging lovingly to heavily muscled thighs, he ran his hand casually over the heavy morning shadow on his face. His utter maleness swamped her senses. Intense desire unfurled deep in her belly. Alexis swallowed thickly. He was devastating to her senses.

"Good morning," she finally answered, speaking carefully. She was afraid the wrong words would rush out. "How are you feeling?"

He smiled. "Isn't that my line?"

Her lips twitched. "I'm fine. At least I got some sleep. I'm sorry I don't have an electric shaver to offer up. You're welcome to use a disposable one if you wish." She shrugged. "That's all I have."

"Not to worry. I'll go home and clean up before going anywhere." He walked toward the coffeepot. "Besides, I find the lack of a man's razor encouraging. May I have a cup of coffee, please?"

She flushed at the comment and her lack of manners.

"Sorry. Sit down, and I'll pour." She waved him toward the tiny table. She filled two mugs and retrieved the milk from the fridge. "The sugar is over there." She pointed to the plain clear bowl at the end of the table. "No razor is encouraging?" she questioned cautiously, not sure she wanted to know what he meant.

"Yes. You aren't accustomed to having men sleep over. *That's* encouraging."

Her face burned hotter. She didn't know what to say. For some reason, she felt he deserved the truth. Maybe it was because he'd cared enough to stay and to watch over her. "I haven't had a relationship since my sister got sick," she said quietly.

He slowly lowered his cup, staring deep into her eyes.

He's making me nuts.

Then Kevin reached across and tilted her chin up, until she was forced to look at him. His eyes twinkled. "Very encouraging."

Dear God. Her heart flip-flopped, before racing on again. She pulled back to a safe distance, rushing into speech to cover her reaction, hating the telltale heat washing over her cheeks. "Sorry, I only have toast for breakfast. I haven't gotten around to shopping."

"Just coffee's fine."

His intense gaze was unnerving. She glanced quickly at him and away again. "Thank you for coming to my rescue. Stefan too," she added, as a sincere afterthought.

Kevin nodded. "Stefan said we were to meet at his house this morning. Does that work for you? I didn't think you worked Saturdays."

Alexis nodded, slightly daunted at the prospect. "That's fine. We can grab something to eat on the way."

"That works. Maybe I will borrow your razor before we leave after all."

THE LATE MODEL truck was parked in the shade under the drooping willow tree, waiting.

"You're late."

The young man slid into the cab. "I came as soon as I could get away." He shifted nervously on the posh leather seat, his hand resting on the door handle, hoping, planning to make an early escape.

The automatic locks snapped down. He jerked involuntarily. Damn it.

A disgusted snort was his only answer.

"Look. I don't really know anything. I'm just a rookie. No one tells me nothing."

The older man's cold gaze cut through the excuses. "I have something to tell you. Make a bigger effort. You're only of use to me if you can supply valuable information." He paused a moment. "What can you tell me about this body from the garden?"

"That one's bizarre." Relaxing slightly, as if realizing he might have something to offer after all, the rookie answered, "The whole office is buzzing about this case. As far as they can figure, the little girl had been embalmed and may have even been buried, before being brought here and reburied."

"What?" The figure behind the wheel pursed his lips in a soundless whistle. He stared out the truck's window for a long moment, then turned his black gaze on his hapless young victim. "I need more," he snapped. "Call me tonight." He turned the key and started his truck. The sharp *click* of the locks being released echoed through the air.

Not having much in the way of options, the rookie officer nodded. He'd been in trouble before and had gotten out of it. But this time? … He had to find an answer to this mess and fast, or he'd lose everything he'd worked so hard for, and he'd be back where he started—on the streets.

STEFAN SETTLED INTO his easy chair in the solarium. He needed a few minutes to unwind before Kevin and Alexis arrived.

She needs help.

Bold, concise, and irrefutable. That the warning came from someone no longer in this world in no way mitigated its truth. Stefan sighed. Rotating his neck and shoulders, he eased some of the tension building in his muscles. *I know.*

What will you do about it? The energy wafted through the room, its female voice imperious—impossible to ignore.

Stefan tilted his lips into a small smile. As much as he enjoyed his abilities and this female ghost who refused to leave him alone since he'd started working with Alexis, he wouldn't be dictated to. *Don't be pushy. They're on their way. We'll sort it out when they get here.* Stefan removed the lids from several of the small ceramic pots in front of him, creating just the right blend. *You might want to hang around and join in the session.*

Like she's ready for that.

Stefan grinned, knowing she was right, but also knowing that there was little anyone could do to make Alexis ready.

Let me help her. I know him. I know what he's like. I can warn her if it gets bad. The energy settled in front of him. *I love her. I need to help her, like she helped me.*

Stefan sighed. *It's not a good idea.*

Maybe not, but I have to. She needs me.

NO EXPENSE HAD been spared in creating a healing, soothing space for Stefan. So talented, yet tormented with overwhelming sensitivities, Alexis saw the small touches that had been added for his comfort—extensive use of soft pastels, overstuffed cushions, stereo system piping music into every room. A soft instrumental in the background.

"Alexis, when you're ready."

Alexis grimaced, putting her tea on the table. It was time, like it or not. No more trying to focus on anything but the matter at hand. Stefan and Kevin had waited patiently, while she'd attempted to settle herself. But fifteen minutes had gone by, along with their patience. "I'll tell you what I remember."

It didn't take long to recite her short crystalline memories of the night before. "Because the nightmare had been so vivid, so powerful, it took several minutes for me to realize I was awake and safe in my room." She stopped, swallowed convulsively several times, before continuing in a low voice. "Only I wasn't safe. The same evil presence from my nightmare was in my bedroom, waiting for me."

"Could you see it?" Kevin asked, his face alive with curiosity.

"No. The room was dark, full of shadows." She paused again, closing her eyes for a moment. "But I heard him. I don't know if he spoke in my head or aloud in the room." She clenched her trembling fingers tightly in her lap, trying to hold it all together. "He said I was wise to be afraid and to stay away from his Daisy."

"Daisy?" Kevin bolted to his feet, quickly coming to her

side and bending close to her. "He actually said her name?"

Alexis nodded. "Yes, he did, and, from her voice, Lissa must have known of him, of his presence on her side." She stared at Kevin and Stefan in growing horror, as she realized what that meant. "Surely Lissa can't be in danger? She's dead." Her voice rose. Alexis couldn't do anything about it. Irrational fear for her sister chilled her skin to an iciness that quickly worked its way deep inside. "Oh, dear God," she whispered. "Is her soul in danger?"

Kevin wrapped his forearm around her shoulders, tugging her close in a protective hug. Alexis leaned gratefully into his warmth, craving security. How long had it been since she'd allowed herself to be held and comforted?

"*Shh.* ... Your sister is fine. Her soul is fine." He squeezed Alexis gently before releasing her.

"God, I hope so." Relief washed through her. Then a slow burn of realization hit her. "You know what makes me so mad?" She glared at both men. "I was almost comfortable with these weird events happening and the psychic-ability thing goin' on, you know? Almost okay with it all, and then this happened." She hopped to her feet and paced around Stefan's living room. How plainly the space spoke of Stefan's personality. Sparse and clean, yet soothing.

"This is all happening too fast. I can't get a handle on it." Alexis stopped in front of Stefan, her hands fisted on her jean-covered hips. "You mentioned a signature. Just what is that?"

He took a sip of tea, while he collected his thoughts. "Everyone has an individual energy pattern. Like DNA, there can be no two energy patterns the same. These are signatures of your soul. Once recognized, they can be used to track someone on both sides of existence."

Alexis stared at him, appalled. "You mean, follow?"

He gazed back at her solemnly. "Follow." He paused again, obviously considering something. "This person read your signature on the other side and returned with you."

"So now he knows who I am and how to find me?" That was too much. She slumped back down to her chair in defeat.

"Possibly, and possibly not."

"What does that mean? Why is everything so cryptic?" she cried out. Pain and confusion battled together in her mind. "A madman ghost out there knows me, but I don't know him or what he intends to do."

"Yes, you do." Both Kevin and Stefan jumped in together.

Alexis looked at them in bewilderment. "I do? How? I didn't see him. I don't know how to read his signature. What can I possibly know about him?"

"Tell me. If you were ever in the same room with him, would you sense that same evil again?" Stefan asked.

"Definitely." The answer flew out. "But that doesn't mean I would know where it was coming from."

"With time, you will. Just as I can," Kevin reassured her.

Kevin had never mentioned his skills before. She was curious. "Is that why you showed up at the park the first day we met?"

He nodded. "I knew someone needed help. I opened my mind and let this same 'knowing' find you." He grinned. "Of course what I found was a little unexpected."

She grimaced, remembering the mud-spattered mess she'd been. "Does that technique always work?"

"Here's the trick. These skills will work for you if you work with them. You need to be centered before you start, or it's much harder to understand what you're seeing and perceiving."

Alexis winced. "It sounds like a bad sci-fi movie to me."

"Just like this 'evil' presence is your imagination?" Stefan laughed. A large cushion hit his shoulder before landing on the floor beside him. "Thanks, I appreciate a second one." Calmly he added the pillow she'd tossed to the one he was already using. Alexis glared at him in frustration.

The two men waited for her with understanding and compassion written on their faces.

The main question burned away deep inside. "Why would he warn me to stay away from Daisy? What is he doing to her?"

Stefan said, in a determined voice, "That's what we'll find out."

"I'D LIKE TO state, for the record, I think trying to contact Daisy about why this guy is holding her is a bad idea. Even if Lissa can help Alexis, I still say it's a *really* bad idea." Kevin stood before Stefan and Alexis. His hands clenched on his hips, he radiated disapproval.

Alexis had come to see this stalwart stance as his policeman mode. When she recognized it, she could almost see him in action against the worst of the criminal elements—and winning. A formidable foe.

Damn, not only was she attracted to this man but she also respected him. Not good. Up until now, she'd viewed police officers in the same way as she had hospitals. She'd feared them.

"It won't be easy either." Kevin's frown deepened. "I might help, but this could go south in a really bad way."

Stefan walked the couple steps to stand in front of Alexis, reaching out to hold her hands. "Do you want to go ahead?"

Alexis closed her eyes, abruptly shutting out their conversation. Did she want to take this step? More to the point, was there a choice?

Kevin's harsh voice broke through her musings. "You don't have to try this. It doesn't have to be this extreme."

"Have you ever tried doing it in a different way?" she challenged him.

"Yes. I've been forced to search for victims of a killer on the other side," he answered shortly, his chin locked into position. "I survived, but the whole thing was a bad deal."

"Ouch," she murmured, at the tortured look on his face. "What other options are there? We need to contact Daisy. Find out what hold he has on her. I also want to find a way to loosen his hold on me. I have to try."

Kevin looked at Stefan. "Are there any ways to do that?"

Stefan let out a tired sigh. "I don't know," he admitted. "You know as well as anyone, damn it. There are no certainties in this business."

Kevin slammed his fist in the heavy cedar beam at the entrance to the living room. "Do what you want. It's not like you'll listen to my warning. Unfortunately."

"Does that mean you're leaving?" Alexis struggled to keep her voice calm and steady, but, inside, her stomach sank. It was important for Kevin to stay, though she couldn't explain why.

Kevin snorted in disgust. "No, I'm staying. This way, I can watch every stupid step."

She threw him a hurt look, before turning to look wistfully at the unlit fireplace. There was a chill to the summer afternoon that even a fire couldn't warm, but she'd have loved the welcoming comfort the dancing flames could bring. She rubbed her arms unconsciously.

Kevin grasped her by the shoulders, turning her away. "Go sit down. I'll light the damn thing for you."

"And I'll get the wine. We'll need something stronger than tea." Stefan walked into his kitchen, leaving the pair alone.

Kevin stacked kindling in the blackened fireplace. Smoke residue blanketed the brick mantel, giving it a cozy, well-loved look. Alexis tried to ignore him, as she settled on the cotton cushions of the futon and closed her eyes. Her stomach flip-flopped with nerves, ignoring her command to calm down.

"I don't want you to get hurt." Kevin's brusque tone accented his words. "And this course of action is likely to do just that."

Fear wobbled through her voice. "Thanks for being concerned … and the warning. I'm aware it's dangerous. I think the spirit I met last night is out to get me—to kill me even."

"And you think meeting him on the ethers will stop him? What lunacy is that? Besides, Daisy may not know anything helpful. Spirits often don't. This could be a wasted trip." Kevin's voice rose.

Alexis shrugged. How could she explain such a feeling? "Maybe. But I want to try. I felt like his prey. And I hated that."

"That he knows about your connection to Daisy is disturbing in the first place. But this makes your evening jaunt insane. I know you want to understand. To control this so you're not a victim, but last night should have shown you how hard this craziness can be."

"Precisely why I want to go back there." She swallowed painfully. "Maybe it will be easier now that I do know."

He lit the paper with the burning match. After a second's hesitation, the flames fired up, consuming everything in their path. Kevin watched the fire, still crouched in front of the hearth. "You're a rank beginner compared to him," Kevin said, his aggravation and fear spiking his voice up to a dull roar. "Stefan walks on both sides when he has to, but he never takes a casual stroll." He spun around to face her.

Stefan reappeared, bearing a wine bottle and three glasses. He poured the wine. "Take it easy, Kevin. You didn't listen back then either."

Kevin stood aggressively before them, a muscle in his tight jaw twitching, as if to some inner debate, until finally he lowered his head, acceptance written on his face. He stayed still and silent, before reaching up to rub his forehead. "Fine, let's get it over with, … meaning, talk to Daisy and then get out before you're recognized."

Damn him for his wording. This entity had felt distant and not quite real up until now. Kevin's words brought the entity into the present, big-time. Several soul-searching moments later, Alexis realized she didn't have a choice. She had to do this. *Something* wouldn't let her do otherwise. Instinct? Intuition? Or just the hope that Daisy would know *something* useful? Now if only Alexis could get at what that was.

Within minutes, the lights were dimmed, the fire roared, and, in true Stefan style, they all sat comfortably on the floor. Lit candles completed the warm, intimate look of the space, as did the half-drunk glasses of wine.

Stefan calmly and quietly directed Alexis's mind.

"Visualize the same path that you follow in your meditations. Take a walk through the door to the beautiful, calm, sunny meadow. Feel the sun on your face, the breeze in your hair. Smell the flowers blooming around you. See Lissa waiting for you on the other side. Walk toward her, happy and full of joy at seeing her again." Stefan's smooth velvet voice spoke calmly, pausing at times to allow her to slip deeper and deeper. "Now that you're relaxed and happy, open the door and set your mind free."

Alexis appreciated the two men's presence. She'd been this far in a few times during practice but had never allowed herself to go farther while alone. Until she'd followed the path into her dreams last night.

Stefan's calm voice guided her. "See yourself in the same meadow full of wildflowers. Use the light as your guide. Know I am at your side. See the path you've traveled and know Kevin stands at your back."

Alexis smiled, tilting her face upward, as she enjoyed the freshness of being free. She knew few people would understand this sensation—no words truly described it. She found herself trying to store memories for later. The fresh smell of air, taken in through nostrils that weren't there, colors that brightened and blended at will, no longer regulated by the physical constraints of vision and reality. Heat or coolness, it all depended on where she allowed her thoughts to flow. It was unique and incredibly addictive. She realized her earlier meditations, where she'd thought she walked freely, had been simple explorations. Unlike this time.

Focus.

Trust Stefan to keep her on track. Almost instantly, she found herself in Lissa's meadow, as she'd come to think of it. Happily she called for her sister.

Alex! I'm over here.

The two sisters hugged and laughed for joy. Alexis knew she was only in her meditative state, but her sister seemed so real. According to Stefan, she was real, just not in the same reality as Alexis.

Hello, Stefan. Lissa glowed with an incandescent light, as she recognized the presence with Alexis. *Thanks for helping my sister.*

It's not as if I had a choice, he said humorously.

Lissa's laughter tinkled lightly. *When you're on this side of the physical plane, it's a pleasure to find someone like Stefan to talk with.*

Is that all you were doing? Up to now, I thought you were nagging me to take care of Alexis. Stefan materialized as a luminous glow, his dry sense of humor unmistakable.

Alexis found it difficult to accept the totality of the experience. A whole other world was out there. All she was missing was Kevin. … Otherwise this reality seemed perfect. Alexis started. Could Stefan and Lissa read her mind here?

Lissa's laughter rang free. *All your thoughts are totally open here. What you think, I hear. It's simple.*

Stefan's voice cut in. *Not only your words but every thought is visualized and transmitted.*

As her mind hooked on to that new information, the images surrounding her wavered—the edges started to dissipate.

Keep your focus! Stefan ordered.

Alexis snapped to attention. *Sorry.* She immediately recognized her returning clarity was the result of her improved concentration.

You're doing good, sis. Lissa's warm smile wrapped her in a translucent hug. Alexis couldn't help but shiver in pure delight. Visits with her sister were priceless. Her focus blurred.

Focus, Stefan snapped. *You can visit with her later. She damn-near haunts my place.*

Lissa's laughter filled the air.

Alexis grinned.

Are you ready to get to work? Stefan once again cut in.

Yes, but can't we stay and visit for a bit longer? Alexis felt she'd only been there a second or two. How long had it been?

But suddenly she felt it. The air was changing, becoming thicker, cloying. On cue with the air's changes, the sun slid behind a large gray cloud that suddenly appeared. A shadowy darkness moved toward them.

No time.

Lissa turned from Alexis to Stefan. *He knows you're here. Make sure she's protected, Stefan.*

Alexis. Stefan's voice sharpened. *Stay in the light of love and stay focused. You can do this. Your abilities are strong, just untried. Keep your focus.*

The sunlight went out. Alexis spun around, searching the area. When she turned back, Lissa had disappeared.

Where is she? Alexis spun around, anxiousness crawling over her skin.

She's gone. Now are you ready to contact Daisy?

No sooner had her name floated out on the ethers than the child's tiny frame, dressed in the same party dress, solidified in front of them, as if by magic. Fear contorted her face. *He's coming. He doesn't like it when I visit with you.*

Stefan's calm voice controlled the conversation. *Why?*

He wants me all to himself.

Daisy ... Alexis hesitated. The child turned those huge blue eyes her way.

What? The child's high-pitched voice was sweet, ghostly, and extremely unnerving. Which, considering where and what Alexis was doing, seemed exactly as it should be.

Focus!

Shit, she'd done it again. Alexis concentrated harder. *Daisy, you said you stayed, so he wouldn't hurt other little kids.*

Yes.

Stefan's question than floated through the air. *How long have you been with him?*

Forever, Daisy answered, looking around the meadow nervously.

Alexis had to ask, *Did he kill you?*

I don't know.

Daisy! The peremptory order, from nowhere and everywhere, shocked them all.

Daisy vanished. She just poofed into the air. Alexis spun around, looking for her to reappear.

Stefan? Alexis called out. She could no longer sense his presence.

She felt a moment of lonely silence, before his faded whisper broke through her doubts. *I'm here. Give me a moment.*

Alexis waited restlessly. This was no longer a comfortable experiment.

Loneliness enveloped her. Nervousness dodged her heels. On the heels of that thought, the air around them went smoky gray. Alexis couldn't see her hand in front of her face.

Stefan whispered harshly, *Stay calm. He's here.*

She already knew that. Her skin screamed, as a million spiders crawled over her nerves. Everything evil materialized in one deep black oozing fog.

Hellooo there, my dear. You don't listen well, do you?

Alexis shoved down the fear and steadied her spine, taking a deep breath. She refused to be intimidated. *Apparently not,* she answered calmly.

Unholy chuckles wafted around her. *Fine with me.* Deep blackness reached for her.

Alexis took a step back, but the ooze kept coming. Her fear rose, threatening to overwhelm her. Her throat clogged, choking her, as if he controlled the very air she breathed. The intensity of the situation increased with her thoughts. She fought against it, struggling to stay calm and aware. She couldn't allow him the upper hand.

Focus! Stefan shouted.

Her spine snapped ramrod straight. Right. She could handle this.

Instantly, before she could do anything, the overpowering essence of evil lessened. She could breathe again. With each passing second, the air was lighter and less intense.

Horrible laughter greeted her thoughts. *Don't think you can stop me. Your fear is my joy. You misjudged your skills and mine. You won't make that mistake again. Neither will I.*

Horrific pain reached out and clawed at her, reaching inside her mind, twisting and churning through her brain.

Focus! Stefan yelled to her through the black whirling mist.

Macabre laughter drowned him out. *She can't. She's not strong enough.*

Yes, Alexis, you are. Stefan's disembodied voice supported her in the blackness. *Don't let him do this. Don't fight. Trust in me and think yourself to the other side of this.*

Alexis heard their comments in the distance, but it was so hard to make sense of them. There was so much pain. It crippled her. Oh God, he was in her head. … She couldn't do it. She couldn't fight him. He was too strong for her.

No, he's not. You can do this!

She screamed, a horrific tearing sound that brought the man sitting beside her in Stefan's living room to his feet. She couldn't make herself stop. All the fear and agony kept pouring from her, until the air was filled with her never-ending wail.

CHAPTER 10

"ALEXIS!" KEVIN CRIED out. "Come back. Come back to me."

Hoping she heard him, Kevin repeatedly relayed instructions. "Damn it, Stefan—help her!"

"I need a moment." Stefan's thin reedy voice came from his prone body, where it had collapsed during the last part of the journey. "Keep calling her."

"She's not responding." Kevin's heart pounded away inside his chest. God, what could he do? He had to help her. Touching her physically was out of the question; he had only one option.

He jumped into her mind—and fell headlong into the long stifling black night of her fear.

Alexis?

Kevin, she whispered in agony. *My God, this hurts. You didn't tell me it would be this bad.*

He's blocking you. It only hurts if you let him. Damn it, Alexis. Don't give in. Surround yourself with white light. Boot him out.

Off in the cold smothering blackness, Kevin could sense the other shifting presence. The asshole. *Alexis, sense my anger. Feel how pissed off I am.* Kevin waited a moment to sense her probe. When it wasn't forthcoming, he snapped out, *Do it now.*

He waited anxiously for the first magical touch that would show him that she was there and listening. Faint and trembling, a whisper of her energy moved toward him. He waited until it touched him. *Now feel our connection. Really feel it.*

I'm trying, … she whispered.

Damn it, don't try—do it! And I mean now, he ordered.

Got it. You don't have to shout, she snapped weakly.

Damn straight I do, he answered, slightly mollified. *Now use that anger to clear a path through the blackness.*

I'm pushing at it.

Again he cut in. *Don't bother. Use the anger to understand what he's doing. Your fear is crippling you. Once you understand what he's doing to manipulate you, your fear will ease, and he'll have no power over you.*

Almost instantly the black fog started to dissipate. Alexis's disbelieving laughter broke through. *Oh, wow. Now I see.* The strength of her conviction matched the pace of the disappearing fog.

Do you see what he was doing? He was using your own fear to build that fog.

She sent him a warm hug. Her thanks hung gently in the air all around the two of them.

Home now.

KEVIN WATCHED ALEXIS slowly return to the present. She would be damn sore tomorrow.

He reached out to stroke her arm. "Are you okay?"

She tried to reassure him, them. "I'm fine. Really I am. I'm very tired though, and almost feel a disconnect with my body. And you're right. I had to experience that to believe it." Alexis looked at Stefan curiously. "Just what *did* happen to you?"

Disgusted, he answered, "My own fault, really. I split off, used one part of my consciousness to help you and another to track him. Unfortunately he's good—ancient-with-years-of-experience good. While he was using your inexperience to his advantage, he went after me and kicked me out. Something he could only do because I was functioning in two levels at once, and, therefore, each piece of me was only half as strong."

Alexis stared at him. "You can do that?"

Kevin couldn't believe it. Stefan had some mad skills, but this? This seemed too far out to be real.

"I've been working on it." Stefan reached for the wine bottle to top up their glasses. He waited several moments, before adding, "And not very successfully apparently. It was a little disconcerting to be kicked out of the ethers so easily." He shook his head, muttering under his breath. "I'll have to work on strengthening the energy to each piece. At least in this instance, trying this technique was the right thing to do."

A dual snort escaped both Kevin and Alexis. They looked at each other in surprise; Kevin winked at her before turning to stare at Stefan.

"How do you figure that?" asked Alexis.

"Because of what I learned." He waited, a bright-eyed look on his face. He tapped away at the armrest. Waiting.

Lifting the wineglass for a sip, Kevin eyed him over the rim. "Okay, I'll bite. What did you find out?"

"He's earthbound."

Kevin leaned forward, roaring, "What?" His voice dropped to a shocked whisper. "That's not possible."

Alexis glanced from one man to the other. "I don't understand. Many souls are earthbound, aren't they?"

Stefan stated simply. "He's not dead, Alexis. This asshole is as alive as you and me."

THE THREE EXHAUSTED people quietly sipped their wine. Fatigue hung heavily in the air.

"I don't get it. What does this mean?" Alexis's befuddled mind couldn't understand what Stefan's findings meant. "What difference does it make if he's alive or dead?"

Kevin, in full detective mode, answered, "It's possible he murdered little Daisy and has kept her spirit captive. She can't escape him, even in death." He winced, frowning into the bloodred liquid swirling in his glass.

She cried out, "Oh, my God! Is it even possible to keep a spirit captive?" Alexis's voice rose in horror. "That poor child. How could things like this happen?" Alexis felt another of those solid foundational beliefs of life and death, that she'd always counted on, now rocked unsteadily. Abruptly she said, "We have to help free her."

Both men looked at her, their faces stern but unsurprised. Stefan spoke first. "I wondered how long it would take you."

"We have to."

"We will. Don't worry, Alexis. We'll help her," Kevin said, his voice soothing and calm. "But we need to do it properly. This isn't something we can just jump into."

"Maybe, but it feels like we need to move quickly." Tension gripped her. A sense of pressure built. From where? From the asshole? Or was she still experiencing that weird sense of disconnect from her body, from reality?

Everything had shifted. Changed. The rules she'd lived by had been wiped out in a single slash. This was a whole new game—again.

"The more you develop in this area, the more you'll see and experience what you'd believed was the impossible." Stefan looked over at Kevin. "That might explain Daisy's body."

Kevin studied him. "Meaning?"

"What if he did murder her, then following the burial proceedings, he stole her again for his own purposes? Perhaps he needs that physical connection or proximity to lock her down here with him? And, no, I have no idea how. It shouldn't be possible, but …" Stefan held up his hand to forestall their exclamations. "I know it sounds 'out there.' But this case is beyond weird."

Twisting his head to the side, Kevin studied his friend. He nodded slowly. "I don't know how he's keeping Daisy under his control, but, *if* he needed her body to do so, then what you suggest might be possible. It's also possible he just *thought* he needed her body. We have to consider there might be other victims. Or that, as we now have her body, he might go after new victims."

A heavy silence filled the room.

"So he had to murder her to do this? Or could she have died accidentally?" Alexis hated the idea of the child suffering.

Stefan pondered the concept. "Could be either. He must have been close to her both physically and emotionally, I'd think, in order to have the connection he needed at her time of death. But I don't know for sure. This is a new one for me."

"If hers was an accidental death," Kevin said, "it would

explain why there's no file."

"Right, but there could be other reasons that you haven't found her in the files. For example, she may have been dead for much longer than ten years." Stefan continued, "That's just one possibility. What if she was murdered in Florida before being moved here? You'd have to contact every county in every state across the country."

"But that's not likely though, is it? Why or how, for that matter, would anyone move a dead body across the country?" Alexis stared first at one man and then at the other. "Surely he wouldn't move it more than a short distance?"

"You forget that she's been embalmed, meaning, she could travel for a longer time without the same level of decomposition that a newly deceased body would have. He could have frozen her for a time. Even long enough to complete the move. After all this time, it would be hard to prove that action either way."

The last vestiges of warmth left Alexis's face, leaving her chilled deep inside. Alexis's stomach heaved. How could someone be so evil? At least with death, a person's suffering was thought to be over. Should be over. She closed her eyes.

"Alexis." Kevin placed a comforting hand on her knee.

"I'm fine," she whispered, after a moment. Opening her eyes, she found both men studying her, concern creasing their faces.

"I can't let him do this!" The words exploded from her unintentionally, but she meant them. She would *not* leave Daisy in the clutches of this maniac.

"Stopping him won't be easy," Kevin snapped. "You have no idea what we could be facing—how difficult this can be."

"Did you?" challenged Alexis. "Back when you first got

into this stuff, did you really know what the hell you were in for?"

"More than you do. I'd already spent years in hell on the force. This only showed another dimension of the horror I'd seen many times before," he shot back. "You're an innocent. You don't have to let monsters into your world. Get out while you can."

"Can Daisy?"

Kevin glared at her. Alexis knew she'd brought up the one point that Kevin couldn't argue. If they didn't help this child, who would? Quite possibly no one else out there could even understand . . .

"Damn it." Kevin's quiet acceptance whispered through the room.

A heavy sigh slipped from Stefan's chest. He straightened. "Then we have a lot of work to do."

IT WOULD BE Kevin's pleasure to nail this bastard. But what if Stefan was right, and Daisy hadn't died in the state of Oregon? A nationwide search could turn up thousands of cases. Kevin flung his pen down in frustration.

"Problems?" John Prescott, the mayor, stood in front of him—looking for all the world like a casual visitor, except for his white-knuckled grip on his briefcase.

"John. How are you?" Kevin half stood, reaching to shake his hand. Then he motioned to the empty chair in front of him. "What can I do for you?"

John fell into a defeated slump on the chair. "I'm glad you're here. Damn it, Kevin, I received another note today."

"What?" At John's worried nod, Kevin held out his hand. "Where is it?"

The briefcase clicked open to reveal a Ziploc bag with the offending paper secured inside. It was small, printed on loose-leaf paper, written in block caps, very simple.

"*Confess*," Kevin read the single word aloud, in confusion. "That's it?" He looked over at John in disgust. "Whoever he is, he's not very imaginative."

"I couldn't care less about his creative writing ability. I just want him stopped!"

John's fear and outrage was palpable. Kevin felt the waves reaching across the desk, engulfing him. He found himself, not for the first time, studying John's face for signs of guilt or, at the very least, hidden knowledge. He saw nothing. Stumped, he stretched back and propped his feet on the desk. *What the hell was going on here?*

"I need you to put an end to this. Sandra doesn't know about these notes, and I don't want her to find out. You know she doesn't handle life well at the best of times. Damn it, we just straightened out her medications again." John's frustration dwindled down to fatigue. "Hell."

As he ran his hand over his face, it was evident the months of never-ending worry had worn him down. And his fragile wife was another big concern. John sat quietly, staring out the window for a few long minutes.

Kevin waited patiently, quietly observing the changing emotions on his friend's face.

"My son Charles turns thirty this weekend. The last thing we need is to have something go wrong at the huge gala event Sandra has spent months planning. It sounds like the whole damn town has been invited. It's been too much for her, but she insisted on doing this. I wonder if Charles even appreciates it?"

John got up and paced around the small office. His short

steps clipped along in military style. "I was on my way to visit my brother, Glen, when I found this damn thing. Now I don't dare drive until I calm down. I'd probably get road rage and snap at some innocent," he said with a half laugh.

Kevin watched calmly, though his senses piqued with curiosity. A little whisper of intuition spoke, telling him he should be noticing something more than the obvious. *But what?* A disgruntled-father issue? A victim-of-blackmail issue? Or just a frustrated-man-with-too-much-on-his-plate issue? Kevin looked up, ever watchful. "How is Glen doing?"

"Glen?" John shrugged. "He never changes. How can he, hooked to life support as he is? I should sign the damn papers to let him go, but I just can't, even if it's been almost twenty years. If there's any chance he's in there still, I have to give him that chance. He's my brother, and I love him. God, that was a tough time in my life."

Kevin couldn't imagine how devastating that car accident must have been for the whole family. John's brother, Glen, had been a vegetable ever since. John continued to visit faithfully, finding a measure of comfort in the contact. Who could blame him for keeping that relationship with his brother alive, if he found comfort in it?

"At least you have him in a great home, where he receives round-the-clock care."

"True enough. He'd lived in Bradford for years. He never liked California. When we lucked out and found him this bed, there was no question it was what he'd want."

There was a moment of silence, then John faced Kevin, this time with a real smile. "Come to the party. You'll enjoy it. Besides, I'd feel better having you keep an eye on the proceedings, just in case …" He strode to the door. "Saturday afternoon. We'll see you then."

Kevin stared at the empty doorway. Something was wrong with this picture. But what?

Hell. The answer continued to elude him. With the note still in its plastic protector, he headed to the lab.

ALEXIS SLUMPED AGAINST the large rock garden, too tired to get up. Content, she surveyed the last flower bed. She'd been practicing her plant-growing skills every day and saw the difference now. The flowers hummed with joy. Several people had stopped by recently to comment on the glorious colors of the blooms.

Scott walked up to her. "Glad to see the plants are reaping the benefits, lass." He turned his electric blue eyes on her and grinned. "Let me know when you're going to move into the healing arts. Your work is a fine recommendation." Pure mischief gleamed down at her.

"What type of healing do you need, you big oaf?"

"Why, to heal my broken heart, of course, lassie. It's fair hurting with unrequited love."

She chuckled. "I doubt it. More like the legion of broken-hearted women you've left behind needs healing," she teased. Her colleague's attractiveness to women was legendary.

"What can a man do? So many women in want of a good loving. I'm helpless before their needs." His grin deepened, as if caught in the memories of too many hot loving nights.

Amazed, Alexis savored the rare glimpse into the devastating attractiveness of her longtime friend. She shook her head to clear her mind, with a new understanding as to why so many women willingly and easily took the walk into the night with Scott. It took away her breath. "Whew. Scott, I feel like I barely escaped unscathed."

"And don't you be forgettin' it." He nodded sagely, his grin never dimming.

"Go on with you. Your ego needs no more stroking."

"True. I came to see if you were wanting to go for a pint?" He looked slyly at her from the corner of his eye, watching for her reaction.

Alexis looked up. He positively glowed with leprechaun anticipation.

"Right." She punched him lightly. "What's the matter? Are you between women right now? Has someone not succumbed to your legendary charm? You need me to keep you company? I know. You've met someone …"

Scott's face turned beet red.

Alexis stared at him in astonishment, before collapsing on her back into the rich green grass. She howled with joy.

Scott glared down at her. "That's enough, that is."

"Not nearly!" Alexis tried to stop, but a few more chuckles slipped out. "How perfect. Even better, your reaction tells me that she matters to you. So who is she?"

"What reaction?"

"Normally you'd be laughing with me." Alexis smiled up at the big teddy bear. "Instead, you're embarrassed and uncomfortable. You care." Her lips twitched into a fat smile. "You're falling in love."

"I am *naw*!" He snapped out the words, horror in his eyes.

That did it, Alexis rolled around on the grass in delight.

"Stop that." His big mitt swatted at her playfully. "I'm not falling in love. I'm too old for such nonsense."

"You're never too old to fall in love. And it's bloody well

time."

From her prone position on the grass, she watched a strange look of comprehension slide over his face. He hadn't known. He was beautiful, smart, and the best friend a girl could have, yet he hadn't known what falling in love was like.

Truly he deserved to find someone, and Alexis would get a lot of mileage from it. She grinned. "So," she said nonchalantly, "who is she?"

The clouded confusion disappeared instantly. "Oh no, you don't. I won't tell you." He turned away from her and looked around, as if just returning to his senses. "I need to think on this." He strode over to his truck and drove off.

Alexis sat up, staring at his dust in shock. "Hey, what about our beer?" But he was long gone. Alexis got to her feet and brushed herself off, looking down the road at the dusty cloud from his truck.

Damn. She'd have enjoyed going for a pint tonight. It was past time to go home. Late and gloomy, the rain that had been threatening for several days now started with light droplets. She still needed a good ten minutes to finish up. Would the skies be kind enough to wait before dumping on her? She noticed several other workers heading home, after shutting down the heavy equipment for the day.

"See you tomorrow, Alex," one of the operators yelled from his pickup, as he pulled away.

She tossed him a goodbye wave. By the time she was ready to leave, the black clouds rumbled menacingly, making her look around nervously. For the first time, she realized she was alone. *Odd.*

Normally that never bothered her, but today the strange electric feel to the air sharpened her uneasiness.

A brilliant flash lit the sky, followed quickly by a resounding clap of thunder. The skies opened, sending down sheets of rain, as she raced to collect her tools.

"Shit." Alexis raced to her truck and threw her tools into the toolbox. The black sheet of rain washed out her vision, as she tried to stab her key into the door lock. Guiding the key with her other hand, she finally made it inside and pulled the door shut.

"I don't believe it." A river covered her windshield. She grabbed her sweater from the passenger seat and vigorously rubbed her sopping hair with it. A couple tissues left in the glove box were enough to wipe down her face. "Where did that come from?" she muttered to herself. She turned on the engine. Thankfully it purred to life. Now, if she could only see, she might get home.

The headlights shone eerily silver on the wall of rain. Her red truck picked its way carefully through the parking lot to the exit. "Damn it, I could've been home by now," Alexis muttered in disgust, hunching over her steering wheel to peer closer. What was on the road ahead? Alexis slowed her truck to a crawl.

Quicker than she'd thought possible, the object loomed directly in front of her. A huge rock? A person? She couldn't tell. She squinted and leaned closer, her nose almost touching the glass when it happened.

The object smashed into her windshield.

Alexis cried out, slammed on the brakes, throwing her arms up protectively against the impending collision.

Only it never came.

Alexis peeked out apprehensively, her ragged breathing almost covering up the heavy pounding of her heart.

And it had waited for just that lull and immediately

smashed through the windshield.

Alexis screamed.

Only the glass never broke.

There was nothing. Except for the horrible sounds that slipped out the back of her throat. She choked her whimper back, until the silence was deafening.

Alexis opened one tightly squeezed eye. Whatever it was had sealed itself against the glass. Shocked, Alexis reared back as a doorway appeared in her windshield. She swallowed several times, as her mind tried to wrap itself around this new development. Shivers rippled through her.

Alexis's breath caught, as the strange doorway morphed into an old black-and-white movie in front of her. She didn't think she wanted to see what was to come, but she couldn't close her eyes, paralyzed to do anything but watch the movie roll on.

Her windshield opened into a hallway with another dingy carpet and gray walls, but the paint chips and cracks on these walls were bigger. The sounds started up suddenly, startling Alexis, as she was assaulted with yells and cries of fear. She clapped her hands over her ears, but she couldn't look away.

Her training with Stefan allowed her, in a small way, to detach. Not enough though. A horrible inner knowing told her something ugly was about to occur …

Focus, damn it. Remember your breathing. If there ever was a time to practice her lesson in detachment, this was it. The cries of fear turned to a child's screams of pain, and the yells became angry bellows. Someone was beating a child. Could this be Daisy? Or a vision of another child?

Uncertainty helped her distance herself even more. She pulled back mentally and changed to a wide-screen view.

Instantly she stood in a ratty bedroom, as someone left the room. All she saw was a scuffed black shoe as the person walked out. The child sobbed uncontrollably on the bed.

A little boy.

Alexis's heart wept. Crumpled into the mussed blankets, the child wrapped his arms tightly around a pillow. Sobs racked his slight frame.

Alexis's eyes shut, as his sorrow and pain overwhelmed her. This vision was the oldest yet. But for Alexis—the pain was fresh. When she could finally bring herself to open her eyes again, hot tears clung to the corner of her eyelashes.

The vision was gone.

CHAPTER 11

"WHAT HAPPENED?"

Alexis wasn't surprised to hear Kevin's voice at the end of the phone. In truth, she'd half-expected it. She tucked her slipper-covered feet up on the couch beside her. She'd barely made it home before the numbing cold and tiredness had hit.

"I had another vision." Quietly and as emotionlessly as she could, she told him what she'd seen. "I think this has to be related, but I don't know in what way. All I can tell you is this one seemed to happen a long time ago."

Kevin listened intently, seeming to hear and to understand all she hadn't expressed. "You're receiving more visions, so there could be more victims involved. Are you okay now?"

"Yes," she whispered, needing and appreciating his understanding and the explanation. "Why are the visions so painful? Why can't they show me happy times?"

"That's the whole point of these visits. These people are in pain and need help to finish business here, so they can truly pass on." Kevin's soothing voice went on to explain some of the research that had been done in this area.

Alexis listened with only half an ear. She could only imagine what a lifetime of feeling other people's pain would do to her.

"They will either destroy you, or you will learn to deal with them."

It took her a minute to realize she hadn't voiced the question, but he'd answered it anyway. She closed her eyes. "That might become irritating one day," she said.

"By then, you'll set boundaries, telling me what I can or can't do. Not to worry. For the moment, this transparency is a good thing."

"By the way, when I had the vision, did you know?"

"I knew you were experiencing something emotionally painful. My sense told me it was happening. But it also told me the vision wasn't dangerous, so I didn't come to look."

"Right." She shook her head at his words. "You make it seem so simple."

She shifted on the uncomfortable couch. Dressed in her nightclothes and bundled under her heavy robe, she was almost warm. Almost. It might be time to invest in thermal underwear if this continued. At least until she learned to cope better.

"WELL?" ASKED THE man impatiently. "I haven't got all day. What did you find out?"

"Sutherland's got nothing." The younger man almost bubbled over with his news. Finally he had something to offer. Maybe it would make this guy happy enough to leave him alone. He straightened his shirt collar.

"And?"

The young man leaned forward conspiratorially. "He's searching the databases for unsolved cases involving murdered children."

"All children?" the man asked, his searing gaze making

the other man nervous.

"No, he's focusing on little girls called or nicknamed Daisy." He snickered. "What kind of a name is that?"

"Daisy!" An odd look transformed his slick features, as the man silently contemplated the news. A heavy pent-up breath gusted out, and he whispered, "At last."

He said nothing more, but a curious light filled his eyes.

STEFAN PULLED INTO a small spot so far off to one side it was almost on the grass. He gave her a sidelong glance. "Ready?"

She stared at the massive estate's grounds, jammed with vehicles and people. As she stared at the mess, she started to understand just how much she hated crowds. "Why are we here again?"

"Because Kevin called, asking for our help. It's the mayor's son's birthday, and the family is throwing him this massive party. I told him that I didn't want to attend, but he's looking for something that could be wrong on this psychic plane. So …"

"For the mayor's son's birthday party?" She took a deep breath. "I guess, if Kevin asked us to check out something, then we need to help out if we can."

"Look at it as practical experience."

"Right." With a sigh, she opened the door to Stefan's jet-black BMW and stepped out.

People filled the landscape in all directions. She wouldn't have minded joining the group of young boys playing basketball in the monster-size parking lot.

Stefan's lethal male grin perked up her spirits. She couldn't help but smile back.

"Much better. It doesn't do my ego any good to have an unhappy woman on my arm."

She tossed him a disbelieving look. "You're too damn gorgeous for that."

"True," he answered smugly, startling a laugh out of her.

He placed his hand on the small of her back and guided her through the crowd. "At least this conversation distracted you enough to get you in here."

Alexis looked around in disbelief. She was already in the middle of the damn crowd. This man was dangerous.

Stefan moved slightly in front of her, magically clearing a path for them. She couldn't see what he was doing, but the warmth of energy flowing outward from his body said he'd done something. *Damn.* She so needed to learn that trick.

"Alex," boomed a thick Irish voice from across the room. "I didn't think you'd be here." Her barrel-chested friend rolled toward her, parting the crowd, before planting himself directly in front of her, arms open wide.

Alexis laughed and walked in for her hug. "Hello, Scott. How are you?"

"Bloody fine, lass. How are you? I couldn't believe my eyes when I saw you." Scott studied the man at her side. "What's this? Did you bring a date?" he drawled, his eyes wide, as he assessed Stefan. "Well, now. I wouldn't have thought you were into models."

Alexis snorted. "Not likely. Scott, this is my friend and mentor, Stefan. Stefan, this is my boss and friend, Scott."

At the word mentor, Scott narrowed his eyes and reassessed her companion. Slowly the huge shaggy head nodded, as he recognized what he was looking for. "Good. It's nice to meet you. For helping out my Alex"—Scott held out his hand to shake Stefan's—"I thank you."

The two men seemed to come to a silent but instant understanding. Alexis could only shake her head at that whole male-protectiveness thing.

"Come on. The food is over here. Let's get you some lunch." Scott's burr rumbled through her ears, his words blending and merging with the crowd around her.

God, she hated social scenes like this.

KEVIN WATCHED ALEXIS and Stefan meander through the crowds, an apparent twosome. He frowned. *Damn it.* They looked entirely too comfortable together.

Jealousy didn't sit well with him. He didn't have much experience with heavy emotions. All his relationships, to date, had been light and easy. Like the one he'd had years ago with Mandy. He glanced over at the petite redhead, who had turned to speak with someone else. No spark existed between them anymore, but it was nice to see her again. He often ran into her and her son, Kyle, around town, but he hadn't spent any real time with them in years. He'd intended to stop by more often, but …

Sandra, the hostess, stepped forward. "Kevin, how are you? We so rarely get to see you these days." Sandra smiled her little girl's smile, making her appear years younger than her mayor husband. She tugged Kevin to the back of the house and into the full library, where many political friends surrounded John. Some would have said attending this function was politically correct. Others would have said it was simple networking. Regardless, far too many were in attendance to try to sniff out dirt.

Kevin accepted the offered beer. "So, John, where's the birthday boy?"

Several other heads nodded at the question, looking around for Charles. Though, at thirty, one couldn't really call him a *boy* any longer.

"He's here, probably surrounded by women. You know how it is when you're young and single." John smiled with fatherly pride.

The men grinned. At that point, someone tossed out the topic of single-child syndrome, starting up a whole new discussion.

"They are usually more assertive, taking what they want in the world."

"You mean, more spoiled, expecting everything from the world to be handed to them."

"Here, here. And on a silver spoon, no less." The good-natured wrangling went on around him.

Kevin tuned most of it out. His senses, both natural and supernatural, searched the group, trying to find signs of unease. When his gaze landed on John again, he felt the wave of pain, even before it reflected itself on his friend's face. John looked distinctly uncomfortable with the conversation and was hedging away. Who could blame him? It was obviously too close to home.

"John, it's too bad about your daughter," said one older man. "It does my heart good to see you and your family getting on in the world so well. The wife and I are awaiting our first grandchild." The speaker beamed, as his news caused a flurry of well-wishes and other personal stories.

John winced at the mention of his daughter, a ghost of a reaction that slipped past fast.

Kevin kept his eye on John, while filing away the news that John had had a daughter. *Had*, because John had told him that his son was an only child. John's expression was quickly masked after one baleful look at the beaming man, who basked in those compliments.

Surviving another ten minutes with the discussion, Kevin then escaped to the other side of the house to the buffet luncheon and the coffee service. He bet Alexis was more than ready for a cup.

"Did you get yourself something to eat, Kevin?" Sandra popped up at his side again, ever the good hostess, making sure that everyone was taken care of.

At his smile and nod, she murmured, "Good, good," and moved on. Some older ladies were gossiping on the far side of the buffet, and Kevin watched as Sandra headed for them. He heard snippets of their conversation.

"Daughter would be an adult now, wouldn't she?"

"Yes, I think so. Wasn't there something suspicious about her death?"

"Ruled accidental, if I remember correctly," chimed in another of the main society leaders.

Eager murmurs of condolences contradicted themselves, as everyone waited with baited breath for more gossip.

"*Shh.* She's coming." The frantic whisper silenced them all.

Amazed, Kevin noted how the whole group simultaneously donned cheerful smiles before facing their hostess. Sandra appeared to not have heard, although how that was possible, he didn't know. Maybe she just didn't want to hear.

The ladies on the other side surrounded Sandra, bubbling away with compliments over the social gathering.

Right, as if they cared. While Kevin didn't have much use for gossips, he knew enough to pay attention. You never knew where the next lead would come from.

He struggled with the bits that he'd learned. He himself

had only been in town for seven years. He wouldn't have heard about the child's death if it had happened decades ago. It must have been incredibly painful. Not to mention Glen's accident happening in there somewhere. A lot of hurt for one family.

Still, something bugged him about both issues. He made a mental note to take a closer look.

THANK HEAVENS BEAUTIFUL gardens were here. Alexis desperately needed out of the packed house and into the world she understood and loved. Any events with crowds were stifling, but this one more than most. An air of covetousness by many of the guests made her want to gag. It wasn't about the structure of the estate but more about the living energy of the place. Stefan could explain the feeling much better, but, for her, the place had the smell of hidden secrets.

Not her style at all.

When Charles introduced himself to her, she'd felt like a fool. She hadn't even known who the birthday boy was. And, from the snippets she'd heard, she had thought Charles to be a child, not a tall, slim, fully grown man a couple years older than her. With the mad crush of people inside the house, she'd jumped at Charles's offer to show her the grounds.

Yet the farther they moved from the house, the more she realized she'd made a mistake. Charles was … too smarmy, … too intimate, … and way too pushy. Every time she put distance between them, he quickly regained his lost ground.

It was ludicrous. He was so opposite from her taste, … and his persistence almost made her cringe.

And, if he didn't get his frickin' fingers off her, she would cause some serious damage. She'd never been one to tolerate being mauled.

Several times she looked around the garden for someone she knew, but the two of them were slowly drifting away from everyone. Great. If this jerk tried to kiss her, she was liable to belt him one, birthday boy or not.

"Let's head back," she said nicely but firmly. "I never did get my coffee and a piece of your delicious birthday cake." She swiveled back the way they'd come, only to find he'd slipped around to stand in front of her, and he was much too close.

The hot sun poured down on them. Alexis hated it today, feeling overheated and a tad angry. His next comment made her even more so.

"I never got my birthday kiss." His words oozed, his smile made her skin crawl.

Masculine charm aside, he was as attractive as a wet bullfrog in slime. Not that she had anything against actual frogs.

"Sorry," she snapped. "I don't do birthday kisses."

"Oh, I think you will. Do you like our new home? This estate is basically all mine. There's no other family member who counts." He wafted a leisurely wave across the impressive grounds. "Most women would be delighted to spend an afternoon with me."

That did it.

"But I'm not most women. This …" She wafted her own arm sarcastically around. "This doesn't impress me. I wouldn't spend an afternoon with you ever. If you don't move out of my way, I'm liable to puke all over you. *You. Make. Me. Sick!*"

She shoved past him. Arrogant asshole. *Who the hell did*

he think he was?

She quickly returned to the back garden. With her head down and her thoughts still in a fury, she didn't see who was waiting for her at the end of the path.

Kevin stood, holding two coffees, a whole gambit of emotions running across his face. He'd obviously heard her. Alexis watched him quickly mask his gleeful amusement. He held out her cup of coffee. "Shall we?"

Silently she accepted the cup and strode forward, happy to have him beside her and even happier to put more distance between her and the degenerate she'd left behind.

As they walked closer to the house, sounds of yelling and shouting rushed toward them.

Kevin sped up, almost running by the time they'd reached the house. Alexis heard him mutter, "Damn it, now what?"

A sentiment she echoed.

He entered the house, but she waited outside the glass porch doors. From her position, she saw several men crowd around Kevin, all talking over each other in an effort to be heard. Scott seemed to be in the middle of them. Thankfully the glass kept the words out of her hearing. She really didn't want to know what was going on.

"Yes, you do."

Alexis pivoted to find Stefan standing slightly behind her. She hadn't heard him approach. "How do you do that?" she asked irritably. "You're almost a phantom."

A ghostly smile appeared, exasperating her even more. Sudden thuds, and even louder yelling, turned her attention back toward the house. It sounded like the argument had jumped to a whole new level.

"Why do I want to know what this is all about?" She

nodded at the chaos going on inside. Kevin actually held an irate Scott, keeping him separate and apart, while several other men held two other men away from him. Of course a fight was an open invitation to an Irishman.

And Kevin seemed to think he had Scott under control. What a joke. Scott must be calmed down or Kevin would be flying through the air, detective or not.

Alexis grinned at the image in her mind. "They almost look like they're having a good time in there."

"Not all of them." Stefan joined her at the glass doors.

"So what's going on that I need to know about?"

"Threats and blackmail, suspicions and fears." Stefan continued to stare into the room. His voice thinned and lengthened in a weird parody of a tape suddenly being reduced to half speed.

It sounded beyond weird. Alexis looked at him curiously, recognizing the change in energy patterns around him. He was lost in a vision of his own.

He'd told her that sometimes he had no control over them. The realization had startled her. Knowing it was the same for her made her protective of Stefan in this defenseless state. Alexis shifted closer. Dropping her voice, she asked, "What do you see?"

"Pain, betrayal, loss, grief, … murder." His voice trailed off, leaving the last word as an eerie hook.

"Murder?" she demanded. "*Who? When?* Talk to me."

And, just like that, Stefan was back to normal. "I would if I could, but I have no idea what that was all about."

Alexis studied him, checking deep in his eyes to see if he really was back. The lopsided grin he gave her as he recognized what she was doing convinced her to believe him, as nothing else could have.

"Alexis!" came the yell from the other side of the glass.

The two looked, Kevin motioning both of them inside.

"These two need to go to the hospital to get checked over." Kevin pointed out two middle-aged men, both sporting bloody noses. Kevin's voice was clipped and irritated. "And Scott needs to get his head checked out."

"*Achh*, there's nuttin' wrong with me head." Being upset, Scott had slipped back into a heavy burr.

"No, just with what's in it," Alexis snapped, eyeing the blood drying on his temple.

"I'd call this in, but they don't want the police involved. What a surprise," Kevin added drily, giving the two older men the once-over. She sensed that Kevin didn't know either of them well. Both of them had the grace to blush in embarrassment. When Kevin pinned Scott in place, now that had been comical. Scott actually shuffled his feet like a shamefaced child.

As if just noticing the crowd still hanging around, Kevin called out over their heads, "Show's over, folks. Go back to what you were doing and forget about it. They were just fighting over their golf scores."

That elicited a wave of laughter. In a town like this, golfing tournaments were a way of life. If there was one fight the populace would believe in, that was it.

Alexis watched, wondering what his announcement had to do with her.

"I'll take them to the emergency room. I won't be back." He pulled Alexis off to one side. "Why don't you come along?"

"To the hospital?" At his nod, she pulled away. "I don't think so. I don't like those places."

"I didn't mean for it to be for fun. I meant to help me

with these two and Scott. He might be more manageable with you along. He's still pretty riled."

"Not bloody likely," she retorted, amazed at his assumption. Scott, in fighting mode, was a scary sight, indeed.

Still, a few minutes later, she somehow found herself in the middle of the back seat of Kevin's truck between the two older men. Scott sat in the front seat, half turned to face her.

"If he hadna 'cused me, then I wouldna thrown the punch." Scott's accent had thickened again, making him next to impossible to understand. "But I didna do it."

"Do what?" Alexis looked to the two men beside her for an explanation. With none forthcoming, she pinned Scott again. "Scott?"

"He 'cused me of writing a word on the mum's writing board."

"A word?" she asked cautiously. *All of this over a word.* She caught Kevin looking at her in amusement through the rearview mirror. She rolled her eyes in disgust. "What kind of word?"

The kindly gentleman on her right, sporting a bleeding cut to his nose and what would eventually become a beauty of a black eye, answered, "We saw him by the board, and mistakenly thought he'd been the one to write 'confess' on it."

"Confess?" Bewildered, she could only look around the vehicle full of men. *Who'd fight over that?*

"There have been some weird notes left for the mayor. The main message in all of them has been for John to confess something. When we saw Scott here at the board, we thought we'd found the bastard who'd been sending all these notes."

"I told you. I didna see the word. I dunno who wrote it,

ye daft mon."

"And I accept your word now." One of the older men gingerly reached up a hand and explored the mess of his face.

Alexis couldn't believe it. "What? He pounds your face into the ground, so now you'll listen to him?"

They all looked at her in surprise. "Of course," was their collective answer.

They were all nuts.

The emergency room was quiet for once. A welcomed relief, as that meant there'd be no wait. The two older gentlemen were examined first. Both had minor injuries and, after being cleaned up a bit, were released.

Alexis sat beside Scott in the waiting room, thinking on the strange afternoon. So much for practice sessions at the party. With the fight, that had brought everything to a halt before she'd even had a chance to ask Stefan about his plans. She certainly hadn't picked up anything odd. Other than the arrogant SOB birthday boy.

A tall woman in scrubs approached. She stood in front of Scott, her hands on her hips, as if she were about to deliver a lecture. "Well?" she demanded.

Alexis was surprised at her attitude. Not the usual bedside manner of nurses. The attractive woman openly studied Scott. It was obvious he recognized her. His face changed from a man to that of a boy in the midst of a scolding. Amused at the revelation, Alexis kept watching.

Now Scott was actually blushing—even mumbling incoherently.

It took her a minute to catch on, but, when she did, Alexis couldn't stop giggling. Scott sent her a disgusted look, silently telling her to be done with it.

"I'm sorry for laughing. I'm Alexis." She hopped off her

waiting room chair and held out her hand to the nurse.

The nurse smiled a classy, enduring smile. Alexis was impressed. Scott had found himself a lady this time.

"I'm Moira," she said, with a lilting Celtic accent.

Ahh. That explained it. She was from his home country.

Moira turned to the grumbling Irishman with a heavy sigh. "Let's go, ya big lug. We needs ta take a look at your head."

"Now, Moira. Isn't anytin' wrong with me head. I just took a wee blow, and look." He tilted his head to show her. "Almost no blood."

Moira wasn't having any of that. She ignored his pleas and steadfastly tugged him into a small cubicle.

Alexis, watching the two of them wrangle and spar as they moved off, was surprised and overjoyed for her friend. If anybody deserved a good woman, it was Scott. For the last couple years he'd been stalwart in his role as Alexis's friend, protector, and, if need be, ass kicker. He'd been heartbroken over the news of Lissa's disease, visiting often during her illness, bringing laughter and light to a family who had too little at the time.

At the funeral, he'd cried—because Alexis couldn't.

Now it looked like he'd found the mate to his heart.

Anticipating their happiness made Alexis feel alone in a way she hadn't felt for a long time. Stupid really. Scott was a friend, not her own life partner. By rights, she could gain another good friend in Moira. But this development was another change in her life, and she had enough of that to deal with already.

Funny how she'd used the term *life partner*. That had been Lissa's phrase. 'One day you'll find your life partner and realize that you will never be alone again.'

Did she believe it? Patiently Alexis sat in the long hallway, where sounds of the hospital moved quietly around her. Yes, she did believe it. She wanted someone to share her thoughts, to hold her at night, to wake up to in the morning, … maybe even, down the road, to have children with.

What would Lissa have thought of Kevin?

THAT NIGHT ALEXIS prepared for bed as usual. Although more moody than normal, she dropped off easily.

Her dreams started out cheerfully enough. Then without warning, *his* voice drove through her happy thoughts, bringing with it a darkness and a smothering sensation. She twisted on her bed, agonizing in her struggle for breath. The smell of death, rotten with desolation and fear, permeated her mind. Her fight continued, as if she fought for her very life.

Somewhere in the middle of the fog and the horror, words mixed and interspersed with her pain and fear. A child's disembodied wail followed her journey through the black of night. *He's hunting again.*

As Alexis raced back to the safety of her room in her dream, his cold hollow voice drove through her senses and left her soul quaking with his words.

It's not your turn yet, … but soon, oh, very soon.

CHAPTER 12

STEFAN SAT IN his solarium, enjoying a few minutes of peace. A necessary interlude after all he'd been through. He picked up his cup of chai tea from the small Japanese table.

Boo!

"Jesus!" he roared, as hot tea streamed over his leg. He sprang to his feet, dancing and shaking his legs free of the hot liquid. Glaring at Lissa, he said, "Did you have to do that?"

She grinned. *Yes.*

"I thought you weren't into haunting people," he muttered in disgust, as he pulled the still-warm cloth away from his skin. "This definitely falls into that category." He settled back down and wished, not for the first time, that he wasn't an open communication system for those on the other side.

She's having nightmares every night.

"Many people have nightmares. Alexis will need to deal with this, as she has all the other issues." He glared at Lissa, wishing for a return to the peace and quiet he'd enjoyed a few moments ago.

It won't happen.

Stefan knew better, but he didn't need to boot this spirit out of his space. She was hurting. The same as Alexis was hurting. And he couldn't seem to help himself from helping.

It's him.

"Until he does something more than torment her, our options are limited." He sighed heavily, running his long fingers through his blond hair. "In the meantime, she's getting stronger every day, and that makes each additional day a gift." His words hung there, before slowly fading on the summer evening air.

Her voice dropped to just above a whisper. *I know. I just wish there was another way.*

In a gentle voice, he said quietly, "So do I. So do I."

IT HAD BEEN days since Stefan had told them that he was certain that this asshole was earthbound, yet, since then, they'd learned nothing new. Alexis had searched the ethereal plane, with what little skill she had, and had left the detective work to Kevin. They still hadn't identified the skeleton she'd found.

But she was hoping to change that. She wanted to check schools, birth and medical records, whatever it took, to see how many children who'd resided in the community of Bradford over the last thirty years, or in Portland for that matter, had the name of Daisy. It was such an unusual name, she couldn't imagine there being many, if any at all.

Kevin had his police database, but she wanted to double-check that against vital records. Yet she had to do it manually. No complete online record had been created to date. The county officials had online records on the more recent births/deaths/marriages, etc. It took time to input all that.

At the end of the day, Alexis headed to the public library. She'd gone in early to work in the gardens, given the high temperature forecast for the day. She also appreciated the early end to the day's work. It was barely one p.m. She thought the peaceful atmosphere of the library would be a good place for her to do her research. At least that was her hope.

Instead she kept looking behind her, as she roamed the stacks, searching for information. She had the horrible sensation that something was stirring on another plane—in the world that both fascinated and terrified her. It was bad enough she always had to worry about two-legged predators, but now she knew ones could walk around outside their bodies. And, if that thought didn't get her nominated for the freak award, nothing would.

That she could communicate with her sister on any level was a joy and … unnerving. She loved the closeness, that whole reconnection—particularly when it was something she'd believed could never be.

But the rest of what she'd learned was pretty horrific.

And it was happening now again. Shudders and cold sweat trickled down her chest. Tension built, her palms sweaty. She turned to search behind her. Something was getting ready to blow, only she didn't know what.

Or when.

But it would be nasty.

Like someone would die.

Die?

Since when had the vague impression crystallized into a single word? This bastard continued to torment her, stalk her even, … as if he were ready to pounce. The anticipation created a sick kind of darkness that had taken over her days. She couldn't explain it very well. But it was as if he were taunting her, telling her that he could do what he wanted, and she'd be helpless to stop him.

It was hard to concentrate. To think. This energy, this person had taken over her life.

She glanced around. What if that had been his plan from the beginning? Making it impossible for her to think this through. Could he be doing something to her? Like putting blocks in her mind to stop her from going down a certain pathway? And how terrifying would that be? And why would he? To keep her from discovering something? From seeing something? From understanding something?

And again she looped back. What could it be that he didn't want her to discover?

What could this person really want? A rich businessman always went after more money. A real estate mogul always went after more properties. A serial killer always went after more victims …

And the cry the other night had said the person was hunting.

Hunting what? The obvious answer was *more victims.*

Was that what this was all about? While Alexis was distracted, he was choosing his next target. So that she couldn't see the victim? Communicate with his victim? She didn't know how or why she knew that, but suddenly she did. And she couldn't get that thought out of her mind.

The same vague uneasiness filtered through her again. Somehow she was inviting trouble, if she didn't back off. Again, nothing specific, just gray impressions of dire consequences. His haunting words, *Your turn will come,* still tormented her sleep.

Several hours later, in the public archive section of the library, she slammed down her pen on the notepad, letting her head drop to her forearms in defeat. She was getting nowhere. She closed her tired eyes for just a minute.

Evil swept past her.

Fear slid up her spine, rooting her in place. Oh, dear God! *He is here.*

With her heart pounding, Alexis sprang to her feet, attracting curious looks from several other people. She gave them only a cursory look, enough to know they weren't who she searched for. At least she didn't think so.

Instinctively leaving her computer and books in place, she circled the main floor of the large library, searching to find the energy she hoped she'd recognize. It was the busiest time of day. With nothing more than intuition and a driving urgency, she moved from right to left, feeling the evil ahead of her, rapidly moving farther away.

She headed down the hallway toward the washrooms and a series of other doors. Alexis stood indecisively in front of the multiple choices. Just then the door to the men's room opened, and two men, deep in conversation, exited. Her breath exhaled in a gush. She sucked in another one. Deeper, harsher, louder. She cast a quick look around. She was alone.

Flushing sounds echoed deep within the same room, indicating more occupants. As she stood there uncertainly, she sensed lightness, a lessening of the heavy energy. The energy was dissipating. He'd gone. She rubbed the goose bumps on her arms. How could he just disappear like that? A choked laugh escaped. Who knew what this asshole could do?

Quickly she retraced her steps, trying to understand. Had he felt her following him? Did he know who she was?

Or was his presence here a coincidence?

And coincidence wasn't something she was real strong on.

She returned to her spot at the table and collected her

laptop and papers before escaping to her truck.

Once in the driver's seat, she leaned back and tried to relax. Uneasiness continued to niggle at her senses, weaving in under her chest, causing her breath to catch on frissons of fear.

She closed her eyes in an effort to regain her center of balance. Instantly the inside of her truck disappeared, and she found herself in a tiny dark enclosed space. She opened her eyes, thinking she was still inside her truck. She was wrong.

Trying to talk the bile back down into her stomach, she slowly explored her surroundings. Claustrophobia dragged at her consciousness, as her arm gradually slid up the wall in front of her. Her eyes grew accustomed to the lack of light.

Her hand? Tiny fingers wiggled at the end of a fragile hand.

Oh my God. It was tiny, the hand of a child. She was caught inside a child's body. The vision had an antique look to it, making her think this scene happened a long time ago. Not that it mattered. It was as fresh to her today as it had been to the child. She closed her tiny teary eyes and wept. Emotionally it was brutally different. This poor child was terrified. A whole different child. Curled against the pain and terror, she'd wedged herself in a corner. Alexis felt dampness between her legs. The tiny waif had wet herself.

Pity welled from deep inside Alexis. The poor thing. Tremors racked the thin frame. The odd sob broke free.

Stefan had tried to teach her to back off emotionally, so she could regain mental control. She sent the little girl comforting thoughts, wrapping her in a warm hug, as Alexis surveyed the small dark space. Above her head, the shadows slowly formed into the underside of multiple hangers full of clothes.

She was in a closet.

The door stood to her right. In truth, the child's body was wedged against the hinges. She knew, without looking, that the door would be locked. But what was on the other side?

On the heels of that thought, Alexis found herself on the other side of the door.

Free from the little girl's body, Alexis felt her mind wanting to stretch and to shake off the human confines. She felt neither human nor dead, just caught somewhere in-between. An incredible experience—one that, given different circumstances, she'd love to explore.

Glancing around, the room appeared to be a bedroom, the walls a dull purple. The bed was too painfully neat. Tucked under the top cover slept a raggedy teddy bear, waiting for its owner's return.

The child's return.

In its sparse state, nothing about the room could bring joy to anyone.

Alexis pivoted to look to the closet. Not only was the door locked but a block of wood had been jammed under the door handle. The child couldn't leave until she was released.

If she were released.

The bile fought to reach the top of her throat. Alexis was slammed back to present time and the interior of her overheated truck.

What an idiot. She'd parked in the sun, and the windows were closed. She'd been out a long time. Too long. She squinted through the hot glare of her windshield and shrieked.

Kevin's distorted features stared at her through the glass.

He pulled open the driver's door, yelling at her. "What fool stunt are you up to now? Are you looking to get heatstroke?" All the while he tugged her arm, half pulling her from the vehicle. "Of all the idiotic things to do! God, you need a keeper."

Leaning against the side door with the cooler air washing over her, Alexis realized just how hot and oxygen-starved she'd become. Everything blurred, even his words, as they ran over her in rapid abrasive tones. And he wasn't about to give her time to rest or adjust either. He dragged her, none-too-gently, down the street to a sidewalk café, and shoved her roughly into a white wrought iron chair.

"Stay here. I'll find something cool for you to drink." He stalked into the dark interior of the building, reappearing quickly with several bottles of juice. "Here. Drink this." A cold bottle of orange juice smacked into her still numb hands. "I said, drink," he growled, still pissed.

She stared at him, then at the bottle. He was right; she needed this. The icy zest hit her numb taste buds, snapping them back to awareness, as the cold juice flowed down her throat. Alexis shuddered.

"Much better." Kevin watched, eagle-eyed, as she finished the bottle. "Isn't it?" he barked. At her nod, he relaxed into his chair.

"Thanks." She took another long drink and had to admit it did feel better. Curiously she asked, "How did you happen to see me?"

He shot her a disgusted look. "You were transmitting again." He gave her all of another minute to rest and recuperate, before continuing, "Now, just what the hell were you doing?"

She studied his grim face. She could count on him saving the day, whether she liked his methods or not. Her problem lay in what to tell him.

"Don't even think about it!"

Startled, she widened her gaze. "What?"

"Don't even think about lying to me."

She glowered. "I wouldn't."

He snorted. "Like hell you weren't. I can see your brain checking out its options right now." Kevin leaned forward, his ire snapping to the forefront. "Spill. What the hell were you doing?"

"Research!" she snapped. "I was doing research at the library, when I thought I felt him close by." Alexis wrapped her arms around her middle, as the remembered sensation rushed back through her.

"Him?" He leaned forward, his eyes narrowing. "Where? Here?" Intent and cold, his voice sliced through her silence, as his eyes skimmed the parking area.

She waved down the street in the direction they'd come. "In the library," she whispered, suddenly so tired she couldn't think. Hating the fatigue and the shock threading her voice, she straightened and infused a confidence and a strength that she didn't feel into her voice. "He was in the library. I was focused on my research, when this horrible sensation *wafted* past. It took me a moment, then …" She winced against what she knew was to come. "I went after him."

"What!" he roared. Several other customers looked over in concern. He looked around, quickly lowering his voice. "What do you mean, you went after him?" he asked in an ominous voice. "Are you nuts?"

"We've already established your opinion of my mental

health, thank you." She reached for the second bottle of juice and took a long drink, the sharp citrus firing straight into her brain. "Okay, so it wasn't the most sensible thing I've ever done. But I don't know who this guy is, and it's only recently come home to me that this *asshole*"—she paused—"is alive and well here in Bradford."

He glared at her.

She tried again. "I believe he's on the hunt for his next victim. At least that's what I'm feeling." She took a deep breath against his next reaction. "Then he'll come after me."

She didn't get the bellowing she expected. Instead, his face paled to a stark white, throwing the planes and angles of his face into harsh relief.

Kevin slumped into his chair. "He's coming after you? When did he say that? Since when have you been communicating with him?" He studied her weary face, then added quietly, "Start at the beginning, and leave nothing out."

She did, slowly and carefully, gradually bringing him up to date on the latest odd developments in her life.

"That's when I came back to the present, hearing you pounding on the truck window," she concluded.

"Are you sure about him hunting another victim?"

Alexis shuddered. "Maybe because I'm speaking with Daisy, he feels he's losing her. Maybe he's hunting for a replacement. I don't know." She took another long sip of the cold liquid. "There was an aged quality to the vision, like it happened a long time ago. I don't have any evidence of that, just a feeling. I think this killer has been operating for a very long time."

Shifting in his seat, Kevin studied the crowd walking by. After a long silence, he finally said, "We don't *know* if there were other victims."

Rubbing her temples, she snorted in disgust. "Like hell we don't. Daisy is one, and I think I've seen three other children. *At least* three others," she amended, thinking of all the shadowy faces in her visions.

"But that's all supposition," he said. "And I need something concrete to go on. Like a body."

"You have one child's body," she cried out. "Why can't you find out about her? Hasn't she paid enough? Haven't they all?"

"Easy." Kevin reached over and captured her hands gently, compassion and caring written on his concerned face. "We're working on it. It takes time."

Alexis clenched her fingers, unintentionally squeezing Kevin's hands. "I can't stand that she has no home."

"I know that, honey."

Honey? Rough skin rasped across her soft palms. Tingling, arousing, yet comforting at the same time. Alexis stared, mesmerized as his strong fingers evoked sensations she hadn't felt before. Who was this man who moved her so? Why had he come into her life now?

"Let's go. I'll take you to one of my favorite places for a couple hours. You need to get out of town for a bit." He held up his hand to forestall her arguments. "I'm not asking you to come. I'm telling you." He stood, holding out his hand.

Alexis glanced up at him, more than a little surprised at this sudden development. "I just want to go home and rest."

"I know. But this is a special place and just what the doctor ordered." He smiled smugly.

"Now you practice medicine, I suppose?" Her sarcasm had no effect on him.

He pulled her to her feet and tugged her in the direction

of his truck. "Part of the job description. Let's go."

Scant minutes later, they were in his truck, heading out of town. The miles of suburbia gave way to miles of green forest. Alexis couldn't remember the last time she'd gone in this direction. Maybe never.

Listlessly she watched the rapidly disappearing miles. They'd turned onto a well-traveled dirt road, heading into a deeply wooded area, with second-growth trees and long meadows. She'd heard a chain of small lakes were in the area but hadn't taken the time to check them out.

The truck bounced over a rise, and the whole vista changed. Alexis gasped, as sparkling blue water opened up in front of her. "*This* is gorgeous."

Kevin smiled at her. "You haven't seen anything yet."

And he was right.

A large stream flowed down the mountain behind them through a series of small glistening pools. It resembled a blue sunlit necklace, winding down to feed the incandescent jewel in the valley.

"Oh, my God." Alexis exited the truck and raced to the water's edge. The musical laugh of the moving water refreshed her soul. Fresh air refueled her senses as nothing else could have. "What is this place?"

"It's private property." Kevin came to stand beside her. "I'm building a house back here in a grove of trees."

It took a moment for his words to sink in. "You mean, you own this piece of heaven?" At his complacent grin, she shook her head in disbelief. "I didn't even know that something like this existed." Alexis turned slowly, trying to take it all in.

"This has been in my family for generations. Everyone enjoyed coming here, but I'm the first to want to live here."

They walked upstream a few hundred yards. Kevin showed her rock steps, leading into one of the pools. "I have many happy memories from here."

"I believe you. It's spectacular." In fact, she was deeply shocked that someone could own this and yet not find a way to be here every available minute.

"Construction has gotten much easier with the times. I'll be bringing power down here. The foundation is complete, as is the well. Do you want to see?"

"Do I ever!"

They walked over to the deserted site.

"Have you got a contractor building this for you?" She saw signs that someone had been working. Tools were neatly stacked off to one side. Yards of lumber for framing sat ready under the trees, the much-needed generator in plain view but tucked farther underneath the branches.

"Yes, but it's a buddy of mine, so he works on this when he doesn't have other work. He's putting up a double garage for someone else today."

Good. Alexis was glad to not have noises marring the silent beauty of this place.

"Do you want to go for a swim?" he asked, smiling broadly.

Crestfallen, she looked over at him. "I didn't bring a suit."

Despite the words, the water drew her back to its side. She wanted to immerse herself in the cool crisp ripples. Did she dare?

"I'm going in. You make up your own mind."

Startled by his words, she turned to face him, only to stop in shock at the sight of his beautifully muscled behind. Dear God, Mother Nature at her best. A moan of delighted surprise escaped—the sound brought his head around sharply.

He grinned. "Like what you see, do you?"

Raw heat washed over her face, but she refused to look away. Keeping her eyes on him, she admitted softly, "Oh yes."

"Enjoy," he tossed back cheerfully, taking care as he stepped on the stone stairs and descended into the rippling water. "But wouldn't you prefer to come in yourself?"

"I'm thinking about it." In this setting, with just the two of them, alone in nature, it seemed natural to be nude. As it was, she felt overdressed, hot and decidedly uncomfortable. Without allowing herself to think of the consequences, she stripped off her clothing. The cool air instantly soothed her overheated skin. She sighed in relief. She glanced over at Kevin, but he rested against a large flat rock, his eyes closed.

Inexplicably she was miffed. To hell with it. She strode, with a confidence she didn't feel, to the water's edge, gasping in shock at the temperature of the water as she slipped in. Cool waves lapped at her skin, as she sank down to settle against a smooth rock, grateful to close her eyes and to relax.

CHAPTER 13

HE WAS NO angel, for heaven's sake, and she'd test the strength of a saint. Although he'd hoped she'd follow his lead and loosen up enough to join him in the water, Kevin hadn't dared to believe it would happen. For all her wholesome, natural look, she held herself in tight control, as if fearful of letting go.

He couldn't resist sneaking a quick glance.

God, she was beautiful! Long and lean from many hours of physical work, tan marks highlighted the secret areas of her body she kept hidden from public view. Gentle waves reached up to caress her heated skin as she slowly sank, inch by inch into the water. But her nipples, oh God. His eyes slammed shut, and he focused on controlling his breathing.

No force on earth could stop him from opening his eyes for a quick second look.

Damn him for looking in the first place, and damn him for not looking sooner. The water already lapped at her breasts, lifting their delicate weight to float on the gentle waves. Kevin shuddered, grateful for the swift current that would at least distort her view of his arousal. His eyes slid closed once again, taking with him the incredible erotic memory of her expression, when she'd first felt the cool water enveloping, caressing, and cooling her skin. That look would feed his fantasies for a long time.

He'd love to have Alexis be more at ease with him. She needed to relax more, to smooth away the constant pinched look she always carried—a look he presumed had been there since her sister's death, if not before. She'd isolated herself inside a tower of pain, refusing to rejoin the world.

Now that she was taking her first tentative steps, he really wanted her to enjoy her life … and he wanted to be in it in some capacity. He didn't know in what capacity or where he wanted this relationship to go, just that he wanted a chance for them to move forward together.

ALEXIS STRETCHED OUT. The gentle current washed away the many layers of stress that had built up slowly over the last few weeks. With the blue sky, hot sunlight, and incredible water vistas surrounding her, nothing resembling ghosts or evil was allowed.

She was thankful for the respite.

She was also getting cold.

They'd been resting in companionable silence for several minutes, maybe even longer, but, without any movement to warm her up, the chill had started to settle in.

"Had enough?" Kevin called to her.

"I think maybe. I'm almost numb," she answered, not opening her eyes. Splashing sounds warned her of his approach. Casually she shifted, allowing the water to hide most of her. She was no prude, but the energy between them already hovered at a flashpoint. It didn't need any starter fluid.

"Can't have that." He stood in front of her, concern written on his face. "Let's warm up in the sun."

He held out his hand.

Alexis looked at his outstretched hand carefully. It was such an innocent gesture but fraught with hidden implications. Shivers raced down her spine.

He waited, his palm still outstretched.

Why was she making such a big deal out of this? Because it was a big deal—at least it was for her. Her hand moved on its own accord, sliding into his much bigger one, mocking her indecisiveness. She watched, shocked, as her fingers nestled contentedly into his. *How dare they?*

Easy. They'd bypassed her mind and had followed her heart.

Shit!

He tugged her gently to her feet and into his arms.

Ice met fire. Heat seared her cool body, igniting flames of scorching passion. Kevin held her snug against him from chest to thigh, wet skin to wet skin, causing heat to smolder inside. Her breath caught, as her nipples shifted against his lightly haired chest.

"Are you all right?" he whispered against her hair.

"I think so, but I'm getting cold," she answered, slightly out of breath.

"Impossible. I'm burning up." He laughed lightly only it slid quickly into a groan.

Startled, she searched his face. Color flushed his high cheekbones, tension pulled at his very skin. But his eyes, oh, dear God. Deep, metallic, and mesmerizing, she felt them reach inside her soul, searching, seeking, asking something of her.

Kevin lowered his head, sealing her mouth with his. Flames ignited her, warmed her from the inside out. A moan escaped on a breathless sigh, when he lifted his head ever-so-slightly, before dropping once more to take her mouth in a blazingly passionate kiss.

Steam should be rising around them, Alexis thought, as her mind floated in a daze. He turned her fully against him, sealing her from breast to hip, before sliding his tongue deep within the sweetness of her mouth.

She ceased to think at all.

His erection prodded insistently against her belly, unfurling a deep throbbing in hot rolling waves. She moaned again. Dear God, his hands! They slid from shoulder to hip, then back again, pressing her closer, each wet slide bringing more shudders.

"We shouldn't be doing this," she protested faintly, when she finally could.

"Like hell, we've been heading here since you climbed out of that ditch."

"No," she protested weakly, as his hand slid around her shoulders to her chest, sliding downward to rest on the rounded top curve of her breast. Her eyelids closed, as continuous tremors turned her spine to jelly.

"No?" he questioned in disbelief.

"That's not what I meant. Hell, I don't know what I meant."

He resumed his assault on her senses, trailing tiny kisses across her cheeks and up over her eyelids. His touch was tender and comforting. "*Shh,* you think too much." His tongue traced the delicate lines of her flushed lips. "Just feel. Anything this good can't be wrong. We need this," he added fiercely, using hot kisses to accent his words.

She leaned against him, unable to formulate a coherent sentence when her thoughts could only center on one thing—his hand was too high. Rising on tiptoe, she shifted so his fingers lovingly cupped her aching breast. She moaned in relief, tilting her head back in acquiescence as sensations overwhelmed her.

Kevin took advantage of the soft skin presented, sliding delicate kisses down her smooth throat. Her moans changed to soft gasps.

"What?" he whispered in her ear. Delicately he traced the shell shape with his tongue, slowly, sensuously reawakening nerve cells that had lain dormant for years.

Snuggled tightly against his chest, Alexis was treated to a symphony of sounds as Kevin's heartbeat boomed through her, his own ragged breathing inexplicably reassuring her. She laughed in sheer joy, a tinkling lightness that echoed over the waves lapping at their bodies. "Nothing, nothing at all."

He lifted his head to look at her. Then he grinned, revealing pure male satisfaction. "I'll have you know this is considered to be a whole lot more than nothing, my dear," he teased her.

A startled laugh burbled out. "That is not what I meant!" she protested with a giggle.

He smirked. "Good, my manhood is a delicate issue, and this is cold water."

His grin was pure dynamite and, as such, blew any remaining resistance right out of the water.

While he watched, she stretched upward in a feline movement, sinuously rubbing her belly and soft curls against his eager, welcoming body. "There doesn't appear to be anything delicate about this at all."

His shoulders shook, as chuckles rumbled through his large muscled frame. In pure delight, the two of them smiled, enjoying the moment.

Until their eyes caught and held—in a promise of much,

much more.

Instantly laughter died, and passion rose between them.

This time when he took her mouth, nothing was tentative about it … or in Alexis's eager response.

Lost in her passion, Alexis was only minimally aware of being propelled up against a cold barrier. They stood flush together while water swirled and rippled around them. Kevin pulled back slightly.

"No," she whimpered, searching for him with her fingers.

"*Shhh,* it's all right. I'm just moving you up and out of the water."

True to his word, he lifted her onto a large flat sun-warmed rock. Before she'd realized what had happened, she was stretched out under the hot sun. Gracefully she arched upward, enjoying the sun's warm kiss on her chilled skin.

"Sex kitten," Kevin whispered, as he splashed up beside her on their warm bed, receiving a smug feline smile for his efforts. "Damn, but you're gorgeous."

That startled her. Alexis knew she was okay to look at but had never put any stock in her looks. That he was enchanted inordinately pleased her.

"Thank you," she responded shyly.

His infectious grin caught her sideways, breaking her own smile free.

As her lips curved upward, Kevin's eyes dropped to follow their slow tilting movement. His eyes deepened to a smoky gray, and his face flushed, highlighting the planes and angles of his features.

Alexis's stomach tightened and twisted in anticipation. This man overwhelmed her senses as none had before. There was no room for anything else but him.

Time stilled. Receded …

Alexis reached up and tugged him down to her.

His lips branded her with his heat. Hot and cold contrasted and blended, covering her mouth in a molten heat that moved and caressed, before pressing deep, forcing her lips open. Lava washed through her, as his tongue stroked and explored the inner recesses.

No, there were no fireworks or horns blowing in the background. But there was an incredible undertow in the sexual current that grabbed hold and dragged her under.

His hands stroked, cupped, and caressed, as they journeyed over the sun-warmed valleys of her tingling body. It was a delight to be touched with such caring. Alexis lost herself in the enchanting sensations. For years, she'd been the caregiver, the one dishing out the comfort and love—so much so that she'd forgotten the joy of being on the receiving end. She reveled in it now. Arching and twisting, she moved under his ministrations, turning up the heat between them with her unbridled pleasure.

"You love this, don't you?" he murmured against her cheek, as he nuzzled her. "You're more sex goddess than you realize." His hands continued to stroke and to pet her, moving from one sensitive spot to the next.

"It feels wonderful," she admitted softly, an unaccountable shyness washing over her, as if she'd let him in on a great secret. But, as tensions twisted tighter and higher inside her, coherent thought was no longer possible. She explored his body with the same abandon. Soon his gasps blended with hers, as the two forgot about words and communicated with the more intimate language of lovers.

This was no short intense coupling, but a joyous taking of time to get to know and to learn each other's secrets. A time of caresses given and accepted, as the two lost themselves in the joy of soul-touching intimacy.

Time had no meaning, and, indeed, with the sun beaming down on their overheated bodies, it seemed to stand still. But eventually they could hold off no longer, and Kevin took control. Holding her soft, warm gaze with his own, he shifted, until he was between her spread legs, propped on his elbows. He waited, … silent.

As if he waited for permission, but, at this late stage, that seemed unnecessary. Puzzlement and confusion had her drawing back from the passionate edge, where she'd precariously balanced.

His large hands cupped the sides of her head, holding her, so he could gaze into her passion-soaked eyes. "I want you with me," he whispered.

That brought a hiccup of a laugh, followed by a groan, as her sensitized nipples nestled deeper into his curly chest hair. "I couldn't possibly be any more with you than I am now."

"Not true," he whispered.

Confused, she looked him. *What did he mean?*

"Open your mind and let me in."

Understanding lit tiny flames in the dark depths of her eyes. "You mean, you're actually asking this time?" she teased.

He pressed his hips teasingly against her pelvis, and the feel of him made her eyelids droop. She tilted her own hips helplessly upward.

"Open up, and let me in."

That suggestion of a duality was her undoing. Needing the physical completion that his body could bring and curious to know what new experiences the blending of their minds could add, she visualized a door in her mind and consciously opened it.

Sensations tossed her high into a sexual reality that overwhelmed, while, at the same time, it drove her right back to passion's edge. She read his thoughts, knew it was his sexual passion that she felt—all of it mixing and blending with hers to push both of them even higher. Colors and heat exploded around them.

Their bodies blended into one and so did their distinctive colors—both becoming something else again, something better, brighter, and far more powerful.

Alexis, poised on the cliff's edge, cried out, as her mind overloaded. Her body twisted frantically beneath his.

"Don't think. Just feel." Kevin's comforting voice was a lifeline through the turbulence of her inner world.

Trusting in him, she clung to his energy, as she let herself fall from the cliff. Dimly she heard his cry, as he dove after her.

For a long moment, she sensed nothing but his voice, his energy … and, dear God, his body. Possessed in all ways, she wouldn't and couldn't have asked for anything different.

"Now you're mine," he whispered, his voice full of masculine satisfaction. How could she argue? He was right. She was his.

The overwhelming possessiveness made her smile. Allowing that to go unchallenged had to be the result of complete satiation. She couldn't see any other circumstance in which she'd have allowed it. Right now she was too happy to care.

Her eyes drifted slowly shut, and she slept. Her spirit smiled, when he slid over to lie protectively beside her on the hard rock surface in the sun.

"TIME TO WAKE up, sleepyhead," murmured the insistent voice.

Alexis murmured her displeasure and tried to roll away from the disturbance—but nothing doing. Something warm and smooth stopped her. The bright sunshine made opening her eyes difficult. But, as a shadow moved over, she opened her eyes to find Kevin smiling down at her.

"How long was I out?" Alexis wished she could think, but it was difficult when she felt so lethargic.

"Just under an hour. I wanted to let you sleep longer, but I don't want you getting sunburned. Some very tender parts are exposed right now."

That reminder had her sitting up in embarrassed surprise. She flushed as she realized what she must have looked like. Totally replete, she'd brazenly slept like a child of nature. Surreptitiously she glanced at Kevin, unnerved to find him watching her intently.

"None of that," he said firmly. He stood and held out a hand. "Let's go for a quick swim, then head back into town. I think you've had enough sun for today."

And other things, his voice implied. But she really didn't want to think about that. Tonight, when she was alone, she could revisit all the uncertainty whirling through her head.

She eyed his outstretched hand. This was a little too reminiscent of his earlier invitation. To have concerns now would definitely be a case of too little, too late.

Reaching up, she accepted his help, and they walked silently into the cool water. He was right, she realized with surprise. The cool water had a bite, as it reached for her sun-kissed skin. Seconds later it became a soothing tonic. She might need to put on some aloe vera cream at home.

As she floated, she realized that other parts of her were in dire need of some attention too. Her back was scraped from lying on the rock, and her tender inner muscles were aching from the unusual activity. She'd be sore in the morning.

"Are you all right?" Kevin's concerned voice broke through her reverie.

She smiled self-consciously. "I'm just realizing what parts of me will be uncomfortable tomorrow."

A startled laugh erupted from him. "Not too sore, I hope. Next time we'll find something other than hard ground to lie on." He dunked his head, breaking through to flip water droplets everywhere.

She felt inordinately pleased by his words. So there would be a next time, would there? That was good. *Wasn't it?*

Half an hour later, they were dried off and dressed. Kevin had found an old towel tossed to dry over the bushes. Alexis didn't really want to think about who might have used it before her, but neither could she put jeans on over wet skin.

She hated the drive back to town. They drove back in silence. Every mile felt like ten. Like the return to reality from their fantasy world, it left her feeling insecure. This was all new for her. She didn't know how to act. She didn't know what to say, so she said nothing. Alexis felt Kevin's gaze on her several times but avoided looking at him.

They pulled up beside her truck, still parked outside the library. Kevin keyed off the engine and turned to face her. "Take it easy for the rest of the day. You've been through a lot lately. Today was special for both of us." He stroked her hand gently. "I'll call you tomorrow, okay?"

Alexis nodded mutely. Where the hell was her cool casual attitude when she needed it? Then where was her understanding of this relationship when she needed it either?

But, in the heat of the afternoon, no reassurances had been handed out. No discussion of a future mentioned. And she didn't think she could do short-term with him. Not successfully.

Not without getting badly hurt. And she was afraid she'd just opened herself for that anyway.

CHAPTER 14

KEVIN WATCHED ALEXIS flee. There was no other word for it. She was swiftly putting as much distance between them as she could. He wondered if she realized it. Instincts had taken over, and she'd bolted. On the drive home, she'd started out sitting in the middle of the bench seat, but, by the end of the trip, she'd almost wedged herself up against the door. He didn't think she was aware she'd done so. He'd restrained himself from going into her mind, although the temptation to delve for the answers had been hard to resist.

With a heavy sigh, he watched her truck race from the library lot and disappear into the traffic.

Damn it. His fist pounded the steering wheel in frustration. He shouldn't have let her sleep. He should have woken her up like he'd wanted to and made love to her again. But he knew she'd be sore from their earlier lovemaking. Instead, he woke her because he didn't want her to be sunburned.

Damn him for that decision. When she'd woken up, everything had been different. She'd immediately started rebuilding her walls, and then he hadn't known how to get back to their earlier closeness.

He shouldn't have let her leave like that either.

Decision made. He slammed the truck into Reverse and backed up. Just then his phone went off. "What's up?" he growled.

"A six-year-old girl didn't make it home from school."

"Shit!"

Two hours later, he switched to much stronger words. A full-scale search had been organized, an Amber Alert had been sent out, and, so far, they'd found nothing.

Several times he'd tried to contact Stefan, but he wasn't answering his phone. Telepathically he wasn't home either. That usually meant that Stefan had holed up with his paintbrush. When he finished a session like that, he usually contacted Kevin on his own.

Usually.

A sick feeling told Kevin this was a kidnapping—or worse. That before the night was out, it could be a murder. He'd driven around town, opening his senses to search on all levels but with no luck.

His cell phone rang.

"Stefan," he said, as soon as he heard the tired voice on the other end of the phone. "I need help."

AT DINNERTIME, ALEXIS puttered around in her apartment. She wasn't scheduled for a practice session with Stefan that evening, and it was a good thing. She didn't know what was wrong. Her energy had fallen below low. She felt like she'd left it behind or had had it siphoned off. She collapsed on the couch and closed her eyes.

As soon as she did, faces and noises swamped her in a mad chaotic vision. The sheer volume deluged her, drowning out any hope of making sense of the images. She couldn't sort out the voices either. Pissed and tired, her beleaguered mind finally had enough. She yelled to the empty apartment, "Stop!"

Dead silence overcame the room, now thick with tension.

Just what the hell was going on?

A frantic child's cry cut through the air. *He broke his promise. You have to help her.*

Alex spun to the left. Daisy stood a few feet away, her form thin and wavering. Bright sparks surrounded her, making her look more nightmarish than ever. Several other small shadows collected at her side. Pale faces, almost recognizable but not quite. One was the boy she thought she'd seen in an earlier vision.

"Daisy, help who?" Alexis cut to the point.

The little girl. He has her. Daisy zapped out of the room. Her companions disappeared with her, leaving a very scared and confused Alexis.

Instinctively she picked up the phone and called Kevin. It was busy. After several failed attempts, she called the police station but couldn't get through there either. What was going on? She turned on the television to catch the evening news.

And heard that a child had gone missing.

Terror swept through her. The madman had a new victim.

Alexis huddled in the corner of the couch, her knees tucked to her chin, and tried to bury her head. So much evil was in the world. She didn't think she could stand it.

Like you've got a choice. Damn it, Alexis, get yourself under control. You're transmitting in Technicolor, and we're trying to work! Stefan's voice slashed through her pity party.

Alexis's tears vanished. She wasn't alone in this—even if it took an occasional boot from Stefan to remind her.

She leaned forward, realizing what they must be doing.

She snatched her phone and dialed Stefan. When he picked up, she didn't even give him a chance to speak. The question rushed out of her mouth. "Stefan, can I help? Tell me what to do."

Just moments ago, she didn't think she could handle even living in this world; now she understood it was the inability—the helplessness—to do anything that had bothered her. But, if she could help stop this asshole, well, that was a completely different story.

"Kevin?" Stefan asked. He'd put the phone on Speaker, lending a tinny hollowness to his voice.

"She's not ready for this."

Kevin's words pissed her off and instantly made them combatants again. "Shut up, Kevin. You don't know what the hell I might be ready for."

"Neither do you."

"Really? Well, Daisy just told me that the same asshole who is holding her has this little girl and that I need to help her."

A fraction of a second of silence passed, before both men exploded. "What? When? What did she say?"

"Damn it, Alexis. You should have contacted us immediately."

"I tried," she mumbled. "Your phone was busy. It was only a few minutes ago, and she didn't say anything else."

"But she did confirm that it was the same asshole?" That was the detective in him speaking again, needing to nail down the facts.

"Yes."

"Shit."

A soul-weariness to Stefan's voice worried Alexis. "Can you find her, Stefan?"

"I've been looking but, so far, … nothing."

"Is he blocking you?"

"Yes, I'd say so—or, if not blocking, at least putting up a different energy to hide behind."

"Same thing," cut in Kevin.

"Can Daisy help with that?" Alexis asked.

"She might be able to," Stefan said. "Can you connect to her again?"

Alexis didn't know half the time if she was speaking aloud or thinking in her mind. Their conversations had become so complex, so strange, yet so intimate on these different levels. Their thoughts and hers blended to become one. Weird. And she held the phone in her hand to complicate matters even further. "I can try."

Kevin broke in hurriedly. *Not alone. Go to Stefan's house and let him help. I have to continue with the search. Let me know if you learn anything.*

Alexis's mind instantly lightened, becoming empty and feeling lonely in a way. To know that someone was with you so intimately was something she was starting to enjoy. It gave her a sense of belonging that she had never experienced before.

Do you want to come here, or shall I come to you? Stefan's words were neutral, but Alexis could sense the fatigue flowing off him in waves.

"No, don't come here. I'll be at your place in a few minutes. Put on the coffee."

With that, she grabbed her keys and headed back to her truck.

STEFAN'S DOOR WAS wide open when Alexis arrived.

Nothing suggested foul play, but she found herself approaching cautiously. She couldn't resist a sigh of relief that Kevin was at work. She couldn't deal with her own confusion over him at the moment, much less explain it to him. And he'd want an explanation sooner or later.

"Hello? Stefan?" She took a couple steps inside, even though she got no answer. The room looked, as always, sparse and clean, everything in its place. Where could he be?

"Stefan!" she called out louder. "Are you home?"

"Back here," he called from the rear of his house.

She walked through to find him comfortably seated on the bench in the center of his back garden. "Stefan? Are you okay?"

He grimaced. The early evening light cast long shadows in his face. It was hard to see details, but his face glowed in the weird light, solemn and intense. "I will be."

"That doesn't make it any easier though, does it?" Alexis sat down beside him, concerned at the melancholy look to him. "You think she's dead, don't you?"

He looked at her in surprise. "Not at all. It's just that I've seen this so many times before, and they usually end badly."

"It's not like you to be so negative."

"I call it realistic." Stefan suddenly stood and motioned her back to the house. "Let's go see if we can make a difference."

They settled into the living room. Stefan immediately started to follow what Alexis now recognized as his work ritual. Once tea was poured, they each relaxed for a few minutes. "Where do we start?" she asked.

Stefan looked at her, his head tilted in consideration. "Why don't you tell me?"

She looked at him questioningly. Where should they start? With Daisy? Or with this asshole to see if they could find out something on their own? She closed her eyes to turn inward.

And found Lissa standing inside her mind.

"*Aacck!*" Startled, she opened her eyes. Lissa sat cross-legged beside Stefan. How did one get used to that?

"Maybe we should ask my sister?" Alexis suggested drily. "She might know what we can do."

Stefan grinned at Lissa. "Her? Now what could she know that we don't?"

Ghostly laughter lit up the room. Alexis's heart lightened proportionally. It was so good to see her sister again. Lissa looked over at her knowingly. Alexis grinned. She couldn't help being delighted at these meetings. Lissa had stayed for her. It couldn't last forever, but, for now, ... their time together was a joy. And, of course, being on the other side of the veil meant Alexis could go visit Lissa. "Let's get down to business."

She's alive. But that's all I know. Lissa's voice was faint and reedy.

"Is it the same man?" Stefan asked.

Lissa's faint form nodded weakly. *Yes.*

"Why this child?" Alexis asked.

There is a connection. I just can't tell what kind.

That made sense, but it wasn't enough to go on.

"Anything more specific?" Stefan asked. "Can you see her? Can you see where she's being held?"

Only that he's stashed her in a dark place, and she's scared. I can't see her. I get the odd spike, as her overwhelming fear bleeds onto my plane.

Stefan nodded. "Good enough to start. Do you want to

begin, Alexis? I'll watch your back."

Alexis agreed. Getting comfortable, she followed the rituals Stefan had drilled into her. Within moments, she'd escaped the physical world to walk through her favorite meadows. Lissa now walked beside her.

The meadow slowly changed, moving into a stark, desolate landscape. Alexis consciously worked on her thoughts to manipulate the scenery back to something more pleasant, but nothing would shift.

It took a moment to understand. This wasn't her world. It was his. Had he noticed her presence already? How could he not?

I don't think he has seen you. I think you've picked up on him intuitively. Lissa looked around as if it all made sense now. *That's why we're here. This is his place.*

Alexis froze, as the first tendrils of remembered fear snaked up her spine. From a long distance away, Alexis heard Stefan's calm, steady voice talking to her.

Focus, Alexis. This is a good sign.

Says you, she muttered. The air around them deepened, thickened, and filled with a rank odor. Her nose wrinkled against the smell. He must know they were here.

No, I don't think so. Just as affected, Lissa had lowered her voice to a whisper.

Then what's with the scenery? Alexis asked. They continued to move cautiously forward. It was hard to breathe and even harder to see.

Stefan's voice rang clear and succinct in her head. *Did you hear what you just thought? You aren't breathing or seeing in any physical sense to begin with. In this dimension, you can clear your surroundings with your mind. That's his projection, but that doesn't have to be your perception.*

Oh, hell, you're right. Instantly the air cleared and began to smell bright and fresh again.

With her new understanding of her personal control, she formulated a beautiful rock to sit on. Sitting comfortably, Alexis brought up the image of the missing girl she'd seen on television. With Lissa at her side, Alex focused at a deeper level than she'd ever tried before. Deeper and deeper she went, searching for a connection that would take her to the child.

She whistled through long tunnels and around corners. She floated, flew, and raced through different scenes in a mad search that took on a life of its own. Without warning, she found herself falling into a black hole. The only viable sense left to her was sound.

What she heard was heart-wrenching sobbing.

Alexis reached deep for control, detaching as completely as she could, in order to bring her other senses back into use, and found a frail child awkwardly crumpled in a corner. Her poor face, half covered in straggly blond hair, was buried in a moldy blanket. Alexis searched the gloom for details, anything helpful to indicate her location.

An odd hum echoed from somewhere, and the room oozed a stale mustiness. She couldn't tell if it were an actual room or some other containment. She needed to find something soon. No telling when *he'd* show up.

Alexis gently brushed the child's forehead. She didn't want to scare her, but the child needed comforting. Outside of a simple flinch, the girl didn't recognize the motion for what it was. No surprise there. Taking an extra second, Alexis consciously pulled some of the fear from the little girl's energy. Alexis's own heart rate picked up, as she absorbed the pain and fear into her own space. Shuddering slightly at the ripples of nastiness, she dumped it from her system as quickly as possible. She ran a light sweep over her own aura and swept out the negative energy, as Stefan had explained to her. A simple-enough mental process now that she knew about it.

Pulling back slightly, Alexis shifted to the other side of whatever barrier was hiding the child. The interior space disappeared. She now floated above an unrecognizable highway, looking down on evening traffic. A van drove steadily below her, an ancient white van with smoked windows. Was that it?

Alexis felt her energy fade. Wasn't much more she could draw on. Desperate to have something concrete to take back, she gathered the last of her energy, zooming in on the back of the speeding van. The distance widened rapidly. She strained to the limits of her abilities. It took every bit of effort, but, with one final burst of speed, Alexis surged down, barely catching several letters in the license plate.

Got it!

She hit the end of her spiritual rope. A huge vacuum sucked her backward through an endless tunnel. This time her journey was much faster, spinning her helplessly in a rotating tunnel, accompanied by endless blinding noise for too long of a time.

Until she was slammed back, once again, into Stefan's living room.

"ALEXIS?" STEFAN'S SOFT, caring voice called to her over and over. "Take a moment to bring yourself back. Slowly return to this plane." It took several long minutes for her to recognize he was stroking her shoulder gently.

"I'm back." Her voice cracked, grating against the serenity of the room. Nausea rose, then calmed in a big ocean wave. Her vocal cords seemed awkward and rusty. "*That* was a rough trip."

"Is there any other kind?" He waited a minute before asking, his voice barely hiding the hint of anxiousness, "Did you learn anything?"

That brought her quickly around. Sitting up too quickly, she collapsed back down again. "Oh, my head," she groaned.

"I said, take it easy for a bit. It's always worse after a bad trip."

"You need to contact Kevin." She took a deep breath against the pain battering away inside her head and then quickly related what had happened.

Even as she winced, she recognized Stefan's inner shift. He'd already opened communication with Kevin. Almost immediately Kevin was in her head, confirming the parts of the license number that she saw and the type of van being driven.

You're sure you didn't get a description of the driver? Kevin's impatient voice demanded.

"No," she whispered painfully. Her head was killing her, the tempo beating between the lobes of her brain. Kevin's questions weren't helping. God, she wished he'd disappear, at least until she felt better.

Stefan pivoted sharply to look at her.

"What?" she asked, confused by the strange look on his face.

"Did you do that on purpose?" At her look of incomprehension, he added, "You just shoved Kevin out of your mind and slammed the door." He grinned, winking at her. "You should hear him now."

Her head did feel better. How odd. She smiled wanly, hoping Kevin wouldn't hold it against her. "Maybe I did, but I didn't know that's what I was doing. My head's been killing me since I came back from that astro trip. His telepathy was making it worse." She shrugged in bewilderment, adding, "I couldn't stand it." She hadn't meant to shove him out though. In fact, she didn't even know that was something she could do.

"So you gave him the boot? Congratulations, you just took your next step. From now on, we'll require your permission to enter. Keep that in mind, any time you're in trouble."

That gave her pause. Several times she'd welcomed their unexpected presence in her mind, reassuring her that she was never truly alone. Now what would it mean? "Will it be difficult to open the door?"

"Like now, no real way to teach it to you. It will open, or it won't."

"Lovely," she muttered. It had better not refuse to open when she was in trouble. Of course she could always scream at them. That had worked so far. Stefan's wry look told her that he understood her thoughts regardless. "You can read my mind but can no longer talk to me in my mind, until I learn to open that door? How does that work?"

"It doesn't take a telepath to read your mind right now. There is also a big difference between reading your mind and speaking in your mind. Think receiving versus transmitting."

Alexis raised her hands in disgust. "Whatever. When does this ever get easier?"

"Never!" His final word was succinct and to the point, with the added implication of *get used to it.*

IN ANOTHER PART of town, an old beat-up car pulled into a very popular watering spot. Unfortunately this town sported several bars that stayed open well into the night. The young man, casually dressed in jeans and a T-shirt, quickly walked through each, searching for the asshole, before heading back to his car and driving on to the next bar. Grim satisfaction settled on his young features, each time he failed to find his suspect. It was possible that he'd missed him, but he didn't think so.

He didn't know quite what to do about the information when he found it. He needed proof of this man's activities first. If he could find this asshole first, it could give him an edge. Maybe enough to get his life back. Grimly the young man continued his search.

He had to find him before anyone else got hurt.

ALEXIS LIE QUIETLY on Stefan's couch. She'd recovered, only to find herself in an odd melancholy mood, feeling tired and chilled, the remnants of recovery mode. Today had been traumatic, to say the least. A long hot soak in her bath would help, but she couldn't leave Stefan's until she knew they'd found the little girl.

Fatigue weighed heavily upon her, and she closed her eyes. Had it only been this afternoon that she'd had such an incredible interlude with Kevin? Unbelievable. It already seemed like days ago. She sighed.

So far, they'd heard nothing.

Stefan returned to the living room, this time bearing a platter of fruit and cheese.

"You don't need to take such good care of me, Stefan. I'm not helpless."

"I'm enjoying it. Besides, after the day you've had, this should help." He carefully placed the full platter down on his low table—missing the odd look that came across her face.

"My day? What kind of day have I had?" she asked in confusion.

He snorted at her forgetfulness. "Don't forget that hiding something from a psychic is difficult at the best of times—and impossible when you're an open book anyway."

Her face burned.

He grinned at her.

"I didn't want to think about it at all," she mumbled sheepishly, too embarrassed to look him in the eye.

"So don't. Deal with it instead. Not to worry. I won't probe for details. That's private."

He spoke so nonchalantly that it gave her pause. She hurriedly reached for a bunch of grapes, uneasily aware of just how much information he could have accessed, if he'd so chosen. "Thank you for that."

"Anytime. I might tease Kevin about your wild afternoon but not you, never you."

She rolled her eyes at him. Heat still warmed her cheeks. She couldn't imagine how Kevin would react to Stefan's teasing. But then he'd been dealing with Stefan for much longer.

"But he hasn't had very many relationships during this time either."

"I thought you had to have permission to read my mind now," she asked, irritated.

"No, just to enter it. A small difference."

Alexis shook her head at the hairsplitting. She popped a grape into her mouth and tried to sort through the difference Stefan talked about.

"The van has been spotted at the mall, just on the outskirts of town. What is that place, Cottonwood Mall or some such thing?" Stefan's distant voice interrupted her musings.

He looked off in the distance as if receiving more information. As she watched him, Alexis could almost see the silent communication going on.

"Cottonwood Mall?" Alexis chewed on her bottom lip, anxiously watching Stefan's face.

"Kevin's en route and will call later." Stefan blinked several times and returned calmly to the food in front of him. "Eat up. You need to rebuild your strength."

They enjoyed their simple meal and chatted quietly.

"Stefan, what type of side effects do you have after your psychic trips?" He didn't answer. She looked up at him. "Stefan?"

Stefan stood frozen, his hand hanging in midair, a chunk of cheese halfway to his mouth, a glassy look in his eyes, giving him a vacant, not-at-home look.

Jesus, he looked scary. Alexis swallowed hard several times, all the while watching him. "Stefan?" she whispered cautiously. "What is it? What do you see?"

Unexpectedly he answered her. "They've found the van. And the child."

"Oh, thank God." Alexis was elated. It was a far better outcome than she'd feared might come of this night. "Is she okay?"

Stefan continued slowly, almost hypnotically. "The child was drugged but appears to be unhurt. An ambulance is on the scene."

"What about the kidnapper? Did they catch him?" She urged him to provide more.

Stefan went deeper inward. "No," he whispered dejectedly. "They didn't get him. He wasn't in the van." He paused for a moment, his eyes rolling upward. A moment later, they rolled back down. He slowly continued, "I'm searching for him."

Alexis held her breath against the pain knifing through her. The bastard was still loose.

"He's nowhere." Stefan slowly opened his eyes. "For just a moment, I caught a whiff of his energy. Incredible anger, madness even. Then he was gone."

"But, if he's losing control, wouldn't it have been easier to find him?"

"Theoretically, yes. But, in this case, he *isn't* losing control. He's coldly, terrifyingly, and dangerously *in* control."

"More treacherous than ever, you mean?"

Stefan stilled, staring at her somberly. "There'll be a horrific backlash from this night."

Alexis stared at him, as painful understanding came crashing in.

The asshole would find a way to retaliate.

CHAPTER 15

KEVIN CLIMBED WEARILY from his truck and trudged toward Stefan's front door. He could have called, but, this way, he saw Alexis at the same time. And he needed that contact tonight. She might prefer space, but he was scared to give her too much. So, here he was, incapable of walking away.

"Good evening, Kevin."

Kevin startled at the sound of his name. "Sorry, Stefan. I must be half asleep."

"Half something, yes. But I'm not sure it's asleep."

Kevin flushed, shooting his friend a dirty look. He got a cheeky grin in return. Kevin pushed past him, calling back, "Where is she?"

"Who?" asked Stefan, a little too innocently as he followed casually behind.

"Alexis!" Kevin called out.

"*Shh*, she might be asleep," Stefan cautioned.

"Now you tell me," Kevin said in a much softer voice, as he walked quickly through the hallway and into the living room—where he suddenly stopped.

Alexis slept, curled up like a kitten on the couch, with a soft mohair blanket tossed casually over her legs. He winced at the deep shadows under her closed eyes.

Hopefully finding the child unharmed tonight would go

a long way to helping her recover. "How was she earlier?"

"Pretty wiped out," Stefan answered, nodding toward the kitchen, so Kevin would follow him. Once there, he put on water for a cup of tea.

"Skip the tea. Do you have any beer?" At Stefan's nod, Kevin pulled open the fridge and grabbed himself a cold one. He removed the cap and took a long pull, before turning back to face Stefan again. "We lost him."

Stefan was compassionate in his silence. He gazed steadily back at Kevin, waiting.

Damn. Kevin wished he could be so calm. He wanted to pound something. "Did you pick up anything on him?"

Stefan shook his head. "Not really. I caught just the faintest scent of him in the mall." He paused and then forced himself to continue, "He's almost insane in his fury."

"That's to be expected."

"But not like this. He's after revenge."

Kevin looked at him sharply. "What do you mean?"

"I picked up some bits. It's almost as if he believes you stole something from him, and now he'll look for something of yours to take in revenge."

"But does he know it's me?" Kevin looked out the window thoughtfully. He hadn't expected this twist. If Stefan was correct, it seemed incredibly personal. Adding weight to the idea that he probably knew the killer.

"My impression is that he does. Besides, your name has been all over the media. It would be hard not to know you're handling the investigation."

"Interesting."

"What's interesting?" Alexis's voice broke through the intense silence.

The two men pivoted. Kevin walked over and pulled her

into a warm, comforting embrace. "How are you feeling?"

"Better." She looked up at him solemnly. "Or at least I will be when you confirm the little girl is okay."

"She is." Kevin smiled with satisfaction. "She's in her mother's arms as we speak."

Alexis closed her eyes in relief, letting her head drop onto his chest. Grateful, Kevin held her close, allowing his cheek to rest on her hair. After a few minutes, she disentangled herself and moved over to give Stefan a quick hug. "At least something good came out of tonight."

Stefan led the way back into the living room. "Kevin, any idea why he chose this girl?"

"Not yet. But neither the mother nor the little one are in any shape to talk. Tomorrow I'll speak with them again." Kevin sat down beside Alexis. "Are you working tomorrow?"

She looked over at him in surprise. "I'd planned to. Why?"

"I wondered if you wanted to come with me to meet the mom and little girl."

Alexis was shocked. "Why? I'm not the police. That's your job." She was so surprised at his question that she missed the grin on Stefan's face.

"News flash, Alexis. Remember all the headlines? 'Psychic Helps Police Find Abducted Child'? Guess what? That's you."

Alexis stared at the two men, as comprehension hit. Dear God, they were right. She'd just assisted in her first police case. A groan erupted, loud enough to be heard over the men's laughter, as she collapsed against her chair. "Shit! I don't want people to know."

"Calm down, Alexis. It's not the end of the world. No one will really know it's you—this time," Kevin said.

That horrified her even more. "And they had better not find out!" she cried out. "Yes, we found the little girl in time but …" She slapped her hands flat against her thighs. "But the asshole is still free. He'll just go after someone else. What if we can't save them?" Thoughts tumbled through her mind. Just the thought of meeting the little girl scared Alexis. No way she wanted to be involved to that extent.

Except she already was.

Kevin broke in, his voice soothing and stabilizing. "Which is why it would be a good idea for you to go away and to visit a relative for a while instead. If this guy finds out that you helped us, he could decide to come after you."

"I don't think he's too worried about waiting. He already said he would." Anger washed through her. Alexis glared at the far wall, trying to contain her temper. She should be afraid at the idea. Instead it just pissed her off. How dare he make her a victim? Stefan had an odd impressionist painting hanging on the wall. She concentrated on that. She'd noticed it before, but today it seemed more vibrant, alive almost. In trying to block out Kevin's words, the picture drew her in. How odd.

"Alexis?"

The colors twisted and shifted, mixing rapidly, even as she watched. Bloodred and stark white—blood flowed over jagged bone. The image struck home. Someone would die. Pain, intense white lightning, struck her in the abdomen, the agony of it doubling her over.

"What is it, Alexis?" Both men rushed to her side. Kevin crouched anxiously in front of her. "Alexis, what's the matter?"

"The picture," she gasped. "On the wall."

They both looked at the painting in question. Stefan got

up and walked over to it. Everything appeared normal now.

"What about the picture?" Kevin asked. His gaze roved over her face.

Alexis tried to reassure him with a smile, but it was difficult. "It looked like bones and blood. An image. Maybe of something to come. But it's gone now. I had the feeling someone would die."

The pain had eased but not her understanding. Her ability constantly forced her to adjust now. A few cautious breaths later, the pain had reduced to a mild ache.

Had that pain been from the image? She gently rubbed her stomach. When would her life return to normal? Could a normal life ever exist for her again?

"Not likely," said Kevin, his eyes full of understanding.

"You're reading my mind again."

"You're transmitting again," came his sharp retort.

"Was not," she responded childishly. It certainly felt like he'd been in her mind. Still was. She concentrated for a quick second and mentally booted him out.

"Thanks, at least now I know the last time was no accident," he said bitterly, pulling away from her, hurt etched on his face. He snagged his beer and walked back into the kitchen. The door slammed behind him, announcing his departure to the garden.

Alexis looked over at Stefan in concern. "I didn't mean to hurt his feelings."

"I know, which doesn't change the fact that you did." Stefan sat down beside her. "It's difficult to learn boundaries in this field. You have to decide what you're comfortable with and stick with it. You and Kevin share a special bond now. He just wants to keep you safe.

Alexis latched onto the main issue. "Bond?" she asked

tentatively.

"From the first time the two of you met, an intuitive bond existed, which has strengthened with time. There is one between the two of us, only different. Now, because he could, he used that link to make sure everything was okay in your world. He knew that, when you finally had some control, you *could* kick him out, but, until then, he wanted to keep tabs on you. Keep you protected." Stefan held up his hand to forestall her indignant outburst. "Before you blow, you knew, on a subconscious level, what he was doing. He couldn't have forged that link without your permission."

"What happened to the link after our love, … ah …" She stopped, flustered. "What happened to the link now?"

"A physical joining strengthens the mental or spiritual link. It's up to you two, but it can become almost permanent."

Alexis didn't know what to think. "Almost permanent?" What a mind-blowing concept.

"Right."

"Does that mean, like, we're 'special' together? As in 'forever' together?" Alexis couldn't get her mind wrapped around this. What she could understand damn-near blew her mind—and her heart. "The thing is, I'm not sure that's what I want. That I'm ready for that." And maybe not with Kevin. And his job. She'd lost so many loved ones already. She didn't know if she could live with the fear of him heading off into danger every day.

Did she even have a choice any longer?

Kevin's caustic voice cut through her speech. "I suppose you just wanted to scratch an itch, huh? Gee, thanks. … Nice to know I was of some use."

Heat flushed over Alexis's features before draining away,

leaving her chilled and wan. "That's not fair."

Stefan's calm voice stepped in, easing some of the tension in the air. "Be nice to the lady, Kevin. This is between the two of you."

"She's the one who brought it up with you."

"I was trying to understand why you were hurt when I closed the door in my mind. That's all." Alexis's voice lowered to a soft, vulnerable pitch. "Now I'm wondering just how the afternoon even happened. It was so unlike me. Did you ...?" She broke off, not sure what she wanted to ask.

But Kevin knew.

Angry disbelief blasted back at her. "What?" he roared. "So now I'm an unscrupulous seducer of young women. I get them under my power, and they're helpless to resist! Do you really think I used some kind of hypnotic suggestion on you?"

His obvious disgust and sense of betrayal shamed her. She didn't think she'd meant that ... Although she didn't think he was to blame, a part of her still felt uneasy. Never would she have seen herself doing what she'd done so casually. That it could be something incredibly powerful, like fate, destiny, or even—God help her—love, wasn't something she could look at right now. It was much easier to hide behind her anger than look at the rest.

She knew the two men were watching the emotions flicker across her face. She kept her mind closed off. She had to sort this out without prying eyes, no matter how well intending they might be.

Kevin snorted in disgust, grabbed his coat, and stormed to the front door. "Thanks for the beer, Stefan. I'm gone. Maybe I can still grab some sleep tonight."

The door slammed behind him.

Stupidly she felt hurt that he didn't say goodbye. What an idiot. He was pissed at her and maybe rightly so. That still didn't change the fact she'd have liked a goodbye hug and kiss after what they'd shared earlier today. Even though she had second-guessed—out loud—whether, for her, it was right or wrong.

She sighed and looked at Stefan, who watched her with one eyebrow raised.

"You could have said goodbye too, you know?" Stefan said quietly to her.

Once again she flushed. "I didn't think of that in time," she said quietly. She stood to gather her things. "Kevin's right. We should both be trying to follow his example and get some sleep. Morning will be here soon." She glanced at the living room clock and grimaced. "Very soon."

With a quick hug goodbye, Alexis walked slowly to her truck.

Way too late, she remembered the *almost* in Stefan's shocking revelation on being bonded. Just as shocking was the realization that such a bond was too precious to lose.

What had she just done?

~

THE SPORTS CAR ripped up the long drive, screeching to a dead stop, as if a drunken driver had slammed on a brake. Charles smiled. The lights were out. The good mayor and his wife were already in bed. They'd never notice his return, the recalcitrant son. Slamming the car door shut, he sauntered casually toward the sprawling mansion. Glancing around, he thought he saw another vehicle hiding under the trees at the fence. He laughed. Not bloody likely. No one would dare trespass on his daddy's all-important property.

Too bad.

He'd been tempted several times to smash his car into the front of the stone-cold building, but knew it wasn't worth the reproach and the reminders that would continue forever.

Almost walking straight, he made it inside the front door.

"Hello. Anyone still up?" He hoped not. He wasn't in the mood for more tears and lectures about his lack of career or his heavy drinking—especially not today. He closed his eyes against the pounding headache. God damn them anyway.

There never seemed to be a reason for these headaches, but they'd been killing him for years now, since he was a teen, in fact. Early on his mom had taken him to doctors and had tried hard to help him, but then, when nothing seemed to work, she had given up.

"Hello," he called out a little less quietly. Still no answer. Good.

"Keep it down, Charles," his dad called from the library, his voice boozy. "Your mother is asleep. Will you join me for a nightcap?" His father stood in the doorway to his study, drink in hand.

Asshole. Jesus, his old man was a royal bastard. One of these days, the mayor wouldn't be so cocky. Still, Charles had to maintain the status quo. He accepted the proffered scotch, before sitting down beside the fire. "Any news from around town?" he asked, smiling.

John stilled. "About what?"

Charles shrugged, tugging his tie loose to dangle down his shirt. "I heard something earlier on the news. Something about a missing child."

"Oh, that. The child's been found safe and sound." John lifted his glass of scotch in salute and took a healthy pull. "Don't know what we'd do without Detective Kevin Sutherland. He found the vehicle where the child was being held. Unfortunately the kidnapper is still at large." He shook his head sadly. "Terrible story."

"But the little girl will be okay, won't she?"

"Yes," John reassured him. "They found her in time." He looked over at his son curiously. "By the way, where were you earlier?"

"What? Oh, I was just driving around," Charles mumbled into his glass.

His father looked at him closely. "Did you go to the mall tonight? That's where the child was found."

Charles stared at his father. *Why the hell had he asked that?* "You don't think I had anything to do with her disappearance, do you?"

"No! No, of course not." But John focused on the swirling amber liquid in his glass, refusing to meet his son's gaze.

Sourly Charles looked at the hint of suspicion on the other man's face. "What about you? Did you go out earlier tonight?"

The other man's face paled, then flushed in fury. "What? My behavior has never been in question."

"But then your constituents don't know everything about your world, do they, Father?"

Horror and pain flowed from the liquid haze in John's eyes. "Why do you hate me so?"

No answer was forthcoming. Charles felt a grim satisfaction for putting his father firmly in his place again. But he knew his father would get his revenge soon—he always did.

He was big on that.

CHAPTER 16

SCREAMS OF TERROR woke Alexis in the middle of the night.

They were hers.

In bed, sweat soaked her silk camisole, and her heart pounded inside her chest. Oh God. What the hell was that? She was in her room but not. She was awake but not.

She was caught somewhere in-between.

The difficult day had roller-coastered her heart and mind into one endless tumultuous ride. Exhaustion had finally married the two into an uneasy truce for the night. Trembling in a crossover between psychic journey and sleepy wakefulness, Alexis didn't know where she was—or why.

Bitch!

Recognition and terror shuddered through her small frame. He was here, in her room. She curled up against the headboard, frantically searching the dark corners of her room.

Damn right, it's me! Thought you'd spoil my fun, did you? A macabre laughter floated through her gray world. *Well, guess what? I found something to entertain me anyway.* More haunting laughter echoed in the darkness. *Or should I say, … someone?*

Alexis woke fully chilled to her soul. She'd never understood the phrase "in a cold sweat." Now she did and wished she didn't. Her throat rasped painfully with every breath. She didn't know what had just happened but knew it was important.

Automatically her mind reached for Kevin. Her mind zeroed in with perfect aim. It took several scary moments before the phone beside her rang.

"What?" growled back his disgruntled voice. "Why the hell did you wake me in the middle of the night?"

"He was just here."

"Who?"

His question alone explained his lack of wakefulness. Alexis waited patiently for it to kick in. It didn't take long.

"Him? The suspect? Was ... He's gone? Are you okay? What did he say?"

Quickly she reassured him and related the asshole's words, emphasizing the tone of voice. "He sounded so satisfied, exultant even. I'm scared, Kevin. I think he's killed someone."

The long silence on the other end revealed Kevin was digesting her words. "That's not a total surprise. We saved the girl. It made him angry. But, if he's killing for revenge, then his behavior is escalating."

Alexis's hand tightened around the phone. She took a deep breath and expressed what really bothered her. "Maybe. I think he's picked someone you or I know, trying to make it personal."

Sudden silence filled the room. "I hope not, but no way to know until the call comes in. Get some rest. You'll need it."

Rest? Not likely. No way she would close her eyes again. That asshole could be waiting for her.

KEVIN FOUND IT impossible to go back to sleep. The initial heat at the sound of Alexis's voice had dissipated into anger. It was easier than dealing with the hurt inflicted last night. He still wanted to kiss her mindless—or at least until she had no doubts about the two of them. He'd never been much of a talker and knew he was reaping the reward of letting her run away yesterday. He'd seen her barriers go up, had sensed her insecurity, and didn't know how to return to the closeness they'd shared earlier. He'd let her run. If the call about the child hadn't come in then, … well, … at least she was talking to him this morning.

Immediately his mind returned to her message. His mind flitted through everyone this killer could target. There were too many of them. After an hour of going in circles, he finally got up and made coffee. It was just after four in the morning. Too early to start the day but too late to grab more sleep.

While sitting with his first coffee, his neck started itching. He opened his consciousness slightly. Awareness slammed into his senses with incredible intensity, letting him know the problem had been there a while, but he'd just tuned in.

Quietly he closed his eyes and opened his mind wider. He wasn't as good as Stefan yet, but he could usually search the scope of his county to pinpoint the area of trouble.

Next he went high and broad, looking for the black cloud, only to zoom back down into a corner of town he knew only too well. The question was, how did the killer know it too?

He hovered about the familiar two-story brick house. His breath whooshed out of him. His heart squeezed painfully before clamping down tight. He couldn't catch another breath. Mandy, the beautiful young lady friend, his former lover and Kyle's mother, lived there. One of the best people Kevin knew.

Now death had moved in.

Kevin returned to his living room, exhausted. He buried his face in his hands. Tears, hot and painful, welled up. Pain sat on the edge of his soul. God, he didn't want to go forward with this day.

Are you okay? Stefan's sleepy voice wove through Kevin's fatigue.

"No," he answered sadly. Too tired to use telepathy, and knowing the coming day would ask more from him than any day in his life, he'd spoken out loud and let Stefan do the work.

What's the matter? The sleepy voice was compassionate but not worried. Already he understood the emotion flowing through Kevin's mind, even if he didn't know the circumstances.

"The killer got personal last night. Very personal."

Waves of sadness vibrated between them as he allowed Stefan to watch the movie on continuous replay in Kevin's mind.

I'm sorry, Stefan murmured gently. *If it makes you feel better, I think that finished the killer's fury.*

"I agree, or I'd be standing watch over Alexis right now."

He waited no longer.

His fellow officers had all the sleep they would get this night.

He drove to where Mandy lived, at the end of a quiet residential block. Everything looked normal on the street. Years ago, when their relationship was going nowhere, they had decided to be good friends. Kevin had seen Mandy and her son many times over the years, the last time at Charles's birthday party. He'd always enjoyed seeing how Kyle had changed as he grew older. Now he just wished he would find the little boy alive.

He already knew Mandy wasn't.

Shit!

He walked up to the front door and knocked.

A crushing sense of evil permeated the air.

"Hello? Anybody home?" The front door was locked. He pounded loudly, hoping for Kyle's sleepy voice. Walking around to the back of the older house, Kevin looked carefully for any sign of forced entry. Mandy's car was parked in the back alley and was cold to the touch. She'd been home all night.

He rapped loudly on the back door. Nothing. The pit in his stomach solidified. He knocked once again, before calling out, "Hello? It's me, Kevin."

No answer. After pulling on gloves from his pocket, he tested the kitchen door. It opened easily. He pushed the door open wider. With his first step, the metallic smell filled his nostrils, and expectancy of the pain to come overwhelmed his soul. He knew he shouldn't enter. But he couldn't help himself. What if he'd been wrong? If there were the slightest chance that one of them was still alive, he had to help them. Several carefully placed steps led him into the kitchen and then to the small hallway. Kyle's room was empty.

And destroyed.

It was slow to come, but his police training kicked in, allowing him to peruse the room again. The killer had been pissed.

Kevin searched quickly, but he found no sign of the boy. Relief warred with hope and terror as he glanced down the hallway.

What were the chances Kyle hadn't been home last night? If he'd been the killer's target, the man would be pissed to not find him. That would explain why the child's room was smashed. And why the killer had gone after Mandy, why his victim hadn't been a child. The child hadn't been available.

Kevin didn't want to walk in any farther but knew he needed to check on Mandy. All the wind escaped from his lungs as he looked on the battered and bloodied body of his friend.

"Christ!" More prayer than invective, his heart cried for her.

She hadn't died easily or quickly.

Kevin ran back outside for fresh air, his stomach heaving. He did finally regain control, but with it came a blinding red haze of fury. This was an insane act of revenge.

The killer had declared war.

Kevin wouldn't rest until the animal was put down—one way or another.

But first, where was Kyle?

ALEXIS CHECKED HER watch several times during the day, while working at the main park. Kevin hadn't called with news. She'd expected a call.

But no such report came.

Alexis tried to phone Kevin at work on her lunch break, only to reach his voicemail. She didn't bother to leave a message. Neither did she attempt to contact him, as she had in the middle of the night. The door to enter his mind was closed. She'd used her baby skills to check. And maybe she deserved that, after blocking him yesterday.

Alexis lost herself in her gardens for the rest of the afternoon. She wallowed in the healing comfort of her plants. Several people wandered around, enjoying the beautiful sunny day. Mothers sat on benches, watching as children scampered about happily.

Alexis watched one group arrive in a dark sedan. A warmly dressed mother-daughter pair exited. A tall suited male stayed by the car, watching. The females must have been boiling hot. The little pixie of a girl tugged on the collar of her coat trying to loosen it up. But her mother held such a tight grip to her hand, Alexis saw there'd be no loosening in any direction.

"We only have a few minutes to visit, honey, before we have to leave. This is just a quick goodbye stop."

"I know, Mommy. I wanted to see the pretty flowers once more before we leave."

The mother smiled lovingly down on the pretty girl. "Say goodbye then, so we can go." She turned, in a nervous manner, to peruse the open spaces surrounding the park and took a step closer to her daughter.

Alexis watched, trying to understand. Her heart was touched, as the little girl bent to smell the flowers and to caress the petals of a bright, perky daisy. This was why Alexis did what she did—so the people could take the beauty and the healing spirit of plants into their own hearts. The little girl looked slightly familiar, but Alexis couldn't place her.

"You do love those daisies, don't you, sweetheart?

The little girl nodded. "They're special."

Alexis's heart hitched.

The young woman smiled lovingly down at the blond cherub. "Absolutely. I'm sorry. It's time to go."

The child beamed up at her mother. "That's okay."

As the child turned to walk away, her profile shone clearly. Alexis gulped. In her heart she knew this was the kidnapped child from the van. The one she'd been hesitant to meet. She slumped to the grass, watching as the two strolled through the winding flagstone paths toward the man and the waiting car. The bond of love shone from them both.

And yet their auras had a ragged edge, and Alexis felt a tight, locked-in connection that could stifle. Hoping to help, Alexis swept over both auras of mother and child, pulling the pain and fear into her own space. Instantly the energy around the two lightened, the edges smoothing out, and a slight glow began to weave joy around them. The mother's smile brightened a little, and she stood more relaxed.

Alexis did a swift cleanup of her own aura, dumping the negative energy, before it could affect her.

Warmth slid through her as she watched the child she'd helped rescue last night leave with her mother. Both happier and more at peace with the world. This answered one question. Alexis now knew why she'd continue to do psychic work. She'd do what she could, when she could, … and maybe help save others, … like this child.

Were the gardens the connection between the kids? Did they share the same love of the flowers? She didn't know how these psychos thought—perhaps he'd noticed this tenuous connection all his victims had to the flowers. Deep in thought, she tugged at the fingertips of her gloves and pulled them off to reach for her cell phone. Damn. Hers was at home on the charger. She had to let Kevin know.

Scott was wielding a shovel on the far side of the park. Alexis wandered in his direction, hoping to use his cell phone.

"Hey there, beauty. How've ya been?" His booming voice reached out for her before she'd made it halfway there.

She was helpless to stop the silly grin. Damn, she liked that man. "I'm good. How's the local lothario?"

A cheeky grin beamed at her. "Oh no, I'm not answering that question."

"What's the matter? Did she break up with you?"

"I'm not talking." Burly arms crossed resolutely over his huge expansion of chest, accentuating his words. But his chin jutting defiantly in the air caused her to break out laughing.

"I'm just teasing you, sweetie. Keep your lovely lady to yourself for a while. I can always go to the hospital and invite her out to tea."

He spun around quickly, his huge blue eyes bulging in alarm. "Ya wouldna, … would you?"

"Maybe. Of course, if you let me use your cell phone right now, I might reconsider."

The item in question appeared lightning quick in her hand, causing another round of giggles.

She punched in the numbers and waited. "Detective Sutherland, please." Scott waggled his raised eyebrows at her. Alexis rolled her eyes and walked a few steps away.

"Alexis, I can't talk right now."

She rushed into speech. "Kevin, I just saw a mother and little girl here in the gardens. She looked like the little girl from the van. Could it be them?" Alexis listened to Kevin's confirmation of what she already knew. "She really loves the gardens. I think there has to be some connection."

"Thanks, I have to go." He hung up.

"Damn it all. Anyway." She glared at the silent phone in her hand.

"I don't think he's listening to you, darling," Scott teased, motioning to the dead phone clutched uselessly in her hand, while she continued her one-sided conversation with empty air. "Or are you so good now that you no longer need any technology?"

If he only knew.

CHAPTER 17

STEFAN SEEMED STRANGELY preoccupied that evening. He didn't mention a reason, so she didn't ask either. She kept an eye on him though, as they enjoyed the first few sips of Stefan's traditional tea. An odd look settled on his face. Alexis eyed him curiously. "What is it? Did you come up with something?" She couldn't stop the dread from sneaking into her voice. "Stefan, what aren't you telling me?"

"Did you listen to the news?" Stefan's voice held a sadness to it.

Alexis looked at him sharply. "What news?" But inside, she already knew. It was just the details that had to be filled in. "Who died?"

Their eyes met and held. Stefan broke away to bow his head. "An ex-girlfriend of Kevin's. Her son wasn't home at the time. He'd had a sleepover at the neighbor's."

Alexis sank slowly down beside him. *Oh no.* Her stomach clenched and heaved. Dear God, what kind of monster was this?

"A thwarted one."

Alexis gulped several times, before whispering, "I suppose that makes as much sense as anything. Poor Kevin."

Stefan picked up his teacup and took a sip. "He found her."

Shards of agony pierced her heart. How terrible for him.

Kevin must have gone through hell. That had to top the list of things she never wanted to experience. Finally Alexis became aware of Stefan's careful scrutiny. She moved to break the silence. "Have you learned anything about the killer?"

"Some. I know I'm up against something unique. He's stronger, more cunning, and has years of experience remaining undetected. I have one advantage though. He's not used to being hunted on the other side."

"Good. At least that gives us something."

"We'll need much more than that."

At the same moment, they heard a car pull up out front.

"Kevin?" She raised an eyebrow at Stefan. He nodded.

They waited, listening for the approaching footsteps, then for the door to open.

"Good evening, you two." Kevin leaned against the archway to the solarium. Dark shadows sagged below his bloodshot eyes.

Alexis wanted to run over to hug him. Something held her back, but she couldn't explain what. "I'm sorry." She eyed him carefully. A black mantle of depression had settled on his shoulders, with a white-lipped, pinched fury just below the surface. She eyed him warily.

His head nodded in a sharp jerk. "Thanks. I gather Stefan told you?"

"A little." It was as if they were strangers, exchanging polite banter. "What's happening now?"

"Everything!" Kevin's expression chilled. "We're doing everything we can, thank you."

"I know that. I didn't mean to imply that you weren't." She stopped one second before confessing, "I'm sorry. Maybe I did, but only because I'm scared and worried." Alexis shrugged defensively. "People are dying. Always before, I've put my trust in the police to find a speedy solution." She looked between the two men, nervous, uncertain, and ashamed of her feelings. "The thing is, this time I feel like I'm supposed to be part of the solution, and I feel like I'm failing everyone."

"No one knows about you or your abilities. There's no expectation that you'll—"

"Except me." She twisted her bracelet nervously. Her insecurities had no boundaries tonight.

Kevin clamped his large hand down hard on her fingers.

Startled, she realized that her fingers were twisted and snarled in her bracelet. "Sorry, I'm not myself. I think it's time I went home. Maybe I can get some sleep tonight."

Before she reached the front door, Kevin joined her. "I'll take you home."

"No, it's okay. You're tired. Besides, I'll be fine."

He turned her by the shoulders until she faced him. "Maybe, but I don't like the idea of you going home alone."

She couldn't resist. "Okay, but I don't want to leave my truck here. If you want, you can follow me home. Make sure I get there safe." Opening the door, Alexis walked to her truck.

"Fine," he said shortly.

As Alexis drove home, she worried about what to do with him, when they arrived at her place.

Minutes later, she exited her truck and waited, while he parked beside her. On their way to her apartment door, she pointed out the hallway where the odd psychic incidents happened.

"This hallway looks a lot like the one I saw in the vision in the ditch, but I don't know. Maybe the whole world is filled with long dingy gray hallways."

He walked into the dark living room behind her, shutting the door with a resounding *click.* "I checked out past tenants. Nothing popped."

Alexis walked over to the lamp, wondering why there was no light answering all her attempts. "The lights aren't working." She tried the wall lamp against the window. "Odd."

This time, she headed for the kitchen and flipped the wall switch. "Oh, great. Like I need this."

"What?"

"A power outage." She slung her purse to the kitchen table. Damn, she wanted a hot bath.

"How can that be? The elevators worked and the hallway lights were on." Kevin moved carefully around the darkened apartment. "Was everything okay earlier?"

"Yes. I made dinner and had tea. There were no issues then."

Kevin unclipped his gun, surprising her. He motioned her to get behind him. Only she didn't understand, causing his motions to become more frantic.

"Kevin, what's the matter?" she whispered.

He held up his hand, as if to keep her quiet.

"Surely this is a simple utility issue. Isn't it?" she whispered again.

Kevin never said a word, but he grabbed her arm with one hand and her purse with the other. She snatched up her cell phone still in the charger on her counter.

"*Shhh*," he whispered, tugging her to the front door, then shutting it quietly behind them. He lost no time hustling her straight back out to their vehicles.

"We're taking mine. Get in."

She scrambled into the front of Kevin's truck without protest. She sat quietly, while he called the station. By the time he'd finished the conversation, a cruiser pulled up with two uniformed men inside.

Kevin waved to them and pulled out onto the road.

Alexis waited a moment. "What was that all about?"

"I didn't tell you before, but Mandy ..." He choked up slightly, then continued, "Mandy, the woman who was murdered yesterday? ... When I arrived at her house, the house had no power either. Yet all the neighbors' houses were fine."

He shifted the truck one gear higher. He glanced over at her. "Alexis, there's a good chance he was coming after you tonight."

Alexis swallowed hard. Wouldn't she know if the killer hunted her? And, if she didn't, what good were her psychic abilities? When she'd finally calmed enough to speak, what she said surprised them both. "Why didn't you search more thoroughly then?" she said indignantly. "We could have caught him."

Kevin looked over at her in astonishment. "It's the 'we' part that's a concern. I deemed it more important to get you out safely first. Those officers will check it out."

By the time she'd processed the concept of cops going into her apartment, they'd reached Kevin's house.

"I'll make some calls, once I get you settled in." He followed her to the front door of his small cozy house, tucked behind an evergreen hedge.

Alexis barely noticed where they were. She was still reeling at the implications of the killer seeking her now.

"Alexis?" Kevin reached out and snagged her into a close hug. "Hey, it'll be all right."

"How can you say that?" Nothing would ever be right again, … until this asshole was caught.

"This is just a precaution," he reminded her. "Maybe I overreacted, but I'm not taking any chances. I saw firsthand what this asshole is capable of. You won't be his victim—ever." He squeezed her tight before stepping back. His voice grim, he promised, "I won't let that happen."

That made for a sobering shift back to reality. "I'm really sorry about Mandy." She watched sorrow deepen the lines of his face.

"Thanks. … So am I. I'm also grateful the bastard didn't get his hands on Kyle. That's why I'm not taking any chances."

"Fine." She followed him into the hallway and stopped in her tracks. "Oh, wow!"

His house startled her. Huge flower pots held an overwhelming array of tropical plants in all sizes, textures, and every shade of green. Every windowsill was laden with an assortment of cuttings and flowering houseplants. The pièce de résistance was ivy that crawled halfway across the living room ceiling, wandering down to a huge dining room. Waves of welcoming energy surrounded Alexis as she walked through the main floor.

"They're beautiful," she whispered reverently. Her smile broadened, as the warm energy visibly strengthened in response to her appreciation.

"I thought you might like them. I hadn't realized you could communicate with them quite so effectively." He looked at the plants he'd lavished with so much care. "Unbelievable! They already look happier." He walked into his kitchen, checking out his plants in bemusement.

"You've done a wonderful job. I'm sure you know that

already." Alexis trailed behind him, a little confused by his reaction. "I didn't mean to barge in on your territory. Plants just react whenever I'm around."

He spun around, surprise lighting his face. "I'm not upset with you. I'm in awe. I've never seen so much raw power in someone so unaware." He walked over to the fridge. "Do you want a beer?"

"No, thank you. I'm so tired that would finish me."

"Will you sleep?"

Alexis felt the intensity of his gaze, knowing he was gauging her on all levels. "Stop that!"

"Yep, definitely need sleep. Follow me." He led the way to the set of stairs they'd passed on their way into the kitchen. "Up here are the bedrooms." The top of the stairs opened into a cozy nook and several doors. He pushed open the closest one. "This is the one and only guest room."

Alexis walked into a simple but comfortable-looking room. She looked around. It seemed generic, almost had a hotel look to it.

"I don't get many visitors. At least not many who sleep in here."

She shot him a dry look. How was she to take that comment? But he'd already moved toward a second door. "Your own bathroom is in there. Do you need anything else?"

You.

No, she didn't dare. She would not be the one who opened that discussion. "I'll be fine, thank you."

"Great. We'll sort everything out in the morning. For now, you're safe." He walked back to the hallway. "Get a good night's sleep. I'll see you in the morning."

Then he was gone.

Alexis gazed at the empty doorway. She really would sleep alone tonight. She'd wondered, anticipated, and worried over the night to come. Now she felt inexplicably disappointed.

Without any nightclothes or toiletries, her evening ritual took mere seconds, allowing her to crawl into bed before her energy fled completely. She remembered to follow Stefan's evening preparations and dropped off into a deep sleep.

DOWNSTAIRS, KEVIN REACHED for a beer. It would be a long night. But he had to stay focused. If the bastard knew about Mandy, then locating Kevin's home was an easy next step.

Alexis hadn't seemed interested in spending the night in his arms, and he'd been looking for any sign of encouragement. But then he hadn't exactly shown any interest either. She'd have to make that next gesture herself.

But it was too early for her. Damn and double damn. She'd gotten that stupid idea in her head about him using some hidden advantage against her. He snorted. Yeah, right. All he'd had was his overwhelming need. Every time he saw the damn woman, he was hungry for what they could have together. His constant state of arousal made it difficult to think clearly around her.

He'd tested the door to her mind once, but it had been firmly closed against him. For her safety, he needed it open. With her guard up against him like this, he couldn't even talk to her about it.

Once this was settled, then …

His watch beeped, reminding him of the time.

He quickly dialed his office. There'd been no word on

Alexis's apartment yet. Kevin sat down for the long evening ahead.

It left plenty of time to think about Mandy and about what would never be again. Most of all, it left plenty of time to think about the bastard who'd destroyed her son's world. Kevin took a drink of his beer and raised the bottle briefly in homage to Mandy. That this asshole had chosen an ex-girlfriend of Kevin's likely meant the killer was someone who knew Kevin, and possibly someone Kevin knew. Sure, a stranger could have asked around. … Mandy's name could have come up in conversation. But, in a town this size, it was just as likely that Kevin knew Mandy's killer. He'd seen her last at John's party. His stomach soured. Had someone seen them together?

Kevin closed his mind to the images that tumbled through his heart. Pain welled up. Kevin brutally slammed aside the images and took a hefty drink. The beer soured on its way down his throat. Kevin wouldn't let anyone else get hurt, especially not Alexis—if he could help it.

A scream ripped through his house.

ALEXIS, DID YOU enjoy my sweet revenge? I thought you'd like to see what I can do. Shall I show you more?

No! Alexis stood in the middle of a black tornado. She was lost in time and space. She had no idea how she'd arrived in this hellhole or how to leave it. Horrific images swirled around her. Faces appearing, then disappearing, as others took their place. Other victims, other deaths. The force of the furor blinded her to all else. *No! Stop! No more victims, please. I beg you.*

Her wail of agony ripped through the energy vortex,

making her tormentor laugh with joy. *They aren't victims. They are my guests. For all of eternity.*

Not all of them. Surely not. He'd only killed Mandy for revenge—hadn't he? Was she now one of his guests?

Yes, all of them. I've enjoyed this little hobby of mine for decades. Since I was a young man actually. I was never caught. Never even a suspect in all those child murder cases. I took a break in there, but now I'm back, … and your turn is coming.

The images circling her increased, the wails and cries of his victims drowning out her hearing. The crescendo of pain and agony built until she couldn't stand it. Her horrified scream slashed through the house and woke her up.

Sobbing for breath, she trembled in shock under the twisted covers. She recognized Kevin's wary approach to the bed. Her teeth were chattering so uncontrollably that she didn't think they'd ever stop.

Kevin sat down on the edge of the bed, looking her over carefully. "I didn't want to approach you too quickly. That can be dangerous. Remember?" A large palm cupped her cheek tenderly.

Alexis leaned into it, gratefully accepting the comfort. "I'm so cold," she whispered. Her fingertips were a curiosity, bluish-gray in color, probably a perfect match for her lips. The chattering showed no sign of slowing either.

"Move over," he whispered huskily. "I'm coming in." He pulled back the warm blankets and slid under to lie beside her. Without giving her a chance to argue, he snuggled her tightly against his chest. "Just concentrate on getting warm."

He felt so good and so right.

She lie still, accepting his comfort, until his body heat finally started to chase away the chills. "He spoke with me.

He said my turn was coming," she whispered against his chest.

Kevin's arm tightened around her.

"All his victims were screaming and crying out for mercy. A mercy they never found. So many victims over so many years." As the horrible shrieks echoed in her mind, the tears started to fall. Knowing she had to get it all out now, she quickly repeated the conversation. Her voice dropped to a whisper, before choking into sobs.

Kevin let her cry, but she couldn't seem to stop them.

"*Shh.* ... Stop now. That's enough. You'll make yourself sick." His hands stroked her back and shoulders, over the T-shirt she'd worn to bed. "*Shh,* it's okay, honey. Please stop."

When his words had no effect, he shifted her and dropped comforting kisses on her cheeks and eyelids. "Please, Alexis, stop."

She opened her eyes and solemnly gazed up at him. Somehow she'd ended up stretched out beneath him. The intimacy of the situation struck her.

He was right where she wanted him.

Something in her eyes must have shown her thoughts for his gaze warmed in response.

"Are you feeling better?"

She didn't trust her voice, choosing to nod instead. He dropped yet another kiss on the corner of her lips. "Are you sure? I could kiss you better here." He dropped a kiss on the other side of her mouth. "Or here." Another kiss landed on her nose. "Or even here." This time, a kiss closed her eyes with his sweet touch. "Anything to make you feel better."

"You're missing the one place which needs it the most."

He hesitated, then dropped to angle a soft kiss on her nose. "Are you sure? I don't want any doubts later."

She smiled warmly. “No doubts in the morning.” She’d have to explain her feelings, her confusion … tomorrow. Tonight they needed this. They needed each other.

“Good.” Holding her gaze, he lowered his head and laid a burning, explosive kiss on her lips.

Oh God, she’d missed him. Only as her heart melted under his loving touch did she recognize this as a homecoming—something to think about later. Right now, her brain was turning to mush.

“Is this better?” His lips continued to travel, distracting her from his words, as she followed his pathways with intensive interest. Nerve endings were once again alive, igniting sensations, warming her with their heat.

“Almost.”

“Am I getting closer?” His lips whispered down to the nape of her neck.

“Definitely.”

“How about here?” He descended farther, catching the loose neck of her T-shirt with his teeth and pulling it down to get better access.

She murmured in anticipation, her body twisting and turning with a will of its own. “Almost …” she whispered achingly. “You’re almost there.”

Kevin shifted onto his knees, letting the bedding fall down his back. Large warm hands slid under her shirt, moving the offending material up to her chin. As he exposed her full breasts, he ducked his head and took one plump nipple deep into his mouth.

She arched off the bed in response. “That’s the spot.”

He murmured, satisfied, and proceeded to feast on the bounty spread before him.

Alexis slid quickly under his magical spell, forgetting all

else. Only one thing existed for her—him.

She didn't know when her T-shirt joined the scrambled bedding on the floor or when his clothing flew haphazardly to join the rest. She only knew that, for those few seconds, she was lost without him.

"*Shh*, I'm here. It's okay, baby." His warm hands took her back under in a sexual haze that had no beginning and no end. It had only him.

In the dark of night, they burned with a light of their own, which sustained them throughout the long hours until morning.

CHAPTER 18

"I'M AWAKE," SHE murmured, her eyes still closed against the coming morning.

"The day is upon us, whether you're ready to face it or not."

"*Not* is my choice." But her luscious lips smiled. She snuggled closer, loath to answer her body's call for the bathroom. "I'm trying to ignore my bladder already."

"I know the feeling. Somehow I don't think that works for long." He hugged her, then loosened his arms and slowly stood, stretching the kinks out of his spine.

She peeked up at him, only to have her eyes pop open wide. "Are you sure you don't want to come back to bed? It'd be a shame to waste that."

After last night, not even those words popping from her mouth of their own volition could embarrass her. Kevin was strikingly beautiful to her at any time. In his early morning aroused state, he was dynamite.

"I wish. You do realize it is almost nine. Are you supposed to work today?"

At her nod, he sighed. "Unfortunately so do I." With those words, he walked into the bathroom and a cold shower.

Watching his rear walk away did nothing to slow down her heartbeat. But he was right. Today was not a holiday or a weekend, and she was now officially very late. Searching for her cell phone in the chaos of her room, she called Scott.

"'Bout time, you called. Rick's been asking where you were. I told him that you'd gone to see the doctor, being still upset over the murders and such. He didn't like that much."

"Thanks, Scott." She tried to cover her huge yawn, but he heard it.

"Did you have another bad night then?"

Alexis smiled at the concern in his voice. How to excuse her night without letting everything slip? "I had a few bad moments. I'll explain when I get there in half an hour or so."

After ringing off, she made a beeline for the bathroom and her solo shower.

When she finally raced down to the kitchen, dressed in yesterday's clothes, and ready for work, she was grateful to accept a travel mug full of rich coffee. "Oh, thank God. You're a lifesaver."

"Do you want me to drive you to your truck or directly to work?"

She checked her watch. Her half hour was past gone. "Straight to work, thanks." Maybe she'd be lucky and could slip in unnoticed. If there were guardian angels, she hoped one was watching out for her and would keep Kevin's presence undetected.

If such angels existed, they were on their early lunch break when she arrived at work.

Several of the men stood around, drinking coffee, when they arrived—including Scott.

"Good morning, Detective." Respectful greetings flew in his direction. No one said anything to her.

"Thanks for the ride, Kevin." Alexis waved casually, studiously refusing to look at the men. She rolled her eyes at

Kevin, sparking his huge grin.

She headed for the garden on the farthest corner of her area, knowing Scott would be on her heels. She wanted to separate him from his cronies. Shyness had definitely taken over.

Whatever. She could only hope he'd let it slide.

Yeah, as if.

"Good morning. So you had a bad night, did you?" Scott's gruff voice half teased.

"Yes, you could say that." She looked over at him casually, catching the curious look on his face. She smiled. "And, yes," she drawled slowly, "Kevin made the night much better."

"Well now." Scott rubbed his hands together gleefully. "It's about time."

Alexis couldn't help it. She broke out laughing. He'd been pushing her in this direction for a long time. He should be happy. "And you're right. It was time."

His booming laugh reached across the gardens. "Good for you." His face closed down with a sudden worry. Alexis watched in amusement.

"You won't jump into this too quickly, will you? You're a little off balance, vulnerable even, right now. I wouldn't want anyone to be taking advantage." Scott latched on to this new concern and wouldn't let go.

Alexis walked closer to reassure her gentle giant of a friend. "I am taking it easy. I know things haven't exactly been normal. As far as the Sight goes, well, the detective has several abilities of his own. Actually," she added, with a resigned look, "he's far more skilled than I am."

"That might be good. He could help you." Scott spoke cautiously, as if wording his thoughts carefully. "He wouldn't be having any special power over you, now would he?" He narrowed his eyes in concern.

"No," she answered slowly. "Though, when you can go into each other's minds, an element of helplessness or vulnerability is involved." She shrugged. "What do I know about relationships and what men will do to get into a woman's bed?" She looked at Scott teasingly. "That's your specialty, isn't it?"

Scott's eyes narrowed even farther, as a detached inward look washed over his face.

Alexis got a little alarmed. "Hey, I'm teasing, Scott. I didn't mean to imply anything." She stretched out to rub his shoulder reassuringly.

"No, but I do know what men might do, being one *meself*." He snagged her into a big bear hug. "And now I'm more than a little concerned about what a man with extra senses and insider knowledge might do."

"Nothing. He'd do nothing. Don't worry."

"Sure." Scott brushed it off, but the look in his eyes left her with lingering doubt.

"Don't you do anything stupid, do you hear me?" Alexis asked.

"Me?" he asked too innocently.

Not feeling reassured by his tone of voice, Alexis dropped the pleading for now. "Shall we get some work done? I have to do something to justify my pay."

"Especially because Rick was here earlier."

"Right I forgot." Alexis tucked her hair behind her head, more than a little bothered at being found lacking at work once again. "What did he say?"

"He wants to see us in his office at the end of the day."

THAT STATEMENT LINGERED heavily on Alexis's mind. By the time she had completed her day's work, it was later than normal.

"Alex? Are you ready for your meeting with Rick? I was asked to attend too."

"Sure, why not. If I'll get chewed out, it might as well be now."

"Don't go there, chippy. It won't help, you know?"

"Nothing will help," she grumbled, as she brushed off her clothes, resolutely determined to get the meeting over with, her temper intact.

When they arrived at the office, they found something entirely different than expected.

The mayor and Kevin—in full detective mode—were already in Rick's office. Their raised voices were too loud to be ignored.

"Sounds like fun," Alexis grimaced. She didn't need a full-blown confrontation.

As they approached, snippets of conversation were easily heard.

Rick's voice was the clearest. "She's the one who might pose a problem, damn it."

"She won't. We'll see to that," Kevin said easily. "We need your cooperation."

"What difference will that make?" A loud snort echoed down the hallway, followed by Rick's disgusted voice. "*She's* the one who won't cooperate."

Alexis looked over at Scott in concern. She had no doubt the female they'd mentioned was her. Scott raised his eyebrows, motioning her to the door first. "Shall we?"

With a comical look in his direction, she rapped loudly, interrupting the ongoing discourse on the other side.

"Who is it?" Rick's imperious boss voice made Alexis's hackles rise.

"It is 'she.'"

A moment of dead silence ensued, while Scott rolled his eyes at her inappropriate humor.

The door opened abruptly. Kevin stood there.

"A job promotion? … Detective to usher perhaps?" she murmured for his ears alone.

"Maybe you should take a lesson in subservience. It would be good for you." He motioned her inside.

"That'd be a waste of time," Scott quickly interjected, pushing Alexis none-too-gently farther into the room and past Kevin. He turned to face his boss and said, "Hey, Rick. Are we disturbing you? I didn't know the mayor was in here with you two. We can come back tomorrow, if that's a better time."

Rick glared at Alexis. "What's the point? She'd disturb me just as much tomorrow."

"Nice to know I leave such a lasting impression." Alexis couldn't stop the snappiness in her voice. Rick always brought out the worst in her.

Kevin said, "Enough. This is official business."

"Then it doesn't involve us. I thought Rick wanted to see me." She quickly stood again, anxious to leave the men alone. "We can do this another time."

"Sit down." Kevin's voice brooked no argument.

Startled, Alexis obeyed, turning to face him.

But it was Rick who spoke. "Alexis, Detective Sutherland wants you to leave town."

Alexis froze. She narrowed her green eyes at Kevin, who stood there with his arms folded across his chest. He was waiting for her explosion. Well, she'd be damned if she'd give it to him.

"Why?" There. That was simple and adultlike.

"The power loss that you experienced last night was isolated to just your apartment."

"And …?"

"There's evidence to show that whoever staged that power outage was the same person involved in yesterday's homicide."

Scott's indrawn breath had her reaching out to him. She offered him a tentative smile. "I said I'd had a bad night."

"But you weren't telling all, were you, lass?"

She rubbed his shoulder. "It would have upset you."

"That be the truth." Scott turned to Kevin. "You must think she's been targeted, if you want her to leave town."

"But I can't leave town. I have a job and a paycheck to collect," she snapped. Those weren't the real reasons, but she'd be damned if she'd explain in front of Rick. Besides, they would *not* gang up on her.

"Which is why we're here." Kevin looked over at Rick and then the mayor. "Would you like to take it from here?"

"You are to go on 50 percent paid leave, until this is over." Rick didn't want to continue, but, at the sharp look from the mayor, he sighed in disgust and added, "Under duress, I promise your job with the city will be here, waiting for you."

The look on his face was almost worth being in this position. He'd been forced to play this hand, and he didn't like it one bit. He'd like her gone for good. "Thanks for the generous offer, but I'm afraid I'll have to refuse."

A tiny minute of shocked silence ensued before everyone jumped on her.

"Like hell!" roared Kevin.

"Don't do anything foolish here." Scott squeezed her shoulder.

Rick smirked. "I told you. She's the one who won't co-operate. She never does."

Alexis knew she had to stay. She hadn't had time to sort out how or why. And maybe she didn't want to look that deep. In ways she didn't know or understand, she had to be here. She had no other option.

"This would only be for a few days," the mayor said, speaking up for the first time. Alexis hadn't even seen him standing slightly behind Kevin. "I have every confidence in our police force. Detective Sutherland has always come through for us before. No reason to doubt that he won't this time either."

Was he for real? Alexis couldn't believe the politically correct drivel that sprouted from his mouth. It's not that she didn't believe Kevin would do his best. But this murderer was something else.

Kevin spoke again. "Thanks for the vote of confidence, John." He smiled winningly at her. "Alexis, you must see how imperative it is that you remain safe and that we can focus on the investigation without the distraction of watching you every moment."

Her look of innocence fooled no one. "I have the utmost confidence in your abilities. I'm sure you can find a way to make that happen without sending me out of town." She nodded at the mayor. "I agree wholeheartedly that our city is safe under the watchful eye of Bradford's Police Force, especially Detective Sutherland."

"Shit!" Kevin looked at her, disgust on his face. "You won't cooperate, will you?"

Alexis took an inventory of the men's faces—only one

gloated happily. Rick had been right about how she'd take the news, and he loved being right.

"Nope. I *need* to be here."

Both Kevin and Scott narrowed their eyes at her. It wasn't the time or place to ask questions.

To that end, Scott half lifted her from her chair. "I'll take her to the pub and talk some sense into her."

Before Alexis realized it, she'd been ushered back out to Scott's truck. He never said a word, until they were seated in their usual corner of the smoky room and held big frothy mugs. "Now what the hell is going on?"

Taking her time, Alexis explained the series of odd events that had precipitated staying at Kevin's last night.

"Not good news. Something's gone bad in this town, Alexis. I wish you'd listen to them and leave." Heavy wrinkles lined the burly Irishman's face. Scott cared sincerely about the people in his world. Alexis was one of those. "Please get out of town, Alexis."

"Scott, it isn't that bad yet." Alexis didn't quite get the reaction she'd been hoping for.

He leaned closer, until he was almost in her face. "Were you planning on waiting until it got right bad then?" Sarcasm glinted in his eyes. His voice rose in a crescendo until he was almost shouting. "And how were you gonna know when that is? When you're dead perhaps?"

"All right. *Shhh.* You're attracting attention. Calm down, Scott." Gently she stroked his shoulder. It took a few moments before the giant settled back down again.

"The thing is …" Alexis paused to collect her thoughts into a coherent pattern. "I don't know what to tell you, except … I *have* to stay." She studied his face. "Something's been bad here for a while, and it's just now rising to the surface. When it goes to hell, I'm supposed to be here."

"This be the Sight again?" Scott shook his head, stumped. "You can't be alone anymore. I can stay with you during working hours, but what about the rest of the day and night?"

"I could ask Kevin." Alexis looked into her beer, wrinkling her nose. "But I don't want to depend on him to that extent."

"And I'm thinking it's too late to worry about that now," Scott teased. "You've already made a choice. All that's left is to see how it works out for you."

Alexis frowned. What a great way to put it. And what would Kevin think of her decision?

BACK AT THE office, Kevin spoke with two younger officers.

"I need you two to dig up everything we have on a serial killer who may have operated in this area close to thirty years ago. We suspect he targeted children who spent a lot of time in the city's gardens. The cases were never solved, the murders stopped after a decade, and the killer never resurfaced. I want names of the victims, a list of suspects at the time, pictures, … especially pictures of the victims, if we can gather those. They would be in the cold case files." He shifted. "A few people are still left on the force who might remember added details. Pick their brains. I need everything and everything now. Before you go, what did you two find on Mandy and Kyle leading up to the murder?"

The senior of the two started. "We've compiled the information from the interviews of the neighbors yesterday. Apparently nothing noticeable happened during the day, but neither had been seen after dinner. Kyle attended school, then went to his friend's house afterward. He stayed for dinner and then called his mom around seven p.m. and convinced her to let him stay for a sleepover. The victim had put in a full day's work and apparently went home and stayed there. Her coworkers had nothing useful to add." As he finished, he looked over at his partner.

The younger man, Allen, picked up the story. "We did pick up several full and partial prints. We might get lucky."

Kevin grimaced. Not likely but they could hope.

"The coroner's report isn't in yet, and, so far, there's no news on the forensic material. We found several hair samples that might lead to something useful, but those will take time and will still require something to match them to." Allen shrugged, as if to say, *What can you do?*

The three men discussed their next steps, before going their separate ways.

Alone again, Kevin watched the late afternoon sun wash his town in orange. His neck itched. That scared the hell out of him. Several minutes of searching the ethers still gave no explanation as to the source of the itch, … but he was sure the vibe came from the same killer they were trying to track down. Kevin recognized the energy pattern. Closing his eyes again, he freed his mind to search. This time he sensed nothing.

He returned to the stack of paperwork on his desk. Nothing else to do but wait.

CHAPTER 19

ALEXIS SPENT A weird evening with Kevin last night, as her guard. Not as her lover. She sighed deeply, as she took a short break the next morning, wishing she had coffee to go with it. Instead, she sat down under a maple tree and worked on Stefan's lessons. First off was to see if she could reach out and touch Stefan. With little effort she saw him in her mind. She grinned. Then stopped and her smile fell away. She focused harder. His energy was pale, almost translucent. She didn't like it. *Stefan?*

She got no answer. More worrisome was the absolute lack of movement in his form.

She pulled out her phone and located the number she needed. "Hi, Kevin," Alexis couldn't believe the relief she felt at hearing his voice. She glanced around the park. Scott stood a short distance away, speaking with another gardener. She lowered her voice. "Something's wrong with Stefan. I can't reach him, and I can barely feel him. His energy is weird. Off somehow." She quickly explained, adding, "I'm heading out there now."

"I'll meet you there."

By the time she'd explained the situation to Scott and had made the drive to Stefan's house, Kevin already stood on the front step, knocking.

"Why don't you break in or something?" She waved her

arms toward the windows.

He shot her a disgusted look. "Just because *you're* impatient doesn't give *me* the right to break in."

That did it. "Look. We know something is wrong. If the police don't have the right, how about caring friends?" Her hands rested on her hips defiantly.

"Calm down. I just got here. Stefan hasn't even had a chance to answer the bell." He watched as she headed around to the back of the house. "Hey, where are you going?" He followed quickly behind her. "Alexis, what are you doing? *Alexis?*"

"I'll knock on the back door of course. You stay there."

"Like hell."

Alexis ignored him. Several knocks on the back door produced no results. She peered through the darkened windows, searching for any sign of life within.

Then she tried the doorknob. It wasn't locked. Knowing she didn't have the right, she pushed it open anyway. "Stefan!" She stepped into the silent house. "Stefan, it's Alexis. Are you home?"

Kevin came up behind her.

"*Shit.*" Alexis spun around in fright. "You scared the crap out of me."

"Calm down. You're terrorizing yourself. Stand back." He stepped in front of her and entered the kitchen.

Alexis studied his movements as he stopped and surveyed the area. He sniffed the air cautiously, before moving on. She followed slowly.

In the living room, Stefan laid on his hardwood floor, wrapped in his favorite wool blanket. He looked to be sleeping, except for his utter stillness. Was he even breathing? She reached toward him …

"Don't. Remember? We can't touch him."

She looked at him, puzzled. "He needs help. How can we help if we can't touch him?" She watched, even more puzzled, as Kevin approached slowly, wafting his hands in an odd manner, almost stroking the space around Stefan.

"What are you doing?" she whispered.

"Checking out his energy. Stefan is off in the ethers."

"But he's okay, isn't he?" Alexis approached from the side, yet stayed behind Kevin. She sank slowly to her knees beside Stefan. His energy seemed odd. "He's surrounded by pure white light," she whispered in reverence.

"He's incredibly powerful." Kevin looked back at her. "He's been practicing that new technique of his but didn't give me many details. Now I wish he had."

"What can we do?"

"Watch over him." Kevin got up and took a step back. "At least that's all for now."

Alexis didn't like the sound of that. She preferred action to inaction any day. Besides, this didn't feel right. Using her inner eye, as she'd been taught, she looked over Stefan's prone body. His energy, although white, was faint and pale. It did not brim with a vital life force. "Something's wrong. His energy is very low. His silver cord is pale and thin, almost nonexistent."

"You can see that?" Astonished, Kevin crouched down to take another look.

"Yes. He's not loose in the ethers. He's lost, period." Alexis followed the wispy trail as far as she saw it, but it dissipated a few feet away from Stefan's body. She laid on the floor beside Stefan. Apart, but close enough to touch him, if she needed to. "How and why, I have no clue."

"What are you doing?" asked Kevin warily.

"I'm going after him," Alexis said simply and closed her eyes.

"Do you know what you're doing?"

"I think so."

Her comment received only a snort and a caution. "Be careful."

That made her smile. "Always."

This time, she had a trail to follow. Blocking out everything else, she zeroed in on Stefan's faint signature. It went on forever, traveling through a permanent light fog. She continued moving faster and faster, until she could no longer tell how far she'd gone.

Had she become as lost as Stefan?

Finally the thread thickened ever-so-slightly. With that concrete improvement, she increased her speed. The miles whipped past. There had to be another way to do this. This passage seemed endless.

On the heels of that thought, she reached a huge solid wall. *Solid? Here? How could anything be solid, yet cold to the touch?* Alexis carefully explored the obstacle. She still had much to learn. But this just didn't make sense. Could it be a blind to confuse her?

It vanished. Just as quickly another took its place. Stefan had to be on the other side, but was he the one putting up the barriers—to keep her out? Or could there be someone else trying to keep Stefan in there? Either way, it wouldn't work.

What could she do? Stefan's energy! She needed to focus on him. Wrapping Stefan's lifeline in love, she warmed his energy with her own. Using the same methods she'd perfected over the years with her plants, Alexis surrounded his cord with bright green energy.

She could sense the difference immediately—again she was surprised by the ease of that accomplishment. Nothing in this area worked the way she thought it would. As the surrounding energy continued to warm, so too did the air. The fog lightened and slowly lifted, allowing Alexis to see where she was.

Stefan stood in front of her. Pale, tired, and too insubstantial to be considered healthy, but he was smiling. Alexis grinned back in relief.

"Can we go home now?" she asked.

"Almost."

"Almost?" she asked, astonished.

"Yes, I came here for a reason, and I'm not quite done. *You* have to go home." He looked behind her. "Now."

At that, a heavy shove snapped a surprised Alexis backward and pushed her right out of the psychic field. And into her physical body.

Alexis sat up in Stefan's living room, moaning, as the room spun around her. *This could take some getting used to.*

"Alexis?" Kevin squatted beside her. "Are you okay?"

She was dazed but looked up at him, nodding slowly. "I think so. I just need a minute."

"Take your time."

Alexis heard the relief in his voice. Poor Kevin. She hadn't exactly considered him when she'd plunged in after Stefan.

Kevin's large hand cupped her elbow to support her, as she attempted to rise. "Easy, easy." He led her over to the couch.

"I'm okay." She collapsed onto the forest-green leather. "I found Stefan."

"And?" Kevin asked sharply. "What's he doing?"

"He didn't explain. He said, he wasn't finished. He shoved me back, saying I had to leave." Alexis looked around Stefan's living room. "So here I am."

"Good." Kevin walked out of the room.

"What are you doing?" Alexis called after him.

"Making tea."

Of course they'd all picked up the habit. It made sense, in a way. She had to admit a cup of tea would be welcome. They needed to stay up and wait for Stefan to return.

Alexis crashed on the couch, after the second pot of tea.

She woke several times in the night to check on Stefan. But found only minimal change. When Alexis woke early in the morning, cold had seeped into her bones. She opened her gritty eyes slowly, trying to place her surroundings. As memories flooded back, she leaped up to check on Stefan.

He seemed the same, only he wasn't. *What was the difference?* Alexis walked around his body that still laid in the same position. Not even a hair was different. But something had definitely changed.

"What's the matter?" A tired Kevin joined her, still rubbing the sleep from his eyes. He stopped suddenly and narrowed them in concentration. "He's back."

"What?" Stunned, Alexis looked from one to the other. "How can you tell?"

"Can you see his cord?" For the first time, Kevin reached out and touched Stefan. There was no reaction. He checked Stefan's pulse. "He's barely alive."

Kevin reached for his cell phone, starting a process that left Alexis stunned by its speed. Less than an hour later, she sat waiting, once again, in the place she hated most. The hospital.

The waiting room was full. Feeling wrinkled and badly

in need of a shower, Alexis sat squished between a screaming child and a family who looked like their world had just collapsed. Alexis could sympathize. She'd spent many long hours in this place, trying to hold it together, hoping against hope for a miracle that never came.

Only on Lissa's last day had Alexis finally accepted the reality of what was happening—finally acknowledging she could do nothing to stop disaster from destroying her world once again. Four hours later, Lissa was gone.

"Alexis!"

Caught up in her memories, Alexis jumped up and raced toward Kevin. "How's Stefan?"

Kevin stilled her hands, making her aware for the first time that she'd latched onto his shirt with a death grip, almost shaking him. She took a deep breath and prayed for the return of some of her famous detached control.

"He's in a coma." At her horrified gasp, he quickly added, "The doctors say he'll be fine. Stefan's specialist is on his way. When he's assessed him, we'll know more."

"Specialist?" Alexis's breath caught in her throat. "What specialist?"

Kevin shrugged noncommittally but didn't explain.

She sighed. It didn't really matter, … except she hated waiting for answers.

"Come on. Let's get something to eat."

Minutes later, Alexis stood outside the hospital, staring up at the early morning sky. It seemed a long time since she'd had a normal peaceful day to enjoy the sun and the blue sky. She wanted this horror to end.

THE NEXT DAY was crap. By the end of it, Alexis was ready

to kill her wonderful daytime bodyguard, Scott.

Kevin shook his head as he unlocked her passenger door with the click of a button. "What is your problem?"

"Today, everything," she snapped, as she sat in Kevin's truck. How to explain the torture of having Scott hanging at her elbow for the entire day, too concerned to let her out of his sight. She loved the man dearly, but his constant presence had become downright irritating.

"Let's go see Stefan." Kevin smiled at her. "Maybe that will help switch your mood."

After being shadowed all day, she'd love some time alone. But Stefan came first.

"Come on." Kevin herded her through the front door of the hospital. Alexis walked past the reception area and headed straight down the left hallway.

"Uh, Alexis. Where are you going?"

Alexis turned around to find him stopped at the reception area. She stood, confused. "I thought we would see Stefan. What's the matter?"

"Alexis?" He pointed to the opposite hallway. "Stefan is down here."

Alexis flushed, unwelcome heat warming her cheeks, as she realized that, from habit, she'd headed toward Lissa's old room, … even after a whole year. "Damn it," she muttered, as she approached him. "Sorry."

"Don't be. Habits die hard. You spent a lot of time at Lissa's bedside, didn't you?"

She smiled sadly at him. "That seems a long time ago."

The two approached Stefan's private room. As she did, she realized Stefan had become a close friend, though, when she thought about it, she realized she really hadn't seen much of Stefan's world outside of his kitchen, living room, and solarium. She'd never been invited to view his studio or his finished works, other than the one piece. Someday she hoped to be welcomed into his inner world.

"When he's ready, he'll show you."

She shot Kevin a dirty look. "Quit reading my mind."

"I didn't have to," he replied smugly. "Lately your face is an open book."

"Then quit reading my face."

The two approached Stefan's bedside cautiously. He looked the same, except for the various machines surrounding him and the IV in his arm.

Her heart sank. Her hand automatically moved to her throat.

"Look beneath the surface."

With a startled glance at Kevin, Alexis complied. A blue haze surrounded Stefan's prone body. A shifting, almost shimmering energy that moved around him, over him … Her gaze widened. *And through him.*

"How is that possible?" she whispered.

"A very powerful healer is working on him. Her name is Maddy. She runs a special program, not all that far from here." He smiled. "I'll assume, now that he's in her hands, Stefan will be just fine."

Alexis reached out, hesitated for a moment, and then covered Stefan's hand. "He's cold," she said quietly.

"He's fine." The voice from the door surprised them both. A doctor walked in, holding out his hand to Kevin. "Detective Sutherland, nice to see you again."

"Hello, Dr. Radnor. What can you tell us about Stefan?"

"I'm happy to say his condition is essentially a deep exhaustion. Whatever he was doing wore down his life force completely."

"He'll be okay though, won't he?" Alexis hadn't realized anyone could get as ill as Stefan from simple exhaustion.

"Oh, he's in a coma," Dr. Radnor said. "It's his body's defense mechanism, which allows him to recover and to heal." The doctor walked closer. "He's just taking a very long and a very deep nap. I suspect he'll stay like this for another day or two, then slowly come out of it."

The doctor took a closer look at the two of them. "You two look almost as bad. Go home and take care of yourselves. I don't want you to end up in here with him."

Kevin smiled his thanks, and, after confirming they'd head to Alexis's place to pick up a few things, he ushered her out ahead of him.

The old apartment building was not welcoming or warm. She unlocked the door and entered with Kevin. As she walked into her living room, Alexis became aware of her exhaustion and wished she could go straight to bed. She was relieved Stefan would be fine, but, at the same time, her emotions were all over the place.

A few steps inside her apartment, she froze.

The energy was all wrong.

Or maybe it was her whacked-out emotions? Right now she didn't think so.

Someone or something had intruded her space.

Police or the asshole? Not that it mattered. She felt violated. All she wanted was to get out of here. She grabbed a few of her clothes and walked out.

CHAPTER 20

AFTER STOWING HER clothes in Kevin's spare room, Alexis returned to the living room, feeling a little lost.

"I'll sit on the porch and have a beer. Do you want one or would you prefer something stronger?" Kevin offered, as he walked over to a cupboard. "There's scotch, rum, and even a little bit of brandy left."

"Brandy would be nice, thank you." She didn't like the uncomfortable tension she'd felt since they'd returned to his house. They were involved in a relationship of some kind. She just didn't know what she had to give, nor did she know what she wanted from it.

He handed her a large balloon glass with the amber liquid. "Do you want to join me outside or take it up to your room?"

Alexis hesitated. The beautiful evening would soothe her soul better than hiding away in her room. "Sure, I'll come out for a few minutes."

The stars were bright on a deep velvet sky. They more than sparkled, they put on a beautiful jeweled display.

The longer she sat and watched and sipped, the more Alexis felt her tension drain away, leaving her mellow and relaxed. A heavy sigh escaped.

"That came from way down deep."

"It did." Calm seeped into her body. "Why haven't you

married?" She hadn't meant to ask that, but, once the question was out, she was glad she did. Had he never wanted to? Had his job been a mitigating factor? How did women do it? Watch their man leave for work each day, never knowing if they'd see him again?

Despair welled up at that thought … No, being involved with a police detective, … that wasn't a life Alexis wanted.

"I don't know. I guess, so far, it just never worked out. I've gotten close a couple times, but not quite that far." He spoke easily.

She smiled in relief. His lighthearted tone convinced her that his heart had yet to be touched.

"What about you?"

Alexis shrugged dismissively. "Like you, I never reached that point."

The evening silence lengthened and deepened comfortably around them. After the highly charged sexual encounters between them, and the panic and the horror of recent experiences—both psychic and grounded in the real world—she felt this time of peace was a joy. It made her realize how abnormal their relationship had been to date.

"Are you ready for bed?" Kevin asked gently.

"*Uhm …*"

A few minutes of comfortable relaxing silence passed; then Kevin broke the silence. "Can you make it back up to your room?" Kevin teased.

Only this time she didn't respond. Alexis, too relaxed to speak, fell asleep under the stars.

Kevin smiled, as he lifted her and brought her to her room.

THE NEXT DAY, Kevin stood in the doorway to Stefan's hospital room. His friend's waxy looks weren't encouraging. Instincts had brought him here. He'd called earlier, only to be told that there'd been no change. Kevin couldn't ignore his inner direction and had come to see for himself.

Come in. Don't just stand there.

Kevin smiled, relief and pleasure lighting his face. Damn, it was good to hear his friend's voice, even if only in his head. "How are you doing? Can't say you look too good from where I'm standing."

Then you'd better sit. I'm fine, or I will be, when I get some energy back. That's the closest I ever want to come to total burnout.

Kevin grabbed the visitor's chair and sat down close to the bed. "That's because the next step is death. As you, better than anyone else, know."

True. Stefan's voice was faint, making it hard to understand. Even so, the determination came through clearly.

"What the hell happened to you?" The words burst out with such force, they even surprised Kevin. "Did you go hunting him? Did you see him?"

No, but I saw some of the things as he saw them. When he let me.

"When he let you? Are you saying he knew you were there? I don't like the sound of that." Kevin leaned closer, checking out his friend's color.

Once in a while, he would pick up on me. His energy is erratic. A lot of old energy is around him. He's been doing this for a long time, but he's still learning. Or learning new tricks. Stefan's internal voice stuttered to a stop. The communication obviously required tremendous energy.

"Do you know who he is?" Kevin's voice was sharper

than he intended. He looked around to see if anyone might have come in. He'd sound like a nutcase talking to himself.

They were still alone.

No, but a cop is helping him.

"What? Who?" It couldn't be. He didn't know all the men at the station as well as he'd like, but it curdled his stomach to think of a deception like this.

A young one. Check it out. Stefan's voice was getting fainter and fainter. *Today.*

"I will." Kevin hesitated, hating to ask more of his friend. But they were out of time. "Did you learn anything else?"

His pattern is old, decades old. Yet a long period of inactivity for some reason. His victims were always children, … until Mandy. Something odd about that energy, something new. A renewed excitement, like he's coming back to a favorite sport. Find him. Stefan paused painfully, gathering the needed strength. *Before he finds someone else.*

With those last words, the telecommunication trailed off into a faint echo of Stefan's former energy.

Kevin walked back to the door, with one last look at the still form on the hospital bed. "I'll come back tonight."

Bring her. Faint but decisive, Stefan's voice brooked no argument. Neither did Stefan need to clarify who he was talking about. Kevin already knew.

"I will." With that, he walked out and headed back to the office. At the office, the captain waited for him. "My office. Now."

Kevin frowned. He waited until the captain shut his door and took his seat at the desk.

"What the hell is going on?" Captain Gosling glared at him. "I received an anonymous phone tip today about someone in the office leaking information about a recent homicide."

Kevin whistled softly. A homicide could only mean Mandy. Speaking slowly, he said, "It's hard to believe anyone here would do that."

"I know," came the somber answer. "If one of our men had anything to do with this leak, I want *him* caught."

So did Kevin.

The captain watched for Kevin's reaction, then nodded. "Precisely, and that leads to the next problem. I don't know why the tip was offered, how accurate it is, or whether it's just an attempt to discredit the office, but we need this checked out and fast, before Internal Affairs hears about it."

No argument there.

In the privacy of his office, and armed with Stefan's tip, Kevin made a list of all the rookie officers on staff, including the two who were no longer attached to their division. The experienced officers didn't come under the heading of young—as far as Kevin was concerned—so he bypassed those.

That left eight names in all. The two who no longer worked in his office, he tentatively crossed out. One worked out of New York now, and the other had transferred home to Alaska. He'd focus on the other six. He'd known two of them for years. Both young men had grown up here. They both came from working families. Neither had excelled at school, but both had done a reasonable job. One was particularly athletic, and the other enjoyed sports at the community level. Overall, nothing about them raised warning flags.

There were four more. The first was a particularly enterprising young man, who could go far with the right connections. The second, with a so-so average personality, could go either way. The other two he didn't feel he knew at all. The third one spent most of his free time working with Kevin's former partner. The fourth he knew only by sight.

Which one of these betrayed the force, and why? What would cause a young man, starting out in his career, to risk it all and to quite likely end up in jail? Had this person done this willingly? Kevin hated to think so. But otherwise, what pressure could be applied to make someone do something like this? Blackmail? Extortion of a police officer was not a new thing. But what could the leverage be?

Kevin pondered the scenarios, before picking up the phone and calling the captain. Quickly he explained about Stefan's news, rapidly running through his points and the research to date. "Any suggestions, Captain? Do you know anything about these guys that would suggest where to look?"

"Not really." The older man pondered the news thoughtfully. "But I hope you're right about leverage being used. It would be easier to accept. He could even be protecting a family member."

Kevin stared off toward the far wall, then said, "I think I'll bring them in and see what shows up."

"Do it fast. We're running out of time."

Only two of the young rookies were at the office. Kevin called them in, one at a time. With each, he asked for a rundown of the cases they were currently working on. As it was no secret that Kevin had a hand in suggesting promotions and shifting personnel within departments, both men quickly complied.

Kevin listened attentively, while he probed their energy fields, looking for anything that made them appear culpable.

They both were innocents, as far as he could tell. Their minds and energy were wide open. He didn't think they were capable of deceit at this level—but he'd been wrong before.

He thanked them both and let them go with words of appreciation for the jobs they were doing.

His notebook was rapidly filling with rough information on the possible suspects, when a package arrived on his desk. Nancy, the long-time clerk from the front office, smiled down at him. "Directly to you. No stops and no other eyes. Those were your instructions, weren't they?" She grinned at him, watching as he ripped open the heavy padded envelope.

Finally.

"Thanks, Nancy." In midrip, he stopped and looked at her pointedly. She raised her eyebrows but obediently left the room, shutting the door with an exaggerated movement.

This was the information he'd requested on John's family. He couldn't believe the difficulty he'd had to get this material.

He opened it, pulled out the copied material he'd requested, and started reading.

"What the hell?" he whispered.

Moments later, he put down the sheet of paper in shock.

A heaviness settled in his stomach, as he tried to digest the details. There had been many different accusations of child abuse concerning their daughter, and neighbors complained of screaming and fighting—all over the last four years they'd lived in Redding, California—even a statement from the little girl's physician.

Intuitively Kevin knew John had paid to hush up any suspicions of foul play. Money might have saved John decades ago, but today he held a position in public office. If this leaked out, they'd crucify him. It wouldn't matter if John hadn't been the bastard who'd dished out the child beatings, the suspicions alone would finish him. No wonder he'd left town.

Was this what the blackmailer wanted John to confess to? Or was it for something worse?

A paragraph caught his eye. According to the case file, the child had fallen from a tree in the front yard, suffered a broken neck, and died several days later. Everyone in the family had been questioned, but the death had been declared accidental, and the case closed. The little girl had been eight years old.

He shuffled through the documents, looking for the start of the problems. There it was. Four years before her death. That was the first time where suspicion of abuse was noted in the file. She'd died thirteen years ago.

That fit the time line too.

This then is where the whole mess started—years ago.

~

ALEXIS FELT THE mounting pressure. Nothing specific—but the heavy atmosphere and the constant tension drained her. It was the same for the townspeople. Everywhere she went, people looked suspiciously at each other, seldom maintaining eye contact or stopping to talk.

After finishing lunch with Scott, they returned to the gardens. Alexis heaved a sigh when she saw Rick waiting for her. What could he want now?

"As you refuse to leave town, I have the perfect job for you. It will keep you safe and out of sight. I want you to clean up last year's paperwork." Rick smiled at her evilly.

Alexis spluttered. She couldn't even form a protest because her mind had frozen. *Paperwork.* A year's worth! He knew she hated that type of work.

Scott's lips twitched. When he finally grinned at her, Alexis shot him a look of disgust. He could at least help her out of this mess.

"I know you'd like to stay here and have Scott as your babysitter, but, believe it or not, he has other jobs to do. And one of them is a meeting now with the city planners for the new building to start next month."

"*Ach*, hell, I forgot." Scott groaned. "Sorry, Alexis. It's not something I should miss."

"Why can't I go with you?" She'd enjoy being in on some of the planning decisions for the new section. Actually that idea perked her up.

"No need. You'll be totally safe in the office. No one could find you under all that filing." Rick was savage with his satisfaction. Turning back to Scott, he said, "Take her down and leave her there. Call the detective and let him know."

Filing? Oh, hell no.

IT WAS AN unbelievably long afternoon. No one had filed the time cards, supply lists, or myriad other papers in months. By the end of the day, she was ready to scream. *"Arrgh!"* Alexis threw her pen across the room. Dry laughter hit her ears from the doorway. She looked up to see Kevin, leaning casually against the doorframe.

"Have you come to rescue me?" she demanded. "Otherwise I might just have to hurt you."

"I think this job suits you." Kevin took a seat on the one chair that wasn't fully covered in reams of papers. "A desk job."

"Like hell."

He sat across from her, with a cheeky grin, but heavy lines creased his face. He opened an envelope he'd brought and slid out several photocopied pictures. "Can you look at these and tell me if any of them look familiar?"

Alexis frowned. Pictures of children. A good half dozen but the quality was poor. She shuffled them apart, so she saw them better … and froze. Tapping the picture of one young boy, her heart ached as she whispered, "Him. I saw him in one vision."

Kevin nodded, his face grim. "Any others?"

She studied the others, before singling out the photo of a young curly haired girl. "Her, I think. But I am not as sure of her as I am of the little boy. She looks different in the picture."

"How about the rest?"

"I haven't seen all that many clearly. Several are always hanging around Daisy in the background, but I haven't gotten a good look at them." She separated out three more photos. "I think these ones as well. But," she cautioned, "I can't be sure."

Kevin smiled. "Don't worry about it. These children all disappeared over twenty years ago. Their cases were never solved. A serial killer was suspected to be in the area, but the information back then didn't travel as quickly as it does now. The killer was never caught. Instead, he just went quiet."

"And he never resurfaced?" How odd. She watched, as Kevin collected the pictures—the first tangible evidence of her visions. Until now, the children in them had faces but no names. That kept them in the realm of being almost imaginary, as if she hadn't really seen them. Now there was no refuting the facts. She pointed at the one. "What's his name?" she asked, suddenly needing to know.

He narrowed his gaze, considering what he'd been asked. "Eric. Eric Mason."

That fit, sort of. "These kids I see, were they all murdered?"

He shook his head. "Not necessarily. Spirits can stay here for many reasons. It's possible you are connected to any child who is lost."

That made her feel better.

A sudden smile brightened Kevin's face. "One good thing happened this morning."

At her sudden interest, he nodded smugly and said, "Yep, I talked to Stefan."

"He's awake?" she asked, jumping out of her chair and reaching for her purse. "Let's go!"

But Kevin didn't move. "No, he's not awake."

Confused, she moved to stand in front of him. "But you spoke to him?"

"Yes, but only telepathically." Kevin slowly stood and stretched, the envelope in hand.

"How is he?" She studied the fleeting nuances on his face.

"He's fine. Very tired and he'll need several more days of rest—but, considering what he's been through, he sounded okay. He wants to speak with you." He walked to the office door, before glancing over at her. "Aren't you coming?"

She preceded him from the building.

"Don't you have to lock up or something?"

"I hope someone steals it all," she snapped. "It would serve Rick right."

ONCE INSIDE THE hospital, they came face-to-face with Scott's beautiful Moira.

"Hello, Moira." Alexis walked up to her and held out her hand. "We haven't been introduced but I'm—"

"Alexis. Scott's *bin* telling me about ye." The Scottish woman smiled a friendly greeting. The two women shook hands. Moira turned to Kevin. "Good day to ye again, Detective Sutherland."

"Hello, Moira. How's our patient?"

"He's the same. No change as far as I know. You're welcome to visit." She waved them in the direction of the room, then grabbed her charts and headed down a hall.

Stefan remained in the same position as when Alexis had last seen him.

"He looks better." A wealth of satisfaction wove through Kevin's voice.

"Does he?" Alexis studied the prone body curiously. "He doesn't look any different to me."

Kevin glanced at her in amusement. "That's because you're looking with your eyes."

Embarrassed to be reminded, Alexis checked out Stefan's energy. It was much stronger, a smooth, calm whiteness that spoke of peace and gentleness. It wasn't back to its full vibrancy, but, if he continued to improve, he wouldn't need to be here too much longer. "He's pretty vulnerable like this, isn't he?"

Her wording caught his attention. "He wasn't attacked or anything. I doubt he's in danger here. Are you picking up something?"

"No. Not really. He just looks so vulnerable." She walked closer to the bed, taking up Stefan's fine artistic hand. His skin was warm and smooth, with a healthy pink color. She curled the long fingers around hers, as if he were grasping her hand on his own.

You don't need touch to know that we're together.

Alexis laughed aloud. "Now that's where you're wrong. I do. It's you who doesn't need to touch."

Nonsense. If you'd wanted to, you could have spoken to me anytime. You just need more confidence in your abilities.

Alexis listened to Stefan's warm, teasing voice in her head. She lifted his hand and dropped a kiss on the knuckles. "It's good to hear your voice again."

Not half as good as it is to hear yours. Are you okay, after your trip in to find me?

Alexis smiled at what already seemed like a week-old memory. "I am, and thanks for showing me some of your much more advanced skills."

No problem. I thought I could accomplish something over there. But I overestimated my abilities.

"Or you just burned up faster than normal because it was new and more difficult to attempt than anything else you'd done." Alexis backed up a bit. "At least, *I* find things go better on the second attempt."

I needed you here to warn you. This bastard checks in on you all the time.

What! Kevin's voice ripped through Alexis's mental space, making her wince at the tone and volume. Damn, that hurt.

You heard me.

"In what way is he watching?" Alexis asked curiously. Just what was this asshole capable of? "And why?"

He likes to know where you are, what you're doing. Not only on an energy level. He's often out physically keeping an eye on you.

That sent shivers down her spine. A stalker. That added a whole new dimension of creepy to this mess. "But why? Why me?"

He's scared of you, of what you can do to hurt him.

Alexis was stunned. "I can hardly do anything compared to you. Even Kevin's abilities exceed mine."

"I'm not so sure about that," Kevin said quietly. "You don't realize how far you've come and just how many areas you've just barely touched on, … so far."

It had never occurred to her that her abilities might worry a predator. It wasn't something she even wanted to think about. Stefan overrode her worries with a completely different observation.

It's your ability to communicate with his victims that disturbs him. He's afraid of what they could tell you. Stefan's voice became even fainter. *Information that will give him away.*

"Why? It's not like they've told me anything useful. Why would he start worrying now?"

"Actually you've helped quite a lot," Kevin said. "You're the one who pinpointed the license plate that allowed us to rescue the child. And it was you who recognized that Stefan was in trouble."

He knows he was careless in the beginning, before he learned to hide his tracks. He's scared you might find something from back then that could give him away.

Alexis didn't know what to think.

For whatever reason, those who passed at his hand are contacting you. Stefan's voice weakened, became thin and reedy. His ability to converse was almost gone.

Kevin stepped in to take control of the conversation. *Stefan, is this why you asked to see Alexis, or is there something else?*

She ... She needs to meet the rookies. With that, Stefan's voice faded into the distance, leaving a blank emptiness in the room.

CHAPTER 21

"ROOKIES?" ALEXIS WAS puzzled. She looked to Kevin for understanding. "What did he mean?"

"Come on. Let's go. I'll explain on the way." He gently untangled Stefan's hand from hers, tugging her toward the hallway. Outside, they headed for the parking lot, almost running.

Kevin slid into the driver's side and started up the engine while Alexis settled in the passenger seat. Without saying anything, he pulled out of the lot and drove through the main part of town. The sun shone heavy in the late afternoon sky, giving everything a wavy, surreal look, as glimpses of it flashed by. Suspicious, Alexis studied Kevin's sassy grin. He was up to something.

While she contemplated just what that could be, Kevin pulled up to a Chinese restaurant. Alexis started to get out, but he stopped her.

"I'll go in and pick it up."

Surprised at that, she watched him exit the truck, then came back a few minutes later with the food. Takeout worked. They needed to talk, and he'd said it was easier to do that at home. This probably meant his home, given the circumstances. But he continued to surprise her as he drove through town and headed on out again. With rising delight, Alexis realized where they were headed.

Relief, greater than she could have imagined, settled inside her as Kevin turned onto the well-worn dirt road leading to his lakefront property. She needed this, had craved it even. The natural surroundings filled her with peace and not only because of the memories of their passionate interlude. Simply said, the beauty of the place suited her soul.

Once there, they parked and got out. The layers of tension dropped off, as they made their way to the water's edge. Alexis sighed happily, as she dropped down onto a flat rock and divested herself of shoes and socks.

"Brrr." The water chilled her hot, sore feet. She couldn't ignore the impulse to roll up her jeans and to let her toes dangle in the water. Dropping her jacket on the rock behind her, she proceeded to use it as a pillow.

"Oh, this feels so good." Alexis moaned in delight. She even went so far as to pull her tank top up to her ribs and loosen the button on her jeans.

"Don't let me stop you from stripping down to the skin. Have a swim if you want."

"Nope, don't want to, but neither do I feel like moving again for a while. Do you mind bringing dinner over here?" Alexis never even opened her eyes as she spoke, but seconds later she heard him approach with the rustle of the paper bags. The rich aroma of Chinese food caused her stomach to growl, loudly announcing its neglected state to a very amused Kevin.

"Dinner is served, m'lady."

"*Uhmmm*," she murmured sleepily, refusing to move.

"Eat first, nap later." Kevin opened the various tubs and boxes.

She rolled over and reached for the plate he held out. It was the perfect picnic.

Working through her dinner, she realized that Stefan's continued improvement had given her peace of mind. She couldn't imagine moving forward with this psychic stuff without him. Besides, he'd claimed a spot in her heart too.

How quickly she'd adjusted to this new reality. She munched on her dinner thoughtfully. She hadn't given much thought to her future, since Lissa's passing. At the time, she felt her continuous existence was a punishment, not a gift.

For the first time in a year, she understood just how many gifts she'd been given. It was sobering to realize how long she'd walked around in a fog of grief. Lissa's death may have been the reason, but it was no excuse to continue.

"Heavy thoughts again, huh? You're the darnedest one for those."

She eyed him wryly. "It's that time of life for me."

"You're too young to have a midlife crisis. So what's the issue here?" Kevin's voice took on a coaxing tone. "Come on. Spill the beans."

"I've already lived a lifetime in many ways. If I want a *mid*-midlife crisis, I will have one," she said in a light voice. "Actually, I've decided it's time to move."

Kevin straightened at her unexpected announcement. "You mentioned something like that before. But where?" he asked cautiously.

"I don't know yet, but I know I need a change," she mused. "Being here makes me realize how a space can improve or dampen my state of mind. My apartment's doing nothing for me. I need a welcoming space again. Maybe I'll start my business back up or start a different one. I need to think on it a bit more. Do I keep my job, go to part-time, or find something different altogether?" She watched him fill his plate for the second time. "Suggestions?"

"Don't make a major change until this mess is cleared up," he advised. "Everything is out of whack for you right now."

"These changes aren't new ideas." She gazed over the sparkling pools of water, glistening in front of them. The cooler evening, combined with the slight breeze off the water, dampened any desire she might have had to swim. Even so, the amazing view soothed her aching soul. It was such a spectacular view that healing energy literally surged through her, leaving peace and contentment in its wake.

"I need something like this. So much pain and sorrow has been in my life to date. This"—she motioned with her arms—"or something like this would help me heal, when I come home." She could tell from his face that he understood what she was trying to say. "My heart needs a place to rest and to rejuvenate."

"That's partly why I'm building here. Some days, because of my job, I feel like I have nothing more to give." He stared down at his half-eaten food. "The things I've seen …" He shook his head. "Many evenings I've driven out here to just sit and forget." He smiled with deep understanding. "It makes the rest of what I do easier to deal with."

Alexis stood suddenly and brushed off her pants. "I thought about contacting a real estate agent to see if something comparable is out there. Preferably with a house already standing on it." She surveyed the area. "Are any trails to walk out here?" She slid a teasing sidelong glance at him. "You never did show me around the last time we were here."

He got up, grinning at her lighthearted reminder. "We had more pressing issues then. Let's go this way, and I'll show you my world."

THE HOSPITAL VISITING hours were winding down. Slowly groups of people made their way to exits all over the vast building. It had been an ordinary evening for most people. It was a welcome chance to say hi to loved ones and to bring them something to brighten their stay.

Dressed casually, the tall, slim man walked through the hallways. He knew how the system worked here. The nurses tended to ignore the comings and goings at this hour, for they knew that visitors could be the bright spot in the day for the people forced to stay behind. If one or two laggards came in during the evenings, anyone with half a heart turned a blind eye for a little bit longer. Their rounds would start soon enough, and then they could chase the last stragglers out the door. So finding someone walking around the halls past visiting hour wasn't exactly a suspicious event.

Which was fortunate.

He strode down the halls with purpose. As he passed the nurses' station, he didn't even receive a questioning glance. Perfect.

A large set of metal shelves were at the far end of the hall. Both clean laundry and dirty laundry sat heaped in their respective places. As he approached, he saw a white lab coat tossed over the edge of the dirty bin. Without a thought, he snagged it and quickly put it on.

Look at that. It wasn't even a bad fit. If not knowing who'd worn it, or where, made his skin crawl, he ignored that. It was necessary, and he'd be damned if he'd turn down the unexpected gift.

When he reached the correct door, he glanced about surreptitiously and saw the hallway was empty. He pushed open the door and stepped inside.

The room was empty but for the single occupant. It appeared to be the right man. Tonight's visit was all about removing what could be a potential problem. It didn't matter so much if he killed the wrong man, but, if he left the right man alive because of uncertainty, that would be a serious error in judgment.

But, from where he stood, he recognized the man's energy. It seemed frail, almost nonexistent. Maybe he'd die anyway. No, that wasn't likely. This asshole was too tenacious to die.

On his own.

He shoved his hand into his pocket. Now, should it be the needle or the pillow?

ALEXIS LOVED THE scent of pine trees. The rich aroma wafted up with every step.

"We used to come here every day in the summertime," Kevin reminisced. "My cousins and I ran around out here for hours …" He turned toward her, his face lighting up, as if to say something, when suddenly the color drained from his face, and he fell to his knees, gasping in shock.

"Kevin!" Alexis reached for him, dropping to her knees to support his weight. "What's the matter? Kevin? Talk to me, damn it." She'd never seen him like this, and she didn't like it. He'd always seemed so strong.

"Stefan," he whispered, digging his fingers into her arms.

She leaned closer to hear. "What about Stefan? Is he okay? Kevin, talk to me." She helped him to the ground, as the shadows deepened around them. "Is Stefan in trouble?"

Kevin nodded, now gasping for breath. "I have to help him." His eyes rolled up in his head, and he was gone.

"Kevin!" There was no answer. "Oh God! Now what the

hell do I do?"

Call the hospital!

Alexis barely deciphered Kevin's faint telepathic message. She was galvanized into action. Her fingers grappled for a cell phone. She punched in the numbers still permanently emblazed in her mind.

She couldn't believe her luck. "Hello, Moira, is that you? This is an emergency. Please run and check on Stefan. If there's … Moira? Moira, are you there?"

Alexis looked down at the cell phone. There'd been a *clunk*, followed by faint hospital sounds, leaving her to assume that Moira had literally dropped the receiver and run.

Odd, you'd think she'd have questioned Alexis. But then, as Alexis's mind worked through the oddity, she realized Scott had probably told Moira about Alexis's odd abilities.

Abilities? Could she use them now? She closed her eyes and thought of Stefan. She tried to reach out, but all she saw was a maelstrom of energy contained in such a way that she didn't know how to penetrate it. He'd said she could reach out to him anytime. She just needed more self-confidence.

She tried again to reach Stefan. Nothing. She saw movement. Action of some kind but she wasn't a part of it. She had to trust in Kevin. And Stefan.

With the shadows deepening and darkening by the minute, Alexis didn't know what else to do. Hang up the phone and call back or wait? There was no decision to make regarding Kevin. She couldn't possibly move him on her own. She disconnected the hospital call. She eyed the phone in her hand and then dismissed it. Kevin wouldn't thank her for letting others know. As he'd watched over her, she could stand guard for him.

She sat down on the cooling ground to wait. Damn, she hated that corpselike look on his face.

After a few minutes, she redialed. "Hello, is Moira there? … No. Do you know where she's gone? … Okay. I just phoned in an emergency in room 207 but was cut off. Could you please check on them?" She tried hard to keep her voice cool and controlled. Inside, panic ruled. What could have happened to Moira? "Fine. Yes, I'll ring back in a minute."

Now she had to wait again.

Gloom no longer gently enveloped them. Chilly darkness had settled in instead. There was no change in Kevin. She didn't dare join him; there'd be no one to protect the two of them. She had to trust that the two men could handle whatever hell they were in.

The wait seemed interminable.

Several times, she called the hospital. Then someone picked up, "Bradford General Hospital. How can I help you?"

At least someone had answered. "I need to speak with Moira, please."

"I'm sorry. She is unavailable at this time."

"What? I just spoke to her less than ten minutes ago. She went to check on a patient for me."

"I'm sorry. I only know that she is unavailable."

"Has she been hurt? You don't understand. I sent her to check on a patient who might have been in danger."

"I'm sorry, ma'am. Maybe you need to contact the police."

Alexis snorted. "The police are already on it, you idiot," she snarled into the night, as she ended the call. She glared at the man still prone beside her. "Well, Kevin, isn't it time to come back?"

Silence. She tried to look into his mind. And came up against his walls. No entrance for her there. Damn.

"Now what?" She spoke aloud, finding comfort in the sound of her own voice. The answer came in a flash. Scott.

"Hey, it's me, Alexis." Quickly she explained what had transpired. "They just said she's unavailable. Scott, I'm scared something's happened to both of them."

"I'm already in the truck and heading down the road. I'll be at the hospital in a couple minutes."

"Call me." She gave him the number.

Again she waited. The underbrush rustled off to her left. The night creatures were foraging for food. She shivered in the cooling air. By now, the two of them were in total darkness. Why couldn't Kevin have collapsed by his truck? She had no idea how far up the trail they'd traveled.

Long minutes later, Kevin's cell phone beeped, scaring the bejeezus out of her. "Alexis, it's Scott."

"What did you find?"

"Moira apparently fell and hit her head. She's still unconscious."

"What!" Alexis was stunned. That didn't feel right. Intuitively she knew something had happened, but falling and hitting her head didn't fit. "Where did it happen?"

"In the hallway outside of your friend's room."

"Damn." She hesitated to ask but knew she had to. "Scott, has anyone checked on Stefan? That's why Moira went there in the first place."

"He's the same. There's been no change."

A huge sigh of relief escaped. "Thank God. I'm thinking Moira might have interrupted an attack on Stefan.

"And she was assaulted instead?" Scott roared, his burr

thickening with his anger. "That's naw good, that isna."

"I'm hoping he's gone." A horrible thought occurred to her. "Or else he's waiting for a second chance at Stefan."

Shocked silence came through clearly.

"That's it. I'll be staying right here for the night."

Alexis nodded. "That's probably a good idea. If you can, would you mind checking in on Stefan as well?" She looked down at the still male beside her. "We'll get to the hospital as soon as we can."

If and when Kevin woke up.

Is this how he'd felt when she'd tried to track Stefan into the ethers? She hated this being-left-behind stuff. It was damn scary. The waning moon flitted through the treetops, adding a surreal, eerie tone to the evening. She sensed Kevin out there, working in the ethers. She saw his energy busy doing something. And how weird … and wonderful was that. How quickly she'd become used to him there. That connectedness.

She hadn't expected him to take up residence in her heart, but, so far, he showed no sign of making a quick exit. She still couldn't believe the speed in which everything had happened. Her heart might be comfortable with it, but her mind was troubled. Males were such foreign animals in her world.

Damn, what could Kevin be doing?

"I'm here." The masculine growl lifted her heart. Relieved, she bent over his beloved face and dropped a kiss on his nose. "Hey, how are you doing?" She smiled tenderly. Even in the dim glow of moonlight, she saw his weary grin.

"I'm okay. Just tired." He struggled into a sitting position, rested a moment, then lunged upright.

"Hey." Startled, Alexis fell back in surprise. "Aren't you

the one who always says to take it slow and easy when you come back?"

"Yeah, but that's when it's you." He reached down to help her up.

"And what the hell happened to you just now? It freaked me out when you collapsed."

"Stefan called for help." Kevin held on to her hand and strode off toward his truck, pulling her with him. "We have to go."

Alexis practically ran to keep up. Her heart pounded, while her mind still grappled with the rapid shift in events. His behavior scared her. "Why? What's the matter? Is something wrong with Stefan?" His long legs ate up the miles. He didn't waste any of his precious energy on speech.

"We're heading there now. He should be fine, but I'll put a guard on him overnight."

"Oh, good."

Every once in a while, the moon popped up between the treetops to give them a glimpse of the world around them. It was enough.

During the trip back to Kevin's truck, Alexis listened as he made several calls—none of them eased Alexis's anxiety. By the time they'd reached his truck, they were almost running.

Once at the truck, he hopped in and barely waited for her to buckle up before he hit the gas. Gravel spit out behind them as he spun the truck around and gunned it. Once on the main road, it actually felt like the problems were rushing toward them, pulling them faster and faster into the crisis awaiting them. A police cruiser was parked directly across from the Emergency entrance. Not an alarming sight in itself, but, with a multitude of officers milling about, her alarm bells rang a notch louder.

Once they parked, several of the police officers walked over to Kevin.

"Sir, we've been waiting for you. No sign of an intruder. Mr. Kronos appears to be stable."

Kevin nodded, never slowing his stride as he covered the length of the hallway in record time. Alexis ran to keep up.

At Stefan's door, yet another officer stood guard. "Kevin, the doctors just went in. I don't think you're supposed to …"

Kevin cut him off with a look and walked in. Alexis followed. Two doctors were deep in discussion. An officer stood at the wall behind them.

"Hi, glad you finally got here," the officer said, with a smile.

Both doctors looked on as Kevin nodded curtly and walked straight to the bed to stare down at his friend.

"Kevin, he's fine. Whoever tried to do this didn't succeed."

Alexis looked over at the one doctor who'd spoken. "What do you mean? What did they try?"

Dr. Magill, according to his name tag, held up an evidence bag containing an almost full syringe. He handed it over to the officer behind him. "This was found on the floor."

"What is it?" Kevin eyed the amount left in the syringe with a practiced eye. "Is there any chance he received some of it?"

"We've taken blood samples, but the results won't be back for a bit. With no change in his vital signs at this point, we assume not." Dr. Magill looked at their patient. "He's being closely monitored. He's a very lucky man." The doctor studied Kevin, adding, "He had a very capable friend." At Kevin's sharp look, he nodded, as if confirming something. "Now it's up to the police. Maybe you can sort this out."

"Don't worry. I'll get to the bottom of this."

No one in the room doubted that for a minute.

Alexis stepped closer to Stefan and gently stroked his hand. Kevin wrapped an arm around her.

"His skin has a waxy, undead appearance," she whispered.

"He's fine. Come on. Let's check on Moira."

They didn't have to go far. Scott had heard the commotion of their arrival.

"How is he?" The big Irishman stood protectively in Moira's doorway. Concern and worry blended with the flames of his ire.

Alexis understood. Someone he cared about had been attacked. Alexis silently dared that bastard to return. Alexis walked up and hugged him. "They think he'll be fine. The consensus is that the intruder was interrupted before he could carry out what he came to do."

"Aye. Chances are, Moira took the brunt of it."

"Has she woken up yet?" Alexis was sorry for sending the poor nurse into what had obviously been a dangerous situation. Her concern had been for Stefan.

"Don't you be worrying none. You did the right thing."

Scott's rough pats on her back had her smiling—the bloody big ox. "Still, I didn't want her hurt."

"Yet, it could have been so much worse," Kevin reminded her bleakly. "They've both been lucky." Scott still barred the doorway with his bulk. Kevin raised an eyebrow and nodded to the interior. "May we come in?" he asked sardonically.

Scott flushed. Kevin was still a law officer. The bigger man moved aside and led the way to her bedside. Moira was sitting up, waiting for them.

"Good evening, Detective. Is my patient okay?"

"He appears to be," Kevin quickly reassured her. "Thanks for checking on him."

"No problem." Moira shifted in bed, wincing in pain. "I don't think I did much good though." She waved Scott away as he moved to help her. "I'm fine. It's just a wee bit of a headache."

"Do you remember what happened?" Alexis asked, steering the conversation to the main issue. She walked to the other side of the bed and sat down on the visitor's chair.

"Not really. I remember what you said, then racing down the hallway, wondering who was visiting Mr. Kronos …"

Alexis interrupted. "He had visitors?"

"Well, I thought I heard a noise, so I figured he must have had someone in there. I walked in, but I must have slipped and hit my head when I went down. I don't remember more than entering the doorway. I never even saw who was in the room."

Scott's voice sounded black as hell. "I think someone hit your head for you."

Moira looked startled. From watching her face, Alexis saw that, the more she considered it, the more reasonable that possibility appeared to her. "It's possible, I suppose. I've never slipped at work before. I thought a spill of some kind made it happen."

Kevin shook his head. "No evidence of anything like that." He stepped closer, checking out her color. "Has the doctor checked your head?"

"Yes, I'm fine, and I want to go home." She glared at Scott. "Scott won't let me."

"Yes, I will but not alone."

The stalwart Irishman wouldn't budge and with two such stubborn characters, they were at an impasse. Alexis hid her smile. These two were good together—or would be, if they ever got a chance.

To that end, Alexis suggested, "Moira, it's probably a good idea to let Scott stay on your couch overnight. The extra protection wouldn't hurt, and you shouldn't be alone after a head injury." Alexis saw Scott nodding his head, emphatically agreeing with her.

But Moira's next comment wiped his smile right off. "Except he wouldn't stay on the couch."

"Aye, I would," he protested in hurt tones. "I won't be going where I'm not invited."

Moira shot him a look of disgust.

He looked so innocent, but even Alexis saw the leprechaun peeping out, fooling none of them. "He'll stay there," Alexis stated emphatically, looking over at the Irishman, now standing defensively with his burly arms across his chest. "Scott's an honorable man." Alexis's tone left no doubt about what she'd do if it didn't turn out that way.

Kevin burst out laughing, garnering looks from them all. "Welcome to having your days numbered, my friend."

Scott blushed and mumbled under his breath, "Danged women."

"What?" asked both Alexis and Moira.

"Nuttin'," the Irishman snapped back and glared at the three of them. "She's going home. You two can leave anytime."

"Actually, you two men can leave. Alexis, would you

mind giving me a hand to get dressed? I'm not sure I can bend to put on me shoes."

"Sure." Alexis glared at both males. "Out!"

The two men left, both grinning like mad monkeys.

"You do that well," murmured Moira, as she sat on the side of the bed, catching her breath.

"Practice." Alexis grinned at the woman she knew instinctively she would come to know and to love quite well. She bustled around the room, collecting Moira's things. "Seriously, if you *were* attacked, the intruder might worry that you did see him. I think it's unlikely, but let's play it safe." She brought over her shoes and squatted to slip them on the unsteady woman. "Let Scott be protective."

"I don't much like the thought of someone coming after me," Moira admitted.

"Nobody does. But we have a murderer in this town. We're getting closer to him every day, and he knows that, and he's starting to make mistakes. So don't *you* make any before we get a chance to catch him."

The women stared somberly at each other.

Alexis smiled at the raised brow and the stern look from the other woman. "No, I won't."

CHAPTER 22

BACK IN THE truck, Alexis yawned widely. "I'm tired but not enough to sleep yet."

"It's the adrenaline rush. Afterward, you're fatigued but not sleepy. Which is a good thing right now." Alexis's color was good, so Kevin didn't worry too much. He probably looked worse.

He pulled into the police station and parked. Turning to face her, he said, "A couple rookies are on tonight. Stefan suggested you come meet them."

That woke her up. "Any idea why Stefan wanted me to meet them?"

In truth, he wasn't sure what to tell her. "I'm not sure." They exited the truck and headed inside. He needed caffeine. The trip to the other side had exhausted his energy reserves.

Several officers called out greetings as they passed. Kevin stopped to talk to a couple of them, catching up on anything he might have missed. At the same time, he was handed a large stack of messages—more than a few from John. Kevin felt the shadows in his world deepen. Fatigue pulled at him. This was getting to be a bit too much.

"Problems?" Alexis broke his reverie gently.

Kevin looked at the woman who'd become a beacon in his world. He hadn't planned it. He hadn't really wanted it. But here she was, and he knew he couldn't walk away from such a precious gift. He needed her.

He wrapped an arm around her shoulders and tucked her close against him. She needed him too. If she'd just accept what they could have together … She was close to that point; he felt it, but, at the same time, he sensed a part of her wanted to hold back. She still didn't recognize and accept how essential they both were to the fabric of each other's lives.

SITTING IN THE chair across from Kevin's desk, Alexis sipped her coffee. She couldn't stay focused. Her mind was exhausted and slow thinking, … coasting. It made her process information slower. Along with that, her emotions were running high.

Kevin appeared to be struggling. Given the mess with Stefan, the murder of his former girlfriend, and this asshole killer, that came as no surprise. If he'd been a woman, she'd have suggested a good cry. This new insight into his crazy life was both a gift and a responsibility that Alexis recognized and now honored.

Compassion swelled her tender heart that felt more open and touched than she could remember being in a long time. She knew it was because of the recent changes in her life … and because of Kevin. He had yet to grieve for Mandy, and, therefore, the pain had built up inside. No tears were allowed to escape, so she wept for him.

Alexis tugged Kevin's grief inside her heart, to ease his pain, then released the energy to the universe. Fat tears welled up at the corners of her eyes, before slowly starting their descent down her cheeks.

"Alexis?" he asked in confusion.

She couldn't answer. The emotional edge cut too deep. All she could do was let the tears roll and hope it helped to heal them both. Slowly she rose, walked around the edge of the desk, and waited. He moved, as if to stand, worry creasing his face.

She shook her head and crawled into his lap. Tenderly she covered his heart with the palm of her hand, tucking her head into the crook of his neck. Kevin wrapped his arms around her tightly, holding her close.

They stayed motionless for long minutes.

Alexis didn't know why she did this. She only knew she couldn't ignore her instincts. Stefan had been right. She was driven to help. She just didn't know what skills she could offer otherwise. She didn't know the difference in energy terms between receiving, transmitting, and healing. Maybe they were all different methods to achieve the same thing.

Sinking deeper into his psyche, she sent the energy to circulate along his meridian pathways, allowing the soothing energy to enter his system. To stroke and to calm as it traveled throughout. Kevin had showed her maps of these energy lines on the body. She didn't have all of them memorized yet, but she'd learned the main ones. On the return path, Alexis drained away Kevin's depression and pain, absorbing and then releasing them, as Stefan had taught her.

Many long minutes later, Kevin sighed, a heavy, heartfelt release of pain and tension. He squeezed her tight once, then released her. Only then did Alexis allow herself to smile. Now she knew he felt better. She had made a difference, and any words to the contrary she'd dismiss as male ego talking. This is what she needed to do with her life. She wasn't sure how or in what way, but it had to include making people feel better.

And you can.

Alexis tilted her head back to smile up at the tough, capable features above her. "Really?"

A knock on the door interrupted their privacy. Alexis shifted over to the chair by the window and watched as Detective Kevin Sutherland collected himself and went into action.

And what action it was.

Alexis could have been a ghost for all the attention he paid her over the next hour. Rookie after rookie came through the door. They were asked a few terse questions, their answers cataloged, further questioned as needed, then the officer dismissed.

What the officers couldn't see, and what totally amazed Alexis, was the efficiency of the energy search Kevin did of each man within the first minute after entering the office. Not one of the men noticed when their energy fields were searched—a quick dip in and out, then on to read their energy patterns. Within seconds, Kevin had a rounded view of each individual's world and insight as to whether Kevin needed to do a much closer interview.

"Where's Arnie?" Kevin asked the young officer, sitting in the hot seat in front of him.

"I don't know, sir." The officer wiped his brow nervously.

Alexis felt sorry for the uneasy young man. She'd already determined that Kevin had found nothing to be suspicious of with him. She waited for Kevin to speak.

"He's here somewhere. I need you to find him and to send him in." Kevin looked up from the papers in front of him and pierced the hapless young officer with his questioning gaze. "Understood?"

"Ah, yes, sir." The young man exited in a rush, banging into the chair in his effort to escape, but he soon left them alone.

"Ouch," Alexis murmured, trying to be quiet.

Kevin still heard her. "What?"

"You're the very devil to them, aren't you?" Alexis made the comment casually, never expecting the response she got.

"What are you talking about? They aren't afraid of me."

She couldn't believe what she heard. "Like hell they're not. Every one of these guys was incredibly edgy in here."

"Oh, that." Kevin casually dismissed the base reactions from the men. "It's the situation, not me."

"I see." But she didn't. "If I were one of them, I'd be terrified."

He glanced over at her in surprise. "Why?"

"I don't know. But they sensed something. They all ran out, as if Satan himself were after them."

Kevin stared off into space, considering her words. "Maybe it is the scan. It's not something I would normally do, but the circumstances are anything but normal." Soberly he looked back at Alexis's understanding face. "A murderer is out there. I have to stop him before he kills anyone else."

Alexis stood and stretched. "Don't you think you're being a little hard on yourself? You've already stopped two attacks."

"It's still definitely a concern." Kevin picked up the phone and used an outside line. "Good evening, John. Yes, I know it's late. I need to go over some information that I have. No, not tonight. In the morning—say, nine? Good. Thanks, and have a good night."

When Kevin hung up, the phone almost dropped from

his grasp.

Alexis watched curiously but couldn't understand all the undercurrents. She'd just decided to ask him when the door opened to admit yet another young police officer.

She couldn't say why, but her spine stiffened, and every sense went on alert. Alexis slipped back to her place by the window, watching the man intently.

He appeared to be a bit older than the others.

Rough justice and street wisdom were written all over him. This young rookie had survived a difficult childhood. But he hadn't come out unscathed. He'd built one hell of a no-holds-barred shell to hide his scars.

But could he be hiding something else?

DAMN IT TO hell anyway.

That stupid bitch of a nurse! He hoped she had a hell of a headache. Had she seen him? He didn't think so, but it could be a huge mistake if he were wrong. He'd have taken care of her later, but that bloody Irishman had sat on guard until she'd been ready to leave.

He didn't know what to do now.

Turmoil circulated through his mind in a never-ending spin cycle, bringing on a hell of a throbbing pain at his temple. This was piss-poor timing. He hadn't wanted to move up his timetable just yet. His damn rookie hadn't provided enough information. And then the asshole hadn't answered his phone all evening.

The longer he sat and thought on the problem, the madder he got. If they wanted to force his timetable forward, fine. And, if that damn ghost whisperer wanted to be next, then that worked for him too.

KEVIN MOTIONED THE young man farther into the room. "Hi, Arnie. Thanks for coming in. Take a seat." He waited for the rookie to comply before adding, "This is Alexis Gordon. Alexis, this is Arnie Morrissey." Kevin watched the two nod politely at each other. If Alexis was on the stiff side, he let it pass.

Within seconds, Kevin's energy reached out, only to be instantly rebuffed. Kevin sat back and perused the tight-lipped face in front of him. "Arnie, is something bothering you?"

"No, sir."

His whole persona came across as too cold and hard for one so young. Kevin found it incredibly painful to watch. "You've been a good cop here for the last …" Kevin picked up the file in front of him. "It's been almost nine months now, hasn't it?" He eyed Arnie over the top of the folder.

Arnie only nodded.

Kevin wondered what it would take to break such intense self-control. Though brittle and edgy, he suspected it would shatter under gentle pressure. Kevin looked at Alexis. She looked ready to burst. He nodded.

Alexis blurted out, "Arnie, does the word *blackmail* mean anything to you?"

Arnie paled to an ashen gray. Fear made his eyes look like black marbles. His clenched fingers turned white at the knuckles.

Kevin barely hid his surprise. He'd have to remember to ask where that word had popped out from … and why. But first, he turned his stern gaze on the young man. "Arnie, tell me about it."

The poor man swallowed several times, tried to speak,

but gave up before the words could make their way out. His downcast gaze dropped to the floor.

"You can take a few minutes to collect your thoughts but realize no one is leaving until we understand just what is going on here." Once again, Stefan had been right.

Arnie visibly swallowed hard several more times before giving up the ghost. He slumped against his chair in defeat. "I didn't know how to tell you," he whispered painfully.

Both Alexis and Kevin leaned forward to catch his barely discernible words.

"Tell me what?" Kevin let his voice soften. Experience guided him. It would be so easy to have everything go wrong right now. He could only hope Alexis would stay quiet. "Arnie? Tell us what?" he coaxed. "Are you in trouble?"

Arnie looked at him, a world of despair in his eyes. "I tried so hard. Honest I did."

"I believe you," Kevin said.

ALEXIS BELIEVED HIM too, although she couldn't explain why. Sincerity and dismal realization permeated the air. Arnie had meant what he'd said, and somehow he'd still failed to avoid what was happening. Her heart went out to him.

"I thought, if I could fix it, I wouldn't have to lose my job. I love being on the police force. It feels so good to be doing something positive after all those years of being on the wrong side of the law. But someone found out." The troubled young man paused. Frustration and anger boiled over. His fist slammed against the arm of the chair. "Damn it, it's just not fair. Everything was going so well."

"What's not fair?" asked Alexis quietly. "Just as important, what did someone find out?"

He looked at her briefly before turning away. "I have a record. Someone found out." He shrugged, as if the rest of the story was obvious.

It took a minute to sink in.

Kevin sat back. "You're being blackmailed?"

Arnie nodded, refusing to meet his gaze.

"You're right," Kevin said. "You should have found a way to tell the captain or me. Someone who could help." He leaned across the desk. "Arnie, despite whatever mistakes you have made, you have to tell me the whole truth now." He stared at the face across from him. "Do you understand?"

"I understand." Arnie straightened up in the chair. He leaned forward earnestly. "That's part of the problem. I don't know his name."

"Can you identify him in any way?"

Alexis wouldn't believe otherwise. She knew his answer would tell her a lot about this rookie's character. To deny this would mark him a liar and would give them a completely different set of problems to deal with.

"Yes." He looked up at his superior in resignation. "I know what he looks like, where we've met and …" He hesitated.

"And?" snapped Kevin.

"I've tried following him but haven't had much luck."

Alexis could appreciate that he'd tried to do that. She might even have done the same.

"What information did you give him?" Kevin asked, curt and to the point.

"Originally he just wanted little stuff, like how many staff worked here, how many senior officers, that kind of thing. I thought it all quite odd, but none of it was high-level security stuff, so I didn't worry about it." The young man shifted uncomfortably on the hot seat.

"And then?" prodded Kevin.

"He started asking questions about different cases. When the little girl's remains were found at the city park, he really started bugging me for information. I had to report in almost daily about anything connected to that case. For a while, I thought he might have been a reporter. But he isn't. I checked the local rags." Arnie stopped again, then continued, "He seemed eager, almost anticipating the news. If I didn't have anything, he'd be furious. Once, he found something new out on the evening news. I'd been so busy that it never occurred to me to call him. He was furious about that and wanted to know about the autopsy report of the child."

"Did he offer anything about himself?" Kevin asked.

Alexis sifted through the odd bits of information. Was this blackmailer just a busybody or someone eviler?

Arnie started to shake his head, only to stop and consider. Then he spoke, as if thinking aloud. "There was one funny thing. He lit up when I mentioned the name Daisy. But I didn't know what that meant." Resignedly the young man looked at Kevin. "Does this mean I've lost my job?"

"I can't say yet. It's not up to me." Kevin's expression closed down, giving no indication of his thoughts.

"Something very positive *could* come out of this," Alexis interjected. She knew it might not be her place, but Arnie was young. Maybe they could turn this around.

"In what way?" Kevin asked.

Arnie's hopeful gaze locked on hers.

"Can't we use Arnie's connection to this person to set a trap?"

Both men considered her point with a dawning realization.

"Sir?" interrupted Arnie hesitantly. "I think he's involved in much more than blackmailing me."

"Like?" Kevin spun back to face the hapless young man.

Alexis watched Kevin zoom in on Arnie, putting the poor man back on the spot.

Arnie shifted uncomfortably. He wiped his damp palms on his pants. "The night the little girl was kidnapped, I went looking for him. I had a gut feeling he might be involved."

"What!" Kevin's lethal voice split the air. "Why didn't you say something then?"

"I didn't have any proof," Arnie explained. "I still don't. But his reaction to the name was over the edge. I put two and two together …" Arnie, seeing Kevin's stance wasn't softening any, tried again. "He seemed to know so much about it already. Later it occurred to me that the news report wasn't that detailed."

"Right." Kevin stood. "You are to meet the police artist now. I want a composite sketch within two hours." Kevin walked to his door before turning back. "Are you sure there's nothing else you can tell us?"

Arnie hesitated. "Once I saw his car parked outside the mayor's house."

Kevin slammed his door shut again and stormed back to his desk. "Is this man young or old?"

"Early thirties maybe. Five foot eleven, slim, well dressed."

"You do know what the mayor looks like?" At Arnie's immediate nod, Kevin eased back a bit but not much.

"It wasn't him. I'm sure of that."

The description Arnie gave twigged something else. Kevin cocked his head as he studied the young policeman.

"What about his son? Would you recognize him?"

Arnie shook his head.

"That's the first photo we need to show you. Where else have you seen this guy? What's the license plate, and what kind of vehicle does he drive?" The next words burst out in a half bellow. "And why the hell did you not come to me with this information before?"

The rookie sank deeper into his unforgiving chair. "I thought, if I could solve it, then I wouldn't be kicked off the force."

"Did you ever suspect that the man you gave information to was involved in the recent murder of a young mother?" A muscle twitched in Kevin's cheek as he pinned the younger man to the spot.

"No, never!" Arnie appeared sincerely horrified at that idea.

Alexis believed him. And, in her mind, it changed his culpability.

Arnie continued with his protestations. "I wouldn't do something like that, honest. You have to believe me. I just didn't know what to do."

"Idiot!"

Alexis winced at the one word guaranteed to get her back up. "It makes sense, Kevin. Not for you, and maybe not for me, but for someone who feels they've done something wrong. They want to fix it before anyone finds out."

"Who asked you?" Kevin snapped.

"I did," she said cheerfully, fully aware of the shocked fascination coming from Arnie as he watched their exchange. "Maybe Arnie was right to be afraid. And right about the other … As long as he didn't give out something major, maybe this can be fixed." She smiled reassuringly at Arnie, presenting a confidence and an authority she didn't feel. There would be repercussions from Arnie's actions, but she had no idea how severe they'd be. From the look on his face, Arnie'd already assumed the worse.

"This *is* in your hands right now, Kevin." Alexis smiled gently. "What you do from here on in affects everything."

Kevin glared at her, his eyes laser hard. "Damn it, Alexis. You can't fix everything."

She smiled. "But *you* can fix some things."

Arnie gawked at her, as she continued.

"I know *I* can't fix everything. But you have authority to minimize the damage, Kevin. Talk to the captain about Arnie first, before anything else." She nodded at the still figure in the chair. "This young man's future doesn't have to be destroyed." At the look of hope on Arnie's face, she held up her hand. "But reparations do have to be made. Otherwise this can never be left in the past."

Alexis looked at the still-pissed Kevin. "Did the department know about Arnie's past, when he was picked, trained, and then put on the job within this force?"

At Kevin's grudging nod, Alexis turned to face Arnie. "Did you hide something else from the department when you made this career step?"

"No, nothing. I was shocked they accepted my application. Thought maybe my file hadn't been looked at closely enough or something. I had worked hard to clean up my act but figured my past would go against me. I thought that maybe they didn't know all of it, when they let me into the training." He shrugged at Kevin.

"Drugs, alcohol abuse, grand theft auto, prostitution all before twelve. You did three years in juvenile hall, then lived in a halfway house for a year, with rehabilitation and retraining for another year after that." Kevin's cold recital made them both stare in stunned amazement. Kevin shuffled some papers on his desk. "We decided that you'd had enough time and had chosen another way. *Our way.* We put our faith in you. A small department like ours has the ability to make these kinds of choices, ones that a big city police department can't."

The look on Arnie's face was as painful to look at as the recital he had just heard.

"Arnie, what went on in your early family life to send you on this path?" Alexis knew something had happened back there. And it needed to come out. Now. How she knew, she couldn't say.

The young man spoke dismissively. "The usual. Broken home, abuse, parents both alcoholics, mother a prostitute. What's to say? It was hell."

"No, there's something else," she prodded. Pain oozed from a hidden cavity in Arnie's soul. Alexis couldn't stand it. "Something hurt you badly and eventually sent you on this pathway to become a cop. Something inside you needed to pay retribution or maybe …" Alexis paused, feeling her way, yet knowing the storm inside Arnie could break with her next words. "Or maybe because you needed revenge?"

Kevin looked at her in shock. "What are you getting at, Alexis?"

Needing to see something, anything else but the torment being released from his soul, she turned toward the window, overlooking the sleepy street outside. Behind her, she heard the young officer's gulps and sobs of a long-held agony.

"Jesus." Kevin's ire had quickly been replaced with understanding.

Alexis had sensed when Arnie dropped the barrier, hiding a lifetime of betrayal and pain, leaving his past wide open, exposed. She didn't want to look, and Kevin could easily see the details for himself. Hell, psychics anywhere in the world could have accessed the information with Arnie transmitting so loudly.

Then he told them in words. Arnie said he had a younger brother he'd doted on, until he'd died. Arnie explained he had been looking after him. They'd gone into a large mall. Arnie wanted to pilfer some candy and left his little brother to sit on a bench just inside the store. When he came out, the younger boy was gone. He'd gone through the automatic doors to pet a puppy waiting outside. When the puppy had run, he'd followed, directly into the path of the oncoming car.

"Oh hell." Weariness marred Kevin's features as he slumped in his chair. He walked over to Alexis. The two stood, not touching physically but wrapped in the comforting energy of the other, while giving the other man time to adjust to his disclosure.

"Sorry." Humiliation and embarrassment colored Arnie's voice.

Alexis sighed at the sad story. "Don't apologize. We each have had times when the pain is so bad that we can do nothing else but let it pour out."

"But you need to tell us the details." Kevin's voice was still cold but now had a thread of compassion running through it.

Broken, but still willing, Arnie explained again, in detail.

Alexis waited a few minutes after he fell silent to allow him to recover a stronger grip on his self-control. "I suppose you thought, if this came out, no one would let you stay here?"

"I was supposed to look after him. Keep him safe. It's all my fault."

His confession confirmed her guess. That was the problem with old abiding guilt; it ruled your actions forever. "Well, it won't. We all have demons, Arnie. Yours are more difficult than some, but no one here would judge you for it."

"*He* did."

Kevin spun away from the window to glare at him. "*He* knew?" Two quick steps took him to the front of his desk. "How could he know? Did you tell him?"

Arnie reared back, away from Kevin's intensity. "Uh, no. I didn't tell him. He already knew. He scared the hell out of me."

Alexis smiled at the past tense usage. The young man still looked terrified, only now Kevin was the looming danger.

Kevin picked up his phone, barking an order to have an officer report to his office pronto. Waiting for the knock on his door, Kevin stood, opened the door, and spoke to both officers now. "Okay, Arnie, I want you to start from the beginning and go over every word from every meeting." To the senior officer, Kevin said, "I want full descriptions with sketches of the perp's face, details about vehicles and locations where Arnie met him. This guy has a pattern, and I want to know what it is." Standing with his hands on his hips, he added, "And I need someone to find a picture of Charles for Arnie to see. Fast."

The senior officer nodded and led Arnie into a private room to take his statement. The police artist was on standby, but hopefully she wouldn't be needed.

Kevin called the captain and filled him in. Finally something had shifted.

As Alexis waited, she almost nodded off. God, she was tired. She wondered when they'd be heading home.

"I know you're tired, Alexis." He pondered the problem for a moment. "I can send an officer with you to my place, or you can grab a couple hours sleep here. We have two rooms with cots in them." He grinned at her. "Actually, we have a whole jail full of them."

"Thanks, but no thanks." Alexis considered the not-so-great options.

"Or I could have a cot brought into my office," he suggested with a raised brow.

Right on cue, Alexis yawned again. "Did we eat tonight?"

"Yeah." He reminded her. "Chinese at the lake. Remember?"

She grimaced. How could she have forgotten? This day had been brutally long. "Maybe I could crash here. Are you sure I won't be in the way?" Even as she said the words, fatigue washed over her.

"Not at all."

Kevin quickly ordered a cot brought in and grabbed his stuff to take to another desk.

"You don't have to leave." Alexis hated to move into his space, if it meant moving him out.

"Honey, I have to talk with Arnie anyway. I need to find out everything I can before I meet with John in the morning." He walked over and tugged her gently into his warm embrace. "Lie down and sleep. This could be an all-nighter. We might need your special skills. Rest while you can."

She sent him a look of disbelief that made him laugh. "Like I can help."

"I mean it."

Even as he spoke, the door opened to admit two men carrying a small folding cot.

After the men left, she moved over to the makeshift bed and stretched out on it. There were no blankets or pillows, but she didn't care.

"I'll rustle up a blanket or two for you. Go ahead and get some rest." He left the room.

Alexis did the exercises Stefan had taught her, though she was tempted to just fall asleep. It felt so damn good to shut off her mind. To know that, for now, she could leave everything in Kevin's capable hands.

Within minutes, she'd fallen asleep.

CHAPTER 23

ALEXIS SLEPT SOUNDLY. She didn't wake up until the light crept through the blinds on the windows. Had she closed those? She couldn't remember. Another few minutes went by. She didn't want to get up, but Kevin had to be around somewhere.

"Good morning, sleepyhead. How are you feeling now?"

Kevin sat quietly at his desk. From the look of him, he'd been there all night.

"Did you get any rest last night?" Alexis rubbed her eyes, noticing she now had a blanket and a pillow. Interesting. A shower would be wonderful, … but coffee would be better.

"I caught a few minutes of shut-eye in my chair somewhere between three and four. Not enough, but it will have to do for now."

Alexis shook her head. He couldn't function efficiently this way.

"Don't say it. I already know. But there have been a lot of surprises overnight, and things are starting to move very quickly."

Startled, she could only look at him. "Coffee," she pleaded in a croaking voice. "First coffee, then information."

After several slugs of dark-and-deadly harsh cop coffee, she smiled. The caffeine hadn't had a chance to hit her bloodstream, but just knowing it was on the way made her mental faculties cooperate enough to ask, "Now, what did you find out?"

"Charles is the blackmailer." He waited for her reaction.

"What? That slimy-toad-of-a-birthday-boy blackmailed Arnie?" She couldn't get her mind wrapped around the idea. "It's not that I don't believe you. It's just hard to imagine. Does he really have the brains to pull off something like this?"

Kevin watched her, a big smirk on his face. "I thought you'd say something along those lines. You really didn't like him, did you?"

Alexis looked at him and shuddered. "What's to like?"

"Most ladies don't have a problem with him."

She thought about it. "I'm not so sure about that. He mentioned something when I walked with him. He made it sound like the house, the money, and the prestige all belonged to him, and, if I was nice to him, he might share."

Alexis became the target of Kevin's narrowed-eyed glare. "He said *what?*"

From the overriding disbelief in his voice, she couldn't tell if she should feel insulted or complimented. "He said something else that was odd. Something about no other family that counts." She looked at Kevin.

"His uncle is in a long-term care facility on life support. John keeps paying the bills because he can't stand the thought of letting his brother die." Kevin looked down at the stack of papers on his desk. "Although, from what he's said lately, he's getting ready to sign the papers to pull the plug. Something about it being time to let his brother go."

"How sad. But like I said, Charles is a toad." Imagine feeling that way about a family member? "Would Charles get any money then?" Alexis visibly shuddered at the next thought. "If he is the blackmailer, does it change the direction of your meeting with John this morning?"

He looked startled.

"Sorry." She blushed. "I didn't try to listen in on your phone conversations, but I *was* here in the office."

"I'd forgotten. There's a good chance Charles has been leaving the threatening notes for his own father."

She sat back and stared at Kevin. "Does he hate his father so much?" Alexis couldn't imagine a family willingly doing such damage to each other.

"That's something I need to discuss with John this morning." At her look of interest, he quickly interjected, "In private."

That was only fair, even if she didn't like it.

He grinned.

She shrugged dismissively. What could she say? "What's happening with Arnie now?"

That wiped the smile off Kevin's face. "He's in with the captain now. They're questioning his every move since he started here. His future is up in the air."

"That will be tough on him." Alexis stood stalwart in her defense of the young man. She knew he deserved another chance. But would he get it?

"It's not up to us any longer, so let's concentrate on what we can do something about." He stood with a large stack of papers in his hand. "John should be here any minute."

She glanced at the watch on Kevin's wrist. "Is there a computer that I could use for a few minutes before I go to work?"

A few minutes later, she looked up in time to see John being ushered into Kevin's office. The door shut firmly behind the two of them.

Damn, she wished she were in there.

"GOOD MORNING, JOHN." Kevin motioned his visitor to take the chair across from the desk. He couldn't help but look at his friend differently now.

"I presume you have something for me, as you called this early morning meeting?" John replied, somewhat testily.

"I think so. That doesn't mean you will agree with me." Kevin hadn't looked forward to this meeting. But some skeletons had to be taken out of the closet for another look. "John, I'm sure you felt you had a good reason for withholding this information. But, since reading this old file, I wonder seriously if this information doesn't all tie in with the current blackmail mess." Kevin looked directly into John's bleached-white face.

"Old file?" John asked faintly. All of a sudden, all the pomposity sagged out of him, and he fell back against the chair. "What old file?"

"The old file on your deceased daughter. The accidental death that reads more like a manslaughter case." He watched the expressions flit across John's face, … shock, fear, horror, and pain. The whole gambit raced by. Some Kevin expected, yet some he hadn't, like fear. If John were innocent, he had no reason to be afraid. Kevin waited for John to speak.

"What does that file have to do with my blackmailer?" John's reedy voice slowly regained its former strength, obviously boosted by years of denial.

Kevin found it difficult to stare into those blank eyes. "Maybe everything," he suggested cautiously. "Someone wants you to confess something. Maybe they know about your past and suspect you to be the villain."

"I loved my daughter." He was calm, cold, and unequivocal in this statement of fact.

"Be that as it may, your tormentor may have a different spin on things." He shuffled through the various papers in the open file before him. This would be more difficult than he'd first anticipated.

Silence.

"John?"

The two men studied each other, the breach between them widening perceptibly. It was uncomfortable, this shift from friend to interrogator, but not entirely unexpected. It didn't make the rest of the meeting easier.

"I had another reason for asking you to come in. Someone else was being blackmailed in town."

John leaned forward. "Who?"

"I can't say." Kevin hesitated. "This other person has identified his extortionist as Charles."

For the second time, the color leached from John's face. "What? This can't be. He's a good boy."

Kevin let that one pass. "We bring him in for questioning today." Kevin checked John over, looking for any sign that these shocks had been too much. "Is there any chance Charles is also blackmailing you?"

John looked at him blindly, obviously having difficulty processing the information and what the question implied. Kevin had heard of people seeming to age upon receiving bad news, but he'd never seen it himself, until now. It was incredibly painful, for both the person in question and for the observer. Kevin stood and walked over to the window, remembering Alexis slipping over here for exactly the same reason. It hurt to see such human suffering.

"Could he hate me so much?"

The frailty of his voice made Kevin wince. He turned back to face him. "Would he blame you for his sister's death?"

John shrugged in defeat. "How do I know? The subject hasn't been brought up since we lost her. I tried to make it seem like it had never happened. Otherwise I couldn't stand it." The painful memories obviously overwhelmed the man, making it hard for him to speak. "Charles couldn't think that. I loved her—we both did."

"Was Charles close to her?"

John smiled. "Very. The difference in their ages added to that maybe. She was his special baby sister. They played together all the time, especially in the garden. They loved the flowers. He even had his own nickname for her. Charles went to pieces when she died. He'd already lost his uncle, four years earlier. ... It was a lot for him to deal with. I should have gotten more help for him," John said. "But then we were all a mess at the time. Charles seemed to straighten out after a while." John shuffled in his chair. "Then Sandra collapsed. My marriage almost didn't make it, for the second time, and I know I lost the close bond with Charles." He brushed a shaky hand over his hair. "But for Charles to do this to me?" His head shook sadly. "I just don't believe it."

"Maybe it wasn't him, but he had the access, the hidden knowledge, and the motive."

"What motive?" John turned to Kevin in surprise. "What possible motive could there be?"

"Any number of possibilities. He might want you to suffer for what he believes you did." Kevin waited a moment before plowing ruthlessly on. "There is no statute of limitations on murder."

That finished John. Kevin saw the walls of John's foundation crumble to the ground around him.

"I swear on my mother's Bible that I did not kill my little girl." Tears welled up and slowly rolled down his face. "I loved her. She was everything to me."

John appeared to be telling the truth, but Kevin didn't know what to believe. He'd seen too much in his career as a cop to be surprised by anything. Besides, what did he really know about John?

Kevin opened the file and studied the contents, while John composed himself.

There had been an investigation at the time of the child's death. Her death had been ruled accidental, and the case closed. Kevin checked a couple sheets, looking for the officer in charge at the time. This deserved a follow-up call.

"John, is there any chance, with the understanding that, *if* her death wasn't accidental, and you weren't responsible for your daughter's death, then … could it have been Charles? Is he capable of something like this?"

John didn't look surprised at the question. In fact, he appeared resigned. "He changed when Glen had his accident. My brother didn't die, but he might as well have, as he's been nonresponsive ever since. Charles took that hard. So … I don't know. For almost twenty years, I've wondered. I don't want to believe it. Mental illness runs in the family, and, at one point, Charles needed serious help. We thought he'd improved. Then he would just stop taking his meds. It was a roller coaster ride for all of us. We had to keep a close eye on him for many months, until the doctors could straighten him out again." John stared off into the distance sadly, as if looking down the long tunnel of his own past. "I don't know anymore. The boy I knew couldn't have done it, but then he wouldn't have blackmailed anyone either."

"We have an odd case open right now. Believe me when I say that I wouldn't be asking without good reason, but can you tell me what clothing your daughter was buried in?"

"Daisy? But she's buried in Redding, California." John stared at him in shock.

Kevin's heart hitched. He leaned forward to pin the hapless man in place. "Daisy? I thought her name was Marie Leanne?"

"Yes, yes, it was, but Charles nicknamed her Daisy when she was just an itty-bitty toddler. The name stuck. I think the dress she had on had her name on it."

"Which name?"

"Marie. She was buried in her favorite yellow sundress, with white stockings and black shoes. I had to help pick out the clothes. Sandra was inconsolable at the time. She hadn't been herself for a long time already, but that …"

Hearing confirmation that the body Alexis found was likely that of John's daughter, although necessary for the files, hurt. The next question would devastate John.

Keeping a sharp eye on John's face, Kevin continued, "There is a strong possibility that the body we found in the city gardens could be your daughter. We'll need DNA tests to confirm."

"What?" John lurched forward, before falling back into his chair. The color drained from his face. "That's not possible. I told you that she was buried in the family plot in California. We actually gave her Glen's burial plot because he was here."

"And now she's probably here." Kevin studied John's face. No way John could have faked this response. He hadn't known. The man was shocked and devastated.

"I can't believe it. No one even knew about her. Who could possibly have dragged her from her resting place to dump her alone in the city gardens?" He raised a trembling hand to his forehead. "I can't believe it. I just can't believe it."

"I need to ask for a DNA sample in order to confirm her identity as your daughter. She was found wearing the remnants of a yellow dress with the letter *M* embroidered on the collar."

John shuddered. "Yes, of course. Anything you need."

"We'll also need to talk to everyone in your family, particularly Charles." Kevin studied the older man. "We're picking him up now." He doubted that Charles had the wherewithal to be a killer. He wasn't the kind to get his hands dirty. Blackmail, yes. Murder, no. But then how well did anyone know Charles these days?

A grave robber? Who knew?

John nodded. He opened his mouth to speak, then hesitated. In an almost pleading voice, he said, "I would like to keep Sandra out of this. She's not been very well lately."

"Sorry, John. That's no longer possible."

ALEXIS HOPED KEVIN and the mayor wouldn't be much longer. Even as the thoughts whirled around in her head, the door opened, and John shuffled out. Dear God, what had happened in there? John looked like he'd aged fifty years. And Kevin?—Well, he looked like the cold detached detective she'd first met at the park.

Alexis waited until Kevin looked around for her, before getting up and walking over. "Are you okay?" she asked in concern.

"Yeah, I'm fine. This morning is shaping up to be hell. Are you sure you want to stay?"

"I called Scott. He's rescuing me from Rick's accounting office for the morning. We'll head to one of the parks."

"As long as you stay with him." Kevin then returned to his desk to collect some papers.

Alexis quietly withdrew. He needed space, and she needed freedom.

Ten minutes later, she stood inside the station entrance, waiting for Scott to pick her up. She hoped to be gone before the officers returned with Charles. The thought of seeing him made her skin crawl. Luckily she spotted Scott's vehicle and stepped outside.

Scott's cheery grin poked through the passenger window, as he pulled up beside her. "Hallo, beauty. Waiting for a ride, are ya? Well, git in."

Thank goodness for friends. Alexis hopped in. Within minutes, they were heading to his favorite coffee shop and then on to their gardens. "How was Moira when you left?"

"*Ach*, she was fine. Said she'd check in on your friend, as soon as she arrived at work."

"Good." Kevin had called the hospital that morning, but there was no change. Alexis couldn't help but wonder if more was going on there than anyone knew. Determinedly she shrugged off the negative thinking. Stefan would be fine. She refused to contemplate any other option.

For the next couple hours, Alexis and Scott lost themselves in the gardens. The place was deserted, and a nice light breeze combated the sultry heat. Alexis worked tirelessly, enjoying the return to a normal day.

Scott's phone rang. He checked the number and handed it over to her.

"I've been trying to reach you but only get your voicemail," Kevin said. Alexis detected a fine tremor of tension threading through his voice. At his words, she dug into her pocket and pulled out her phone. Shit. She'd accidentally shut it off. Probably while it was in her pocket. "Sorry. My phone was turned off. What's going on? Did Charles come in for questioning?"

"Hell, yes. He's definitely the blackmailer, but he's adamant about his father's guilt over his sister's death. This will get pretty ugly."

"Could he have had anything to do with Daisy's death?" Alexis waited for Kevin's answer, uncertain about the odd energy she sensed surrounding him.

"Not likely. He'd have been pretty young. We've confirmed Charles' whereabouts at the most crucial times in regard to the kidnapped girl found in the van and to Mandy's murder. But we have more to look into."

Alexis winced. She wouldn't want that job. At the prolonged silence on the other end, she felt the bottom of her stomach drop. She asked, "Do you think, intuitively, that Charles is the murderer?"

"I don't know." Kevin spoke slowly and thoughtfully. "I can't read him. I get a black wall that seems impenetrable."

Alexis had just about rung off, when a thought occurred. "Kevin, I need to ask. What was Daisy's real name?" In the background, she heard papers being moved, as if he were searching.

"It's here somewhere." Another pause came, then he read quickly, "Marie Leanne Prescott."

"Marie. Interesting."

"But also quite common," Kevin pointed out. "I have to go."

"Wait. I know this isn't a question you want to hear, but I wondered if it is possible to contact Mandy?" She bit her lip, wondering if she'd gone too far.

Kevin spoke with great difficulty. "As far as we know, a person who has recently crossed over can't communicate right away. A period of adjustment is required."

That made sense, sort of. "Could Lissa communicate with her?"

"There's a slim possibility, but apparently they can't direct their focus over there, like we do here."

Alexis didn't know what else to say. They were playing a waiting game. Only it was a game in which one person seemed to make up all the rules.

CHARLES WALKED OUT of the police station, smiling, Daddy's pet lawyer at his side. He'd given his statement. His father had, of course, refused to press blackmail charges in order to keep his only child out of jail and out of the news. Charles had also freely admitted to pressuring Arnie to give up any information to help convict his father. Of course the district attorney said they'd be filing charges for blackmailing a police officer. Charles would let the lawyers battle that out.

The police were idiots. What would it take for them to focus on his father? His dad didn't deserve to live after what he'd done to Daisy. It had taken a long time, but Charles believed punishment day had finally come.

His mom wouldn't understand. She didn't seem to be all there, even with the latest round of drugs—something else he could blame his father for. Rather than outright murdering her, his father had chosen to kill her slowly with medications.

At his car, Charles opened the front door and sat inside for a moment, before starting the engine. Even as he smiled grimly in the rearview mirror, a shadow crossed his face.

He frowned. That shadow had been there for as long as he could remember. He didn't know when he had first noticed it. Not that it mattered. The shadow wasn't separate and apart. It was part of him.

Maybe it was the weight of finding justice for his beloved sister all these years. Or maybe it was just another of his many drugs kicking in. Whatever. He didn't mind the shadow showing.

Shadows had dominated his life for the last decade on the inside. Longer even. Why not let everyone else see them too?

Enough hiding had been going on.

It was time for the truth.

CHAPTER 24

IT WAS LATE. Almost everyone would be asleep, lost to dreamland at this hour. Until evil slid in their back door.

Evil didn't rip through, announcing its presence. It slithered in. He should know—he'd perfected the process.

He circled the outside of the house first, keeping to the shadows. Then he approached the back door.

But he was particularly careful now. This was a cop's house, after all. For a cop, his alarm system left much to be desired. Still, a crappy system made his job easier. Faster.

Moving stealthily, the intruder slid through the main floor, taking note of everything he'd need to finish this scenario. Like many plans hatched out of revenge, this one had taken on a life of its own. This meddling trio had shown more talent for causing trouble than he'd thought possible. Good thing they didn't know everything.

And he intended to keep it that way.

ALEXIS HAD BEEN fully prepared to spend another night at the station, but Kevin had been adamant. He'd already worked through one night—he couldn't go for a second. As soon as he'd been able to, he hauled her out for a quick dinner, and then they'd headed home for an early night.

This time he hadn't even shown her to the spare bedroom. He'd excused himself, gone for a shower, and had tumbled exhausted onto his own bed. She'd taken the initiative and climbed in beside him, following him into a deep slumber.

Until something woke her up. Something wrong.

A cold, clammy sweat covered her slim body. She looked over at the other side of the bed. She was alone.

"*Shh*, Alexis. I'm right here." His voice was pitched low and urgent.

Kevin stood next to the closed bedroom door, his bare chest gleaming in the pale moonlight, every muscle tensed against an unseen foe. He'd pulled on jeans and held his handgun at his side.

She slid out from the crumpled blankets, pulling on underwear, pants, and a T-shirt, tugging that down for some measure of warmth against the massive chill shaking her body. "What is it?" she whispered.

"Use your other senses," Kevin whispered back.

The minute she understood what he meant, she felt *him*.

The bastard was close by.

"He's here," she said. Kevin already knew, she realized. She opened her mind yet another sliver. She could almost feel the evil clawing at her throat. She swallowed convulsively. He was so strong.

A soft *thud* from downstairs had Alexis staring fearfully at an equally grim Kevin. Their intruder had entered the kitchen.

"*Shh.* Stay calm." Keeping Alexis an arm's length behind him, he opened the bedroom door to creep into the hallway. Alexis stayed close. She had no intention of being left behind.

Cautiously they moved down the stairs. Alexis feared her

ragged breathing could be heard from the next room. Another step caught a creaking stair. The loud sound pierced the silence, freezing them in place.

Alexis could sense the evil blackness swirling in place below her. Seconds later, she heard the slam of the back door and the fainter echoing sounds of running footsteps.

Kevin jumped the last few risers and raced out into the night after him.

Alexis made her way to the couch and collapsed.

Never before had she felt such malevolence. She needed to put a face to it. In her heart, she knew Kevin wouldn't catch him, although he'd give it his all. She glanced at the clock; it was almost three in the morning. She closed her eyes, resting against the back of the couch.

Then that she felt it.

Stefan's signature.

She couldn't explain it. It seemed like he'd popped in and quickly left again, leaving a straggling trail. Though he was recovering, he'd tried to come to their assistance. But he hadn't quite succeeded—for reasons she didn't want to contemplate.

The impulse to call the hospital couldn't be ignored.

Several times the phone rang, before someone with a harried voice answered.

"Hello, is Moira there?" Alexis asked.

"No. Can I help you?"

"I'm wondering how Stefan Kronos in room 207 is doing? I know it's an odd thing to call at this hour, but I woke up with him on my mind."

"His vitals were checked not quite an hour ago. There's still no change."

"Oh, uh, thank you." Alexis quickly hung up the phone.

She didn't know if that was good news or bad.

"Who did you call?" Kevin walked through from the kitchen, breathing heavily from the exertion of the chase.

"The hospital." She looked around the room with her inner senses. The faint energy had dissipated. "I couldn't shake the idea that Stefan had been here or had tried to come." She shrugged in exasperation. "So I called the hospital. The nurse said there'd been no change."

Kevin closed his eyes and reached out mentally. Alexis watched, knowing exactly what he was doing. In this skill, he was more advanced than she was.

"And?" she asked with raised eyebrows. "Could you feel him?"

"Yes," he answered quietly. "And no." She raised an eyebrow.

He explained further. "I found a mirror image of his energy, but not his energy, as if it's only part of him." Kevin grimaced. "That's the only explanation I can think of for his energy pattern at this time."

"Didn't he say that to split his energy up like that would make each strand weaker than if he'd stayed whole? And he's so weak as it is …" God, just listen to her. Sometimes this whole business was just too bizarre.

"Theoretically, yes." Kevin gazed in the direction of the moonbeams, as they landed on the couch where Alexis sat. "Stefan seems to think that this is not only possible but necessary in some difficult cases, especially where we have to keep track of many problems at once. But it's taken a lot for him to develop the necessary skills."

Alexis heaved a sigh. "I can't even keep track of one thread." She studied Kevin. Damn, he looked good. An effervescent glow surrounded him. Instead of angering him, the nocturnal visitor had energized him. It made no sense. An intruder coming into his house should have pissed him off—only he looked grimly satisfied at this turn of events.

"Do you know how he got in?" Odd that she felt so calm. The sense of evil had passed, leaving no lingering fear it would return. Instead, a sense of peace surrounded them. Definitely odd. "Why am I not more disturbed? Shouldn't I be scared, terrified even?" Her reaction bothered her a lot.

Kevin smiled down at her.

"What?"

"Look around you." His relaxed manner seemed almost amused. What did she not know?

"What?" Confused, she looked around carefully.

"Look again. This time, look with your inner eye." Now there was no mistaking his humor.

Immediately the colorful energy slid into her view—warm, protective, comforting, *safe* energy. Every window had been outlined in this protective alarm. All possible entrances had received the same treatment, with one exception—the rear kitchen door.

"You did that on purpose." She turned to him in stunned understanding. "You left him an open door." Alexis couldn't believe what her mind slowly realized. "You expected him. Not only that …" She eyed the growing smile on his face. "You were waiting for him to show up!" By the end of her statement, she was almost shouting.

"*Shhh.*" Kevin ran his hands soothingly up and down her bare arms, as if trying to calm her.

She didn't feel like being appeased. Instead, she snapped to her feet and paced around the room. Kevin took her place on the couch.

"How dare you set this up and not tell me!" she snapped,

as she stormed around. "Why couldn't you have told me?" He opened his mouth to answer her, but she spoke right over his attempt. "I don't get it. If you were expecting him, why weren't you waiting for him?" She spun around and stalked back to stand by the window, hands on her hips. She was royally pissed off.

Kevin once again opened his mouth to speak, only to shake his head, his face lighting with laughter as she walked right over to him. "You had the perfect opportunity, and you slipped up. I just don't get it." Alexis collapsed on the couch beside him and suspiciously glared at his grinning face. "What are you grinning at?"

"You. You're priceless. You won't even give me a chance to speak." He reached over and pulled her onto his lap. "Now listen." His large hand slipped around to coax her head against his chest. Gently he caressed her hair. "Let's see if I can explain. First off, you were never in any danger."

He ignored the half-buried snort of disgust and continued, "Our bedrooms had a similar alarm. So he couldn't have snuck anywhere without waking us. Next, if I could have caught him tonight, I would have. I did try," he reminded her. "But that isn't the reason why I left the kitchen door accessible. Obviously it gave him a way in. 'But into what?' you may well ask." He waggled his eyebrows in a hilarious Groucho Marx imitation, startling a surprised giggle from her. He explained further. "Into a video camera, which, with any luck, took his picture."

God, she must be tired because it took her a minute to realize what he said.

"Oh my God! You set *him* up! Oh my God." Alexis couldn't contain herself. She bounced up and tugged him into the kitchen.

Kevin went to work immediately. Standing on a chair, he attempted to retrieve the camera. Alexis waited anxiously, feeling positively wired.

"Can we check it now?" Alexis hopped from one foot to the next in excitement.

"No." The camera proved to be difficult to extract, tucked away as it was, inside the glass panel at the top of the cupboard. It took several intricate maneuvers to release it from its hidey-hole. Once safely down, Kevin looked from the camera to Alexis. "How do you feel about spending the rest of the night at the station?"

"Let's go."

A little later, Alexis looked seriously at Kevin, as they whipped through the deserted streets. "Will I ever have a normal life again?"

Kevin smiled at her. "Nope, never."

Minutes later, they walked into the quiet precinct office. Several officers looked up in surprise. A couple made light comments. Alexis tolerated their well-meaning teasing—apparently it went along with the job. Besides, the group seemed to be a fun-loving bunch. If this kind of teasing helped relieve the depression and the tension that plagued their jobs, so be it.

Once inside his office, Kevin turned on his computer and downloaded the images, while Alexis watched. He fast-forwarded to the time frame they wanted.

Alexis waited breathlessly.

Kevin slowed the film down to when they should have arrived home. It would get interesting fast. They'd gone to bed soon afterward.

There.

Someone was coming in the back door. Not much light

shone in the room, and that made it hard to see anything but shadows.

"Got him!"

Alexis couldn't see what though. Impatiently she waited and watched as Kevin cut and cropped, lightened, then darkened the background, as he brought the figure forward. Once again he cropped and enlarged just the head this time.

"Oh my God. It's Charles!"

Or was it? she thought with a frown.

She'd have trouble recognizing this Charles in daylight, as well as in the darkness of night. He was positively horrifying. His features seemed distorted by dark grooves and hollows.

Alexis sat back in shock.

Kevin stayed equally quiet beside her.

Still staring at the picture, she nudged his shoulder. "What's wrong with this picture?"

"Everything and nothing. It's Charles, but not the one I know. It's like his evil twin."

"Or is it just a side he doesn't show in public? Does he have a split personality?" Both were possible. Medical science dealt with these questions all the time, … although their answers were still inconclusive. "It would explain a lot."

"True, but I'm not sure if that's what's going on."

Alexis sat down beside him, focusing on him and his words, instead of the disturbing picture in front of him. "What are you talking about?"

"Look here." He pointed his finger to the cloudy haze around the image's head. "This is odd." He leaned closer, using the mouse to point it out on the screen. "A weird outline is surrounding his head."

"Couldn't that just be an effect from all the cropping

and enlargements though?" Alexis studied the haze uneasily. She hoped it was. Anything else would be bad.

"No, I don't think so." Kevin studied it intently, before adding, "But I'll have to check with our specialists."

"What difference does a cloudy area make?"

Kevin stood as he answered, "All the difference in the world." With the disk in hand, he walked out of his office, leaving Alexis behind to wonder what had just happened.

ALEXIS SAT ACROSS from the three policemen, ready to scream. They were having such a good time teasing her. Unfortunately they hadn't brought her enough coffee yet, so she wasn't handling it well. In truth, she wasn't handling it at all. She'd woken up from her nap sore, stiff, grumpy, craving caffeine—and alone.

Only she wasn't alone any longer. Kevin had left strict orders that the remaining men were to keep an eye on her.

Damn, she wanted to hiss and spit.

It didn't help that they'd filled her in on what had transpired while she slept. Kevin, accompanied by several officers, had gone to pick up Charles for a second time. Only he was nowhere to be found. A specialist had taken a look at the security file from Kevin's kitchen and had said that the weird lighting had nothing to do with the film or what Kevin had done to it.

"Drink up! Kevin said you need at least *three* cups, before you're safe to talk to."

Alexis glared at the speaker but took another healthy slug. "Any new word on Charles?"

"Nothing new. They're still looking."

Alexis nodded. "Do I get to go to the ladies' room without you guys?" At their comical faces, she reminded them drily, "And I will be sure to let Kevin know if I'm not."

"Sure, you can go on your own," said the officer sitting on her left.

One grinned at her from the right. "After all, how dangerous can that be?"

"This *is* the police station," joked the one on her left.

Alexis finished off her coffee, reached for her purse, and excused herself. The bathroom was a definite necessity now. She looked for a clock to tell her the time but couldn't see one on her way. It felt like five in the morning. Her eyes still had grit caked in the corners.

She pushed open the door to the ladies' room and walked through to the large mirrors. Those were definitely bags under her eyes, a sure sign of stress and lack of sleep. She needed this chaos to end before it was the end of her. She yawned. Damn, she was tired.

Then she remembered. Stefan's instructions to safeguard her energy before falling asleep! Had that made her vulnerable again? Dear God, she'd forgotten to follow them last night. She'd collapsed on the cot again in Kevin's office and had closed her eyes.

Unease settled deep in her bones.

She hurriedly used the toilet, washed up as well as she could, and then brushed her hair. Another hit of coffee would go down nicely now. Then she might just survive the day after all. Humor softened her face. Maybe two cups of coffee would make her sociable today and not three, like they'd been warned. Just this once. It wouldn't do to spoil the guys too much.

Alexis headed back into the deserted hallway.

She hadn't taken two steps, when blinding pain ripped through her skull, and she collapsed to the floor.

CHAPTER 25

KEVIN STALKED INTO his office, pissed. He regretted that Charles, the damned weasel, had been allowed to walk out of the station after the last time they'd questioned him. But that was lawyers for you. So far, Charles had yet to be located again. Had he run? If so, why? No way he could have known about the camera. Kevin had set it up himself.

He eyed the empty cot. At least it looked like Alexis had gotten some sleep. He sure as hell hadn't. Long ago he'd become used to working through the night when on a case. He'd tried to close his eyes last night for a few hours, with limited success.

One of the guys walked in behind him. "She's just gone to the washroom. Give her a couple minutes. You don't want to disturb her. She hasn't had her three cups of coffee yet." Kevin glared at Peter, a fellow officer he'd worked with for years. Peter placed a full cup of the same hot heady brew in front of Kevin. "You two have so much in common."

He didn't deserve an answer.

Kevin wrestled with his temper, catching up on what he had missed, finally managing a reluctant smile. "What the hell is she doing in there? I've been back for ten minutes already."

"Don't know." The other man shrugged.

"Who does?" Kevin got up and strode impatiently down

the hallway to the washrooms. Using the men's room first, he returned to knock on the women's door. No one answered.

Belatedly his neck itched.

Shit!

Guilt screamed through his fatigued brain. He should have picked up on the sense something was wrong earlier. He had to find Alexis.

"Did you find her?" called a voice behind him.

Kevin turned to find several concerned fellow officers crowding around.

"No, she's gone."

The entire station ripped into action. It took mere seconds of frantic organization to search the building. When that produced no sign of her, everyone went into overdrive. All officers on duty and a few who weren't joined in. Alarms went out to mobile units, and alerts went out to all surrounding counties.

Alexis was nowhere.

ALEXIS STRUGGLED AGAINST the wave of nausea and pain. She knew she had to fight. It was important. Only she couldn't remember why. For long moments, she worked desperately to reach this seemingly impossible goal. To fight what held her in the fog. The effort burned up her frail energy reserves. Yet the deeply buried instinct to survive couldn't be ignored. She struggled onward, upward, searching for an anchor to pin her energy on. She couldn't see anything, … as if in a vacuum with no senses of any kind—except pain.

She slumped against the cold hard surface, as her urge to

fight waned. The goal of wakefulness that had seemed so attainable a few minutes ago now became impossible. With walls of excruciating darkness pressing down on her, she collapsed into the pit of unconsciousness, only too happy to forget what it was she'd been trying so hard to achieve and why.

UNCONSCIOUS, ALEXIS NEVER roused when the vehicle she was in finally came to a rolling stop.

Good. Charles smiled.

Not that anyone would care. No one cared about anyone or anything other than themselves. At least not for long. People deluded themselves into thinking others cared about them. That lasted for a month or two or maybe even a year or two, … but that's all it was, a facade that everyone saw through eventually.

He preferred to live out of the limelight, unlike his father. God, he hated that man.

It had been too easy to snatch Alexis. After running out of the cop's house last night, he'd parked around the corner and followed the two of them back to the station. At that hour of the night, the place was close to empty. He'd waited until dawn broke. Going in the back entrance in coveralls, as if he were part of the cleaning crew, had been a no-brainer. Besides, the guy he'd replaced wouldn't be telling on him … or anyone again.

Making himself wait until the opportune moment to grab her? … Now that had been hard.

He didn't bother checking up on her in the back seat. Either she'd survive or she wouldn't. It was too late to worry and way too late to care.

Charles drove carefully, not wanting to attract attention. Damn, there was that headache again. He never felt like himself when this happened. He grimaced and reached for the bottle of pills in his pocket. The fucking things didn't work anymore. Why were the headaches so bad these days? Sometimes it scared the hell out of him. He didn't care about dying, but he sure as hell wasn't into suffering through cancer or something equally nasty.

He rubbed his forehead, as the pounding tempo increased. Shitty pills. When would they kick in? He peered outside. The house looked the same. It always did. After all, it was the perfect house for the perfect couple—to hell with the fucked-up son.

Charles chuckled, the sound closer to a cackle. He parked near the garage's side door and entered. The garage was dark but spotless. When had it been anything but? He opened up the back seat, tugging the blanket off his captive.

Still unconscious, Alexis had curled up in a fetal position, her arms tucked in close to her sides. He laid his hand on her neck, checking her pulse. Slow, deep, and steady. One surreptitious glance around, then he tugged her up and over his shoulder. He grunted as he took the full brunt of her weight. Damn good thing she wasn't any bigger.

On the way to the huge storage closet, he grinned savagely, kicking the work table that held spotless tools. The clatter screamed through the cavernous room. Instead of making him happy, he winced as the beat in his temple increased.

None too gently, he lowered Alexis to the cement floor of the closet, the spotlessly clean cement.

God, everything pissed him off today. The freedom to finally act out his plans brought out the submerged feelings he'd spent half a lifetime hiding—even from himself.

Alexis laid crumpled and still on the cold floor. He couldn't waste any time or emotion on her. He had nothing left to give anyone. For years, he'd been a shell on automatic pilot, waiting for someone to throw a switch. Finally someone had.

Arnie.

Quickly Charles finished setting things in order. His final act was to close and to lock the closet door.

Nonchalantly he walked through into the main part of the house. "Hello! Is anyone home?"

The house appeared silent. He knew better. She'd be here, hiding in her bottle. He walked through to the solarium. There she sat, just as he'd expected, all dressed up for company. Company that would never come. She was the epitome of the perfect lady, except for the heavy lacing of Glenfiddich whisky in her coffee, her favorite choice of wake-up drinks.

He'd been close to her—once. He didn't know whether the drugs had sent her off or the booze, but she wasn't often the mother he remembered.

"Good morning, Mother. How are you this morning?"

A faint tremor washed through the older woman. Visibly regaining control, she couldn't quite hide the shudder of revulsion in her eyes as she looked at him.

He smiled nastily. "What's the matter, Mom?" He stressed the title, knowing how much she hated it. "Are you not having a good morning?"

"It's fine." She refused to add more, choosing instead to take a hefty fortifying drink from her cup.

Sitting there, she looked almost perfect. Not a hair out of place. Appearances for her were everything. He almost felt sorry for her—her world was about to bust apart.

On the heels of that thought, his headache lashed out, catching him above the temple. He winced, as agony speared through him.

"I told you to get those headaches checked," she lectured in her patronizing voice.

God, he hated that tone. "And I told you that I'm fine. I won't see any more damn doctors."

"Well, maybe your medication needs to be changed. You are taking it, aren't you?" she asked fearfully. "Remember what happened the last time you forgot?"

Irritated, Charles sat down across from his mother. She flinched. "And, if I don't, what the hell could you do about it? You're nothing but a useless washed-out alcoholic whore."

Pain mixed with faint tendrils of fear filled her gaze. "Are you taking your medication?" she demanded sharply. "Are you?" At his sneering look, she reiterated, "Charles, you have to take it. Do you hear me? Bad things happen when you don't. You're not yourself without them."

Her voice mocked deep into his weak soul. "Don't you mention that again, you bitch." He shoved away from the table, standing threateningly over her. "This time, I've made sure it will be *him* who gets locked up. Not me!"

Sandra's face bleached white. "Dear God, what have you done?" Frail hands clutched her antique gold necklace.

"You'll find out." He gave her a salute of mock respect and turned his back on her, then walked out. "When it's too damn late to change it."

He left.

~

SANDRA'S HEART POUNDED, as terror, never far from the

surface in recent years, slammed into her head.

Dear God, what had her son done now? He was a good boy really. But there'd always been something a little … off … but only sometimes. She loved him so much but was so afraid something was terribly wrong.

She'd always wondered if Charles had had anything to do with her beloved Marie's death. They'd tried so hard to keep him stable. Like Sandra, Charles was … delicate. Not always himself.

And, when he wasn't himself, … she was terrified. Of what he'd do. Of what he'd done.

She gasped in pain. A decades-long torment rose once again to the surface. She had tried to stuff it back down. Down where her other fears lived. The constant bruises, the small accidents befalling her little girl. That horrible intuitive feeling a mother has … that something, … someone was hurting Marie.

And the fear of finding out who. Sandra had drowned those horrible fears in her whisky, hating the suspicion always inside, eating away at her family, poisoning everything around her.

It had been easier to forget it all. To block it out. To black it out.

She clutched her hand to her heart.

It had been so hard to survive all these years after losing her only daughter.

Too hard. But she'd tried. Tried to salvage her marriage, tried to be a mother to her son.

Now her frail, worn-out shell of a woman who'd seen too much, who had been dealt so many lethal blows, gasped and fought for air. The faint gasps finally gave out to a crushing, squeezing compression of her weak heart.

She couldn't think, as a gray fog filled her brain. Blue color slowly overtook the blank whiteness, as she fought for air and against the pain. Stumbling off her chair, she collapsed to the hardwood floor, struggling to reach the phone on the side buffet. She crawled partway, a bit more—was almost to the phone—when a voice reached out to her.

"Oh my God, ma'am. Wait. Hold on. I'm getting help."

The frantically struggling woman never heard the sounds of help arriving. Blackness choked her in an unending constricting torment, until she slipped into blessed unconsciousness.

KEVIN WAS BESIDE himself. He found no sign of Alexis on the physical or ethereal planes. Cruisers were out looking for both Alexis and Charles. With Stefan practicing his new technique, Kevin found it impossible to talk to him telepathically.

He desperately needed his friend's help.

Kevin strode through the double doors of the hospital entrance, heading for Stefan's room. Never in his life had he needed his friend like he did today. "Stefan?" He called out as he entered the peaceful room. "That's enough. I need you. You have to come back. Alexis is in danger or, … or worse," he said.

"I know," whispered Stefan, his voice faint. "What makes you think I can help more on this side than on the other?"

"I don't give a damn where you help, just so long as you do!" Kevin said forcefully, approaching the bed with quick steps. "I can't feel her. Something bad has happened."

"She's there."

"Where?" Relief sharpened Kevin's voice to steel. "You can feel her? Where is she?"

"She's unconscious, caught in the fog between here and there."

"Can you contact her?" Kevin wouldn't give up. "Find out where she is!"

"Take it easy. You aren't helping any."

Kevin forcibly pulled back. Stefan was right—going to pieces now wouldn't get her back. Stefan needed his assistance, not his distraction. "Fine. And, when you can, tell her to open the damn door to me," he said shortly. "What can I do to help?"

"Walk me through what you do know." Stefan's voice trembled with the physical effort. He stirred restlessly on the bed. "I'm not back to full strength yet."

"It's a damn good thing you did wake up, or I'd be tempted to crawl inside your head and force you back." He was only half joking and saw by Stefan's faint smile that he understood. Kevin relented. "Sorry, Stefan. I can't think because I'm worried."

"So quit wasting time and fill me in."

It took a few minutes to give him the scant details. Painful silence followed. Stefan said briskly, "All right then. I'll go look for her, as she did for me."

Kevin had to be content with that.

STEFAN, USING THE closely developed bond with Alexis, finally picked up her faint trail. It wove through dark fog and gloom, as a glowing silvery thread. From his perspective, he could tell she had no idea where she was. There were no visuals.

Odd. If anyone else were involved, Stefan found no indication, no imprint. He pondered this as he zeroed in on her. Minutes later, he felt her warm, comforting spirit. But he couldn't see or hear her.

Using methods he'd fine-tuned over the years, he slipped into her mind.

It was empty.

Shards of icy terror slammed through his consciousness. What the hell was going on? Slowly he pivoted in the brilliant crystal cave of her consciousness. Nothing to see but ice. Sounds were muted, deadened by the vast denseness of the frozen wasteland. Eerie echoes bounced in his head. Fear for Alexis clouded his mind, and he struggled for control. She was in incredible danger. He had to help her. But first, he had to find her in this bizarre space of her mind.

Expectant numbing silence prevailed, a waiting stillness, … for something or someone. Stefan pivoted in disbelief. Dead in front of him stood a specter. He thought he was past being shocked by anything. He still didn't understand how this could be possible. *Who are you?*

Your nemesis.

Yeah, right. Stefan almost thanked the bastard, as his comment returned a sense of realism. This asshole was, and always had been, just one clever son of a bitch. But Stefan wasn't fighting for himself. He was fighting for Alexis and for all those earlier victims. His thoughts, easily heard, echoed through the cavern of Alexis's mind.

Why worry about them? What are they to you? The specter opened his arms wide.

Pardon? Who could not care? Stefan didn't get it.

I used to believe in people, a long time ago. Now I use people just as they used me.

Depths of unrelenting bitterness stretched out toward Stefan. He saw fragments of a huge unresolved history swelling up. Cautiously he asked, *So you blame someone for your rotten life, and now hold all of humanity responsible?*

Don't psychoanalyze me. I know what I'm doing and why. The why is easy—because I can. And because they deserve it. John deserves it.

Macabre laughter echoed hollowly in the odd chamber. Alexis's mind! God, how could he forget! He glanced around. Bizarre stalagmites stretched forever upward around him. He felt as if he stood in the deep ice caves of Norway.

Don't bother.

Stefan pivoted back to full attention. *Don't bother what?*

Don't bother looking for her. She's frozen in her own world. A little parlor trick I've perfected. What passed for a face grinned evilly.

Stefan's stomach revolted. *Frozen?* What the hell did that mean? *Is she dead?*

Hell, no. But now I can do what I want. Use her as I wish and let her go. Of course she'll probably die then. They usually do. He shrugged dismissively. *That's not my concern.*

How did you learn to do all this? Stefan waved futilely around his bizarre surroundings. *It's incredible.*

Thank you.

The specter actually preened—talk about an ego.

I tripped into this accidentally, but, once I realized I could have a life, and a secret life that most of the real world would never know about, I was hooked. Such power. Such control.

He laughed again, making Stefan wince at its mocking resonance.

You still don't understand, do you? I'm whole here in spirit, but in the physical world, my body is useless. Useless! he shrieked. *Do you know who's fucking responsible? For me being hooked up for life? Existing in a world with no control? A victim to his every whim? My goddamned asshole of a brother, that's who.*

Stefan's mind rapidly filled in the pieces of what he knew. Dear God, this had to be Glen, the comatose brother of John Prescott, Mayor of Bradford—in Alexis's mind.

The madman's face twisted. *Now you're starting to understand. Can you comprehend the extent of my relief when I realized I could be free from that rotting vegetable in the hospital bed? My brother must have loved sitting there, drinking my favorite whisky, watching spit slide from my lips, knowing I was locked in a prison of his making. Did I tell you that he caused my accident in the first place? He rammed my car and ran me off the road.*

Angry sparks flew in all directions with his rage. *Asshole. My fucking brother couldn't go out and make his own way in the world. No. He had to take what was mine, so he tried to kill me. And fucked that up too. While I'm here in a coma, he took my house, my cars, even my business. Would he let me go then? Would he let the doctors pull the plug and release me? No!*

Stefan fought for control as the poisonous tirade lashed out at him. The pain, the anguish of betrayal without physical control, had become a hurricane of human emotions. Stefan struggled to avoid the maelstrom. He needed clarity to find the advantage hidden in this man's loss of control.

I've had decades to watch, to learn, and especially to control other people.

The energy force turned violently black and purple with his feelings.

Do you really think John's wimpy useless son, Charles, is

responsible for any of this? He's so weak he has no idea what he's done versus what I've done through him.

More laughter came, calmer this time and all the more eerie when matched with his words.

He was a perfect tool. Easy to manipulate. Easy to make him hate his father. John deserved to lose everything, ... like he arranged for me to lose everything.

Stefan was staggered. How much damage had this embittered soul done? The scope of this diseased mind was too horrific to contemplate.

You'll never know all that I've done. No one will.

WITH GREAT DIFFICULTY, Kevin stayed quiet, as he hovered in the background of Stefan's mind. The truths were too many, delivering more shocks than he could absorb all at once. It was totally incomprehensible. They'd come up against some devious and twisted minds before, but he'd never known someone could physically live confined in a deep coma for decades, yet live freely on the ethereal plane and take over, at will, the physical bodies of others who were weaker.

He hadn't exactly asked Stefan's permission when he'd hitched a ride on Stefan's energy trip. He hoped Stefan would understand. When Kevin hadn't been booted out immediately, he'd assumed all was well, and he'd stayed quiet. This was too crazy. How could they help Alexis now?

The asshole continued to speak.

You see, if you and the nosey cop hadn't butted into my business, then this game could have gone on for another decade or two. But knowing how weak Charles is, I started putting a contingency plan in place, just in case I lose my host.

Host? Stefan asked.

Stefan's surprise matched Kevin's horror. Dear God, is that all these people were to him?

Yeah. You know that I use their bodies to achieve what I want to achieve. If I'm forced to be here in this world, then I'll damn well live it the way I want to.

His demeanor was that of someone casually discussing a piece of paper that, once used, had no value and was discarded like garbage.

Only these people weren't litter.

Finally Stefan asked the question burning inside of Kevin. *Why Alexis?*

That did it.

The blackness deepened to billows of hollow smoke, as Glen struggled to hold his dark image together. *That bitch!* The edges blurred, shifted, and then reformed again. He paused before continuing in a slightly calmer voice. *She's the only one who seemed to find out about the real me. My history. My actions. My motivations. She could actually talk with some of the children. She could sense when I was around. I'd never experienced anything like it before.* He snickered at Stefan. *You could have, if you'd looked, but you're so locked down that I operated under your nose for years, and you never knew.* He positively beamed as he considered his own craftiness.

Kevin felt like vomiting. He swallowed heavily, forcing the bile back down.

Stefan asked cautiously, *Have you been doing this for long?*

Glen laughed. *God, I snatched little children when I was in my twenties and thirties, when I was healthy and whole. I used to keep them for a while before I killed them.*

Stefan hated the thought of a serial killer getting away with these crimes for so long. Kevin's thoughts mirrored the same disgust.

You couldn't have killed very many then, Stefan prodded. *Not if you were never caught.*

Bullshit. I won't give anything away, but you can bet there were over a dozen back then, until my asshole big brother stepped in and decided to steal what was mine. Now that I've learned to live again, I think Charles will develop the traits of a pedophile.

Kevin shuddered.

Where is Alexis now? asked Stefan humbly, as if bowing gracefully to a talent bigger and stronger than his.

Kevin laughed humorlessly. *As if!*

The ripples of mirth slid through Stefan's mind, only to be quickly stomped on, in warning.

She's locked in a closet, the asshole explained comfortably.

Kevin almost lost it. A fucking closet! He barely heeded Stefan's silent warning to stay in control. He closed his eyes, forcing away the horrific image of Alexis's suffering. He had to remain strong, or he'd be of no help.

A closet, that's smart. Presumably she can't get out?

Stefan's friendly conversational tone surprised Kevin. While his stomach churned, and bloodlust blinded his vision, Kevin knew Stefan was calm, cool, and collected. Kevin had never admired him more. Was he still probing the ethers for Alexis's physical location?

Yeah, I left her in an incriminating place, at least for John. His statement seemed to amuse him to no end, as gales of laughter overwhelmed him.

That must have been difficult.

For you maybe, not for me. I've been using Charles and several others to do my dirty work for years. Glen shrugged dismissively. *They made it almost too easy.*

If everything is working for you, why take out John now? asked Stefan.

Maximum destructiveness. I want him to suffer. He's responsible for destroying my life. I'll destroy him. His useless wimp of a son should get the same. I've perfected my next step, which will allow me to enjoy their confusion and pain from the most advantageous place.

Gloating satisfaction oozed from the madman's energy, as his projection shone with pride. His mocking commentary almost drove Kevin to his knees. How many people out there were acting under this maniac's commands? Kevin would have to consider this carefully.

But don't you want them to pull the plug on your physical body, so you can finally find peace?

Stefan continued to talk calmly, almost reverently of the other man's exceptional talent. An ego-stroking that nauseated Kevin, even as he understood the need for it.

It no longer matters what they do to my body. Once my dear brother is taken care of, I will move on to my next host. From my new vantage point, I can do what I want. They probably will pull the plug on their own, if he's not there to continue paying my exorbitant medical bills. And he'll be gone soon. Everything's almost in place.

The words rolled over Kevin in mass confusion. Surely Glen couldn't continue to control these people without a physical presence? Somehow this madman had found a way to make dead no longer mean totally *dead.*

The asshole was still talking, and Kevin had to forcibly refocus. Only Alexis mattered now.

I'm confident that I'll carry on my existence in the same manner. After all, I've had years to work out a solution to this problem. I don't need my body to be alive anymore. I can control more now than I ever could alive. Keen intelligence gleamed through the blackness. *In the beginning, it was a different story of course. But, with endless time for practice, I think I've perfected the transfer. I believe I can make it permanent. Through lifetimes even. Over and over.*

His seeping malevolence wavered, appeared to dissipate, before solidifying once again in front of them. Kevin watched and listened in horrified fascination, as the maniac continued his gloating.

And don't think I'm stupid enough to let you know where I'm going, or how I'm doing this. He smirked at his own superior knowledge. *You'd like to know though, wouldn't you? Too fucking bad.*

I don't understand what you could have done with Alexis. After all, it's her mind we're in now. Stefan kept awe and confusion in his voice.

Kevin waited, breathless.

Of course you don't because you're thinking from the human perspective, not the soul perspective. You have to work on that! he admonished. *Like they say on TV, you have to think outside the box.*

Sorry, it's difficult while grounded in physical life.

True.

The asshole seemed somewhat mollified by Stefan's admission of a lesser status and talent. Yeah, right.

Kevin waited and watched. At the same time, he tried to observe the frozen stalagmites forming the visual of Alexis's mind. He didn't understand—how could this be? Everything about this case could have come from a horror show. Were these surroundings hers or the asshole's? Not that it mattered, but Kevin had to locate her and to help her free herself.

He scanned the space he saw. There! Off on the far wall, back slightly out of view, stood something frozen in the ice. *Alexis*. Excited, Kevin started to tell Stefan, only to be cut off immediately.

I know. You need to get over to her but don't let this maniac know. Stefan's faint whisper came as an impression felt rather than clear words.

Go to her? How?

The ice is Alexis's vision, only she doesn't know it. Become one with it, and you'll become one with her.

Shit. He'd never tried anything like this. It didn't matter. He had to succeed. He had no other option. He didn't know about becoming one with the ice, but he could definitely relate to water. Could he warm the surface of the ice enough to melt it to a film of water?

It was easier than he'd thought. Almost instantaneously, he found himself slithering across the frozen surface, inside the slightly warmer film connecting him to the icy particles that made up the chamber of Alexis's mind. A small part of his brain watched the proceedings in awe. How was such a thing even possible?

He had no time for amazement or shock. That would surely follow, but, for now, he raced through the cold watery flow to help the woman he loved.

CHAPTER 26

ALEXIS FOUGHT THE rising tide of panic. None of this made any sense. Disjointed images flooded her subconscious, washing her in sounds and impressions that refused to fit together. She shuddered under the chaotic onslaught. Pain and confusion blinded her. Inundated on all sides, she fought for clarity.

When clarity finally came, amazement beset her. She existed simultaneously in two planes. Always before, she'd been focused in one energy field, blocking out any vivid awareness of the other. Not this time. That juxtaposition merging in itself seemed as horrifying as it was exhilarating. The panoramic vistas of both realities overwhelmed her with their sharpness.

This lucidity she didn't appreciate, once she realized she was a prisoner in both worlds.

In the physical plane, ropes strangled the circulation in both her ankles and her wrists, and a tight cloth gagged her mouth. Worse than that had to be the awkward position she'd been twisted into. It felt like she was the last item shoved into an already-full closet, before the door was slammed shut quickly to prevent her from falling out.

Right now, falling out would be a welcomed relief.

Tears welled up, as she tried to shift her body. Muscles screamed for relief but could only move scant inches in any direction. The gag pulled the skin on her cheeks, and worse were the few loose hairs caught in the tape over her gag that ripped her scalp with each tiny movement. Defeated, she collapsed to her original position.

She was going nowhere here.

Simultaneously she was transported to the other world. She drifted in and out of sleep and wakefulness. Icy cold surrounded her in this place, where pain and fear inundated her.

This reality was no better.

Imprisoned and suspended in an icicle, she appeared to be in the middle of a huge stalagmite that dominated an icy cavern. Peripherally she registered the presence of others.

Yet something was familiar. What? No, not what—who? *Kevin!* Was Kevin here? She concentrated harder, searching for his tangible thread. *Yes.* She felt his comforting presence. And Stefan's too! Joy pulsed through her. They were both here.

Then she sensed a third presence. *The asshole.*

Numbing coldness encroached on her emotions, fighting with gripping fear. Her captor was here. This last realization, oddly enough, was what grounded her firmly in this reality and made things clear.

He had to be stopped.

Now, through the surrounding frozen wasteland, she felt and, even to a certain extent, saw, the vague outlines of both the asshole's and Stefan's energies.

Stefan's energy looked distinctly odd—tight, controlled, yet wispy. Alexis focused next on his adversary. A malevolent force she recognized straight away—evil oozed from the center of his black heart.

Where could Kevin be in all this? Carefully she closed

her eyes and opened her senses. She felt him but did not see him. She smiled. There he was. He was … everywhere. Kevin existed in the ice that surrounded and supported her, that covered and held her.

Alex? His soft voice rippled through her consciousness. His words slid in at the DNA level. Without sound, without form, only a distinctive knowing that allowed her to understand. And to respond in kind.

So relieved to hear you. Maybe you could explain what is going on? Alexis whispered. Her mind opened wider, as the words slipped out on fragile snowflakes—the link between the two of them made words unnecessary.

True to thought, images played through her mind. Became a movie of what had happened and how they all came to be here at the same place.

That place being inside *her* mind.

Dear God.

Alexis slumped, understanding what her reality had become.

Don't, Kevin admonished.

Don't what? Be depressed? Be afraid? I think I'm entitled to feel a little alarmed over a science fiction war currently being fought inside my head, she said, fear sharpening her voice to that of a razor's edge.

True, but you're not alone, Kevin said. *We won't let anything happen to you.*

His soothing tones washed through her, but she knew better. *Too late!* she lashed out.

It is not. We're trying to find the physical you. Can you help us? Do you know where you are?

In a padded cell? If not now, I probably will be soon, she muttered.

Stop! You are not crazy. Help us.

Excuse me, she snapped. A fraught minute later, she pulled back. He was right. They all needed to keep their wits about them, or she'd never survive. There'd be time for a full-scale breakdown later.

It won't happen, so don't even think about it.

Harsh crystal tones jarred her senses. *What do I need to do?*

Do you have any idea where you are? Did you see anything? Glen mentioned a locked closet.

That sounds about right. I'm jammed behind some kind of wooden door. It could be a closet or a storage locker. That's all I know. I only just woke up. She felt like apologizing for her predicament. Alexis hesitated as his words sank in. *Glen?*

I'll explain later. Are you hurt? Do you need an ambulance? Can you tell us anything else? he prodded.

No, it's too dark to see.

What about smells, sounds—anything distinctive?

Smells … She paused to consider the odd scents that assailed her nostrils. *Car smells, gas, oil. Maybe a garage or a mechanic's shop. Not overwhelming, possibly someone's garage.*

Good, keep thinking. Did you hear anything? Did you feel anything unusual? Think.

Alexis remained silent for a moment, letting the words sink deep into her consciousness. *Movement. I remember traveling, maybe being carried, but the memories are slippery, inconsistent,* she protested. *We can't rely on them.*

Wrong. Even though you were out cold, these sensations were emblazoned on your consciousness. You can tap into them.

If I were to guess, I'd say I was brought here to someone's garage in the trunk of a car.

Good, excellent!

Alexis didn't understand his sudden excitement. *It's not as if I told you anything new.*

But you put things together in a different way, and that made all the difference. I think you're inside John Prescott's garage.

What? Why there?

I think Charles has stashed you there to implicate John. Glen said something about "maximum destructiveness."

Alexis found her focus wavering. It was getting harder to concentrate.

Alex?

His sharp tone forced her attention back to him. *Sorry,* she whispered, *I'm losing focus.*

Alexis, stay awake! Do you hear me?

Barely. Her voice faded away for a moment, before rallying once again. *I think I'm hurt.*

Then she was gone.

"DON'T PANIC. DON'T panic." Kevin raced through the hospital corridors, dodging people and carts, heading for his car and fresh air and his cell phone. "Just because she faded out doesn't mean she's badly hurt," he muttered to himself, ignoring the many fascinated looks from people walking the same corridors.

"Detective Sutherland," Scott called out in a thick Irish burr.

Kevin whirled to see Scott, striding quickly behind him.

"I called out several times, but you must be doing some very hefty thinking to not hear me." He smiled, but thick worry lines showed on his face. "Sorry to bother you, but I can't locate Alexis." He paused for a mere second. "Have you seen her?"

Kevin motioned for Scott to follow him out of the huge building. "She was kidnapped from the police station this morning. I'm on my way to check out a potential lead now."

"I'm coming." Scott barreled beside him, anxious to hear the details. "Don't you be thinking I'm not."

"I wouldn't dare." Kevin rolled his eyes at the huge man. "Get in."

After throwing lights on the top of his roof, Kevin ripped out of the hospital parking lot and cut the corner too close, bouncing over the curb. Kevin felt Scott's sidelong glance, but he chose to ignore it. He used his cell to call Dispatch for backup and an ambulance.

The nightmarish trip continued through town, until Kevin's truck came to a screeching halt, just ahead of the black-and-white backup car. The ambulance also waited for them.

As the two men raced to the front entrance of the house, the door opened, and a stretcher was wheeled out. Kevin stopped, transfixed.

It was Sandra, John's wife.

"What the hell happened?" he asked, his voice sharp with worry. His gaze darted in all directions, as he searched for signs of Alexis.

"Looks like a heart attack. We're taking her in now." The two ambulance attendants maneuvered the trolley carefully down to the waiting vehicle.

"Is she stable?"

"For now, but she needs to get to Emergency."

Kevin nodded. "I need you to wait another moment. We have reason to believe another injured person is on the premises."

Both paramedics looked at each other, before nodding. "Only long enough to get her loaded, or we'll have to come back."

"Done." Kevin didn't waste any more time, he headed into the front foyer, Scott following closely behind. The other policemen were directed around back. Kevin knew the layout of the house, and he headed for the door leading to the garage.

He entered at the same time as the other officers entered through the outside door. Carefully he looked around. The space appeared deserted. A large closet occupied most of the far wall. Kevin couldn't recall ever seeing it open.

A large bolt secured the wooden doors.

"Useless things, these are." Scott reached out a meaty fist and wrenched the whole door off, taking the latch and bits of cheap pressboard with it.

Alexis, unconscious and bleeding from her head, slumped to the floor at their feet. One of the two backup officers raced out, calling for the paramedics, while the other three people bent over her prone body.

"Is she alive?" asked Scott anxiously.

"Yes, she's breathing." Kevin grimly sliced through the tight bindings that pinned her poor arms back. As he did so, a low groan escaped from her slack mouth. Quickly the others took care of the remaining bindings, as a paramedic arrived.

The medic checked her over thoroughly. "She has a head injury, almost certainly a concussion, but I don't see any breaks or major bleeding. Let's get her to the hospital, where they can check her out."

The second stretcher arrived, and, within minutes, they were on their way to the hospital, an anxious Scott holding

Alexis's hand.

Kevin had to stay behind and finish his job.

For long moments, he contemplated the empty driveway and the plume of dust, as the ambulance peeled off. Charles was physically responsible, but was he mentally responsible? Who would pay the penalty for these crimes? More aptly, who should pay for the murder and mayhem? Glen had mentioned finding a new host. ... Could he even be stopped?

Would anyone believe this tale, let alone convict a coma patient of being a serial killer? Shaking his head at the vagaries of fate and the other side of reality he found himself policing, he headed back inside to take care of business.

Charles drove up an hour later and parked in the driveway. Calm and cool, he walked into his father's house, using the front door, calling out, "Hello! Is anyone home?"

Kevin walked out to meet him. "Charles, we need to ask you some questions involving the kidnapping of Alexis Gordon."

The younger man looked at him in astonishment. "What are you doing inside my house? And what are you talking about? I had nothing to do with any kidnapping."

"Eyewitness accounts tell it differently." Not quite the truth, but Kevin hoped to prod him into revealing more than he would have otherwise. So far, Charles's surprise appeared genuine.

"Bullshit! I've been at work all morning. Go ahead and talk to the construction crew about it."

Kevin stopped to consider that. "Someone will corroborate your story? In the meantime, what makes you think she was kidnapped *this morning*?"

Charles looked at him in confusion. Stunned and bewildered, he didn't appear to know what to say. "I don't know. I guess I just assumed it."

Could Charles be ignorant of Glen's actions when being used as a host? It was often that way with multiple personality cases. Kevin nodded noncommittally. "Like I said, we need to ask you a few questions. Shall we sit for a few minutes?"

"I don't want to bother my mother with all this," Charles replied stiffly.

Kevin grimaced at what this young man didn't know. Kevin made it brief and succinct.

Charles didn't adjust well to the news. Bitterly protesting, Charles took a seat in the kitchen. One of the officers stood quietly off to one side and slightly behind him.

Kevin phoned the hospital to get an update on their latest patients. Hearing that all was as well as could be expected, with Alexis still unconscious and his mother still undergoing tests, Kevin updated Charles. Giving the man a moment to deal with the news, Kevin then worked on getting the answers they needed. "Let's start with where you've been since last night."

Charles willingly complied, giving a full and detailed account. If Charles's statement heavily implied that his father had been somehow involved, Kevin ignored that.

"Charles, I need to ask about your little sister's death. What can you tell me about that?"

"The only important thing to know is that my father killed her." He seemed almost relieved, even delighted to say the words aloud.

The door behind them opened wide, and his father entered the room abruptly.

"I certainly did not kill my daughter!" The shock of betrayal laced John Prescott's voice.

This didn't sound good. On the other hand, maybe now they could get to the truth.

"John, I didn't know you'd arrived home." Kevin studied John's ravaged face. "Have you heard about Sandra?"

A shudder rippled down John's back. "Yes. I'd hoped to find Charles here, so we could go to her at the hospital together." He motioned to Charles. "Let's go, son."

Charles sneered at him and stayed seated. "Like you care."

Deliberately staying between the two men, Kevin gave John the update he'd gotten a few minutes ago. "I'm sorry. We need to clear up a few things first." He motioned to another empty chair. "Please take a seat."

John sat down slowly, his outrage at his son slowly replaced by grief. He asked Charles, "How could you think I don't care? Is that why you've hated me all these years? Do you really believe I killed your sister? I loved her, Charles, just as I've loved you all these years." The expression on John's pale face wilted further.

Kevin studied John's features, then scanned his mind. No sign of deception. John appeared genuinely devastated by the accusations of his son and by the news of his wife.

"Like hell. You were always jealous of the bond between Daisy and me." Charles slouched against his chair, turning away from his father.

"Listen carefully." John leaned forward earnestly, trying to make his son understand. "I didn't kill Daisy. She was the light of *my* life!"

Kevin straightened. Maybe now they could find the truth. The evil root. "Do you have any idea who did?" Kevin asked his friend.

John, shamefaced, turned to look at Kevin. "Sandra was supposed to be looking after her. She'd been drinking heavily those days. She'd have blackouts and wouldn't know what she'd been doing, sometimes hours would be unaccounted for. Or so she said. On top of that we couldn't get Sandra's medications straight. I got home from work that day, too late to save my little girl from Sandra's neglect." He hung his head in pain.

"I know what you're thinking. But there was no proof. And she didn't do it on purpose. She wasn't herself. Wasn't responsible for her actions. Please try to understand—I was devastated." He swallowed hard. "Sandra said she didn't see Marie's fall that broke her neck, that she had turned her back for a second. That it was an accident. … At the time, I couldn't think straight and …" He stopped, tears hanging in the corners of his reddened eyes. "And punishing her wouldn't have helped. There's no way to know the truth of what happened that day. And no amount of blame would have brought my Marie back."

Shocked silence hung heavily over the table.

"Sandra's harmless when she isn't drinking, and she's even better when her medications are under control." He glanced between Kevin and Charles, blatantly pleading for understanding. "And I know it's no excuse, but, between Glen's care, my business, a teenage son, and Sandra, … I just couldn't deal with it all." He locked his fingers together, staring down at them. "So I took the easy way out."

Charles sat forward. "What?" Shock and horror shone from his young face. "No! You're lying! No," he said, shaking his head frantically. "You have to be lying!"

"Why?" prodded Kevin, needing to push Charles as far as possible.

"It's just not possible." Charles stood, gripping the edge of the table in a white-knuckled grip. "It just can't be how it happened."

"Because then everything you've done since your sister's death was done for the wrong reasons?" suggested Kevin matter-of-factly.

"Exactly," murmured Charles, lost in his own world. He glared at the father he'd spent a lifetime hating. "You have to be wrong. Daisy was being abused. I saw the bruises, heard her cry at night. I knew it. It had to be you. You never took care of her. And you let that bitch keep neglecting her."

John shook his head frantically. "Don't call your mother that. Still, I can't hide your mother's problems anymore. It wasn't abuse. It was neglect. Sure she might have hit her once in a while but never badly. It was always the booze talking."

Kevin hated the denial on John's face. How often had Kevin heard the same thing from other families? Too often.

When Charles turned, face-to-face with his father, shame, even acceptance covered John's features. There was a sense of waiting for judgment to be passed …

Suddenly John realized what Kevin had said. "What do you mean, Charles did things for the wrong reasons? I don't understand." He turned to his son and asked, "Do you mean those threatening notes? You expected me to say I killed Marie? But I can't confess to something I didn't do."

"It doesn't matter right now." Kevin bypassed John's question, wanting more of his own answered first. "What precipitated your move to this place, so long ago, John?"

He shuddered. "That was a horrible time. The police investigated Daisy's death and finally determined it was accidental." He stopped speaking, visibly holding back tears.

"Even with that ruling, it seemed like the public persecuted us. So I moved everyone here. And, after losing Daisy, I wanted to be closer to my brother."

"I spoke to the police years ago. Tried to get them to take another look at you. But they weren't interested," Charles said.

Kevin sensed there was more to the story. "And Daisy?" he asked John.

"It was so hard to leave her behind, but we needed a fresh start. And Glen needed us too. I felt I could be of more use to the living." John slid a surreptitious glance his son's way. Charles glared at him, obviously not quite ready to give up all his long-held beliefs.

Kevin thought about that. It wasn't uncommon to leave an area for a fresh start. Moving a loved one from cemetery to cemetery was much more difficult. After a moment, he continued, "But that's not everything, is it? The problem goes back further, doesn't it?"

John looked at him in confusion. "I don't understand."

"Tell me about your brother's accident."

"What's to say? He ran his car off the road years ago. He was in his early thirties at the time and has been in a coma ever since. He had an affair with Sandra. Wanted to take her away, but she stayed with me. Though I disliked what he tried to do with my marriage, I haven't pulled the plug. Instead, I funneled tens of thousands of dollars into his care, hoping he might one day recover."

"More half-truths!" Charles interrupted, his fingers drumming the tabletop. "You inherited all the family businesses, Glen's house, his cars, in fact, his whole fortune. What did you have before his accident? Nothing—that's what." He turned his back on his father. "Accident, my ass."

Kevin watched their interaction with interest.

John held out his hands. "No, that's not true. What have I done to make you want to crucify me like this?"

Sarcastically Charles answered, "Nothing apparently, except let my sister be abused at the hands of a raving drunk."

There was no doubting Charles's sincerity. This man truly believed the worst about his father and wanted to see him hang. As Kevin turned to study John's face, an odd black shadow caught in his peripheral vision. Another presence hung around John. *Shit!* It had to be Glen, trying to control the scene. *And damn it.* This was a little out of Kevin's league. Where the hell was Stefan when you needed him?

Right here!

"Thank you!" whispered Kevin under his breath.

Get rid of the other cop.

Kevin called the other policeman over, for a moment of private conversation. Quickly the other man left. Kevin's actions received strange looks from both father and son.

"I have something a little odd to discuss with both of you." Kevin sat down, motioning for Charles to retake his seat, opposite him. "Very weird psychic occurrences are going on here that you both may or may not be aware of."

John stared at Kevin in astonishment.

Charles's face changed, almost a mockery of his former features, and he grinned malevolently. Obvious signs of possession—for those who knew what to look for—became more apparent by the second. As he spoke, there was no longer any doubt. The voice was hard, raspy, and mature, … well beyond Charles's normal voice.

"Finally you'll give me an opportunity to speak. *Hallelu-*

jah." The macabre laughter both fascinated and horrified Kevin. John's face twisted in confused horror, as he stared at his son. He obviously didn't understand.

"What's the matter, brother? Don't you recognize me?" Charles's face seemed to even elongate, shaping itself into a travesty of the more mature man.

"What? Charles, what's wrong?"

The laughter seared John. This time, even Kevin winced at the sound.

"You still don't understand, do you? You simpleton. I'm Glen, right now, … inside Charles. Using your precious weak son for my own purposes. He barely exists in here any longer. But this isn't about him. It's about you. Have you enjoyed my life, brother? The life you stole from me."

John went from disbelief to shock. "This … isn't possible. Is it?" Fearfully he looked from his son to Kevin. "Kevin, please tell me this isn't happening."

"Sorry, it's happening all right." Kevin didn't dare take his eyes off the malevolent manifestation in front of him. He'd never seen anything like it before.

And hopefully you won't ever again, murmured Stefan.

Kevin had forgotten Stefan's presence, faced with this new development. He wasn't sure what either of them could do at this point, except watch the scene play itself out.

"Are you really Glen?" John spoke faintly, obviously not believing what he'd witnessed so far.

"Of course. You never would pull that damn plug, would you?" Bitterness rolled as easily as the laughter had. "For years, I lie there, helpless, while you enjoyed my wealth, my hard work, my favorite whisky. God, I hated you, until I learned how to do this. Just look at what I've accomplished." Again the disembodied laughter chilled the air. "No way you'd have attained even a fraction of my success."

Kevin watched the awareness on John's face change from incredulity to shocked certainty.

John hastened to explain. "Dear God, I always hoped you'd wake up to enjoy a normal life."

"Sure you did. That's why you sold my car collection and disbanded my businesses. What kind of life would I have now? Do you even have *any* of my money left?"

John started to explain. "Well, I have some, but, with the economy and your care, … a lot of it is gone."

"Like hell. You gambled it in high-risk investments and lost most of it."

John tried to protest but to no avail.

"You should be a fucking millionaire many times over by now." Charles—rather Glen—grinned. "Now it's too late. You'll spend the rest of your life as a prisoner, just like you forced me to be!" His voice gained in volume, until, in the end, he was almost shouting at his hapless brother.

"For what? Why should I be punished?" John raised both hands. "I loved you. I spent hours at your bedside. I couldn't bear to let you go."

"For trying to kill me, you jealous, greedy, worthless son of a bitch."

"No, you can't know about that!" John whispered.

Kevin could only stare. Would the shocks never end? He'd never seen a family so full of pain, betrayal, and murderous intent.

"*I* know." Bitterness oozed from Glen. "You ran me off the road, hoping to kill me. When that failed to complete the deed, you felt guilty and refused to let me go. Bastard. Do you have any idea what you sentenced me to? To hear and understand everything but to have no way to communicate? No. You don't."

"You learned to do this"—John gestured at his son—"for revenge?" It was clearly all too much for John to take in. He leaned forward, hiding his face in his hands. His shoulders sagged against the weight of the evidence facing him. "Dear God, what have I done?"

"That's a good question. Just what did you do?" Kevin queried forcefully.

"He's right. I was so jealous," John admitted, guilt and pain dominating in his face. "He had, well, … everything. Both of our parents doted on him. Even Marie may have been his …" John stopped at the snort erupting from Charles's mouth.

"It's true. Everyone loved you, Glen," he snapped. Then, just as suddenly, all the air seemed to *whoosh* out, to deflate him, and he sagged forward. "I didn't mean to hurt you. We were both heading home from a dinner out. A rarity for us. But you'd bragged the whole time about all you had. Including Sandra. On the way home, you were in your fancy car ahead of me." He looked sorrowfully at the other two men. "What can I say? I gave in to a fit of jealous madness and ran him off the road." If possible, John sank even farther. "I'm so sorry, Glen."

"A little too late, brother." Glen snickered.

Enough was enough. Kevin stood and said, "John, let's get you downtown for a statement."

John, beaten, nodded. "What about Glen? We don't even know all he's done."

"That's something we may never know." And it bothered Kevin terribly. How could he stop someone like Glen?

John must have had the same thought. He pulled out his cell phone and automatically dialed a number. "Yes, this is

John Prescott. I need you to fulfill the requirements on the signed request form you've been holding for me. … Yes, that's the one. Thank you. No, I won't be in to say good-bye."

"What? You think you can pull the plug now, you ass-hole! I need a little more time first. Damn you." Charles raced out of the room, the surprise move giving him a head start.

Kevin raced after him, the officers and John at his heels, but Charles ran into his father's study, and opened the drawer on the right-hand side. He scrambled to pull out the loaded gun, as John walked in behind Kevin.

"Charles, don't do this!" John said. "Things are bad enough. Put the gun down. Please, we'll get you some help. Please!"

Charles laughed. This time it *almost* sounded like Charles. "You idiot. Do you really think Glen can take over my mind without my permission? We've been working on this for years. I like what we do when we're together. I didn't at the beginning, but I grew to like the sense of power and control I felt when he was with me."

Kevin knew things had gone south in a big hurry. He had no idea how to stop what would happen next. But his muscles tensed, awaiting an opportunity.

"You know Glen doted on Marie when she was born." Charles shrugged indifferently. "Her death came so close to his new awareness and abilities that, at first, he didn't understand what had happened. She'd come to him in confusion over her own death. It didn't take him long to figure out a way to keep her with him, at least temporarily, while he worked on a long-term solution. Once he figured that out, there was no stopping him." Charles nodded mockingly to Kevin, then continued to explain.

"When I heard we were moving right after Daisy's funeral, Glen panicked. He was sure the connection would be broken, without Daisy's body close by. He couldn't take the chance. And I, … I couldn't leave her behind. So I broke into the funeral home after the staff left and stole her remains that night before the ceremony. With a quick burial and a small private ceremony, no one noticed. Or should I say, no one gave a damn. Except Glen and I."

Charles glared at his father. "Then I wrapped her up in my hockey bag and moved her here at the same time the family moved. You say you wanted a fresh start, but you moved within days of her funeral. That was too fast for Glen to find a way to stay connected, so we couldn't leave her behind. And we had no time to find a better solution." He wrinkled his nose. "Of course that new city garden bed had just been planted, and it made for an easy place to keep her safe, while Glen continued to practice." Charles laughed at his dumbfounded father. "You still don't understand all he's done, do you? He was molesting and killing kids before his accident. You actually did society a big favor by running him off the road back then."

Kevin's stomach heaved, as he remembered hearing that Glen had been a long-time resident of the area.

"Dear God, that's not possible. Not Glen," John prayed aloud at the monstrosity of that belief. "How could he hurt those children? They didn't do anything to him. They were so young."

"He liked them young or old. He wasn't all that fussy, Father." Charles's face deepened, darkened, and he took on the look of Glen.

"I did many things that you have no idea about," Glen

said, Charles's personality submerged. "I kept Daisy with me on this side. I used her love for her precious brother, your Charles, to keep her with me. Even she doesn't know all I did before her time."

"The cold cases on my desk." Kevin shook his head. "Wow, what a family."

Charles pointed the gun at his father. "You never did know Glen, … or me, for that matter. I know him so much better than you ever could. I can't have you changing our system. Glen empowers me. Without Glen, what am I? Nothing."

The gun fired without warning. John fell backward.

Kevin crouched, his own gun in hand. The second police officer who had been hiding behind the door, launched into the room, his gun up and ready. "Charles, put down the gun."

Charles laughed and turned the gun on Kevin. "You can't beat me."

Kevin fired.

Twin pools of spurting red sprang from Charles's chest. Stunned horror filled his face. "No!" he cried out in disbelief, even as his body collapsed to the floor.

John had fallen face upward, one neat round hole in the center of his forehead. Dead. Kevin crouched beside him, futilely checking for a pulse.

"He's gone, Sutherland. No one could have survived that shot." The other cop stood up again.

"I know." Kevin sighed heavily as he walked over to where Charles laid. His eyes were still open but pain-filled and slightly glazed over. Yet, for the first time, his face looked normal—younger and innocent, as if Glen's influence had finally left.

"Kevin, I didn't want to kill him," Charles gasped. "It was my uncle. All my life I watched myself doing things." He panted heavily, his chest gushing more blood. "But I could never stop myself. Daisy, everything I did was for … Daisy. I let him do terrible things, in order to keep her soul safe from him. He told me …" Charles gasped.

"Take it easy, Charles. It's not a concern right now. Help is on the way." Kevin tried to soothe the fatally shot man.

"Like hell." He coughed, bloody foam ringing his lips. "Take it easy on Mom. We won't ever know the truth about my sister now. Mom was drunk so much of the time. … Please let Daisy be free … and safe from him … now." His fingers clenched spastically in Kevin's hand, before falling back, limp, to the carpet.

Charles was dead.

"Sir, I've called the station. Another ambulance is on its way."

Kevin nodded, staring grimly at the sad remains of what had once been a family.

CHAPTER 27

"WHY WON'T SHE wake up?" The pain and uncertainty from the last five days tore at Kevin. The regular doctors had more or less warned him that Alexis might never wake up. Stefan's specialist was out of town until tomorrow.

Kevin couldn't live with that. To think Glen might have succeeded in ruining more lives was unacceptable.

In the last few days, he'd hardly left Alexis's side.

Sleeping in the chair had been an uncomfortable experience. He'd long since taken over the small hospital room, using the hooks for his jackets, spare clothing, even his holster, which hung within easy reach.

He'd spent the long hours talking to Alexis too. Speaking of anything that might tweak her interest—like Arnie being offered a second chance, if he met certain conditions. Kevin spoke of the sad funerals for both John and Charles. He'd even told her that Daisy's remains had been placed in a small plot just outside of town, with daisies decorating the grave.

All to no avail. Alexis never moved an eyelash.

"She can't. I keep telling you that." Stefan sat comfortably on the single visitor's chair at Alexis's bedside.

Perched on the window ledge was Lissa, standing watch as always.

"Damn it." Frustrated, Kevin glared at his friend and

mentor. It was always the same irritating conversation. According to Stefan, Kevin had to go in after her. Only Kevin didn't know how. Which always precipitated the second ongoing conversation.

"Damn it, Stefan." Kevin was ready to tear his hair out. Instead, he satisfied himself with running his fingers through his hair in aggravation. "I don't know what to do."

"Yes, you do." Stefan was adamant.

Defeated, Kevin slumped on the side of Alexis's bed, opposite Stefan. "Okay, let's go over this one more time."

"There's nothing to go over. You have to go in there after her."

Kevin shot him a disgusted look. "Do you really think that I haven't tried?"

"Try again. That's the vision blocking you. This time, come from a position of love and not fear. Go ahead. The bed is big enough."

Kevin eyed the potential space in disbelief. Deciding that he'd have to trust Stefan, he sat down carefully on the bed, turning on his side to wrap his arms around her. She seemed so defenseless and lost. His heart hurt, if he thought about it for any length of time. He closed his eyes and slipped into her mind.

ALEXIS SMILED IN her frozen world. There was really nothing else to do. She'd been here forever, or at least it seemed that way. Day and night had melded and blended into one long stasis state. In truth, reality as she'd known it had long since faded away past the ice and cold. This condition had seeped into her consciousness. Caught and imprisoned, she just existed, happily unaware of ever being anything else, loving the beauty of the fragile wonderland of snowflakes and ice patterns.

Alexis?

Alexis hummed happily as she turned toward the sound. *Hello, Daisy! How are you?*

I'm fine. … The little girl hesitated, watching Alexis curiously. *How are you doing?*

I'm doing good. I'm happy you came to visit me.

The child worried her bottom lip. *Uh, Alexis? How can you be so happy here?*

Why wouldn't I be? Alexis didn't understand what the child meant—and didn't care either.

Because now you're his prisoner.

I'm what? She laughed. *Nonsense. I'm no one's prisoner.*

Slowly Daisy dipped her head. *Yes, you are.*

At first, Alexis let foggy confusion cloud her comprehension, but the longer she gazed at the slowly nodding child, fragments of Alexis's old world seeped in. Recognition and comprehension slowly slid back into her reality. *Is this … what happened to you?* she asked Daisy.

Daisy nodded, her curls bouncing, even as her eyes reflected windows of sadness.

Alexis couldn't believe what she'd so easily forgotten.

That's him. He keeps you in a fog for a while. It helps you to detach from those you left.

Fear spiked through Alexis, stopping her cold. *Am I dead?*

Daisy's eyes commiserated with Alexis's plight. But she didn't answer.

I can't be. No, she added more definitively. *I'm not dead. Dying maybe but not dead. At least not yet.*

Daisy made a tiny, almost imperceptible shrug but remained silent. The truth would be shown soon enough.

Alexis tried to focus. Visions of her other world had been dipping in and out of her mind for a while, but they'd gradually faded off into the distance. Now she deliberately searched for those fragments, drawing them to the forefront.

Focused, she visualized those she loved, as brightly and intensely as she could.

Kevin.

Kevin. … He was worth fighting for.

Damn right!

Alexis smiled. Her visualization was so strong, she could even hear his voice.

What the hell have you been doing? We've been calling for you for days. You never answered.

It was him! Dear heavens, but it was good to hear Kevin's voice.

You scared the shit out of me, he said.

Kevin's gravelly tones shrank the emptiness in her world and lit up her heart. *Damn, I thought I'd never hear your beloved voice again.*

Beloved? I like the sound of that.

But I'll only be happy when you're back, back where you belong. So come home, sweetheart, please!

Show me the way, and I'd love to, Alexis muttered sarcastically.

That gave him pause. *Can't you get home?*

I can't see *where home is.*

Why not? Kevin pressed her.

He's blocking me. I'm trying, but I only get vague sensations of my past. I can feel you, but it's different than everything else in my world here.

I should bloody well hope so. Kevin snorted. *I hate to tell you, sweetheart, but that's your fear talking. He is dead.*

Dead? He is not! His wasted body might be but not that evil soul. Alexis knew that for truth, at a deep, elemental level. She could still feel his pulsing evil presence. No way this was leftover energy from his earthly sojourn.

Kevin rushed to reassure her. *He is. They pulled the plug on his life support system days ago. In fact, I think Glen's funeral was yesterday.*

But she'd have none of it. Instead fear clawed at her throat. She had to make Kevin believe. *He's got you fooled into thinking he's dead, but he's still here,* she enunciated forcibly. *Feel him yourself.*

Kevin's energy flared in disbelief. *It can't be.*

Well, he is. Alexis felt agitation wiping out her calm. The pervasive sense of evil smothered her newfound focus. Not good.

Wait. Kevin's energy distorted, as he went deeper into his own consciousness.

Dread filled the yawning silence. She needed Kevin to believe her. They couldn't lose track of the asshole at this point. If Glen could go underground to such an extent, no telling the damage he could inflict on the unsuspecting world.

He did say something about having a plan to continue his existence. But I didn't believe him because he said he needed a little more time. As Kevin spoke, his voice oddly thinned out. *I never really thought about it, with so much else happening.*

Alexis thought on it furiously. What choices were available to a madman without a body? *He must have found another host, an even weaker one this time—one that would allow him complete control. One he could overwhelm so inclusively that the person only existed to function on a physical level. And to do his bidding.*

Hell.

I'm right. I know it. I think he tried it with me, or … he's planning to later.

Who else would he have chosen? Who was close enough to him to accept this hooks into that strongly? *For just a while. We have to stop him. Alexis, come back home.*

You have to help me. I'm not strong enough to get free and to fight him alone. Once again, apprehension built. Only now there was the added dread of being left alone once again. Maybe forever.

Yes, you are strong enough. I've never seen anyone shine like you have. You are strong enough. You just have to beli—

His energy blinked out.

Kevin? Kevin, come back. What's wrong?

But he was gone.

She didn't know how, but she knew something bad had happened to him. His energy hadn't faded—it had vanished. Just winked out.

Or been vanquished.

Panic set in. The icy cage, instead of being a winter wonderland, instantly reverted to being a prison of isolation and cold. She had to get out. Kevin was in desperate trouble.

She had to help him.

Using everything she'd learned, she reconnected with the reality of the physical world. Stronger and faster, the puzzle pieces finally floated into place with her renewed purpose. But, with every step of visible progress, she had to struggle harder and harder. She had to get to Kevin. Each second she could move forward brought her closer.

Until she came up against a blank wall of deep, thick, impenetrable ice.

No matter what she tried, she couldn't get through it.

Daisy's forlorn face peered at her from the other side. Before, when Alexis had been less aware of her imprisonment, she hadn't seen the density of the ice. Now she knew it was as impossible a barrier to cross as the Atlantic Ocean in a hurricane.

Aggravated and depressed, she slumped back to regroup. Fear kept her nerves firing with continuous panic messages. Her heartbeats thrummed through her soul. She had to get to Kevin.

How, damn it?

Silence greeted her.

It couldn't end like this. The bastard couldn't win. Alexis railed at her world. *Not this time*, she vowed fiercely. *Not this time!*

She directed her fury against the frozen vastness, blasting at her stalagmite barriers.

Again nothing happened.

Her heart wept. She hadn't really expected that to work. It wasn't her style. Her back stiffened; then she laughed for sheer joy. Of course it wasn't her style. She wasn't a fighter. She was a healer. She could receive and transmit energy. And, with that memory, it clicked.

On her new path, she opened her heart and sent out warm loving energy, just as she would for an ailing plant. Thinking it might help, she transmitted a thick broadband of power toward Kevin. Even as the love flowed from her psyche, thick fat droplets of water dripped down the icy prison walls. She turned up the heat, firing warm colors and powerful energy outward at the ice, already cracking under the curing power of her love.

Long seconds later, she was free.

And back in her body.

An almost soundless groan escaped, as she assimilated her mind into her physical world.

No one noticed, so locked were they in the frozen tableau playing out in her hospital room.

Alexis opened her eyes a faint crack, trying to decipher the strange feel to the atmosphere.

Relief swelled in her heart, as she recognized that the heavy weight over her waist was Kevin's arm. Her relief quickly turned to horror. His arm was limp and lifeless. What was wrong? She cracked her eyes open a little more.

Only to slam them closed.

Shit!

Carefully she peeked again. Sandra, wearing a hospital gown, held a handgun in her weak fingers. It looked like Kevin's gun.

Stefan stood mere steps from the smoking firearm. "Easy, Sandra, take it easy. Please, we need to get help for Kevin."

Quiet, Alex!

Alexis started at Lissa's caution.

Kevin's hurt. Help him, but don't let anyone know that you're back. Stefan will take care of Glen.

What? She was still groggy and disoriented. Her mind struggled to adapt. Something about Kevin being in danger? Right. That's what had snapped her back.

Then she sensed what was wrong. Alexis plunged into Kevin's mind and into his body. Dear God, he'd been shot! His searing pain stabbed through her.

Alexis ceased to be in that moment.

She gave of herself and liberated the loving energy of her own body and transmitted it to him. With that, she opened the door between them. Not just the door between their minds but the door between their souls.

Waves of her loving energy poured through him, becoming one with him. Blood seeped through the wound in his side, dripping relentlessly onto her hospital bed. Her energy received the pain, even as she transmitted her healthy energy into him. Mending. Rebuilding. Healing.

Hot energy flashed and sparked, as it encompassed the injury, warming and communicating with the damaged cells. She understood something momentous was happening. A bonding that could only be broken by death … and maybe not even by that.

She transmitted every healing thing she could pull from her energy, his energy, and that from those around her. *Heal. Be strong. Help is on its way. Be one and be whole—join with me. Together we can finish this. Together we are stronger. Undefeatable.*

The lights in the room flickered, as she pulled in even more power to transmit to Kevin.

She shifted slightly, snuggling against his unconscious body.

Groggy whispers echoed through her mind. *Alexis, in case I don't make it …*

Shh! None of that. You'll be fine. Feel the healing, it's unmistakable.

You're in my mind! And my body? Amazement poured off him. *See? I told you. You're phenomenal.*

Her warm energy radiated, laughing in triumph—even ringed as it was with fatigue. *And I will celebrate, when this is over.* She widened the energy pathways, pulling healing energy from the world around her into her space and transmitting the life force for his body to use. She poured all that she was into him. Why the sheets weren't burning with the heat, she didn't know. She turned it up a notch, feeling the drain on her resources at the new demands.

Stop! You're exhausting yourself. I'm fine now. Stop it, Kevin added sharply.

Instinctively she toned down her actions and checked her own energy levels. *I'm okay. I'm trying to read Sandra's energy at the same time.*

What?

Check out what's going on in the room. Her voice wavered. She wasn't strong enough to do this for long.

STEFAN WATCHED THE continuing tussle on both levels as it played out in front of him.

It appeared that the ultimate act of firing the gun had brought Sandra back to the forefront, and she was now caught in the horrifying battle for life, … with Glen trying to control her every move.

Sandra, who'd hidden from most of the unpleasant issues of her life, couldn't seem to bring herself to fire the weapon a second time. The war in her head seemed to be more than she could deal with. She no longer knew who she was, … only who she wasn't.

The struggle was mirrored in the wild expression in her eyes and in her tortuous, snarling features, as the fight continued for control of her physical body.

Stefan and Lissa could only watch, helpless to do anything.

SANDRA, WHISPERED ALEXIS urgently, inside the older

woman's confused mind. *Fight, Sandra. You can't let Glen win. He's taken everyone you love from you. Fight, Sandra.*

I can't, whimpered the tired woman. *I loved him once. He's too strong, and he knows me too well.*

Yes, you can. If you let him win, you will be no more. Fight! Alexis ordered harshly. Sandra had curled up, defenseless, in a tiny corner of her own mind, helpless to continue the unfair battle that Glen was winning.

Forget about her. She's weak, Glen said, and then his harsh laughter amplified ten times over in the small space.

Alexis's fury knew no bounds. This man couldn't be allowed to continue. *Sandra, he killed John. He killed Charles. Don't let him continue.*

What would get the woman's attention? Alexis didn't know the truth, and, knowing that Sandra wouldn't know at this point either, Alexis pulled out all the stops. *Glen killed Marie. He had been abusing her for years before. And he made you carry the guilt for that because you chose John over him.*

That caught Sandra's attention. Her quavering voice asked, *Do you really think he killed my baby girl?*

Pity welled in Alexis's heart. This poor woman. *Yes, Sandra, I really do. Worse, Sandra, he abused Marie before she died by controlling you. He hurt her through you. Over and over again. He enjoyed it. Making her suffer. Making many other children suffer. … Making you suffer. Don't let him live to hurt more children. Sandra, fight! Please!* Alexis pleaded anxiously. Sandra had to stand up for her right to her own life.

But in her mind, Sandra squeezed into the tightest ball that she could be. It was a feeble attempt to protect herself against the villain living in her soul.

Glen mocked her. *What the hell will you do, Sandra? I am in control, not you. Stupid bitch!*

Sandra was flung back against the wall by an unseen power that came out of nowhere, dominating and controlling her, as he would a cringing pet.

But everyone has a breaking point, and Sandra had finally reached hers. Alexis watched the painful video of horrid thoughts pouring through Sandra's damaged mind. How many times had this man controlled her like this, making her do things she didn't remember? Would anyone ever know the extent of the damage inflicted by this madman?

Alexis held her breath and watched anxiously, as Sandra gathered her failing strength for one last battle.

Dismissing Sandra as already lost, Glen redirected his energy toward Alexis, casually flicking her out of Sandra's mind and slamming her back into her own.

There was no time to adjust. Alexis opened her eyes to watch the scene unfold in slow motion.

Sandra lifted the handgun, pointing it first at the couple entwined on the bed, zeroing in on Glen's choice of target, before lifting it in an agonizingly stilted motion to her own head. She held it there, fighting for supremacy, for what seemed like an eternity.

No! came the eerie echo reverberating inside Alexis's mind. At the same time noises filled the room, as Glen fought desperately in his losing battle for dominance against Sandra's will.

In breathless horror, the audience could only watch.

Sandra pulled the trigger.

Blood and brain splattered across the room.

Sandra had won … and lost.

Traumatized silence reigned.

Then the air was filled with sounds of yelling and running, footsteps rushing toward them.

Alexis closed her eyes. What a waste …

Relief, sadness, and thankfulness filled her. It was over.

Exhaustion washed over her, pulling her under. And she let it, happy to sink back into the sea of semiconsciousness, connected as one with Kevin, barely aware and wholly uncaring of the chaos going on around her.

CHAPTER 28

Three Weeks Later

"ALEXIS, ARE YOU sure you're ready for this?"

The group gathered comfortably in a circle on Stefan's living room floor. The ritual of drinks had already been observed, and they were now ready for the evening's work.

Alexis smiled at Stefan. "I'm definitely ready. Besides, I'm not the one who got shot," she teased the quiet man, sitting close to her.

Kevin smiled at her, reaching out to tousle her hair. "I'm fine. I'll get a lot of mileage out of my injury, won't I?"

"Maybe," she agreed cheekily. "At least until the next time."

He snorted. "As it won't happen again, don't hold your breath. Besides, I'm not the one who tangled with a serial killer's twisted mind."

A sobering reminder. "True. That's why it's important we finish tonight's work. Only then will this be over. For what Glen did to Daisy and all those other children, he deserved to be in a coma all those years. But those children need to be freed."

"The children have been there for a long time. If they have to wait a little longer, it won't make that much difference. He can't hurt them now."

They still didn't know how many early victims of Glen's were caught in-between. Alexis hoped they would eventually, but … "No." Alexis was resolute. "Tonight we rescue them and show them the way home."

Some of the victims' bodies might never be found, but, at least this way, she could rest easy, knowing that their souls were free to go on. She hadn't seen the little boy, Eric, since the first time, but she knew he still wandered, lost.

Kevin was following up on several of the other leads, if only to find closure for his sake and for the sake of the children's families. Maybe more victims would surface and maybe not. This was enough for now. She smiled at the two friends who had shown her so much. Lissa sat with them, her form just visible enough for Alexis to see.

She didn't want sadness to destroy their efforts tonight, but she couldn't resist asking, *Lissa, you do know that I'll be okay now, right? … If it's time for you to leave, I'll understand, and I'll be happy for you.*

Alexis dreaded her sister's answer. But, after seeing those children locked in-between life and death and beyond, Alexis knew that, no matter how much she missed her sister's presence, she wouldn't wish that on any soul.

Lissa's tinkling laughter whispered through the room, with the softness of a warm wind. *I'll be here for a little while longer. I'm sure other people could use my loving assistance with their lives.* She looked pointedly at Stefan.

Alexis grinned. Was it her imagination, or did Stefan look decidedly uncomfortable at Lissa's suggested inference? "Then let's begin." Closing her eyes, Alexis opened the door in her mind, then released loving energy waves to create a path forward.

She opened her eyes to see Daisy laughing, running down the path, a string of children following her.

This concludes Book 4 of Psychic Visions:
Garden of Sorrow.

Read the first chapter of *Knock, Knock* …
from Psychic Visions, Book 5

PSYCHIC VISIONS: KNOCK KNOCK... (BOOK #5)
CHAPTER 1

There is no revenge so complete as forgiveness.
—Josh Billings

ICE HIT HER first. Inside and out.

Shay Lassiter woke to find goose bumps marching across her cold skin in the early morning. She tugged up the chocolate-brown duvet she'd thrown off sometime in the night, but even that didn't account for the cold filtering slowly through her waking consciousness. The rest of her brain screamed at her to wake up all the way. *Something was off.*

Morris, the ever-present ghost of her beloved childhood pet, snuggled up close. She didn't understand the miracle of his existence, but she rejoiced in it every day. The deep purr rumbled at her shoulder, making her smile. She was thankful his gentle blue ball of energy sat on her bed most days. She rarely saw him in physical form, but he was always there in spirit—offering immeasurable comfort. Most times, the sound of his engine powered through the small room. That oversize orange tabby had been the size of a small car but had a diesel truck motor for an engine.

The purr shut off.

Shit.

Her internal alarm finally kicked in, as the bedding pressed down on her, confining, where moments before it had been comforting. She threw back the duvet, springing from bed, her heart pounding. A clammy film coated her skin. *What the hell was wrong?*

She spun around, searching her darkened bedroom for the cause of the unease, settling deep in her soul.

No one was here with her.

Last night she'd gone to sleep without a problem. That was surprising because she'd had an argument with her fiancé, Darren, before going to sleep. And it had been a bad one, making her doubt their relationship … again. But still, she knew that discord hadn't created this type of response. Her psyche often chose the wee hours of the morning to wake her up and to chew away at her, but she'd never woken up quite like this. Shivering, she looked down at her cami and boy shorts to see the hairs rising on her smooth skin. Her teeth chattered, as she ran to check the thermostat in her room. It was normal.

Of course it was. It *should* be warm; it was summertime.

She ran back to bed and huddled against her headboard, her duvet high up on her chest.

Shay?

Stefan Kronos spoke; his familiar voice swept through her mind, calming her. He must have heard her silent distress in the night. *Stefan? Something's wrong. Only I can't see what it is.*

I'll check it out.

The emptiness in her mind told her that Stefan had left. God, she didn't know what she'd do without him. He didn't always respond this quickly, but her psychic friend always knew when something was wrong.

Then she heard *it* ...

The *click* of her front door opening, ... then closing. Something moved across her living room floor.

She had an intruder.

Alarm swept through her. *Oh no.* The door had been locked. She'd double-checked it before going to bed. No way anyone could get in.

Unless they had a key.

Shay? Get out of the apartment. Stefan's sharp voice sliced through her frozen state. *A rogue energy is heading toward you.*

Too late, she whispered in her mind. *It's too late. He's inside already. Call for help, Stefan. Hurry!*

Hide. I'm getting help.

"Shay? Oh, hi, honey. I hadn't expected you to be awake." Her fiancé stood at her bedroom doorway, a crooked smile on his face. Darren held up a key in his hand. It gleamed in the slice of moonlight creeping through her drapes. Dressed all in black, he cut an elegant figure. His handsome good looks and confidence had been part of what had attracted her to him in the first place.

Relief swamped her. "Oh, thank God," she murmured and closed her eyes. Her rigid spine relaxed. Nothing to worry about after all. Feeling much better and slightly foolish, she opened her eyes and smiled warmly at him. So happy to see him after their fight and her initial panic.

It's just Darren, Stefan.

Silence filled her mind.

Darren? Stefan asked in a flat voice. *Your fiancé?*

Yes. She gave a small deprecating laugh.

Shay? Then ... why the fear?

Her eyes widened. Good question. "Darren, why are you here at this hour?" She glanced at the clock. "It's two in the morning." She stared at him, confused, as something else registered—finally. "And where did you get the key?"

He shifted away from the door, his smile widening. But something was off about that twist to his lips. A little too tight, and an odd glow added to the toothy shine. "When you wouldn't give me a key, I decided to have one made up on my own."

She blinked. That didn't make any sense. Did it? No. It was wrong. She tossed back her long brown hair, trying to clear her head. And wished her roiling stomach would calm. She couldn't seem to think straight. "Why? I don't understand."

His lips quirked. He tossed the key on the bed. "I know. But I figured that I had to do something. After all, we're fighting more lately. Not making up the same. It's as if we're on the verge of a breakup."

"Oh, I don't think—"

"Stop." He held up his hands. "You know you don't look at our relationship quite the same anymore. Neither do I." His hands dropped, and he shook his head. "You also know you've been spending more time on that damn Children's Hospital project than ever. Even when I said I didn't like it."

Oh, shit. He was breaking up with her. But then why get a key made? And of course she spent a lot of time on that project. It was special. The kids were special. He knew that.

Didn't he?

Why was nothing making any sense right now?

Stefan whispered through her mind. *Shay, something's wrong. What's happening?*

She stared at Darren. *I don't know.*

To her fiancé, she said, "I don't understand."

"I know you don't. That's okay. I can explain." He walked over and sat down at the edge of her bed. "It's too bad though. You're a beautiful lady. Inside and out."

"Thank you, I think?" Shay might be confused, but some truths made their way inside. He'd had a key to her home made without her permission, and he had let himself into her apartment in the middle of the night. Like Stefan had said, something was wrong.

And now she felt more than a little nauseated. And she felt ... slower. Her mind sluggish. As if she were in shock. Or hurt. ... But she wasn't. She gazed at her arms and the rest of her body. She felt weak, faint even, but not like she was injured in any way.

"You don't get it, do you, Shay?"

She stared up at him, puzzled. "No. And I'd appreciate it if you'd explain. This isn't very funny."

"No, it isn't. You ruined all my plans."

She tilted her head and tried to focus. "Plans?"

"Yes, plans." Looking relaxed and at ease, he crossed one leg over the other and then clasped his hands over his knees. "See. I need money. Lots of money."

Feeling foolish and spaced out, she asked, "Why?"

He smiled, a knowing smile. "For lots of things." He tilted his head and looked at her steadily. "Are you feeling okay?"

She tried to swallow, her tongue thick, unwieldy. "I don't know. I feel a bit ... weird actually."

"That's all quite normal. I'm making it easy on you."

Normal. What was *normal* about any of this? "I ... I don't understand."

He gave an exaggerated sigh. "No, I don't suppose you do. So let me make this simple." He stood and walked over to the window. "I need money. You have money. And, if we were together, that wouldn't be a problem. On top of your personal fortune, you control an amount that's unbelievably large. See? That's really attractive. Plus, taking you to bed isn't exactly a hardship." He leered at her. "In fact, that part has been sheer fun. I figured I was in clover. We were engaged—"

"Still are, I thought."

His smile didn't quite reach his eyes. "So you say. See? I understand the female mind. I know that you aren't as happy as you were. And, once that thread of discontent starts, it only gets worse. Our fight tonight was about moving up the wedding day. But you didn't want that. You're hesitating. And that means you have doubts. And doubts are dangerous because they could mean the end of my plans—and make me very unhappy." He moved the blinds slightly. "I can't have that."

He sighed. "I thought I could save you. … I have to admit that even now I'm having doubts …" He cocked his head and stared at her.

She could barely see a softening in his features. A pondering. A weighing of options.

Then he straightened, stuck out his chin, and shook his head. "No. It has to be this way." The moonlight shone in through the crack between the blinds. "Too bad though. You showed such promise."

Shay closed her eyes, as his words and tones filtered through the growing fog in her brain. *Stefan, Dear God, I need help.*

It's coming. Stay with me.

I don't know if I can. I don't know what's happening.

Nothing good! Damn it. I told you someone better was out there.

She would have laughed if she could. Instead a strange lassitude had filled her veins, mixed into her bloodstream. *I can't think.* The buzz of Stefan's thoughts disturbed the clouds fogging her mind.

Shay, read his energy. Shay? Shay! Damn it, stay with me. You need to read his energy.

She didn't want to. It was difficult. She could barely understand Stefan's instructions. Something about Darren's energy. Her head lolled to the side. "What did you do to me?"

"Well, I'm punishing you of course. Actually it's not that much of a punishment. If I thought I could control you, I'd keep you around, but I can't. The decision has been made." He paused and tilted his head. "You're strong, you know? Not as strong as me, of course, but still strong."

He hesitated; his gaze turned inward, as if listening to an inner voice. Then sighed and shook his head. "No. I can't change my plans. If you ever found out what you could do with all that strength, ... if you could be trained to use it properly, ... but no. You aren't trainable. I've seen that already." He walked around the bed, studying her. "It's almost over. See? This is a nice way to go. Just fall asleep, and you'll be gone. But, of course, everyone resists it. Too bad. So sad. Everyone keeps clinging to their pathetic little lives, even when that point is long gone."

Then she got it. *Oh, God.* "You'll kill me?" The fog deepened. She struggled to push it back. To find clarity. To find answers. To find a way out of this hell. Stefan had said, "Read his energy." Not an easy task. The fog thinned slightly, a small victory, and she tried to shift her vision to see Darren's energy.

As she'd done, when things became serious between them. It was almost instinctive self-preservation to do so. She'd discovered he had a few anger issues, a few regrets, some energy heading into his past. A few walls, saying he had a few secrets, but nothing to make her feel like she should delve deeper into the core of the man.

And now she realized her mistake. When it was too late to do anything about it.

She'd believed what she'd seen. The facade he'd presented. And had missed seeing him for who he really was. On the inside.

He was talking again, preening. "You live out your days, worrying about what to do with all that lovely money. Oh, poor you. You were so focused, you never even saw who came knocking on your door. Didn't really see me. Not as I am inside. Only as I wanted you to see me."

She closed her eyes and opened her senses. With her fading strength, it was easier to function entirely on a soul energy level. The physical form was so much harder to sustain and to control as it failed around her.

Clouds of dark black, sickly green energy surrounded him. Like a hard shell, it protected him on the inside, while he … *While he what?*

She couldn't see clearly enough. Fog rolled in. She blinked several times, trying hard to understand. A long cord from his root chakra trailed to … the bed. And then to her. *He'd connected a cord to her.*

That connection, in itself, wasn't the issue. Most people had hooks or cords into others but not like this one.

Stefan's voice murmured deep in her psyche. *Stay with*

me, Shay. The cops will be there within minutes.

Too late, she whispered. *His energy ... It's sick. Deep, dark, diseased. Dying. Stefan, see it for yourself. I can see him. The real him. He's been hiding all this time. Somehow masking who he really was.*

And that betrayal hurt. So much. She'd loved Darren. Had planned to marry him and to bear his children. She had planned to link her life with this man, who now stood so separate from her, watching her die by his own intent. Dear God. How had this happened? How had she not seen the man for who he was?

Because he could hide himself. And his personality is what's sick. He's not dying. You are!

Her thoughts drifted, scattered. *How is he doing this? I feel so weak. It's as if he's draining my very soul.* She couldn't hold a focus. She understood in theory what Stefan had said, ... but reality felt distant. Like this was happening to someone else.

He's opened your heart chakra. Draining your energy in a torrential wash. He'll syphon you dry.

She pondered that bit of information. She should be upset about it. Should probably care. But it was hard to connect the information to its logical outcome—to use it.

You have to do something, urged Stefan. *Don't fight it. Embrace him with love. Start from that power position. Remember? Energy is everywhere. You cannot be drained, if you remember that universal energy flows through you at all times.*

She blinked at the tidbits of understanding as they filtered in.

Know that I am here. Part of you. As he drains you, I'm refilling you with love.

She couldn't move; she couldn't do anything but exist,

caught in a war between life and death. *How?*

Open your crown chakra to the universal energy. Create a spinning loop between your chakras to build power. But protect yourself. Don't let him see you turn the tide of the energy flow. I will start it for you, but you have to help yourself.

His words penetrated more slowly than the energy. By the time she understood what Stefan meant, she was working on her crown chakra, opening it. She already felt the effects, and, bolstered by the rise in her own energy, she immediately picked up the pace, refilling her body, enlivening her soul.

Don't feed the anger. Feed the love. Feel the power in the loving energy. Feel it strengthen you on all levels. You don't have to be his victim.

I can make him my victim. She had to admit, a part of her loved that idea.

Don't. It will change you. It will be something you will never forget. We need to find another way.

There isn't one. We can't hold him off forever, she whispered. *And how else can anyone stop him? Or others like him?*

Stefan's silence gave her the answer. She could stay in this unlimited loop, or she could do something about it. Something lethal. What choice was there? She had to do something before Darren realized what was happening. Shay focused on funneling more and more universal energy through her body, creating a swirling vortex within her. Gaining strength. Gaining purpose. Gaining determination for what was to come.

"How many have you killed?" she whispered, letting her eyes close weakly. He needed to believe she was dying. That he'd won. And she needed to know the extent of the damage he'd inflicted on those around him. To know she was doing the right thing in destroying him.

Darren stepped closer to hear her question. "How many? Is that what you asked?"

"Yes." She kept her eyes closed, focused on the energy pouring through her, gathering, waiting for the right time.

He laughed. "So many. It's really easy, once you understand how. The biggest trick is hiding what I'm doing, until I'm ready for people to know. Like you. You're very intuitive. Very astute. I had to be especially alert in your case. It was good for a while. Kept me on my toes. But tonight I deposited a nice fat check you were kind enough to write out for me." He laughed. "Oh, you don't remember writing me a check, do you? That's okay. I'm great at forging signatures too. I stole the checks a while ago. ... It's not like you'll need them after today."

"How many?" Her voice gained a desperate strength. She needed to know. Even one death was too many. If he'd killed other people, she'd have no problem doing what needed to be done. She'd have to. He had to be stopped before he went on to kill again.

In the far distance, she heard sirens.

"Isn't that nice? You're curious. You can't stop the process now, you know? I chose Friday on purpose. No one will find you until Monday. When you don't show up for work, they will come looking." He glanced around the bedroom. "It's really too bad. I'd so hoped that this would be my forever home." He chuckled. "Odd to think I'm still using that childhood phrase. So few would understand it."

"How many?" she insisted, her voice stronger, as anger stirred dangerously close to the surface. She had to keep herself in check. Had to keep her anger reined in. She had to take him out the right way. Or her actions would be impossible to live with.

He laughed. "Dozens, over the years."

Dozens. And, with that, she knew there was no one else to stop him, no other way to stop him. He had ways of killing people that no one would ever know. That no one would ever understand. That no one would prove. He had to be stopped. And so few people were capable of doing that.

She was one of them. Stefan was another. *Stefan. I need all you can channel my way.*

I'm open and pouring. Do it. We can't hang on like this for much longer.

She opened her eyes and stared at the man she'd once loved. Now her heart was filled with loathing for what he'd done—she hated him with a passion that fed her actions like she'd never felt before. But she had to find a way past that to the core of love from one human being to another. She had to come from a soul level.

She could do that. "Darren."

He looked up at her, a sarcastic smile on his face. "What's the matter, Shay? Aren't you going to plead for your life?" he asked mockingly.

She made it look agonizingly difficult to raise her arm and to motion him closer. And to make that arm drop down weakly to the bed. He thought he'd almost drained her dry and had no idea what she could do. Good. She just needed him a little closer.

He scooted down the bed, his hip pushing up against her thigh. Now, if she could only reach … Her arm trembled with effort as she stretched it out and placed her hand on his chest. Right over his heart.

Barely holding the building energy force back, she asked, *Stefan, are you ready?*

"What did you want to say, dearest Shay?" Darren's

mocking voice floated through the room, surrounding her. Filling her. Firing her actions.

She opened up her swirling vortex. In her mind, she said to Stefan, *Now.*

She looked Darren in his eyes and whispered, "Go to hell."

She channeled the vortex to jettison the stream of loving soul energy forward to his heart—the actual organ—with all the energy that she could manage. With all the caring she could find.

He gasped once, his eyes going wide.

Shock and disbelief flashed, livid on his face. Understanding lit the deep depths of his gaze. But it was too late for him to act. His opportunity was gone, before he ever saw it.

Or, maybe, it wasn't.

Even as his eyes darkened, a firestorm of energy ricocheted through his heart chakra and back into her, burning through her palm as some type of fireball lit the room.

Something else—*someone else*—had joined the fray. And combined, they were stronger, more powerful, and … desperate … to survive.

Shay continued to pour energy, opening herself up to the universe and channeling everything she could access into the fight. *Stefan. What's happening?*

I don't know. Another element has been added. Possibly another person …

Then we can't win, she cried out in pain and frustration. *That's two against two. And they have the advantage. How do we save this?*

Look out! A small blue fireball leaped from her bed and flew into the energy, torrenting through her hand.

No! Shay cried out.

It was too late. Morris, her ghostly feline, had joined the fight—and had turned the tide as his loving, protective energy joined hers. There was a momentary pause, as if both sides were reevaluating the balance of power, and then a deep purr sounded from the center of the maelstrom.

The space beneath her hand exploded.

Shay was thrown back against the headboard.

Darren was flung to the floor.

Regaining her wits, Shay scrambled to her feet to look over the edge of the bed.

Darren's features had frozen, his mouth open in a horrible rictus of terror, and, like a tidal wave after it has lashed a beach and receded back into the ocean, the color had slipped from his skin—leaving a gray wasteland behind.

But he was still alive.

Her heart squeezed tighter. Pain and shock rippled through her.

His eyes dimmed.

And that's when she saw it. A second light inside. A second awareness? A second person? A different part of Darren? How? Was he manipulated? Possessed? Or was this the other "something" that had joined the fray?

She cried out, *Stefan, look!*

But it was too late to stop the process.

A deep sigh whispered from Darren's chest one last time, and his eyelids dropped closed.

He was dead.

Book 5 is available now!

To find out more, visit Dale Mayer's website.

https://geni.us/dmknock

Simon Says...: Kate Morgan (Book #1)

Welcome to a new thriller series from *USA Today* Best-Selling Author Dale Mayer. Set in Vancouver, BC, the team of Detective Kate Morgan and Simon St. Laurant, an unwilling psychic, marries all the elements of Dale's work that you've come to love, plus so much more.

Detective Kate Morgan, newly promoted to the Vancouver PD Homicide Department, stands for the victims in her world. She was once a victim herself, just as her mother had been a victim, and then her brother—an unsolved missing child's case—was yet another victim. She can't stand those who take advantage of others, and the worst ones are those who prey on the hopes of desperate people to line their own pockets.

So, when she finds a connection between more than a half-dozen cold cases to a current case, where a child's life hangs in the balance, Kate would make a deal with the devil himself to find the culprit and to save the child.

Simon St. Laurant's grandmother had the Sight and had warned him that, once he used it, he could never walk away. Until now, her caution had made it easy to avoid that first step. But, when nightmares of his own past are triggered, Simon can't stand back and watch child after child be abused. Not without offering his help to those chasing the monsters.

Even if it means dealing with the cranky and critical Detective Kate Morgan …

Find Simon Says… Hide here!

To find out more visit Dale Mayer's website.

https://geni.us/DMSSHideUniversal

Author's Note

Thank you for reading Garden of Sorrow: Psychic Visions, Book 4! If you enjoyed the book, please take a moment and leave a short review.

Dear reader,

I love to hear from readers, and you can contact me at my website: www.dalemayer.com or at my Facebook author page. To be informed of new releases and special offers, sign up for my newsletter or follow me on BookBub. And if you are interested in joining Dale Mayer's Reader Group, here is the Facebook sign up page.
http://geni.us/DaleMayerFBGroup

Cheers,
Dale Mayer

About the Author

Dale Mayer is a *USA Today* best-selling author, best known for her SEALs military romances, her Psychic Visions series, and her Lovely Lethal Garden cozy series. Her contemporary romances are raw and full of passion and emotion (Broken But … Mending, Hathaway House series). Her thrillers will keep you guessing (Kate Morgan, By Death series), and her romantic comedies will keep you giggling (*It's a Dog's Life*, a stand-alone novella; and the Broken Protocols series, starring Charming Marvin, the cat).

Dale honors the stories that come to her—and some of them are crazy, break all the rules and cross multiple genres!

To go with her fiction, she also writes nonfiction in many different fields, with books available on résumé writing, companion gardening, and the US mortgage system. All her books are available in print and ebook format.

Connect with Dale Mayer Online

Dale's Website – www.dalemayer.com

Twitter – @DaleMayer

Facebook Page – geni.us/DaleMayerFBFanPage

Facebook Group – geni.us/DaleMayerFBGroup

BookBub – geni.us/DaleMayerBookbub

Instagram – geni.us/DaleMayerInstagram

Goodreads – geni.us/DaleMayerGoodreads

Newsletter – geni.us/DaleNews

Also by Dale Mayer

Published Adult Books:

Bullard's Battle

Ryland's Reach, Book 1

Cain's Cross, Book 2

Eton's Escape, Book 3

Garret's Gambit, Book 4

Kano's Keep, Book 5

Fallon's Flaw, Book 6

Quinn's Quest, Book 7

Bullard's Beauty, Book 8

Bullard's Best, Book 9

Terkel's Team

Damon's Deal, Book 1

Wade's War, Book 2

Gage's Goal, Book 3

Calum's Contact, Book 4

Kate Morgan

Simon Says… Hide, Book 1

Simon Says… Jump, Book 2

Simon Says… Ride, Book 3

Simon Says… Scream, Book 4

Hathaway House

Aaron, Book 1

Brock, Book 2

Cole, Book 3

Denton, Book 4

Elliot, Book 5

Finn, Book 6

Gregory, Book 7

Heath, Book 8

Iain, Book 9

Jaden, Book 10

Keith, Book 11

Lance, Book 12

Melissa, Book 13

Nash, Book 14

Owen, Book 15

Percy, Book 16

Hathaway House, Books 1–3

Hathaway House, Books 4–6

Hathaway House, Books 7–9

The K9 Files

Ethan, Book 1

Pierce, Book 2

Zane, Book 3

Blaze, Book 4

Lucas, Book 5

Parker, Book 6

Carter, Book 7

Weston, Book 8

Greyson, Book 9

Rowan, Book 10

Caleb, Book 11

Kurt, Book 12

Tucker, Book 13

Harley, Book 14

Kyron, Book 15

Jenner, Book 16

The K9 Files, Books 1–2

The K9 Files, Books 3–4

The K9 Files, Books 5–6

The K9 Files, Books 7–8

The K9 Files, Books 9–10

The K9 Files, Books 11–12

Lovely Lethal Gardens

Arsenic in the Azaleas, Book 1

Bones in the Begonias, Book 2

Corpse in the Carnations, Book 3

Daggers in the Dahlias, Book 4

Evidence in the Echinacea, Book 5

Footprints in the Ferns, Book 6

Gun in the Gardenias, Book 7

Handcuffs in the Heather, Book 8

Ice Pick in the Ivy, Book 9

Jewels in the Juniper, Book 10

Killer in the Kiwis, Book 11

Lifeless in the Lilies, Book 12

Murder in the Marigolds, Book 13

Nabbed in the Nasturtiums, Book 14

Offed in the Orchids, Book 15

Poison in the Pansies, Book 16

Quarry in the Quince, Book 17

Lovely Lethal Gardens, Books 1–2

Lovely Lethal Gardens, Books 3–4

Lovely Lethal Gardens, Books 5–6

Lovely Lethal Gardens, Books 7–8

Lovely Lethal Gardens, Books 9–10

Psychic Vision Series

Tuesday's Child

Hide 'n Go Seek

Maddy's Floor

Garden of Sorrow

Knock Knock…

Rare Find

Eyes to the Soul

Now You See Her

Shattered

Into the Abyss

Seeds of Malice

Eye of the Falcon

Itsy-Bitsy Spider

Unmasked

Deep Beneath

From the Ashes

Stroke of Death

Ice Maiden

Snap, Crackle…

What If…

Talking Bones

Psychic Visions Books 1–3

Psychic Visions Books 4–6

Psychic Visions Books 7–9

By Death Series

Touched by Death

Haunted by Death

Chilled by Death

By Death Books 1–3

Broken Protocols – Romantic Comedy Series

Cat's Meow

Cat's Pajamas

Cat's Cradle

Cat's Claus

Broken Protocols 1-4

Broken and... Mending

Skin

Scars

Scales (of Justice)

Broken but… Mending 1-3

Glory

Genesis

Tori

Celeste

Glory Trilogy

Biker Blues

Morgan: Biker Blues, Volume 1

Cash: Biker Blues, Volume 2

SEALs of Honor

Mason: SEALs of Honor, Book 1

Hawk: SEALs of Honor, Book 2

Dane: SEALs of Honor, Book 3

Swede: SEALs of Honor, Book 4

Shadow: SEALs of Honor, Book 5

Cooper: SEALs of Honor, Book 6

Markus: SEALs of Honor, Book 7

Evan: SEALs of Honor, Book 8

Mason's Wish: SEALs of Honor, Book 9

Chase: SEALs of Honor, Book 10

Brett: SEALs of Honor, Book 11

Devlin: SEALs of Honor, Book 12

Easton: SEALs of Honor, Book 13

Ryder: SEALs of Honor, Book 14

Macklin: SEALs of Honor, Book 15

Corey: SEALs of Honor, Book 16

Warrick: SEALs of Honor, Book 17

Tanner: SEALs of Honor, Book 18

Jackson: SEALs of Honor, Book 19

Kanen: SEALs of Honor, Book 20

Nelson: SEALs of Honor, Book 21

Taylor: SEALs of Honor, Book 22
Colton: SEALs of Honor, Book 23
Troy: SEALs of Honor, Book 24
Axel: SEALs of Honor, Book 25
Baylor: SEALs of Honor, Book 26
Hudson: SEALs of Honor, Book 27
Lachlan: SEALs of Honor, Book 28
SEALs of Honor, Books 1–3
SEALs of Honor, Books 4–6
SEALs of Honor, Books 7–10
SEALs of Honor, Books 11–13
SEALs of Honor, Books 14–16
SEALs of Honor, Books 17–19
SEALs of Honor, Books 20–22
SEALs of Honor, Books 23–25

Heroes for Hire

Levi's Legend: Heroes for Hire, Book 1
Stone's Surrender: Heroes for Hire, Book 2
Merk's Mistake: Heroes for Hire, Book 3
Rhodes's Reward: Heroes for Hire, Book 4
Flynn's Firecracker: Heroes for Hire, Book 5
Logan's Light: Heroes for Hire, Book 6
Harrison's Heart: Heroes for Hire, Book 7
Saul's Sweetheart: Heroes for Hire, Book 8
Dakota's Delight: Heroes for Hire, Book 9
Tyson's Treasure: Heroes for Hire, Book 10
Jace's Jewel: Heroes for Hire, Book 11
Rory's Rose: Heroes for Hire, Book 12

Brandon's Bliss: Heroes for Hire, Book 13
Liam's Lily: Heroes for Hire, Book 14
North's Nikki: Heroes for Hire, Book 15
Anders's Angel: Heroes for Hire, Book 16
Reyes's Raina: Heroes for Hire, Book 17
Dezi's Diamond: Heroes for Hire, Book 18
Vince's Vixen: Heroes for Hire, Book 19
Ice's Icing: Heroes for Hire, Book 20
Johan's Joy: Heroes for Hire, Book 21
Galen's Gemma: Heroes for Hire, Book 22
Zack's Zest: Heroes for Hire, Book 23
Bonaparte's Belle: Heroes for Hire, Book 24
Noah's Nemesis: Heroes for Hire, Book 25
Tomas's Trials: Heroes for Hire, Book 26
Heroes for Hire, Books 1–3
Heroes for Hire, Books 4–6
Heroes for Hire, Books 7–9
Heroes for Hire, Books 10–12
Heroes for Hire, Books 13–15
Heroes for Hire, Books 16–18
Heroes for Hire, Books 19–21
Heroes for Hire, Books 22–24

SEALs of Steel

Badger: SEALs of Steel, Book 1
Erick: SEALs of Steel, Book 2
Cade: SEALs of Steel, Book 3
Talon: SEALs of Steel, Book 4
Laszlo: SEALs of Steel, Book 5

Geir: SEALs of Steel, Book 6

Jager: SEALs of Steel, Book 7

The Final Reveal: SEALs of Steel, Book 8

SEALs of Steel, Books 1–4

SEALs of Steel, Books 5–8

SEALs of Steel, Books 1–8

The Mavericks

Kerrick, Book 1

Griffin, Book 2

Jax, Book 3

Beau, Book 4

Asher, Book 5

Ryker, Book 6

Miles, Book 7

Nico, Book 8

Keane, Book 9

Lennox, Book 10

Gavin, Book 11

Shane, Book 12

Diesel, Book 13

Jerricho, Book 14

Killian, Book 15

Hatch, Book 16

Corbin, Book 17

The Mavericks, Books 1–2

The Mavericks, Books 3–4

The Mavericks, Books 5–6

The Mavericks, Books 7–8

The Mavericks, Books 9–10

The Mavericks, Books 11–12

Collections

Dare to Be You…

Dare to Love…

Dare to be Strong…

RomanceX3

Standalone Novellas

It's a Dog's Life

Riana's Revenge

Second Chances

Published Young Adult Books:

Family Blood Ties Series

Vampire in Denial

Vampire in Distress

Vampire in Design

Vampire in Deceit

Vampire in Defiance

Vampire in Conflict

Vampire in Chaos

Vampire in Crisis

Vampire in Control

Vampire in Charge

Family Blood Ties Set 1–3

Family Blood Ties Set 1–5

Family Blood Ties Set 4–6

Family Blood Ties Set 7–9

Sian's Solution, A Family Blood Ties Series Prequel Novelette

Design series

Dangerous Designs

Deadly Designs

Darkest Designs

Design Series Trilogy

Standalone

In Cassie's Corner

Gem Stone (a Gemma Stone Mystery)

Time Thieves

Published Non-Fiction Books:

Career Essentials

Career Essentials: The Résumé

Career Essentials: The Cover Letter

Career Essentials: The Interview

Career Essentials: 3 in 1